ALL
SHOOK
UP

ALL
SHOOK
UP

CATHERINE DALY

POOLBEG

Published 2004
by Poolbeg Press Ltd
123 Grange Hill, Baldoyle
Dublin 13, Ireland
E-mail: poolbeg@poolbeg.com

© Catherine Daly 2004

Typesetting, layout, design © Poolbeg Group Services Ltd.

1 3 5 7 9 10 8 6 4 2

A catalogue record for this book is available from the British Library.

ISBN 1-84223-166-9

Typeset by Patricia Hope in Palatino 10/14
Printed by
Litografia Rosés S.A., Spain

www.poolbeg.com

About the Author

Catherine was born in Dublin and spent her childhood in Belgium and Ireland. After qualifying as a pharmacist from Trinity College, she worked in an English hospital for five years. She returned to Ireland in 1996 and lives in Dublin with her husband and two children. *All Shook Up* is her first novel and she is working on her second.

For more information, go to **www.catherinedaly.com**

Acknowledgements

The book's written, the editing's done . . . now for the really hard bit – making sure I remember to thank everyone.

First of all thanks to Denis, who kept me sane(?) and provided encouragement when he was the only person who knew I had embarked on the crazy project of writing a novel. And to my two children, Lorcan and Cliodhna, who learnt that 'working in the home' can mean sitting in front of a computer as well as providing milk and snacks on demand.

A special thank you to my parents Claire and Sean O'Donnell who gave me, amongst many other things, the gift of reading and a love of words – without which I would never have put pen to paper.

To my parents-in-law Jean and Michael Daly, thank you for your friendship and support, not to mention all the baby-sitting! And to the rest of the Daly Clan (Carrick branch), thank you for accepting me as an honorary member.

Thanks to Linda for being my first reader and for

sharing some memorable nights out in Limerick. To Aisling for much support and advice, and to Noelle and Mary for long chatty cups of coffee while we all tried to ignore our kids wrecking each other's houses.

Thank you to my agent Ali for believing in me and to everyone at Poolbeg, especially Paula, Sarah and Brona. And finally thanks to Gaye for being just the kind of supportive and encouraging editor that a first-time writer needs.

For Denis, with my love.
Without you I wouldn't have got this far.

Chapter 1

Maeve braked hard then cursed, as the car in front of her stopped at the amber light. She needed to be in early today. Her husband, Fintan, had offered to take the children, but it was Maeve's turn and to change routine would be to admit she was nervous.

And Maeve wasn't nervous, at least not so as anyone else would notice. She could out-negotiate Peter in her sleep and she'd get a good deal out of him for the sake of everyone in the company.

And if I have to be devious, tough! Maeve thought, swallowing her non-existent nerves further down into her fluttering stomach. We've wasted enough time negotiating – Ofiscom's ready to deal, we're ready to deal and Peter's the only one holding things up.

Maeve looked at the baby strapped into his seat beside her and her face softened into a smile. She stroked his cheek gently with the back of her finger. The only one of her children to resemble her, with dark eyes and straight brown hair, Darragh was struggling to keep his eyes open. He turned his head sleepily towards her, opening his soft mouth against her hand.

Then she glanced at the older two children in the back.

"Take your fingers out of your sister's face, Ciaran! Ciaran! Ciaran! *Ciaran!* If you don't stop that right now . . ." she tried to sound menacing. "I said stop it! Don't make me stop the car!"

Ciaran straightened up.

"I wasn't doing anything, Mummy. Fiona was crying so I tried to make her happy by tickling her."

His father's brilliant blue eyes beamed out of Ciaran's angelic face and Maeve tried not to break into a grin matching his.

"If you can be good all the way to Sarah's house," she offered, "I'll ask her if she'll let you watch one cartoon off her new *Rugrats* video."

Maeve had long since overcome any guilt she felt about using television as a bribe. She reckoned that children were programmed by evolution to torture their parents and anything she could use to even the odds had to be fair.

"All right, but it has to be the *Bug's Life* video, not *Rugrats*!" Ciaran replied, tilting his head to one side. "I saw *Rugrats* yesterday, and it's boring!"

Not for the first time, Maeve wondered exactly how much television her children watched while she was at work. But Sarah was the perfect minder; Ciaran and Fiona loved her, and they came home exhausted and full of stories of trips to the park and games of football. The kitchen walls at home were covered with drawings and paintings the kids had done at Sarah's – and besides, some television could be educational, couldn't it? It never did Maeve any harm, and she was raised as much by John Noakes as by her own parents.

As they pulled into Sarah's housing estate in Stillorgan, Darragh finally gave up his battle with sleep. Maeve knew he'd be in a foul mood when she woke him to bring him in, but that wasn't her problem. Although she hated leaving her kids to someone else when she went to work, there were always those few moments, just after she pulled away, when the car was blissfully quiet.

Sarah opened the front door as Maeve pulled up. As usual, she looked as if she was just dressing when the doorbell rang. A red cardigan hung from one shoulder as she hitched up her jeans and tucked a tiny white T-shirt into an even tinier waistband. Then she ran a hand through her short red hair, making it stand up on end.

She waited while Ciaran, with Fiona in tow, clattered out of the car and into her sitting-room, and then went out to help with Darragh.

"Hi, Maeve, how are you doing for time?" she asked. "I've just put the kettle on."

"Hi, Sarah, sorry, but I'm in a mad rush." Maeve looked at her watch for emphasis. "I'm supposed to be in early, but just as I put my jacket on Darragh threw up and we both needed a complete change of outfit."

"Aah . . . the joys of Motherhood!" Sarah grinned

and rearranged the baby in her arms to minimise the chance of a repeat performance. "Okay then, how about this evening? I need to have a word with you."

Maeve's heart sank. "Oh? What about? Can it wait?"

"Oh, sure it can wait – this evening's fine."

"Alright . . . I should be able to leave early," she promised, getting into her car, relieved that Sarah's problem, whatever it was, wasn't urgent. "We'll have plenty of time for a chat."

But, as she pulled away, Maeve wondered what was on the other woman's mind. It couldn't just be a chat; Sarah never saw the need to plan ahead for that. Maybe Ciaran was acting up and Sarah had read in one of her childcare manuals that his behaviour was typical of a developing axe-murderer. How Anita and Mark had ever successfully reached the ages of sixteen and fourteen respectively, without the benefit of their mother's recent fascination with child psychology, was one of the twentieth century's great mysteries.

Or maybe she was after another pay raise, Maeve thought. The last one was only eight months ago, but Maeve knew she would pay up before the hints got too obvious.

Then Maeve put Sarah out of her mind to enjoy the rest of her drive. Unlike most people she actually enjoyed her commute with its half-hour or so of solitude. She thought about the weekend ahead. She and Fintan were taking Friday off, farming the two older children out to 'the grannies' and hoping that Darragh would sleep for a few uninterrupted hours

4

to allow Maeve and Fintan to spend some time together.

Romance had been on hold in the Larkin household for the past few months, leaving Maeve with a strange mixture of guilt and regret. Towards the end of her last pregnancy, she'd gone right off sex. And after Darragh was born she went back to work early and was so exhausted that she would have questioned the sanity of anyone who suggested there were things to do in bed other than sleep.

Maeve pulled out of the heavy traffic on Leeson Street and turned into the car park in front of Leeson Business Solutions. She parked in the space marked *M Larkin*, then walked up the granite steps of the redbricked Victorian building and into a small reception area, recently painted a gentle primrose yellow. She smiled in greeting at the receptionist who already looked busy despite the early hour.

Leeson Business Solutions was a friendly, family-run firm, founded in the 1960s by the late Seamus Breslin, who had run it until he retired due to ill health ten years ago. Originally his main business was office supplies, but in the '80s he moved the company into computers. When his son Danny joined him from a background in computer programming, he in turn pushed LBS into software. Then, when his father retired, Danny took over and Maeve was the first person he appointed. Her first official role was in sales and marketing, but gradually she became Danny's second in command as she saw opportunities for them to expand and diversify. Now Danny relied on her completely.

The company employed thirty-two people, providing a complete computer and office-machinery service to their impressive list of clients. They had also developed some interesting software, which needed capital to develop further, so Danny had decided to merge with the American giant Ofiscom. In reality it was a buy-out, but Danny was to stay on as chief executive and LBS would keep its own identity.

Maeve was doing most of the work on the merger along with Peter Fisch, a Texan seconded from Ofiscom's headquarters. And although Maeve managed to maintain a working relationship with Peter, she really thought he was a pain in the ass. Too much the stereotypical, thirty-something, company man for her to take seriously. She'd bet any money he sang the Ofiscom company anthem every morning, standing to attention in front of the mirror after flossing his teeth.

Maeve walked into an open-plan office area that had been the hallway and part of a spacious drawing-room in the original Victorian house. Over the rest of this floor, and at garden level below, the building had been extended and adapted over the years to provide a hotchpotch collection of small cramped offices, but with ceilings at the original height giving an impression of space. Danny once told Maeve that when his father bought the building at the end of the 1950s, some of the original plaster mouldings remained. But because he couldn't afford to have them restored and because they were in a state of dangerous disrepair he had been forced to have them ripped out. However, he hadn't

6

touched the main reception room on the second floor so, when there was more money available, it had been transformed into a large bright boardroom with a giant central ceiling rose and an ornate plaster frieze and cornice.

"Maeve, Danny's waiting for you in his office," Danny's secretary, Amanda, called from behind the photocopier. "He knows you weren't due to meet till half nine, but he saw you parking and wondered if you could go in to him now?"

Maeve resisted the temptation to laugh. Her boss couldn't wait to discuss what they were going to squeeze out of Peter this afternoon. She gathered together her organiser and laptop and went into his office. Danny was staring out the window, frowning.

"Cheer up, boss, it might never happen!" Maeve sat in one of the comfortable armchairs near the window and accepted Amanda's offer of a cup of coffee.

"After all the work we've put in, it bloody well better," Danny growled, referring to the merger. Then he turned and grinned. The boyish grin lit up his face and made him look younger than a few months off forty. He was a handsome man with a crop of dark, curly hair cut short. And he was one of those men you knew were Irish before they even opened their mouth – Maeve could never decide whether it was his smile, his gestures or the self-deprecating expression that said that he was going to laugh at himself before anyone beat him to it.

"Don't mind me," he said. "I'm just in one of those 'Oh God, am I doing the right thing?' moods."

7

Danny sat in the other armchair and held out his cup for Amanda to top up.

"Would Dad have approved? I can't get Mum to express an opinion. She says I'm running things now and I've got to do things my own way."

Knowing Mrs Breslin, Maeve reckoned she was even less interested in the goings-on at the office now than she had been when her husband had been alive. Besides, the family stood to make a lot of money from the sale of the company. As did the staff. Seamus Breslin had been a man ahead of his time, who made sure all his employees had a stake in LBS in the form of a profit-sharing scheme under which employees earned 'shares' based on their years of service and performance. It was a stake Ofiscom would now have to buy out.

Maeve sipped her coffee and waited for Danny's mood to lift because, typically, his bouts of introspection lasted no more than a few minutes. Maeve could spend longer agonising over whether she'd ordered the wrong sandwich for lunch than Danny spent wondering if he was making the right decision for the welfare of thirty people.

"I wanted to have a chat before your meeting with The Fish this afternoon," Danny said at last. He always referred to Peter as 'The Fish' outside his hearing. "He says Texas won't agree the figure we proposed on Tuesday and are trying to pare it down further. It's standard negotiating tactics, but you know how much I hate these games." Danny began to dismantle his pen with a frown of concentration. "Still, we must be approaching a figure they'll accept if they let him come that close to an offer." He looked up hopefully at Maeve.

"I think we can still get our figure out of him, if we structure it differently." Maeve pulled out some papers and spread them out on the low table between them. "I'm convinced Ofiscom would accept our figure, except for Peter holding them back, telling them he can do a better deal. So I'll try to sweeten it a bit. Let's tell him we'll accept an offer of two and a half Ofiscom shares for each of our LBS shares *upfront* as long as they'll commit to another share over the next three years for anyone who stays with the firm. Maeve looked to her boss for approval. He nodded slowly.

"Okay, run with that." Danny looked relieved to have made a decision. "It works to their advantage to keep people. And we still have to run this joint after The Fish goes home."

Maeve was going to feel like Santa Claus if she pulled this off. Of course Danny would officially get the credit, but most people knew she had done the hard bargaining. And she stood to make a nice little sum herself, enough to pay off a good chunk of her mortgage, and have a little spending spree.

With the main business discussed, Maeve and Danny spent the next half-hour going over other issues. The company was too busy for its own good at the moment and a lot of Maeve's time was spent re-deploying staff to fill gaps. It made for a crazy time for everyone, but morale was at an all-time high because of the imminent cash windfall.

The meeting wound down and Maeve returned to her own office. She rang her friend Andrea to remind her they were meeting for lunch and then knuckled down to her morning's work.

The early spring sun had brought the warmest day of the year so far, so when Maeve left the office just before one, she decided to walk to Andrea Egan's beauty salon at the end of Leeson Street. Her friend had opened the salon, simply named Egan's, eight years ago on the ground floor of a building owned by her father. He thought he was just humouring his youngest daughter's latest whim, but the space had just been vacated by a previous tenant, so he gave her one year to get the business up and running, and to pay a proper commercial rent. Andrea surprised everyone, putting her failed beauty diploma and two years' sporadic attendance at an expensive hairdressing school to spectacular use. Within six months she was well capable of paying her way, but kept to the original agreement and only started paying rent one year to the day after she had moved in. Instead, she 'reinvested' the money in business development. Which, in Andrea's language, meant supporting her lavish social life and moving with the beautiful people. It clearly paid off, as the beautiful people soon began to flock to the salon. Maeve was never sure if it was Andrea's skill as a stylist, or her encyclopaedic knowledge of the private lives of Dublin's rich and famous that kept her clientele loyal, and the salon now occupied the basement, the ground floor and an office and small private treatment area on the first floor.

It was into the office Maeve was ushered when she arrived. The receptionist, Jane, brought a tray of delicious finger food and said that Ms Egan would be up shortly. As Maeve sipped a fashionable mineral water, she listened to Andrea's high-pitched 'Oooh's' and 'Aaah's' through the floor as she flattered a children's television presenter and extracted an obscene amount of money for the latest Egan hair creation. Then she heard Andrea usher her client to the door and run up the stairs two at a time. Sometimes Andrea's inability to do anything at normal speed exhausted Maeve.

She burst through the door, all five foot ten of her. Slim, blonde and tanned, the kind of woman Maeve guessed she would hate if they hadn't been friends so long.

"Darling, how *wonderful* to see you, it really has been *toooo* long!" Andrea kissed the air beside Maeve's cheek.

"You've ten seconds to start behaving like a normal human being or you won't see me for dust," Maeve growled.

"Oops, sorry! Busy day, busy week, I've been 'in character' for too long without a break." Andrea flopped onto the armchair opposite Maeve, knocking her head on a hairdryer on the way down. "Shit! I'm going to chuck that fucking thing out the window one of these days!"

"That's better," Maeve laughed, "but don't feel you have to swear on my account." It was an ongoing joke between them – Maeve had drastically cut down on her use of four-letter words since she'd had kids, while Andrea, who could curse like a sailor, never did in front of clients.

"So, Madame, what can we do for you today?" Andrea asked.

"What I really need is a good gossip and my roots touched up. Not necessarily in that order." Maeve stretched back in the chair, ready to be pampered.

Twice a month, religiously, the two friends met up. Once at the salon, where Andrea worked her magic over a takeout deli lunch, and once when Maeve took her friend to dinner at whichever restaurant was trendiest in Dublin at the time. Maeve reckoned she had the better half of the deal. She always walked tall and felt beautiful and sexy when she left Egan's, and for a woman only a couple of inches over five foot and very self-conscious about her looks, this was no mean achievement.

As Andrea worked, they both picked at the sandwiches and fingers of quiche.

Soon Maeve's roots were cooking under the drier and, as she enjoyed a manicure, she told Andrea about her plans for the weekend.

"What?" Andrea gasped, a mischievous expression lighting up her face. "You didn't tell me you needed the full romantic-weekend treatment. Cancel the rest of your afternoon and we'll send you home looking and feeling in the mood for *lurve!*"

"I wish I could, but I've a meeting with that horrible Fisch-Man this afternoon." Maeve groaned, pretending to dread it, when really she couldn't wait. "We have to squeeze as much money out of him as possible in the takeover."

"You really will have to explain all this high finance to me some day," Andrea yawned theatrically. "Remind me to call you some night when I've got insomnia. But, if that's all you've got to look forward to, escape as soon as you can, and pop in here on your way home. You need a facial and ideally an aromatherapy massage. Francoise, who started with us last month, is magic with the smelly oils. Not only will you be relaxed, you'll smell irresistible. The ingredients in her oils are some dark French secret, known only to the initiated. Costs a bloody fortune, but I'm going to put her prices up as soon as she has a regular list of addicts."

"I could do with a bit of that,' Maeve sighed, "but I've got to collect the kids today, and Sarah wants a chat – which reminds me, I need cakes to soften her up. So if you're not going to eat all those gooey things wrap them up in a doggy-bag for me – it'll save me stopping on the way home."

Andrea always ordered large quantities of sticky buns for their monthly lunch and then wouldn't eat any in sympathy with Maeve who was always on a diet. Well, not always, but after each child she had at least a stone to lose, so for the past five years it had felt like always.

"What does Ms McEvoy want now?" Andrea asked,

her dislike of Sarah barely concealed. The two women had not hit it off the only time they had met, at Darragh's christening. Andrea, who was Darragh's godmother, had worn a flawless cream suit and enormous hat, and displayed a tan that looked almost ridiculous in Ireland in February. Sarah decided at once that Andrea was a spoilt rich bitch whose business was underwritten by Daddy's money while Andrea in turn resented the way Sarah was always first there with a kiss-better for Fiona or to reprimand Ciaran when he got boisterous in church. She seemed to be implying by her actions that she was more motherly to Maeve's children than their own harassed parent.

"She's probably reached the chapter on how to recognise a dysfunctional family in her *Child Psychology for Dummies* book," Maeve groaned, "and she's going to tell me where I'm going wrong." Fond as she was of Sarah, Maeve could get a little weary of her theories. "Or she's after another pay raise."

Andrea nearly choked on her mineral water. "She wouldn't have the nerve, would she, Maeve? You pay her far too much already. Give her another pay raise and I'll chuck in this place, and take them on myself. It's much better money."

Maeve let Andrea rant until she climbed off her high horse.

"Yeah, yeah, I know," Andrea said at last, "St Sarah the Blessed of Stillorgan is worth every penny, for your peace of mind. You're lucky to have her. A crèche would cost more. *Blah, blah, blah!* I've heard it all before. Just do me a favour and don't tell me if you do give her a raise – I couldn't handle the depression about my lousy career choice."

She finished drying Maeve's hair, then stood back to admire the results.

"There now, Mrs Larkin! No more roots visible. Only Fintan could tell you're not a natural blonde and by the sound of things *he's* about to be reminded in a big way this weekend."

Andrea grinned wickedly and held up a mirror for Maeve to examine her hair.

She had trimmed the ends and Maeve's straight, now blonder hair stopped just above her collar, turning in at the end to frame her delicate oval face. As always after having her highlights redone, her brown eyes seemed bigger than ever. As Andrea looked at her friend she thought it was a pity that Maeve didn't appreciate her own looks. She would have killed to have bone structure like that. But ever since Maeve was only nine or ten and her mother had none too subtly expressed disappointment that her only daughter was going to favour her husband's shorter side of the family and not inherit her own Twiggy-like physique, Maeve had idolised a model of beauty which encompassed height, skinniness and the ability to wear clothes like a hanger.

"Are you sure I can't tempt you to the full treatment? Romantic weekend and all that?"

Maeve groaned. "Don't tempt me . . . maybe another time. Hopefully, we'll get a few more of these weekends. And now that Darragh's weaned we may even be able to book that weekend in Paris we've been promising ourselves since Fiona was born."

"And you might have already been there, if you hadn't proceeded with such indecent haste on to Darragh – 'All-the-hassle-over-with-in-one-go,' my foot!" Andrea was fishing for information as usual. Fintan and Maeve had never admitted to anyone that Darragh was a surprise arrival.

"Wait till you have a few of your own, then you'll understand," Maeve teased back. *"Tick-tock, tick-tock!"*

Andrea's biological clock had grown louder when she turned thirty and she had stopped dating in favour of interviewing future husbands. Although she had plenty of applicants, none survived the rigorous selection process. Few were even called back for a second interview.

"Get out of here, Maeve, before I get nasty and start boring you with the details of my disastrous love life," Andrea threatened. "Socialising for the sake of promiscuity was really *so* much more fun than this hunt for Mr Right. If you were a real friend, you'd poison that cow Cathy Houlihan's coffee next time she was in the office, and release Danny back to being one of Dublin's most eligible bachelors."

CHAPTER 2

Maeve strolled slowly back to the office. She was due to meet Peter Fisch at half two and she wanted to arrive in the building not a second before. He had a habit of ambushing people in their offices, trying to start meetings a few minutes early, thinking this gave him some psychological advantage. No doubt a technique he'd picked up in some management manual.

And sure enough, as she arrived back, Maeve saw Peter disappear around her door. She waited to see how long he would stay in her office. A few minutes later he emerged, saw her and went red. Then he flashed her one of his seductive grins and Maeve was annoyed to note both receptionists looking daggers in her direction. It seemed that every other female in the company had fallen in love with the Texan. Well, Maeve thought as she smiled back at him with a smile sweet enough to make her fillings hurt, *they* didn't have to work with him.

"I'll be right with you, Peter," she informed him in a business-like voice. "I'll join you in the boardroom as soon as I get my things together."

Maeve went towards the door Peter had just come through and was amused to see him perform a little shuffle on the spot as if deciding whether to walk away or hold her office door open for her. She stepped inside before he could make up his mind and, as she turned to close the door behind her, she saw him retreat in the direction of the stairs.

"Right, let's get started," she said five minutes later, as she sauntered into the second-floor boardroom and took a seat at the head of the long, highly polished mahogany table. She enjoyed the flash of annoyance that crossed Peter's face as he realised he had wasted the opportunity to take possession of the seat of authority.

"Danny tells me that Texas didn't buy the figure we agreed on Tuesday and I must say we're disappointed," Maeve continued. "When you were sent over, we were given the impression you were senior enough to make decisions." She waited a second for that barb to hit home before adding, "But I'm sure we can come to some agreement today. If not, I think we may have to insist on going face-to-face with a real decision-maker."

"Maeve, I'm afraid that's not exactly how Ofiscom operates." Peter opened one of his own files, smoothed out the papers and looked up at Maeve. "Any executive in the company, even my boss, can only make a financial decision of that magnitude subject to board agreement. You have my guarantee that any recommendation I make will carry as much weight as that of anyone else the company could choose to send."

Well done, Peter, Maeve thought, you've grown up in the few months we've had you. When he was fresh over from the States, an exchange like that would have had him blustering and aggressively defending himself.

Then aloud she added, to soothe any battering his ego might have taken: "Of course, Peter, I'm sorry if I made it sound like I didn't have confidence in you. It's just that I'm under pressure to get this part of the negotiations sorted out so we can present it to the staff. It's made me a bit jumpy and over-reactive."

"I know, Maeve," Peter purred in his irritating Texan drawl. "We all feel that way, but we must get it right, for all our sakes." He paused for a second, unaware he had been manipulated into feeling he had the moral upper hand. "So let's sit down and see if we can't come to some middle ground."

"Peter . . ." Maeve hesitated as if she were struggling with her conscience, "I don't know if I should tell you about this, I don't even know if it's relevant or anything . . ." She put on a little-girl-lost expression.

"Tell me what, Maeve?"

"Well, it may be nothing, really, only a coincidence, I feel bad even bringing it up."

"Just tell me," Peter smiled, "and I'll be the judge of whether or not it's relevant."

Whack! Maeve had him now, hook, line and sinker. All she had to do was reel him in.

"Well . . ." she took a deep breath then spoke quickly, words tumbling out as if she felt guilty, "I was trying to phone someone from the main office on Wednesday and I kept getting an engaged tone, so I kept hitting redial. Then I went to talk to Colm for a moment, and when I came back, I picked up a different phone. I pressed redial without thinking and . . ."

"And what, Maeve?" Peter coaxed gently. "Go on, take your time."

He was so predictable, Maeve thought. This was almost too easy.

"Well . . . oh God! I feel like the office spy or something, but when I pressed redial I got through to the headquarters of the Technical and Professional Union of Ireland." Maeve stopped for a few seconds then rushed on. "It probably means nothing. None of our staff are unionised – someone was probably arranging to meet a friend for lunch, or returning a call. Maybe they're looking for some new computer equipment, or training or something."

She deliberately allowed herself to babble. The whole story was a fabrication. She knew Peter had an unnatural dread of unions, and would die before telling head office that he'd handled things so badly in Ireland that he'd sent the staff scurrying to unionise.

He stood up and began to pace the room.

Maeve hated being underhand and felt sorry for the man's obvious disquiet, but she was fed up of all the delays. She watched him as he moved over to the window and stared out.

By all standards, he was a good-looking man. He wasn't too tall, just short of six foot, but well-proportioned and clearly fit. His features were attractive – a perfect nose, high sharp cheekbones, and a strong dimpled chin. But there was something missing. It had taken Maeve a while to realise it, but Peter's face rarely displayed real emotion. He could smile, presenting an assault of capped white teeth, but the rest of his face reminded her of a mannequin. When he frowned a small furrow appeared between his eyebrows, but it looked rehearsed. As if he had studied in front of the mirror to produce a look that said, 'I'm not happy with this' without wrinkling his smooth complexion too much.

"Look, Peter, let's forget I ever said anything – this has obviously upset you. I know the staff and they wouldn't go behind my back. There must be a logical explanation to this."

"You were right to tell me, Maeve," Peter said slowly. "I agree, it probably means nothing and we should keep it between us. But as you say – it does inject a bit of urgency into our negotiations."

He was clearly worried, so Maeve went straight for the kill.

"Look, Peter, I've been thinking about would be the best for everyone. You say the board in Texas won't accept the figure we proposed earlier in the week, but frankly we both know that's just a bargaining position. Danny and I have talked about this and we're not prepared to sell our staff short. This is the lowest we're prepared to accept." She pushed a piece of paper across the table at him. She had asked for a total of four shares, rather than the three and a half she had agreed with Danny so she would have room to negotiate downwards. "However, we would be prepared to have a portion of those shares, no more than one and a half shares, retained by Ofiscom in a staff fund to be redistributed over the next three years for anyone who stays with the company. That would solve the itchy feet problem as soon as you take over, and ensure everyone still has a stake in keeping the company profitable."

Maeve knew that most of the staff would sell a big chunk of their Ofiscom shares as soon as they received them, whereas the shares they held in LBS were merely part of the profit-sharing scheme – if you left the company, the shares were bought back at a nominal value.

Maeve watched Peter for a reaction.

After a long pause, Peter said slowly, "Okay, I think I can get them to go for that."

Maeve fought to hold in the gasp. He was going for the full four shares – she should have asked for more!

"Of course this is higher than I was given sanction for, but . . . OK, Maeve," he held out his hand, "I think we have ourselves a deal. Subject, of course, to board approval."

This was just posturing; Maeve knew they were home and dry.

"If everything goes to plan," Peter continued, "we can have the offer drawn up over the weekend, and you can tell the staff on Monday. If you like I can ring you at home tonight as soon as the final decision's made."

"I think I can wait," Maeve grinned. So far she had avoided giving Peter her home number and she wasn't about to weaken. "Let Danny know and he'll get in touch with me."

Maeve felt as though she could have hugged Peter as she tried to hide just how delighted she was by their deal. For all his infuriating posturing, he was quite likeable when he stopped playing games and just got on with things, she decided suddenly.

They finished up and Maeve vanished into her office to dial Danny's private mobile number. He had made himself unavailable for the afternoon so that if negotiations were not going to plan, Maeve could use the stalling tactic of having to check with him. He had appointed her to negotiate, ostensibly so that she could ensure the staff got the best possible deal, but he, his mother, his sister and two brothers were also going to have a lot to be grateful for after this afternoon's work. Between them, they held over three-quarters of the 'shares' in the company as well as a huge cash payment Danny had already agreed, separate from Maeve's negotiations.

Danny picked up the moment Maeve got through.

"Don't you know that a watched mobile never rings?" she asked, laughing.

"Shut up and tell me how it went. Do I order another G&T to drown my sorrows or can I break out the champagne?"

"I thought you were playing golf," Maeve teased. "Don't tell me you've managed to get eighteen holes played already?"

"I sprained my foot on the third," Danny explained. "So I limped straight to the nineteenth for some ice. Silly beggar of a barman insisted in drowning it in gin."

"Yeah, right!" Maeve snorted. "Who's there with you?"

"I'm on my own. The others went on to finish the round," Danny grumbled.

"Well, if you're on your own I feel duty-bound not to tell you anything. If you drink a bottle of champagne on your own, Cathy'll blame me when you roll back to her flat drunk."

"Sod Cathy, she's in London," Danny hissed. Then, as he realised what Maeve had said, he gasped. "Hang on, you did say champagne, didn't you? Tell me all the gory details!"

Maeve filled him in and heard him whoop with delight.

"That's even more than you said this morning!" He laughed. "You're a genius – I think I love you! Marry me and have my babies! Forget Fintan and Cathy, they don't understand us like we understand each other!"

His laughter was infectious, and Maeve joined in. "I'd settle for a share of that bottle of champagne."

"You're on!" he said. "Name a bar in town, take the rest of the afternoon off and meet me there."

"I can skive off at four o'clock. Oh, you're such a generous boss!" Maeve stuck out her tongue at him, forgetting she was on the phone. "Oh, damn! I forgot. I've got to collect the kids today. And maybe it's better to wait till everything's signed, sealed and delivered before celebrating."

"I thought you said you had him landed," Danny said cautiously.

"Yes, I'm sure I have," Maeve reassured him, "but don't count your chickens till you've got them stuffed."

"To hell with caution!" Danny brightened up again. "You're not depriving me of my champagne. Even if I have to drink alone. You have a good weekend and say 'Hi' to Fintan and the kids for me."

Maeve felt slightly deflated, having to go to Sarah's now, at one of the crowning moments of her career. She should be out on the town getting drunk and ending up at some disgusting nightclub.

On second thoughts, maybe she was better off missing that. When Cathy started organising celebrations it could end up exhausting everyone but her. Her main aim in life was to go to as many trendy places as possible in one night. She claimed it was her professional responsibility as a journalist for one of Dublin's fashion magazines.

But hadn't Danny said Cathy was in London? Suddenly Maeve felt guilty. Maybe he really would be celebrating alone. He wasn't mad about most of Cathy's friends, and in the five years they'd been together, she seemed to have managed to distance him from most of his.

Then Maeve shook her head resolutely. Danny was a big boy and not her responsibility. They'd become very close friends in the years since she'd started working for him, but she had own life after all.

She spent about five minutes trying to get through to Fintan at work, because she was bursting to tell someone the good news, but gave up when she was put through to the third extension and was told "Oh yes, Mrs Larkin, he was here a minute ago. I'll just see if I can find him."

Typically, because Fintan was taking the day off tomorrow, he was rushing around the office making sure he had tied up all his loose ends. All his work was planned weeks if not months in advance, but he always seemed to have some crisis at the last minute.

Maeve often thought it was a good thing her husband hadn't ended up in the financial markets. Although he had the brains and the insight to understand the smallest nuance of world economics, he would have been a nervous wreck every time indices moved up or down. Fintan's two brothers were stockbrokers, one in New York, the other in London, and neither of them could figure out how Fintan could have settled for a training job in the bank. Their mother, Niamh, had once confided to Maeve that neither of them had Fintan's intelligence and lacked the imagination to consider a life in which the pursuit of money was not the primary goal.

Maeve packed up her things and sneaked out of the office. She couldn't wipe the smile off her face and didn't want anyone to see her, just in case things turned sour over the weekend. She got into her car, stuck a CD of Vivaldi opera choruses in the stereo, opened the window and sang her way towards Stillorgan and Sarah.

CHAPTER 3

When Maeve arrived at Sarah's, Ciaran and Fiona were in the back garden, playing football with Sarah's fourteen-year-old son Mark. But on hearing her voice they tumbled in from outside, and began climbing all over her.

"Darragh's just gone down for a nap," Sarah said as she filled the kettle. "Will you have tea or coffee?"

"Tea, please. Oh, and I forgot, I've got some cakes in the car." Maeve took out her keys and turned to Mark who had joined them in the kitchen. The boy had some sort of extrasensory perception, making him turn up at the precise moment food was mentioned.

"I'll get them for you, Mrs Larkin," he offered, holding his hand out for the keys. She had given up trying to get him to call her Maeve. "Are they in the front of the car or the boot?"

"Thanks, Mark. They're in the boot. In a huge bundle of silver foil."

Mark hurried out, his eyes having lit up at the word 'huge'.

"So, Sarah. How are things? How's life treating you?" Maeve knew it would take a while for the other woman to get down to what she wanted to talk about, so she geared herself up for at least half an hour's gossip first. To her surprise, Sarah said she'd wait to tell her till the kids were settled with Mark in the living-room so they could talk in private. She was jumpy and nervous, and didn't even seem able to make small talk. Suddenly Maeve was worried.

Finally, with the children spreading cakes all over the wooden floor in front of the television, Sarah took a deep breath.

"There's no easy way to say this . . ." she said, ". . . but I can't go on looking after the children."

There was silence. Then, when Maeve finally got her breath back and trusted her voice to come out in anything other than a squeak, both women spoke at once.

"I don't understand, is there a problem –"

"Honestly, Maeve, if there was a way –"

"No, you go ahead." Maeve was relieved not to have to talk for a moment.

At once Sarah found her tongue again and the words tumbled out as if a dam had burst. "I want to go back and do my Leaving Cert. I'd like to get some kind of formal qualification, and if I don't do it now I might never do it."

"So how much longer do I have?" Maeve asked, forcing herself to face the problem at hand.

"Till the start of July."

"July!" Maeve spluttered, thinking that that was just when she was hoping to be in the middle of supervising the smooth transformation of LBS the independent company into LBS part of a global conglomerate. "Surely the school term doesn't start till the autumn?"

"I know, but the community college is running a course over the summer for people like me who need to get back into the swing of studying. Although in my case it'll be my first attempt at it!" Sarah's smile died when she saw that her attempt at humour was lost. Maeve looked drawn, shocked and several shades paler than when she arrived.

"Oh God, Maeve! Don't look like that. I haven't killed your granny or anything!"

"I'm glad you seem to find this so funny!" Maeve snapped and then immediately felt bad. "I'm sorry. It's just a bit of a shock. I have no idea what I'm going to do. And it couldn't really have come at a worse time – you know what a shortage of childminders there is at the moment."

"Look, Maeve, I hope you don't mind me saying this, but your family comes first, and if Danny Whatever-his-name-is has to manage without you, he will."

Of course it wasn't as simple as that. Maeve hadn't told many people how much she stood to benefit from the merger and that it depended on her still being with the company when it went through. Thanks to today's manoeuvring she had effectively tied herself in for another three years. She didn't feel like explaining any of this to Sarah. Nor did she want to get into a discussion with her over money. As far as Sarah was concerned, any couple with two jobs and a nice house in Blackrock and who could afford a childminder, had more money than they knew what to do with and could easily chuck in one of the jobs.

She felt exhausted and all she wanted to do was go home and cry at the unfairness of it all. But she knew she couldn't. Sarah had become a friend over the past four years and Maeve couldn't walk out now that the relationship took a turn that didn't suit her. So she asked Sarah for details of her plans and put on her listening-supportive face.

"This course over the summer will basically reintroduce some of the main subjects and help us pick what we want to do in September," she explained, "and we'll be taught how to use computers and some basic study skills."

Soon she was back in full flow and Maeve only had to nod, agree and ask the odd simple question to keep the conversation going.

After half an hour of listening, Maeve felt she had done her duty and began to make moves to leave. As she gathered up Ciaran, Fiona and their many belongings, Darragh woke up and began to scream, his indignation only slightly relieved when his mother picked him up.

"Do you want me to feed him before you go?" Sarah offered. "You don't want him screaming all the way home."

All Maeve wanted was to get home and stop pretending everything was fine.

"No, I'd better get going." She rocked Darragh gently against her chest and kissed the top of his head, drawing more comfort from the soft baby smell of him than he seemed to be receiving from her. "Even as it is, I'll probably hit lousy traffic.,"

She buckled the children into their safety-seats and made her escape. Sure enough, there were cars bumper to bumper most of the way to Blackrock. Every time the car stopped moving Darragh began to scream and Maeve felt like joining in.

When the car finally pulled into Abbeywood Close, a leafy cul-de-sac in Blackrock, Maeve was relieved to see Fintan's car parked on the street so that she could pull in to the drive. As she turned off the engine, he opened the door with a grin.

"How's the great entrepreneur?" he asked, kissing her. "I believe you pulled off quite a coup today.'

"Was that only today? It feels like a lifetime ago. How did you hear?"

"Danny sent by a token of his appreciation." Fintan ushered her into the kitchen. There on the table were a huge bunch of flowers and a bottle of champagne.

"I took the liberty of reading the note," he explained, "to check you didn't have a secret admirer." Then saw the expression on her face. "Hey, you're supposed to look pleased!"

Suddenly everything was too much for Maeve and she burst into tears. And once she started there was no stopping her. Fintan looked at her in horror, afraid he had done or said something wrong.

"Maeve, honey, what's wrong?" he asked.

"Sarah's just given notice that she can't look after the children after June! She wants to do her Leaving Cert next year and there's some kind of a preparatory course she has to do in the summer – I don't know what I'm going to do!" Maeve pulled out a chair and collapsed into it.

"You mean you don't know what *we're* going to do," Fintan corrected. "I don't know either, but there's not much point in talking about it right now." An anguished yell in the distance reminded them of the children still strapped into the car. "Look, I'll leave them in the car, grab their bags and bring Ciaran to Mum's and Fiona to your mother's – I'll be back with Darragh in about an hour."

"Not without a helicopter you won't," Maeve grunted. "The traffic's a mess. It took me half an hour from Stillorgan."

"Ouch! No wonder Darragh's in such a foul mood. Well, I'll take them as far as my parents – I'll feed them there, then drop Fiona to your mum in Dalkey."

Fintan's parents lived under a mile away. When they had been house-hunting before they got married, Maeve had tried to find something closer to her mother. But even before the huge price-rises of the mid-1990s, Dalkey had been too expensive for them.

"It'll still take ages. Are you sure you don't want me to do one of the trips?" Maeve asked, not really meaning it. Fintan refused her offer, and after a few frantic minutes of packing all the paraphernalia Ciaran and Fiona would need for the weekend, the house was quiet.

Maeve turned on the hot water heater, poured the remains of a bottle of white wine into one of her favourite long-stemmed glasses and collapsed onto the couch in the living-room. She kicked off her shoes, curled her feet up under her and closed her eyes. She tried to put Sarah out of her mind and to regain some of the euphoria of her success with Peter. Soon her mood lifted and she wandered upstairs to get ready for a long soak in the bath. She searched around for some smelly bath oil, talc and her scented candle.

Finally, with the bath full and the bathroom steamed up and smelling vaguely oriental, Maeve stepped into the bath and sighed as she sank under the water and relaxed in silence.

CHAPTER 4

Maeve wasn't sure how long she'd been soaking in the bath, but her fingers had turned to raisins and the water, while not cold, was more than a few degrees off the scalding she usually liked. She pulled out the plug but, rather than climbing out, hugged her knees and watched the water spiral towards the drain. After less than a quarter of the bath had emptied, Maeve replaced the plug and turned on the hot tap. Keeping her feet clear of the torrent of hot water, she let enough run in to raise the temperature. Usually she would feel guilty staying this long in the bath, but she deserved it, never mind needed it on therapeutic grounds. Hot water was cheaper than therapy.

A key turned in the front door and Maeve braced herself for the onslaught of noise as Darragh and his father crashed into the house. But Fintan closed the door quietly and walked into the kitchen. The baby must have fallen asleep in the car and not woken as his car seat was moved inside. Why could she never manage that, she wondered as she listened to her husband rummaging around in the kitchen.

Then he poked his head around the bathroom door.

"What's cooking in all this steam? It sure smells good."

Fintan was carrying the champagne bottle and two crystal glasses. He kicked the door closed behind him, and parked his bum on the wide edge of their long corner bath. "Mmm . . . nice view! Could I tempt Madame to a glass of champagne? You have time for one in the bath and then I want you out and dolled up. A taxi is calling for us at nine, and will bring us to a surprise location for dinner."

"What about Darragh?"

"Darragh? Oh yes, the baby, I knew I'd forgotten something – I wondered why the car was so quiet." Fintan gasped, put his hand over his mouth in an expression of mock horror, then grinned and added: "I left him with Mum and Dad. Mum'll bring him later and wait here till we get back. So we've got the house to ourselves . . ." He hesitated, then: "Do you realise this is the first time we've had a free house in nearly five years?"

"Shut up and give me a glass of champagne," Maeve ordered, "or do I have to open the bottle myself?"

"I wish you would."

Fintan hated opening anything bubbly since he had knocked a bauble off the chandelier in the honeymoon suite, the morning after their wedding.

"Oh, stop being such a wimp and pour," Maeve mocked, giggling at the memory of that morning eight years ago. The aftermath of that bottle of champagne had been such fun that she almost wished he'd make a complete hash of this one too.

"I can read your dirty little mind, Maeve Larkin," scolded her husband. "I promise to open this bottle professionally – the electrical fittings have nothing to fear." He opened the champagne with a muffled pop, and managed to get most of the inevitable overflow into Maeve's glass. As he handed it to her, she grabbed his hand, and licked his fingers one by one.

"Mmm, I knew you'd spill some, can't go wasting any of this," she said huskily.

Fintan froze, afraid to do anything to spoil the mood – it had been a long time since Maeve had made the first move. The desire in her eyes made his heart pound as she sucked on his index finger, massaging it with her tongue.

Then the phone rang and Fintan groaned. They let it ring and it stopped. After a short pause, it started again.

"It might be urgent," Maeve whispered, giving him back his hand. "The kids."

"Yeah, right. The kids." Fintan crashed his way downstairs cursing under his breath and grabbed the phone.

"Hello? Oh, hi, Anna. Is Fiona settling in alright?"

Upstairs in the bathroom Maeve cringed; her mother had unique timing. Anna had an internal seismograph, tuned in to her only child, which picked up the faintest trace of sexual vibrations across a hundred-mile radius. Very useful no doubt in bringing up a teenager, but Maeve wished it could have been permanently disabled once she got married.

"What? Oh! Ehmm, I was in the garden, and Maeve's in the bath," Fintan blustered. "No, that's fine, I'll bring the phone up to her, and you can tell her yourself."

Maeve cringed even further.

"Your mother," Fintan whispered as he gave her the phone. "She wants to congratulate you on your deal. I might have let something slip earlier."

Maeve glared at him and listened while her mother gushed about her success. Fortunately Fintan hadn't given her exact figures, but now Anna was trying to extract them. Maeve tried to be vague, and to impress on her mother the need for confidentiality, but it was hard to sound serious with Fintan dripping champagne onto her toes and licking it off so she immersed her feet firmly under the water. Fintan sat back and waited for Maeve's mother to hang up. But by the time she had finally run out of steam, Anna Boland had stressed her daughter out to such an extent that Maeve grabbed the bottle of champagne, topped up her glass, knocked it back and got out of the bath. She wrapped a towel around herself and pointed firmly to the stairs.

"I'm going to get ready. Put the bubbly back in the fridge and I'll be down soon."

"But we were in the middle of something . . ." Fintan complained.

"I know," Maeve apologised, "but Mum kind of spoilt

the moment. Anyway, we'll be late for the restaurant." She gave him a conciliatory kiss on the nose.

"We could have re-booked the restaurant. Or cancelled." But Fintan was already on his way downstairs, conceding defeat.

Maeve stomped around the bedroom as she got ready. The first time in months she had felt like jumping Fintan and her bloody mother had to ring! She sat on the edge of the bed and forced herself to calm down. Then, with a short black dress she knew Fintan loved, some sexy underwear and killer heels, Maeve decided she would do her best to rescue the evening.

When she joined Fintan he was in the front room and there were two candles burning on the coffee-table. The champagne glasses had been washed, the bottle was on ice and a George Michael CD was playing on the stereo. Fintan's eyes opened wide in appreciation as he took in Maeve's dress and high heels.

"Wow!" he gasped. "Now I feel somewhat underdressed. Hang on while I see if my tux still fits."

He disappeared and came back a moment later with a cloth to catch the drips off the champagne bottle.

"Sorry, I've put on too much weight since my student days – the tux won't fit. You'll just have to put up with me like this." He was wearing a pair of casual, caramel-coloured trousers and a black, finely knit polo-neck jumper. The polo was tight-fitting and the trousers loose, which somehow made Fintan look smaller, as if *he* had been in the bath and his tall muscular body had shrunk several sizes.

He put down the bottle and put his arms around Maeve. Looking down, their difference in height only slightly reduced by her dangerously high sandals, he said: "Ooh, I *do* like heels. I can kiss you without straining my neck."

He demonstrated at length and when they both came up for air he buried his face in her hair and whispered, "You look stunning. You always do, but you're especially stunning tonight. And you smell good enough to eat."

He pulled back and admired her again, at arm's length.

"Talking of eating, we've precisely fifteen minutes to finish this champagne before the taxi gets here." He filled their glasses, emptying the bottle.

"*Precisely* fifteen minutes? When did you last book a taxi?" Maeve laughed, her mood improved by flattery and a good snog. As she spoke, the doorbell rang and Fintan peeped through the curtain.

"Oh woman of little faith, your chariot awaits."

"That taxi's early," Maeve protested. "I'm not going to knock this back. It's a waste of good champagne." But she swallowed back her drink anyway. Then they grabbed their coats and headed for the door. "Where are we going?"

"The only place I could book into at such short notice was the local Chinese," Fintan said. "Shame about the dress."Maeve stopped dead and looked at him.

"Tell me you're joking."

"Of course I am. Now get out that door, woman, and into the taxi."

He patted her bum and she squeezed his, both of them playful under the pleasant influence of booze on an empty stomach.

When they pulled up outside an elegant Georgian house on one of Dublin's better-known squares, Maeve gasped and her voice took on a reverential tone.

"How did you get a table here at this notice? You usually have to book months in advance."

"Well, I gather they usually keep a table or two for emergencies – you never know when someone important will drop by."

"Exactly, so how did *you* get a table?"

"Very funny. Actually, your mother pulled strings." Anna worked for a PR agency, and always managed to sound more important than she actually was.

"Alright, you're forgiven for spilling the beans earlier. I just hope you've arranged a second mortgage to pay the bill."

"I have a flexible friend. Now that I have a successful, rich businesswoman as a wife, I thought we could start living it up a bit."

Maeve snorted as she proceeded up the granite steps, past the discreet sign declaring the building to be home to the Restaurant Perigord, a fairly new establishment, only open two years. But in that time it had acquired the deserved reputation of serving some of the best food in Dublin. As they pushed their way through the heavy oak door an aroma of grilled meat and garlic met them, reminding them of how late it was, and how they had eaten nothing since lunch.

They were shown to a table in a discreetly lit room, subtly divided so that each diner could only see two or three other tables. This gave the impression of a eating in small, cosy bistro, rather than in a bustling restaurant capable of serving over a hundred per sitting. The music was muted, and, Maeve was relieved to note, classical. They both declined the offer of a pre-dinner drink and studied their menus. After making their selections, and ordering wine, they sat in silence for a minute or two.

"So, what was all that about earlier?" Fintan probed.

"What was what about?" Maeve answered defensively.

"You. Getting so upset. That's not like you.'

The waiter interrupted with the wine, giving Maeve a few moments to frame her answer.

"I guess I was feeling sorry for myself. I'd just accomplished the business deal of my life and Sarah went and rained on my parade. And she didn't see why losing her was such a big deal – she even suggested I should give up work and look after the kids myself." Seeing her husband's indignant face Maeve added quickly: "No, no. She didn't actually say that – just that, if I couldn't find anyone to replace her, then Danny would have to manage without me."

"And of course we both know that to be complete fantasy – the whole company would fold without your capable hand at the helm," Fintan said, taking a sip of wine.

"Nice try, Fintan!" Maeve answered with a wry grin. "But it's not some misplaced sense of my own importance that has me so uneasy." She paused. "It's more that . . . well, maybe Sarah's right."

"What do you mean?" Fintan asked.

"Well, most women, faced with this situation, would take it as a sign that it was time to throw in the towel." Maeve shrugged her shoulders helplessly. "I don't know. Give up work, spend more time with the children. Whatever." She sighed. "I know we never really talked about it, but is this the way we planned to bring up Ciaran, Fiona and Darragh? Both of us working mad hours, farming them out to childminders, only spending 'quality time' with them at the weekend?"

"We don't work mad hours," Fintan protested. "At least not by some standards. And one of us is always home, with the kids, by half five. Besides, we can't afford for you to give up work, especially not at the moment." He shook his head in confusion. He was desperately trying to say the right thing but felt that they had wandered into completely new territory.

"I know all that," Maeve said, "and I'm not arguing with it. It's just that . . . well . . . maybe I feel guilty that I'm not giving up work, rushing home to be a nurturing Earth Mother. Maybe deep down I feel I should never have got myself into the position that we depended on my working. Maybe if I really cared about my children I wouldn't be such a success at work and I could easily leave now."

43

If she had grown a third head, Fintan couldn't have looked more puzzled. Maeve nearly giggled, but was saved by the waiter bringing their first courses.

"I'm not saying I actually believe all that –" she broke off as she sampled her food. "Wow! This is wonderful! Here, try some." She held out a fork with a tiny slice of her warm duck salad served with a warm plum and balsamic vinegar dressing. "Isn't that to die for?"

Fintan nodded appreciatively, then returned to the subject in hand by asking carefully: "Sorry, I've lost the plot, what exactly *are* you saying?"

"Maybe I'm on a huge guilt trip about not being able to give up work," she continued. But, even as she said it, Maeve realised what was really wrong. She was relieved there was no question of her giving up work. She enjoyed her job and wanted to stay on, but something stopped her from saying it out loud. Her need for a satisfying career felt like a self-indulgence she was ashamed of, no matter how many times she told herself her guilt belonged in another generation. So she tried to distract Fintan with a simpler explanation of her earlier upset. "But maybe it's because I was on such a high this afternoon after my meeting that being brought down with a bump hurt more than it should have. I felt sorry for myself."

Maeve wore her 'subject closed' expression and Fintan could see he was going to have to be satisfied with that explanation.

So they talked for a few minutes more about

childcare options, but agreed to let the subject lie until they could look into it properly. And for the rest of the meal they dwelt on the far more pleasant subject of how they were going to spend Maeve's windfall. They talked about the children, as all parents will, no matter how hard they try not to. They discussed their summer holiday plans. They congratulated themselves on how lucky they were. And all said, they had a wonderful, relaxing meal and consumed another bottle of wine after the first vanished sooner than expected.

When they were finally ready to leave, the maître d' had to pour them into the waiting taxi. On the way home they behaved like a pair of teenagers, snogging, giggling and groping, much to the amusement of their mini-cab driver. At least he shut up, rather than lecture them on the state of the economy, politics and the moral downturn of the country. Maeve whispered to Fintan that she would have to remember this technique next time she was being bored to death in a taxi. Then, overcome with her own humour, she shook with smothered laughter the rest of the way home.

They had forgotten that Fintan's mother would be waiting in the house with Darragh, and spotted her coat just before they embarrassed themselves by continuing in the hallway what they had started in the taxi. Although from the grin on her mother-in-law's face as they came into the living-room, Maeve guessed they hadn't been as quiet as they thought they were being when she was groping Fintan as he tried to unlock the front door.

After a few minutes of polite conversation, Fintan

went to walk his mother to her car, and Maeve went upstairs. She checked on Darragh, did a quick job of removing her make-up and washed her teeth. Then she went into the bedroom, draped herself seductively across the quilt and waited for her husband to join her.

CHAPTER 5

Maeve sat up with a start. It was dark and Darragh was whinging in the next room. As she clambered out of bed, she remembered she'd been waiting for Fintan to come up.

Shit! She must have fallen asleep.

Unconscious more like it – Fintan had managed to get her undressed and into her pyjamas without waking her. Surely she hadn't had that much to drink? Maeve added up in her head, and realised she had – and more! After settling Darragh, she went down to the kitchen for a glass of water.

It was just after two, according to the clock on the cooker – no wonder her hangover hadn't kicked in yet. Maeve flipped on the over-counter lights, unwilling to expose herself to the glare of the halogen ceiling lights. She pulled a litre of apple juice from the fridge and sat down at the end of the long farmhouse table that ran nearly the whole length of the wall. She poured a glass of juice and despite her exhaustion was unable to suppress a smile as she ran her hand over the rough pine surface of the table. Each of these dents and scratches told the story of another generation, she thought. Food had been prepared and served here while homework was pored over. Countless newspapers had been spread out leaving a grey shadow at the other end of the table. Maeve knew she should really sand the stain off, but she kept postponing the job, because she loved the feeling of continuity it gave her.

The whole kitchen had been designed to fit around the table. Maeve had chosen pine units, rough-hewn slate floor tiles and a Belfast sink to reproduce the kitchen she imagined this table to have lived in a century ago. The walls were painted white rather than a more modern shade of pastel, and the year Ciaran was born Fintan had found a Wexford dresser in a shop on Capel Street. The deliveryman who levered the huge piece into place had joked, looking at Maeve's swollen belly, that she wouldn't need to buy a cot now – the bottom drawer had no doubt served as bed for countless farmers' children.

Maeve returned to the present and tried to remember how to ward off a hangover. Vitamin C and lots of sugar. Fluids, fluids and more fluids, wasn't that it? She poured another glass of apple juice. As an afterthought, she took two Solpadeine tablets to get ahead of the inevitable living death she would suffer later.

At six, that death became reality. Maeve's tongue

was stuck to the roof of her mouth and her head felt only loosely connected to her neck. She was afraid that if she moved too fast she'd look down to see it roll across the floor.

Darragh was screaming.

Gingerly, Maeve turned to see what state Fintan was in. He was asleep, or 'as peaceful as a baby'! Ha! She shuffled around in bed, directing an 'accidental' kick in Fintan's direction, but he just turned over, sighed and seemed to settle into an ever deeper sleep.

Resigned, Maeve lowered her legs over the side of the bed and made her way downstairs to warm a bottle and to find some more Solpadeine. The tablets she had taken earlier were duds, she decided. No way could they have failed so spectacularly otherwise.

Darragh greeted her with a glorious smile and gurgled happily as she changed his nappy. She handed him his bottle, and tried to put him down again in his cot. Not a chance. This was the start of a wonderful day and if Mum couldn't appreciate it, Darragh would explain . . .

He screwed up his face, took a deep breath, opened his mouth and. . .

Maeve grabbed him just in time.

"What am I going to do with you?" she asked miserably.

She brought him downstairs and, ignoring her guilty feelings, put Darragh in the playpen and switched on the television. To her son's delight, a red Tellytubby began to cavort musically across the screen.

Gently Maeve lowered her head onto a cushion, stretched herself along the couch and pulled one of the children's fleece blankets over her legs.

"Darragh, honey," she mumbled, "you don't realise what an awful mother I'm being right now, but I promise I'll pay for your therapy when you're old enough to resent this."

Within seconds she was asleep, dreaming of strange yellow and red creatures playing in a surreal, hilly countryside.

"Maeve, Maeve. Are you awake? Maeve!"

Maeve pretended not to hear him, but Fintan didn't give up that easily.

"Maeve, are you awake?"

"Go away, and let me die in peace," she snarled, pulling the blanket up over her head.

"Go back to bed, if you're that bad." Fintan sounded as if he was trying not to laugh.

"I can't move," Maeve answered. "All connections between my brain and the rest of my body have been severed by the army of little men with chainsaws and jackhammers who have invaded the inside of my skull. What time is it anyway?" She had only just noticed the television was silent.

"It's half eight," Fintan answered. "When I came in half an hour ago, Darragh was happily watching *Sky News*."

"Oh no!" Maeve groaned. "Another news junkie in the house. One of you is bad enough."

"Actually I missed the financial report," Fintan told her as he helped her to her feet, "so Darragh gave me a quick summary while I put him back for a nap. The Euro's down, and Noo-Noo cleaned up all the tubby-custard."

In spite of herself, Maeve laughed and found the parts of her body she needed to propel herself upstairs.

At around noon, she re-emerged to find life somewhat improved. The house was quiet so she tiptoed past Darragh's room for fear of waking him, but she needn't have bothered. A note on the hall table informed her that father and son had gone to the park to play football. Fintan was determined to have his offspring inherit his love of sport.

In the kitchen the table had been set for a solitary breakfast. There was a pink and white tulip from the garden in a small vase and the morning newspaper beside Maeve's plate. Fintan had defrosted some Danish pastries and there was a huge pile of them in a basket in the middle of the table. It was nearly as good as breakfast in bed!

Maeve switched on the coffee machine, wandered in to the living-room to get her glasses (contact lenses and hangovers don't mix, she knew from past experience) and noticed the flashing light on the answering machine. There were four messages. Maeve debated leaving the phone until she had finished breakfast, but conscience and curiosity got the better of her so she pressed *Play*.

There were two messages from Danny, one last

night, and one this morning, both confirming that the deal had gone through. There was a message from Andrea asking how things had gone with Sarah. And the last message was Fintan saying he was on the way home. At that moment she heard him pull up outside.

"How was the park?" Maeve asked as she took a sleepy Darragh from his father.

"Green. How's the hangover?"

"Idiot, I mean did you have a good time? And I'm feeling a lot better, thanks."

"We had a fantastic time, didn't we, Darragh? He's really picking up the finer points of soccer," Fintan said proudly. "I explained the penalty shoot-out today. He sat in the buggy and watched while I scored at least ten fantastic goals, and he didn't need to ask a single question. Then I showed him how to do headers. That didn't go nearly as well – the oak tree saved four out of six of them."

"How lovely. Did you meet anyone we know?" Maeve asked, wondering how long it would be before the neighbours realised just what kind of a lunatic she was married to.

"No one really, unless you count that French guy, what's his name?" Fintan was smiling innocently, referring to a new client of Maeve's. "The one we took to dinner last month? You know who I mean . . . you were trying to get that big contract out of him. Anyway, I asked would he like to play in goal, but he didn't seem that keen. Left in rather a hurry actually." Fintan took pity when she went pale. Jean-Paul was an important client whom Maeve was due to see again soon. "Only joking! No, we didn't meet anyone."

They put Darragh to sleep upstairs and shared coffee and Danish pastries in the kitchen. They read the papers and then Maeve rang her mother to check on Fiona and update her about Sarah's bombshell.

Anna could come up with no solutions, but she did express relief that she was back working, so she wouldn't have to step into the breach. "Raising you, darling, is as much as any woman could be expected to do in one lifetime."

Maeve grinned at that; her grandmother and a series of au-pairs had always played a much greater part in raising her. Somehow Anna always had something terribly important to do, although she hadn't started in her current job, her first, until a few years after her husband's death. Instead, she took her position as bank manager's wife very seriously. Always immaculately turned out, she helped with all the right charities and maintained a highly visible social life. It was experience that now served her in good stead in the PR business, she was fond of telling people.

Her mother's life was not one Maeve had any intention of emulating. As a young child she had sworn, to the amusement of any adult who would listen, that she would always work and that she would earn at least as much if not more than her husband – if she deigned ever to get married. And as she grew older Maeve also promised herself that she would be more involved in her children's upbringing. It should be possible to do both, she constantly reminded herself in the small hours of the morning. Her father had been the greatest influence in her life and yet he had worked so hard he ended up working himself into an early grave.

Fintan rang his cousin June to pick her brain. With three children herself, she should be a mine of information on the subject of crèches and childminders. She was sympathetic, but not much help. It had taken her so long to sort out her own arrangements that she hadn't the energy to put into someone else's problems. But she came up with the name of three crèches in their area as she taught near where they lived and other teachers at her school used them.

So Fintan and Maeve checked the Golden Pages for other nurseries, Fintan composed an ad for a childminder and by evening they felt they had the problem in hand.

For dinner, they kept to the day's lazy theme, and Fintan went for a takeaway. While he was out Andrea phoned.

"You've been keeping me in suspense – what did that Sarah woman want?"

"Andrea, you need to get a life, if that's all you've had to worry about all day!" But Maeve filled her in on the details nonetheless.

"Wow," Andrea whistled, "you didn't see that one coming. Rotten timing too. What are your chances of replacing her in time?"

"Not good."

"So what are you going to do?"

"No idea yet – we were just going through our options before you called."

Andrea was silent for a moment and then asked, "Did one of those options entail you giving up work?" Much as she wanted to settle down and have children herself, Andrea would freely admit she had no intention of giving up work to look after them.

"No, with the merger, if I give up work now, I'll lose a shitload of money." And I really don't want to give up, Maeve thought – why can't I say that out loud?

"Oh yeah," Andrea remembered. "You had that meeting with Fish-face yesterday – how did that go?"

"Let's say better than expected – I'll fill you in when I have more details."

They chatted for a while and Andrea, always ready with a supply of cheering little anecdotes, told Maeve horror stories about women who, not being able to find the right kind of childcare, ended up chained to the sink until they went stark raving bonkers. They continued talking until Fintan arrived back with enough brown bags of Chinese food to feed the whole road.

The next morning Maeve woke up in a warm, optimistic, rosy mood. She realised that she hadn't lost her sex-drive, but with three kids in the house, she had merely temporarily mislaid it. Remove the kids for a short period, and she could search and locate it. Certainly she and Fintan had enjoyed hunting for it last night. Maeve resolved to make sure they got some time to themselves at least once a month and then she laughed out loud.

If someone had told her eight years ago, when she and Fintan were first married, that she would be making plans for uninterrupted sex once a month, she'd have thought they were insane. Back then they could barely keep their hands off each other. Back then they could have had sex anywhere, even once in the utility room, amongst all the dirty laundry. These days, Maeve was more likely to be on her way up to bed only to suddenly remember the dirty laundry, and then find Fintan fast asleep by the time she had finished filling the machine.

She remembered, shortly after Fiona was born, reading an article in a woman's magazine claiming that the number of times a couple had sex dropped from seven or eight times a week before they were married to two or three afterwards. As Maeve fell short of the lower figure she had been depressed for days and wondered if there was something seriously wrong with her. After a while she had rationalised that the article didn't take children into account, and anyway, who wanted to set their standards by the type of women who replied to sex surveys in magazines?

CHAPTER 6

On Monday morning, Maeve was early for work. She pulled into the carpark at seven and let herself into the office. She was the first in, so she made a pot of coffee and began work. From the pile of messages on her desk, it looked as if she had been missing for a week. She loved the office at this time. The smell of cleaning fluids after an earlier visit from the contract cleaners was soon banished as the coffee machine began to splutter to life. Apart from a muted hum of traffic through double-glazed windows, the coffee machine and Maeve's fingers on her keyboard were the only sounds. Her tiny office felt cosy rather than cramped without the invading telephones, voices and office noise from outside her door that she was used to. And at this time of year, if Maeve got in early enough, she was rewarded by a few rays of morning sun that crept across her crowded but tidy desk, along her shelves and filing cabinets to light the old blue carpet in front of her door for a few brief minutes.

After dealing with her in-tray, Maeve started phoning her list of crèches. She was surprised and soon horrified at the number of places no longer taking babies and she crossed them off her list because she didn't want to separate the children.

At nine Danny appeared in her office, grinning like a schoolboy.

"I've put together a presentation for the staff, explaining the implications of the deal," he said, waving a thick sheaf of slides and handouts at Maeve. "Can you get everyone back here for a lunch-time meeting so that we can give them all the news before they hear it on the grapevine?"

Maeve had anticipated this, and gave her assistant, Colm, a list of people to call. Then she ordered food from Andrea's delicatessen friend and phoned the off-licence for wine. As an afterthought, she added champagne to the order, thinking, what the hell, the company was paying!

In the middle of the morning, Danny arrived back in her office.

"Peter wants to hi-jack my meeting," he sulked. "He has all these Ofiscom slides, showing the value of the shares, all sorts of company propaganda and the reasons they'll be better off once Big Brother takes over."

Maeve tried not to laugh at the petulant expression on her boss's face.

"Tell Peter that as I'm chairing the meeting he should come and talk to me," she soothed, "and I'll see what I can do." She was getting sick of keeping the peace between those two.

She shuffled some papers around on her desk to give Danny the hint that he should leave and let her get on with her work, but he was barely out the door when Peter stuck his head around it.

"Maeve, great! Just the person I was looking for."

Who else did you expect to find in my office, Maeve felt like saying. Instead, she flashed a saccharine smile and asked him to come in.

"What can I do for you, Peter? I take it Danny's told you I've managed to get everyone back here for lunchtime?"

"Yes, that's what I wanted to talk to you about. I gather you're chairing the meeting? Great! I just want to run things through with you. I have some slides I need to share with the group."

"Well, let's see, Peter . . ." Maeve consulted an imaginary running order on her laptop. "I had planned to give a brief introduction and then turn the meeting over to Danny. Maybe if we took a quick break and topped up everyone's glasses, you could close with the Ofiscom presentation. That would end the meeting on a high note." She knew from experience that Peter's presentations erred on the long and boring side of mind-numbing, but hopefully after a few glasses of bubbly, everyone would either already be half-asleep or past caring. As a precaution she added, "I will have to ask you to keep it to under ten minutes. We have a lot of people who have to get back out there to 'bring in the dollars'!"

The phone rang, interrupting her.

"Yes, Colm . . . the manager of which crèche? Oh yes, of course, I'll take that now, one moment." She placed her hand automatically over the mouthpiece. "Peter, do you mind? I really do have to take this call." As he showed no sign of leaving, Maeve sighed and pressed the flashing button on her phone.

"Hello, Maeve Larkin speaking. Thank you for returning my call. I was enquiring whether you have any free places coming up in the near future. You have? Great!" Maeve grinned at the thought that her troubles were so close to being over. "I need places for a toddler, a baby, and a four-year-old . . ." Her face fell. "When am I due? Oh no!" She tried a little laugh. "Darragh's six months old already . . . he *is* the baby . . . oh, I see, well thank you for keeping me on your list." She hung up, dejected.

"Problems, Maeve?" Peter asked, trying to look sympathetic, but only really managing curious.

"My childminder just gave notice that she's quitting and I have to sort something else out before July."

"That should present no problem surely, to an efficient businesswoman like you?" He beamed.

"How long have you been in Dublin now, Peter?" Maeve tried not to sound too exasperated. "Do you never read the papers, listen to the radio or even watch TV? We're in the middle of a childcare crisis!"

"The only newspaper I ever read is the *International Herald Tribune*. And of course the *Financial Times*. As for radio and TV, I couldn't really be bothered, most of it's trash! If I get really homesick, I pick up one of my favourite Texan stations on the Internet. But back to your problem, surely there's plenty of agencies out there you could outsource to?"

Peter took a sheet of paper from the printer, pulled a silver pen from his inside pocket and wrote *Maeve's Children* on the top. He underlined it three times.

"Let's see. What have you tried so far?"

"'Outsource'!" Maeve was still struggling with his last comment. "Peter, these are my children, not some programming glitch in one of our contracts."

"That's your problem, Maeve," he drawled. "You view the situation too emotionally. If you could become detached, take the helicopter view of your arrangements, I'm sure everything would fall onto place." Peter leaned back in his chair. "I'd like to help you get a handle on this problem, Maeve. We could do with a fresh project like this to get us working closer together. What do you say to a brainstorming session on the issue?"

Maeve had trouble deciding if he was being serious, or taking the mickey. Then she remembered who she was talking to and she was forced to conclude he was trying to be helpful. She smiled weakly.

"Thanks for the offer, Peter, but Fintan and I are well into the organisational stages of this . . . project. Now I really must get on with planning what I'm going to say at this meeting. I do *so* want to give your presentation justice."

"Don't worry, Maeve, what I have to say to the

troops will stand on its own merits. But thanks for the sentiment." Peter jumped to his feet and left, grinning.

When she was sure he was gone, Maeve banged her head three times slowly on the desk then looked up to see Colm watching her, an amused expression on his face. She blushed, and fiddled with an open file.

"Don't worry, boss, we all do that after The Fish leaves our presence," her assistant quipped. "In fact it's a relief to see you do the same – some people were beginning to suspect that you'd been around him too much and were losing your grip on reality."

Maeve opened her mouth to give her usual 'Peter's important to this company so we really must tolerate his little differences' speech, but she saw Colm doing his winding-up impression so she decided not to bother. She asked instead: "Did you manage to get everyone back for the meeting?"

"You kidding?" he sniffed. "Everyone's been waiting for this call for weeks. There would have been an uprising if you hadn't come up with the goods soon. I was elected to come and ask you straight out what the hold-up was. I've been holding them all off by saying, 'No news is good news' . . . I just hope it *is* good news." He pulled what Maeve called his 'hungry-puppy' face.

She was tempted to tell him to wait till one o'clock, but decided that there was no harm in having everyone come to the meeting in good spirits. And even though there was only one hour to go, she was sure that anything she told Colm the whole company would know before they entered the conference room.

"Yes, Colm, it's good news," she smiled, "but I'm telling you that as my assistant, and because I trust that anything I tell you in confidence will not go beyond these four walls." Maeve wondered how long his conscience would hold out under that onslaught and gave it five minutes, maximum.

Sure enough, when Maeve, Danny and Peter entered the packed conference room, the atmosphere was buzzing. The food had hardly been touched, but the wine had been savaged. Maeve tapped on a glass to get the crowd's attention.

"Right, before we get started, I'd like you all to help yourselves to food." She pointed to paper plates and platters of cold meats and salads on the long boardroom table. There was an excited but muted hum as people piled food onto disposable plates. There were not enough chairs, so when everyone eventually settled down there were people perched on the edge of the table and on the windowsills. Some of the more enterprising staff had brought their own office chairs with them.

Maeve brought the meeting to order.

"As you are all aware, in order to expand this company, keep competitive, and ensure we all have jobs in ten years' time, Danny decided that we needed to merge with a larger partner, preferably international," she began. "We looked into a number of options and eventually chose Ofiscom. This can only be good for Leeson Business Solutions – it opens up new markets and guarantees the capital we need for expansion.

Ofiscom has already earmarked a number of our software products for further development."

Maeve stopped and took a sip of water before continuing.

"However, what most of you are here to find out today, is how Ofiscom proposes to deal with your rights under our profit-share scheme."

Thirty pairs of eyes were riveted on her and eating stopped, mid-mouthful. As she spelt out the implications of the deal she had negotiated on their behalf, Maeve looked around at her fellow workers. She could see that most of them could hardly believe the windfall they were about to receive. Although they had all been optimistic and rumours had abounded as to what the little company they worked for was really worth, she felt like Santa Claus as nervous smiles split into wide grins. When she finally handed the floor to her boss, Danny got a rapturous applause.

By the time Maeve broke out the champagne, pouring as much on the carpet as into the small plastic glasses, everyone was in celebratory mood. A couple of the older hands came up to Maeve to congratulate her on the deal and to thank her quietly for driving such a hard bargain. When she had taken as much praise as she could handle, Maeve tapped on the side of a bottle to attract attention and called Peter to the top of the room.

It was difficult to bring the meeting back to order, but the Texan didn't seem to mind the lack of attention lavished on his slides. He had nothing new to add, except reassurances that jobs were safe and that there would even be scope for promotions. He spoke for double his allocated ten minutes and Maeve was glad she had set him a limit. When everyone finally broke up to return to work it was nearly three o'clock and she knew very little actual work would get done for the rest of the day.

So she returned to her office and spent about half an hour finishing bits and pieces she hadn't managed to get through in the morning. Then she decided to call it a day and left early to visit two crèches on her way home.

CHAPTER 7

Later that day, Fintan left work at about six and fumed his way along O'Connell Street in traffic that was almost at a standstill.

He watched with envy as cyclists whipped past him and he half-wished he were still lecturing in college which was far closer to home and well within cycling distance. He had given up his academic ambition when he realised he couldn't cope with the political in-fighting and back-stabbing he would have had to indulge in to get a permanent post. Instead, five years ago, when he had hinted he would like to leave the college, he had been headhunted straight away by The Irish Progressive. He took the easy option and accepted the job. He enjoyed his work, but he wasn't as passionate about it as he had been about lecturing and he had to admit he missed all the free time he had used to research the book he had started writing in his college days. His *Irish Economic History* was now gathering dust in its three cardboard boxes of notes, where it had languished since Fiona was born.

Sarah looked flustered when she saw that it was Fintan collecting the children. Although they met at least two or three days a week, they still had an uneasy relationship. Neither would have been able to explain why. Sarah was more comfortable with women, not having had much male contact since her husband left, and although Fintan had initially made an effort to develop the same chatty line Maeve used with Sarah, after a while he gave up.

"Hi, Fintan, come on in. I'll just get the kids." Sarah began to deliver a report on their day. She spoke at high speed, then rushed upstairs to get the baby while Fintan retrieved the two older children and loaded them into the car. When Sarah re-emerged, carrying a sleepy and cranky Darragh, Fintan felt he ought to try to make some kind of conversation.

"Maeve's gone to look at a few crèches on her way home from work today. I hope she has some luck," he said, and then wished he hadn't when Sarah looked so guilty.

"You must think I'm awful landing you in the lurch like that." She looked as if she was about to burst into tears.

"Sarah, I'm thrilled you've decided to have a go at studying," Fintan said quickly. "Maeve and I will sort something out – it just came as a bit of a shock, that's all." He buckled Darragh into his baby-seat in record time and took out his keys for a quick escape. "Really, don't worry about us. We've been very lucky to have you for as long as we have. Ciaran and Fiona will really miss you. I'd say Darragh would too, if I wasn't so sure that that young man's affections lie entirely with whoever fills his stomach the fastest."

They both smiled at his attempt at humour and Fintan made the most of the opportunity to get the car started and down the drive. He felt guilty at the relief he felt when he was out on the road and away from Sarah. Although he hadn't been as upset as Maeve was at the thought of losing her, he was pissed off at the problems they would face arranging alternative childcare. Also, although he hadn't mentioned it to his wife for fear of making her feel worse, he knew the children really would miss the woman who had essentially been their daytime mum for years now.

"Well?" Fintan kissed Maeve and handed a sleepy Darragh to her. "How did you get on?"

"Not great." Maeve had a resigned expression on her face. "Let's wait until we get this lot to bed, then I'll tell you about it."

When they finally sat down to dinner, she began with a sigh. "This is going to be more difficult than we thought . . ."

"Even more difficult, you mean," answered Fintan. "We knew it was going to be tough. But, after all, this is only Day One, so let's not get too discouraged. Why don't you tell me exactly how you got on?"

He had opened a bottle of wine when he saw

Maeve's face earlier, and now he topped up the glass she had almost knocked back in one go as soon as she sat down.

"Well, out of the list of twenty crèches we drew up on Sunday, I've worked my way through fifteen so far and I've drawn a blank. Loads of crèches have stopped taking babies under a year old and two of the ones who do take them asked me when my baby was due." Maeve sighed and pushed her pork chop around her plate. She took a big knob of butter and watched it melt into her potato. "All the managers were very sympathetic, but I got the impression that they considered me slightly soft in the head to be even trying to find place for Darragh at this late stage. Most people have their babies booked in before they're born!"

When she stopped speaking Fintan didn't know what to say. Everyone had heard horror stories about the problems with finding childcare in Dublin, but this was beyond a joke.

"Oh, but there is light on the horizon!" Maeve said, with a tightening of her facial muscles which might pass for a wry grin. "The manageress of Amberley Tots in town said if we were considering having any more children, she would note our interest now, and we would have a good chance of getting a place later. In fact, if we pay a deposit now and tell her as soon as we know I'm pregnant, she could almost guarantee a place for number four. How's that for service?"

"Did any of the nurseries offer to let us book places for our grandchildren?" Fintan asked. "It might be a worthwhile investment and a great wedding present for the kids."

He cleared the plates off the table, although Maeve had hardly touched her food, and then reached automatically for two dessert dishes and dug into the back of the freezer for the emergency tub of Double Chocolate Haagen Dazs. He took a small scoop himself, and filled his wife's bowl.

"Thanks." Maeve started picking chocolate chips out of her ice cream with her fingers. "Seriously though, what are we going to do?" Her face crumpled with worry. "You did put that ad in the paper today, didn't you, Fintan?"

"I posted it on Saturday and I rang today to check they had it. It'll run for three days from Wednesday." He came up behind her, dropped a spoon into her bowl and then began to rub her shoulders. "Don't worry, we'll sort something out. There must be someone out there dying to spend time with our three wonderful children."

Fintan expressed optimism he didn't feel. For the first time, he began to feel some of the panic Maeve had experienced on Friday. Mentally, he reviewed their options. It didn't take long. He cursed the summer job he'd helped his younger sister Orla to get in London. They had always fallen back on her in case of emergency. She absolutely doted on her nephews and niece, and if the worst came to the worst, he knew he could have relied on her to step in for the summer, at least until the college term started back. But this was her first real job, and his parents were hoping that once she got a taste for work, their twenty-six-year-old daughter would finally give up her eternal student lifestyle. She was currently on her second degree, financed by her hobby of website design – the result of her first degree.

"Pity Orla's going to London for the summer," Maeve said, with her uncanny ability to know what he was thinking. "If she'd been around, she might have helped your parents look after the kids. There's no way that they could handle them on their own."

Neither of them even considered Maeve's mother. When she baby-sat, the children all had to be in bed before she arrived, and if two of them woke up at the same time, she was on the phone in a panic, wondering what to do.

"I wonder how Matt will survive without Orla for three months?" Maeve said, changing the subject. Matthew Tobin, Orla's boyfriend, was also Maeve and Fintan's next door-neighbour.

When they first moved in, Orla spotted the gorgeous hunk who lived next door with his parents and suddenly developed an interest in gardening, spending every available opportunity helping to tame the wilderness they inherited from the previous owner. It paid off. One day Matt offered to help Orla stack and light a bonfire, and once she had him, she didn't let go. They had been going out together, with a few breaks, for nearly seven years now. It was very convenient for Maeve and Fintan to have him next door. If Orla baby-sat, Matt usually tagged along, and then insisted on seeing her home, saving Fintan the walk.

"He's enquiring into block-booking weekend flights to London for the summer," Fintan replied with a grin. "The guy has more money than he knows what to do with. You'd think he'd buy a house or something."

It had turned out that Matt shared Orla's love of computers, but had stuck with it and had started his own company. He programmed security into computer systems and was very successful.

"He's not going to buy a house until he knows what Orla's plans are," Maeve answered. "He's terrified that if he buys something here Orla'll think he's trying to settle down and you know what effect that would have on her."

All their previous break-ups had been because Matt had 'got too serious' or pressed her for a commitment. Everyone knew they were prefect for each other, and would eventually end up together – but as far as Orla was concerned, 'eventually' meant sometime far in the future.

"Talking of Orla, she offered to baby-sit for us on Wednesday. I'll get tickets to the preview of that play you wanted to see," Fintan told Maeve.

"Great, we'll actually get to see a play before you read the reviews and tell me how awful it's going to be," she laughed, and then remembered: "Oh no! Not Wednesday. That's the day we have to take Jean-Paul to dinner. Now that I've landed him as a client, Danny wants to keep him sweet until the merger goes through, reassure him that we'll still be able to do the job right for him."

"*We* have to go out to dinner? Surely you don't need me too?" Fintan moaned. "You know how much I hate these business dinners!"

"Oh come on, they're not really that bad, and anyway, you're off the hook. I suggested to Danny that we'd be better off without partners, and he looked relieved. I guess Cathy kicked up a fuss too about having to go."

Maeve had been surprised at that; normally Cathy jumped at every opportunity to dine out and be seen. She always insisted Danny book the trendiest, most expensive restaurants, so she could gather material for her monthly social column. Maybe she was still in London, and Danny had forgotten how long she would be away for.

"This must be the fourth business dinner this month. I hardly ever get to see you anymore." Now that Fintan didn't have to go himself, he was going to kick up a fuss about Maeve going. "I thought you were going to keep those to a minimum."

"I know, love. And I'm sorry," she apologised, "but things should improve when the merger goes through. And Danny originally wanted to have it on Friday – at least I managed to put him off that."

Fintan sensed that Maeve felt bad enough and reluctantly let the subject drop. But he was still unhappy about it. He felt that the pressure of Maeve's extra workload was putting a strain on them as a couple. So far, they had both been careful that the

73

children didn't lose out, but it had meant that their own time together was usually spent in a mad frenzy of sorting out the children and keeping the house in a state fit for human habitation. Although Fintan was proud of Maeve, and admired her drive and enthusiasm for her job, qualities he was honest enough to admit he didn't possess himself, he sometimes felt jealous of the times her job took her away from him. He hated that he felt that way, as if he were possessive and patriarchal, so he tried to tell himself that it was only because he was afraid that they would lose out as a family. But during the weekend they had just spent together, Maeve and Fintan had been close in a way he had forgotten he missed. He was determined not to lose that closeness.

"I won't moan about Wednesday if you promise not to do any work all weekend," he offered. "In fact, I think we should spend the weekend sorting out the garden."

"That's blackmail, Fintan," Maeve grumbled.

Maeve loved the garden, but she hated the huge tidy-up each spring. She could handle the odd bit of weeding, even mow the lawn now and again, but she left most of the other work to her husband.

"I know," Fintan grinned and fed his last spoonful of ice cream to her, "but you'll be glad when we've done it." He wiped the last of the chocolate from her lower lip and kissed her.

CHAPTER 8

On Wednesday evening Maeve got ready to go out for dinner with Danny and Jean-Paul. Jean-Paul Thiebaud was the CEO of a French manufacturing firm about to expand its operations into Ireland. It was Danny who had originally pursued the contract, but he failed to convince the French that they needed LBS's expertise. Six months later Maeve travelled to Lyons to have another go.

There was only one problem – the merger. It had taken a lot of convincing to persuade Jean-Paul that LBS was going to remain relatively free of interference from their American partners. In the end she won him over and came home clutching LBS's biggest contract to date. Now that the final details of the LBS-Ofiscom merger were ironed out, they were meeting to reinforce their position and keep the French on board.

Maeve searched through her wardrobe, trying to decide what to wear. The black trouser suit and gold camisole she had picked out that morning looked wrong now and she flicked through the hangers on the 'good' side of her hanging rail. All day she had been regretting her choice and had decided to opt for a cream shift dress she had bought in France. In a sale, even hugely reduced, it cost more than any other item of clothing she had ever bought. It was simple, chic and just right for dinner with the sophisticated Frenchman. The fact that she had bought it to reward herself for landing the French contract just made the choice more perfect. Perfect except for the fact that the dress was in the dry-cleaner's. After discarding two more dresses, and two suits that no amount of accessorising could turn into anything other than 'Day at the Office', Maeve finally returned to her original choice. Her indecision had left her with only a few minutes to rearrange her hair and touch up her make-up.

Danny had arranged to collect Maeve at half seven, but as usual he was early, chatting with Ciaran in the kitchen because Fintan was in the middle of putting the two younger children to bed. Although normally Fintan would have abandoned the bedtime routine to chat to Danny, Maeve suspected he was making a point. Family life took priority in the Larkin household, even when Maeve's boss was waiting for her.

When she finally emerged, Ciaran was displaying his Pokemon cards to a confused Danny. The poor man couldn't get his head around the concept.

"Ciaran's been telling me all about Pokechus," he grinned. "Fascinating subject. Now I can see what all the fuss is about."

"They're called Pokemons! And Pikachu is the name of my favourite one," Ciaran snorted. "And Daddy's calling me for bed so I'd better go. Night-night, Mum. Night, Danny." He kissed his mother, gathered up his cards and left the room in the superior way only a four-year-old can pull off.

"That put you in your place," Maeve laughed, watching her son sweep out.

As she watched him act all 'grown up' she longed to follow him, enclose him in a bear hug and put him to bed with a long story and a good-night kiss – before he grew too old to tolerate such humiliation. For Maeve suddenly realised that there were only a limited number of Ciaran's childhood bedtimes left, and to waste one on Danny and Monsieur Thiebaud seemed absurd.

"Let's get going," she said reluctantly to Danny. "You go out to the car and I'll follow you out." She went up to say goodbye to Fintan, who managed not to look too huffy when she kissed him.

"Don't stay out too late," he said, only half-joking. "I'll wait up until you get back"

"You sound like my mother," Maeve complained coming up behind him to wrap her arms about his middle. She tickled his chest in a way she knew he could never resist.

"Stop it, you tease," Fintan groaned.

"Hold that mood and I'll get away as early as I can."

"Mmm, good. I'll see you later." He turned and kissed her hungrily on the lips.

Maeve left, happier now that Fintan was in a slightly better mood. She joined Danny in the car and they pulled out onto the road.

"Where are you going to leave the car overnight?" Maeve asked Danny as they drove towards town.

"I'll be driving home actually," he answered, looking straight ahead. "I'm on antibiotics so I can't drink."

"Oh come on, Danny, you don't honestly expect me to keep pace with Jean-Paul on my own, do you?" The Frenchman was fond of his wine and usually ordered a different bottle with each course. Even with three of them drinking, Maeve found it hard going.

"He won't expect you to drink as much as him – you're only a woman!" Danny joked. "Anyway, I was at the dentist this morning and I need a root filling so I'm on antibiotics till it settles down."

Maeve was so terrified of dentists, especially when anyone mentioned root fillings, that her sympathy for Danny just about overcame her cynicism about the convenient timing of his dental infection. He'd done this before, left her to drink with the client, while he kept a clear head and remained in control of proceedings. She fumed in silence the rest of the way into town.

They were meeting Jean-Paul in the bar of the Shelbourne Hotel where he was staying. He wanted to eat in the hotel because he was in such dread of Irish weather that he was terrified that if he stuck his well-coiffed head out the door, it would be drenched in a monsoon-like downpour. The fact that he had been very lucky with the weather, and had experienced in Ireland only the best that global warming had to offer, had not changed his mind.

"Maeve, Danny, wonderful to see you again!" Jean-Paul stood and greeted them loudly. He moved confidently, in a perfectly cut suit and hand-made shoes, an imposing figure despite his lack of height, and several other guests turned to watch his progress across the floor.

"Is not the weather truly dreadful?" he gasped. "When I left Lyon this morning the temperature, she was at nineteen degrees. Here you have only twelve degrees!"

He shook hands with Danny and kissed Maeve three times on the cheeks. She was glad she hadn't brought Fintan as she imagined Jean-Paul lingered rather too long with the third kiss – and strayed dangerously close to her lips with it. And his hair, extravagantly long, but in no way effeminate, brushed against her ear as he withdrew.

"The table it is booked for nine, I think. Will you help me drink this bottle of Sancerre before we go in?"

Danny ordered a mineral water, while Jean-Paul poured wine for Maeve and topped up his own glass. The Sancerre was divine. Jean-Paul certainly knew how to order wine even if, being French, he had a habit of ignoring anything produced outside his native country. They chatted about the weather for a while and Jean-Paul sought their advice about sightseeing in Dublin.

By nine they had done sufficient damage to the bottle of Sancerre and he led them into the dining-room.

Once they had ordered, the conversation turned to the LBS-Ofiscom merger and any possible implications it might have on the contract with Jean-Paul's company. The conversation went much more smoothly than Maeve expected and she began to relax.

By the time their starter plates were cleared, the topic of conversation had moved on to rugby and Maeve was finding it hard to join in. Not only because she had no interest in the sport, but because she was concentrating on controlling the amount she drank. Despite several glasses of mineral water, she felt tipsy. She had no idea how much wine she had drunk because, every time she so much as took a sip, the Frenchman refilled her glass. By the end of the main course, she caught Danny giving her a funny look as she advised Jean-Paul about up-and-coming Irish artists. He had expressed an interest in investing in some Irish paintings, and Maeve was giving him the benefit of her non-existent knowledge. She decided to shut up before she did any real damage.

They ordered dessert, but Jean-Paul told the waiter to wait until the wine was finished before serving it so Maeve decided to take a trip to the ladies' to pull herself together. She looked at her watch for the first time all evening and was horrified to discover that it was after eleven so she phoned Fintan to warn him that she would be late. He announced coldly that he wouldn't bother waiting up for her and asked that she be careful not to make too much noise when she came in.

Maeve sighed as she imagined all the grovelling in store for her. Sometimes she wished Fintan was the work-all-hours businessman and she merely the tag-along wife. It would be much easier to stay at home and sulk, than be the one who had to keep apologising. If the roles were reversed, Maeve wondered, would Fintan apologise, or would he expect her to understand his working late? Maybe it was because she was a woman and a mother that Maeve felt so guilty and kept saying sorry.

She took a deep breath, reapplied her lipstick, ran damp fingers through her hair and ventured back into the dining-room.

When she got back to the table the waiter brought another chair and the two men stood as a tall, very glamorous, redhead joined them. Jean-Paul introduced her as Sandrine, a friend of his, who had just flown in from London. She was an airhostess whose schedule happily coincided with his stay in Dublin. When she remembered how hard it had been to pin Jean-Paul down to a particular date, Maeve found it hard not to smile. Sandrine declined to join them for a dessert, but ordered a side salad, and to Maeve's relief, seemed more than willing to help them kill off the last bottle of wine. But then, to Maeve's horror, Sandrine suggested champagne would be far easier on the stomach at that time of night and Jean-Paul immediately obliged.

It was nearly one by the time Danny and Maeve finally escaped into the cool Dublin night.

As soon as they got into the car, Danny began to apologise.

"I'm sorry, Maeve, I had no idea Jean-Paul would keep us that long. Will Fintan be annoyed?" Maeve didn't answer so Danny continued. "He must be really fed up with all this extra time you're putting in lately. I hope it's not getting to be a problem, is it?"

His apology annoyed Maeve because she knew she was expected to ease his conscience by saying it wasn't a problem. What would Danny do if she said it was a problem? Reorganise his whole way of working? Find someone else to fill in whenever Maeve felt she was doing too much? She was almost tempted to test his mettle, but realised that she had drunk too much and Danny was sober. Not a good time to play games with your boss. Even if he also happened to be one of your best friends. Instead Maeve chose to give him the reassurance he needed.

"Don't worry, Danny, Fintan and I are fine. We're just under a little extra pressure at the moment."

She explained about Sarah giving notice and the problems they were having sorting out alternative arrangements. Predictably Danny made all the right noises and offered to do all he could to help. Which, unless he was going to open a crèche in the already over-crowded LBS premises, was very little.

"Oh, don't worry, I'm sure we'll sort something out," Maeve said, in an attempt to reassure herself as much as her boss. "The ad for a childminder only appeared today, so hopefully we'll have people queuing at our door in no time."

"I'm sure you'll be fine," Danny agreed, "but if

there's anything I can do, be sure to let me know. If you need to juggle your hours around a bit more, I'm sure we can work around it."

"I'm already doing so much juggling I'd get job in the circus," Maeve said wryly, "but thanks for the offer."

For a minute or so they drove in silence. Maeve imagined it to be an uncomfortable silence, so she tried to think of something . . . anything, to say. But the longer it took her, the heavier the silence became.

"How's Cathy?" she asked at last. "I haven't seen her for a while. Is she still in London?"

For a moment Danny didn't answer, but frowned, then grimaced and seemed to be involved in some kind of inner debate. Eventually the need to unburden won over.

"Cathy and I are no longer together," he said. "Or so she informed me by e-mail over the weekend."

Maeve was stunned and slammed her mouth shut with an audible click when she realised it was hanging open. She had never particularly liked Cathy, but she hadn't taken her for that much of a bitch.

"We had some rows over the phone," Danny explained. "Nothing huge, or so I thought – until Saturday when she dropped the bombshell over cyberspace."

"Had you no idea at all it was coming?" Maeve asked, still unable to believe that Cathy had broken it off with Danny after five years. The general consensus was that the woman knew a good thing when she saw it and that it wouldn't be long before she marched him down the aisle – to a life of joint bank accounts and platinum credit cards.

"Not really," Danny said, shrugging. "I knew she was eager to get one of those jobs she applied for in London, but I always kind of assumed we'd work it out, commute between the two cities or something." He failed to add that he had been window-shopping for engagement rings and had intended to pop the question soon. "She claims I'm too set in my ways and she wants to get out and enjoy herself before she settles down."

Maeve suspected that now Cathy had a job in London she was in a bigger sea and wanted to be free to fish. Not that being attached would have presented her with much of an obstacle – Maeve knew of at least one fling Cathy had enjoyed in the past five years, and that was in Dublin, right under Danny's nose. She longed to tell him he was well shot of her, but she knew the wound was too raw. Besides, she always made a point of not trashing exes; you never knew when an apparently hopeless couple would get back together. And then you were the worst in the world for having said such awful things.

"So are you having a break, do you think, or are you actually broken up?" she asked carefully.

Danny snorted. "I'd have thought by the way she delivered the news and the fact that she hasn't returned any of my calls, that it was pretty obvious." He was clearly upset. "The thing that gets me most is that she was obviously just having a good time, when I thought we were getting serious. Now she's moved on to bigger and better things. She doesn't need me anymore, so it's 'Bye, bye, Danny, you are surplus to requirements, pick up your P45 on the way out'."

Maeve was surprised at how bitter he sounded. She didn't want the conversation to go much further because she was afraid that in this mood Danny might say something spiteful he'd regret later. She was relieved when they pulled up outside her home. Danny looked up at the silent house and then at the clock on the dashboard.

"Looks like everyone's gone to bed." He began to apologise again. "I really am very sorry about how late this went on. Tell Fintan I owe him a pint or ten. Do you think he'd find time for a round of golf anytime this weekend?"

Normally Fintan would jump at the chance of a round of golf with Danny but, at the moment, Maeve was afraid he'd rather make a point by turning down the offer. She didn't want to hurt Danny's feelings.

"He said he was determined to get to grips with the big spring-clean in the garden this weekend," she answered, "but I'll tell him you offered and get him to ring you tomorrow."

She opened the door to get out, and then stopped.

"Listen, Danny, I'm sorry about you and Cathy. I know you were really fond of her and now you must be hurting like hell. But it will get better, you have to believe that. Though it's the last thing you feel like hearing right now."

"Yeah, sure. What you really mean is that I'm better off without her. At least you didn't say it."

The weary resignation in his voice saddened Maeve.

"I'm not going to get into an argument with you about this, Danny, no matter how much better it might make you feel to defend Cathy. But you know I'm here at any time, if you want to talk."

"Of course, Maeve, I'm sorry. It's late and this tooth is acting up. It's making me into a cranky old fart."

"You don't need a toothache for that, Danny. You can do cranky old fart in your sleep! But you're forgiven. Goodnight, Danny." She leaned over and kissed him on the cheek, then got out of the car.

Trying to get inside without waking either her husband or the children, Maeve felt like a burglar breaking into her own home. Fintan had not set the alarm, so at least that was one obstacle she didn't have to face. There was a short note on the hall table.

'Darragh's had his bottle. He had a bit of a temperature, so I gave him Calpol at 10pm. Check on him when you get in.'

As if Maeve didn't feel guilty enough. Darragh didn't cope well with any type of illness – he had probably been unbearable all evening. She sighed as she made her way up to the baby's room. He was sleeping peacefully, his arms stretched up over his head, his hands clenched into tight little fists. Maeve loved to watch her children sleep, especially like this, late at night, when she was the only one awake. She stood still for a couple of minutes, watching him. Soon her own breathing fell into step with his as his small chest rose and fell with the steady unconscious rhythm of deep sleep. Then she laid her hand across his forehead to check for a temperature, gently so as not to wake him, but his head was cool and dry. The slight disturbance made him screw up his face in sleepy annoyance and Maeve held her breath. In seconds Darragh resettled and sucked noisily on his soother to restore his interrupted sleep. She rearranged his blanket and crept silently from the room. She checked on the other two children, experience guiding her feet past the creaky floorboards, and found them all fast asleep.

Fintan rolled over in bed to face the wall as Maeve walked into their bedroom. She listened to his breathing, convinced he was still awake, and moved around the room as quietly as she could. If he wanted to pretend to be asleep, let him, she thought. She would rather not face confrontation at this time of night.

Outside, Danny was only just getting ready to drive away. He had waited to see Maeve safely inside the door, and then, when he was sure she was no longer likely to look out and see him, he touched the spot on his cheek where she had kissed him.

For Danny, Maeve was the one who got away. When she first joined the firm her enthusiasm and good humour had captivated him. They became natural allies as he was finding it difficult to be the new kid on the block. The staff were naturally suspicious of the boss's son and the young marketing graduate he appointed, so Danny and Maeve formed an alliance, which quickly turned into a firm friendship. He was wary of asking her out, not only because she worked for him, but because he knew that she was just out of a long term romance which had broken up suddenly only a few months before. He had been relieved when she started dating Fintan, assuming him to be her rebound man.

History had proved him wrong, however, and he had to admit that Maeve and Fintan were one of the best-matched couples he knew. He was genuinely pleased when they announced their engagement. But he still felt an occasional pang of regret at what might have been if only he'd made his move sooner. As Danny watched Maeve and Fintan's relationship flourish, he began to worry that maybe he was being a little too obvious in his regret. Especially in front of someone who knew him as well as Andrea, also Maeve's best friend. He didn't start looking specifically for another woman to throw them all off the scent, but he did decide to put Maeve behind him and open himself up to any possibilities.

He'd met Cathy a few times, mainly at business social events. As a social columnist, she seemed to be at every party he attended and he was flattered by the attention this young, pretty journalist had paid him. He asked her out and was delighted, if somewhat surprised, when she accepted. She was unlike anyone he was used to.

When he was her age, he supposed he must have been like Cathy, with her endless energy and longing to make each night last longer than the previous. But if Danny had been like that, he couldn't remember. And that was the thing about Cathy. She made him feel young and old at the same time. Old, because he couldn't quite see the point of half of the things she and her friends got up to. And young because she was willing to share so many of those things with him. He was vaguely aware that his friends disapproved of her, suspecting that she was after him for his money, status or whatever, but he laughed that off. After all, she was the daughter of one of Dublin's most successful advertising magnates. Surely she couldn't be short of a few bucks?

As his relationship with Cathy deepened he began to ask where it was really going. They met three or four times a week for a meal, or a party, and soon he began to stay over for nights, or occasionally even whole weekends, in her flat in Donnybrook. They had fun together and the sex was great. They never talked or shared things the way Maeve and Fintan seemed to, but then Danny looked at other couples, married couples he knew, and they didn't either. So he came to the conclusion that Fintan and Maeve had a marriage in a million, and that for most people the kind of relationship he had with Cathy was as good as it got.

And it was about time he settled down, although his mother had stopped reminding him of that since he had been with Cathy.

But he still couldn't figure out when things had broken down so completely between them that they had started moving in such different directions. Danny had ambled towards the engagement-ring counter of Weirs, while Cathy flew to London and out of his life.

Now that it was over, although he felt anger, his predominant emotion was relief. And he was frightened at how fast that emotion had taken over. For the first time in his life he had been about to settle for second best. He swore to himself that he would remain single if he couldn't find the woman who made him want to spend every minute of every day of the rest of his life with her.

With a start, Danny realised he was still outside Maeve's gate.

As he drove home he realised he was lucky to have maintained the friendship he had with Maeve and wondered if he had taken their excellent relationship for granted. He would have to remember that she was as human as everyone else who worked with him. And to make sure that her loyalty to him and the company should not be allowed to screw up her private life.

CHAPTER 9

When Maeve woke on Thursday morning, she could hear Fintan and the kids moving around downstairs. She turned to look at her clock and saw that it was quarter to eight. Swearing, she dragged herself out of bed just as Fintan came into the room.

"I turned off your alarm. I reckoned you'd appreciate every bit of sleep you could get." He didn't mention what time she came in at. "I'll take the kids this morning. Do you think you could manage to pick them up this evening? There's a meeting of section heads this afternoon, so I won't get finished before half five."

"Yeah sure, I can manage that," Maeve mumbled. "Thanks, Fintan. And I'm sorry about last night. Jean-Paul really is impossible. Just because he doesn't have to work in the morning, we all have to stay up and entertain him."

"What time did you get in?" Fintan asked slowly.

"After two," Maeve answered quickly. "I didn't look

at the exact time. Danny drove me home; he was on antibiotics so he couldn't drink."

"Convenient for him, wasn't it?"

"That's what I thought. He claims he has to get a root filling. Oh, by the way, he wants to know if you want to play a round of golf with him at the weekend. I said you'd ring him." Maeve held her breath waiting for a reaction and was dismayed to see Fintan's carefully maintained neutrality dissolve into anger.

"So! If I'm a good boy and don't complain when Danny keeps my wife out all hours, he'll bring me for a round of golf," he exploded. "If I'm really, really, *really* good, do I get a McDonald's on the way home?"

"Oh, come on! It's not like that," Maeve protested half-heartedly. "Danny may feel guilty about all the extra hours I've had to put in lately, but the rewards for the work I'm doing at the moment are better than average."

"Money isn't everything, Maeve," Fintan snapped. "It doesn't mean much to Ciaran who was asking why his mum wasn't home to read him the second part of *The Little Engine That Could*. Apparently, I don't do the voices right." He began to make for the door to referee a loud dispute that had erupted downstairs between Ciaran and Fiona.

"Don't walk out like that, Fintan." Maeve tried to keep her temper. "You know I always put the kids first. And besides, you may say money isn't everything, but it'll be a different story when we pay off our mortgage. How many of our friends live in a large five-bedroom house and have the chance of clearing their mortgage? We'll have the freedom to do what we want with our lives. We won't be working for the building society anymore."

"That's an interesting one." Fintan's tone was harsh and cynical as he stopped in the doorway and looked at her. "What *do* you want to do with your life, Maeve? What interests do you have outside your job?"

"I don't believe we're having this conversation, Fintan. What happened to the man who told me less than a week ago that he loved me the way I was? Job and all. The man who was proud of what I'd achieved? Are you having a change of heart? Deep down, I suppose you *really* want me to chuck it all in and wait at home for you – cooking and cleaning, like a perfect little wifey!"

The noise downstairs grew louder and it was clear that without parental involvement one of the children might inflict serious injury on another. Fintan hesitated at the door. He looked almost repentant, as if he was about to say something, but Maeve interrupted.

"Go! Dash off and be the perfect parent!" she said airily. "Your children need you because *I've* obviously been neglecting them. No doubt if I weren't a working mum, Ciaran wouldn't be trying to turn off the television every time Fiona's favourite programme came on. Go down and see to the kids and tell them their mother's too busy with her Filofax!"

She stormed past him into the bathroom and slammed the door; then she rested her forehead against the cool mirror and fought tears. She was furious with Fintan – and with herself for arguing back at him. How dare he suggest she was neglecting her children? What did he expect her to do – toss in her job? A headache began to pound behind her eyes. She tried to forget the wine she drank last night, or rather early this morning, and sorted through the towels strewn around the bathroom until she found a dry one.

Okay, so maybe Fintan was right about the late nights. But did he have to throw it at her like that? Maeve began to feel sorry for herself. She really had no choice at the moment; surely he must see that? Everything would get better in September, she said to herself, repeating it like some well-rehearsed mantra. Once the merger went through, she would have her shares, the workload would decrease and everything would get better.

She heard the front door opening and splashed water on her face to go down and kiss the children goodbye. Fintan was outside buckling Darragh into the baby-seat in the car, leaving Fiona and Ciaran standing in the hall, surrounded by the bags they would need for the day. Maeve kissed the two older children good-bye, told Ciaran to give Darragh a kiss for her and disappeared upstairs quickly to avoid another encounter with Fintan.

She showered quickly, letting the scalding water chase away the last of her tears. She felt like crawling back into bed and having a long cry at the unfairness of her row with Fintan, but instead she clambered out of the shower to examine her eyes. They were slightly bloodshot and puffy, but no more than could be expected after a late night in a smoky restaurant. She put in some eye-drops that claimed to resurrect the most abused of eyes and re-examined them. Slightly better. A bit of make-up and she'd look fine.

At last, ready to face the day, Maeve went downstairs. She was about to leave without breakfast, then decided that there was no point in struggling against the traffic. She would have a proper sit-down cup of coffee and possibly something to eat if she could face it once the caffeine hit home. There was less than a cup of brown tarry liquid in the coffee-machine so she put on a new pot and switched on the radio to catch some news. But the presenter's voice grated on her nerves so she switched to CD without checking what disc was in the player. Then Maeve smiled as Ella Fitzgerald's crooning voice slid out of the speakers, dissolving her tension as surely as oil easing its way into a creaking hinge. She began to tidy the kitchen, swaying to the rhythm of the music while her coffee bubbled.

She thought back over the argument and began to wonder if she'd been unreasonable. Fintan might have been looking for a fight with his comments about Danny buying him off with golf, but Maeve didn't always have to rush to her boss's defence like that. And Fintan's comments about money were no more than she had said herself a thousand times. And finally, when he asked her what she wanted from life besides work, maybe that upset her because she couldn't identify anything quickly enough.

Maeve poured a mug of coffee and stood at the kitchen window, staring out at the spring wilderness that was their back garden. Two days working with the children to sort out the garden for the summer would get them pulling together as a team again. The kids loved to 'help' with gardening, and would fall exhausted into bed at night, leaving their parents with some well-deserved time together.

Maeve felt a lot more cheerful as she climbed into the car for the commute into town.

Fintan dropped off the children and struggled through traffic on his way to work. He was later than usual and his chance of getting parking in the bank's small carpark would be less than zero. Nonetheless he put his plastic pass into the slot on the gate and drove through the raised barrier on the off-chance there might be a free space. To his delight, he saw a blue BMW pull out just as he drove in. It was Hazel Cunningham, human resources manager and Fintan's immediate boss. He remembered she was heading out to the Airport Hotel to take part in a management-training day. He waved as he pulled into her space and she made a face at him.

Fintan liked Hazel. She was one of the most popular managers in the bank and he worked well with her. When he first joined the bank, she quickly recognised him as a gifted teacher and put him in charge of developing in-house training programmes. Not quite as sexy as teaching world economics to third-level students, but it might have been years before Fintan managed to get himself a full-time job in the college. From his position in the bank's training department, Fintan attracted the attention of higher management and had occasionally been called on to give his opinion on economic policy. His grasp of economics came naturally and it was a subject that fascinated him. He often wondered, if he had been just a few years younger, if he had been job-hunting in the improved climate of the late rather than the early '90s, would he have ended up in a more interesting job? He knew he was unlikely to make the break now and he sometimes looked with regret at the high-flying financiers in the financial services centre. But he would be the first to admit that although he had the knowledge and brains to do the job, he didn't have the drive – or the killer instinct.

Fintan walked to his office and checked his in-tray, which was mercifully empty, except for a note from Hazel. She wanted to meet him later that day, but didn't say what about. He put the note to one side and got on with the rest of his work.

But it was impossible to concentrate because he couldn't forget the row with Maeve. What had he been thinking of? Fintan knew that the worst time for them to discuss anything was early in the morning because he was a poor morning person and although Maeve was usually at her best then, she hadn't had much sleep. And he was sure she had a hangover, given the wine fumes he had inhaled when she crept into bed in the small hours of the morning.

"You idiot!" he told himself.

He picked up the phone and tried Maeve's direct line at work, but gave up after two or three busy signals. Instead he rang his mother and asked if she or Orla could baby-sit so that he could take Maeve out. His mother volunteered Orla and laughed at her son for going out a second time in seven days.

"I'm glad to see you're finally paying each other some attention. The kids and work will look after themselves now and again. When you're old and wizened like your father and me, you'll only have each other to fall back on."

This was a favourite theme of his mother's. She thought the sun, moon and stars shone from her daughter-in-law and was constantly reminding her son that he needed to live up to her. Fintan did not like to point out that he would willingly spend ten times the time he did with his wife, if they could only fit it into their schedules.

Just as he was paying for something loosely resembling a chicken salad in the bank's canteen at lunch-time, he felt a tap on his shoulder.

"Hey, Larkin! You owe me a coffee for keeping that parking space for you this morning," Hazel said, grinning at him. "A birdie told me they had seen you heading this way, so I thought I'd better check if you were losing your sanity. You never eat down here."

Hazel ignored the filthy look she got from the restaurant manager who was manning the till. The lack of decent facilities or edible food in the canteen was a subject Hazel never tired of raising at management meetings and the restaurant manager hated her guts.

"I couldn't be bothered going out in the rain to buy a sandwich," Fintan explained, then asked: "How did your talk go this morning?"

"Oh, you know, the usual," Hazel answered. "Most of the people there were middle management, and they weren't the slightest bit interested in what I was saying because they're all rewriting their CV's. So many of them are being made reapply for their own jobs and only so many of them will get to keep them." She looked depressed. It must be hard to be in her shoes at the moment. Popular though she was, it was hard not to interpret her department's name-change from 'Personnel' to 'Human Resources', as signalling that the bank no longer viewed its staff as 'persons'.

"You said you wanted to see me today?" Fintan suddenly remembered the note she had left him.

"Oh, it was nothing important. It just seems like ages since we had a chat." She smiled and took a sip of coffee.

Hazel's chats were famous. She was gifted as a people manager and always sensed when a member of staff was feeling down or had itchy feet. She had one of the best retention records in the country at the moment, no mean feat when no one seemed to want to stay more than a few years in a job anymore. She could persuade the most disillusioned member of staff that there was something worth staying for: a promotion, a change of scenery, or training in a new field. And if she really couldn't keep someone, Hazel was generous with her time in helping him or her find something else to suit them. This reaped its own rewards as some of the bank's best young financial analysts had returned after a stint with someone else. Fintan wondered why she was suddenly so anxious to see him.

"So how's life treating you at the moment, Fintan?" she began.

"I'm fine – you don't have to worry about me leaving quite yet."

"Don't I?" Hazel raised one eyebrow as she asked. "Sometimes I wonder about you, Fintan. You really loved working in the college. I could never quite understand why you gave it up."

"It's no great mystery," he answered. "I was unlikely to get a permanent post in the economics department. I was just drifting from one set of replacement lectures to another, covering for people on sabbaticals or sick leave, and there was only so long I could keep on doing that. Besides, we had a kid on the way, and we got the mortgage on the assumption I'd get a proper job some day." Fintan tried hard not to sound regretful. He knew Hazel would pick up every nuance.

She was quiet for a few moments, and then asked, "So there's nothing on your mind? You're not planning to leave us? You've seemed distant . . . distracted, over the last week or so." She hesitated for a moment. "That day you took off last Friday – are you sure that wasn't for an interview or anything?"

"Hazel, you're too observant for your own good," Fintan laughed. "You'll give yourself an ulcer. I took Friday off because Maeve's been working so hard lately we don't see enough of each other. And if I've been preoccupied this week it's because we've got childcare problems. Our childminder quit and we have absolutely no idea what we're going to do. Every crèche in the city seems to have been triple-booked since the last century and when I put an ad in the paper, the editor suggested I might want to avail of their three-week special, as most people who run childcare ads tend to re-book them for weeks on end. I didn't even tell Maeve that, she's worried enough as it is. I don't suppose a staff crèche would be on the business plan for the bank in the next few months?" Fintan stopped to catch his breath, suddenly aware he was babbling.

Hazel looked at him with sympathy. "God, I'm glad I'm over that stage," she said. Hazel's youngest child was in his teens. "I remember what it was like after we had number three. It got so crazy I had to give up work. All the rushing to and from school, childminders . . . whatever. At least our mortgage wasn't as bad as the debts some people are facing today." She rattled her spoon around her half-empty mug. "It was hard getting used to not having the second income, but once the taxman had taken his share, and the baby-sitters theirs, we actually weren't that much better off when I was working. And our whole pace of life slowed down so much it was well worth it."

"Maeve doesn't really have the option of giving up work," Fintan said defensively.

"Oh God! Don't think I was trying to preach." Hazel went purple with embarrassment. "No, I really do sympathise. I remember what hell it was."

"Our mortgage isn't even that bad," Fintan explained. "We bought our house long before the current price rises, and we're well into repaying it. It's just that Maeve's company is merging with an American giant and she has to stay on if she's going to get any of the share handout."

"She may not *want* to give up work either – don't forget that, Fintan. I was lucky – I quite enjoyed having those years with my children. Some of my friends who stayed home out of necessity rather than choice went crazy. But in one sense, today's women are luckier than ten years ago. It's quite okay to say you're working because you can't afford to give up, but if you stay home, you're then admired for making a stand against a society that's trying to force mothers into the workforce. In my day we had a choice, but then we were judged on whichever choice we made. I was a traitor to the cause by giving up work to look after my kids and the women who chose to stay on at work were considered greedy, working to pay for the second holiday or flash car." She grinned. "You're lucky you're not a woman – we're our own worst enemies."

"I hadn't really looked at it like that," he conceded, "but I suppose you're right, things have changed. And it's true – I doubt Maeve would want to give up work even if we could afford it. She loves working. Always has." He paused then grinned. "Anyway, she earns more than me, so maybe I'll revert to being a kept man. There were times when we were first married, when I was barely earning enough to pay my share of the mortgage."

Fintan pushed aside the remains of his lunch. "But talking of money and salaries – don't you think it's about time we got back to earning ours?"

CHAPTER 10

Maeve flew around the house doing two or three things at once. She fed and bathed the children, read bedtime stories and tried to put a dent in the Himalayan laundry pile. She wondered why Fintan was being so mysterious about going out tonight. All Colm could tell her was that Orla was baby-sitting. Her assistant hadn't thought to take any other details when Fintan left his message, not realising that a baby-sitter mid-week was an almost unheard-of event in the Larkin household.

And then there was that ridiculous e-mail: *Sorry for being such a Misery-Guts this morning – will make it up to you this evening. XXX Fintan.* The whole message had been surrounded in a wreath of lurid red roses that winked at her. Where Fintan had managed to find that, God alone knew. He really spent too much time playing with the Internet.

Silly or not Maeve printed out the e-mail, roses and all, to put in her memories box. It was a while since

Fintan had done something so romantic and it gave her a warm glow for the rest of the day. Every time she thought they had grown too old and familiar with each other to be daft and romantic, he surprised her again.

She reached to the top of her wardrobe and carefully lifted down a large shoebox with the number '4' written in black crayon on the end. This box was filling fast and a fresh one, already labelled, was ready and waiting to take over. The boxes contained a treasure-trove of bits and pieces mapping Maeve's life since she was twelve years old. This one was filled with the children's birthday cards, Mother's Day cards, Valentine's cards and Father's Day cards. There were also some theatre tickets, menus, and orders of service for friends' weddings. Andrea laughed at her when she still carefully collected some item for addition to her collection; she thought the romantic Maeve who collected memorabilia was at odds with the organised career woman she was today. Fintan saw the hoarding differently. He described it as an attempt to catalogue her memories and apply to them the same level of controls as she did to her work. Maeve wasn't sure who was closer the mark, but she knew in the case of fire, once the family were safe, these boxes would be the first things she saved.

She resisted the temptation to leaf through the box as she carefully laid Fintan's e-mail in it and as she replaced the lid she heard a car pull up outside. She went to the window of her son's room and looked out.

"Ciaran, here comes Daddy!" she shouted. "Turn off

the television, go give him a big kiss and then come up here to brush your teeth before bed!"

"But, Mum," came the truculent reply from the living-room, "the video's not over yet."

"Ciaran Larkin, a deal's a deal. I let you stay up after Fiona had gone to bed on condition you'd go straight to bed when I told you to – now hop it! Look, here's Dad!"

From the landing Maeve could see his silhouette through the glazed hall door as he fumbled with his keys.

He burst into the hall.

"What?" Fintan pretended to be shocked to see Ciaran. "Are you not in bed yet? If you can get upstairs before I get my coat off, I'll come up to read a story."

Fintan kissed his wife and shrugged off his coat. He nearly tossed it onto the hall chair, but caught himself just as Maeve's brow began to furrow.

"I'll just hang up my coat then go finish putting the munchkin to bed," he grinned.

Maeve let out a sigh of relief and went to turn off the TV and video. Orla was due at eight so she had barely twenty minutes to get ready.

Ten minutes later Fintan joined her. He came up behind her, as she was struggling to put on a necklace and fastened it for her. His hands lingered on her shoulders and he kissed the back of her neck. She leaned towards him and he lowered his arms to encircle her waist. She wriggled around to face him and looked up.

"I don't know to what I owe the honour of a mid-week night out, but thanks. I'm really looking forward to this." Then she said: "Look, I'm sorry about this morning . . ."

But before she could go on, Fintan put his finger to her lips.

"Shush, you've nothing to apologise for. Go and get ready, we'll talk later. I need to run an idea past you."

He disentangled himself and disappeared into the bathroom before Maeve had a chance to react.

They decided to walk, so that they could both relax and have a few drinks, and they chatted casually about work and the children as they went. Maeve was dying to ask Fintan what his 'idea' was, but she knew from experience not to rush him. After just over twenty minutes of walking, and only a few hundred yards short of the pub which was their planned destination, they reached the Oriental Lantern restaurant and they both stopped in their tracks as the smell of Chinese spices wafted invitingly out the door at them.

"I could easily put away their special set meal for two," Maeve pleaded.

Fintan hesitated only a fraction of a second before holding open the door.

They were ushered to one of the last tables in the large restaurant. They remembered coming in here mid-week five years ago and being almost embarrassed by the amount of attention the waiters lavished on them in an attempt to justify their jobs. Tonight it was nearly quarter of an hour before they finally managed to flag down one of the harassed members of staff to order Tiger beers and a set meal for two. The young French girl who took their order looked as if she could kiss them for keeping it simple. As she left their table, a group of loutish-looking young men in suits began to click their fingers and whistle at her, in an attempt to order more drink. She ignored them and vanished into the kitchen.

"Good for her," Fintan snorted in disgust. "What do they think she is? A dog? How dare they click their fingers at her like that? Were we this ignorant as a race before we crawled out of the slime of depression?"

Maeve sighed – he was off on one of his hobby-horses. To her relief she saw that the loutish group had decided to give the restaurant up as a bad job and were calling for the bill.

While they waited for their food, Fintan fiddled with his napkin, obviously trying to find the words to express what was on his mind. Maeve kept silent and waited to hear what he had to say and eventually he started.

"Maeve, I'm sorry I had a go at you this morning. I was totally out of order. You have every reason to be mad at me." He wore an expression on his face similar to Ciaran when he knew he was in trouble.

"Much though I'd love to, I can't let you take all the blame," Maeve answered, trying not to smile. "I was cranky and tired and I overreacted. But I do think we should have this conversation. It sounds like we both have things to say, so best get it out now, rationally,

rather than next time we're on the verge of a row."
Maeve thought she sounded terribly grown up as she
said this and was faintly annoyed to see her husband
grinning, trying not to laugh. "What's so funny?"

"Nothing, darling, you're right – we need to talk, get
everything out in the open. We need to air our
grievances and rationalise our emotions. Are you sure
you haven't been reading one of Sarah's pop
psychology books?"

"Woah! Hang on a second, you're the one who
brought up the subject in the first place, which you'll
have to admit is pretty much a first for you. Normally
getting your opinion on something important is like
drawing teeth. You let me have my say, agree with me
and then point out later what was wrong with it!"

Maeve found she was getting annoyed, but she
couldn't work out why. Throughout her relationship
with Fintan, she had always longed for discussions of
feelings, emotions and plans for the future. But Fintan
wasn't big into verbalising, and they had got along fine
up to now. Maybe it was because life had been
relatively good to them and they'd never had to face
any major dilemmas or problems. But Sarah handing in
her notice had stirred up a hornet's nest, forcing them
to examine their whole way of living and Maeve wasn't
one hundred per cent certain they would like what they
found.

She took a deep breath, and then continued. "I know
things have been tough lately with all the extra hours
I've been putting in and I appreciate that you've had to

pick up a lot of the pieces I've been dropping. *And* I know you think my whole life revolves around the job at the moment, but you're wrong. You and the kids are much more important. I admit I love my work and I'd hate to give it up. If I had to, I could adapt to life without work, but it's just not practical at the moment. We need the money coming in from the shares, so even if I wanted to, staying at home at the moment is just not an option. I know you said this morning that money isn't everything, but we've got to be realistic." She was beginning to look desperate so Fintan took pity on her and cut in.

"You can forget what I said this morning; I was wrong. I was just mad with you for being out late." He took a few sips of his beer, and swivelled the stemmed glass around on the table a few times before continuing. "I said I wanted to talk to you about something, so here goes . . . and let me get to the end without interrupting,' he pleaded. "If you think I've completely lost the plot, fine. But wait till the end before you tell me. To be honest, I don't know how I feel myself about this, so I won't blame you for thinking I've lost my marbles."

He paused, bit his lip, took a deep breath and continued. "Well, I was thinking that maybe we should have a back-up plan. Just in case we don't find a new childminder."

"Brilliant, Einstein, any suggestions? You know I tried every crèche there was, our parents can't really do much and –"

"Maeve, will you let me finish? You promised."

Maeve decided to start eating although her appetite had suddenly vanished. She needed to do something with her hands to stop herself tapping on the table in exasperation.

"There's been an idea, well, not so much an idea as a vague shadow of a feeling floating at the back of my mind," Fintan said uncertainly, "ever since we had that conversation in the restaurant last week."

"Yes, go on," Maeve coaxed, sounding a lot calmer than she felt.

"You said that we didn't spend enough time with the kids, and that Sarah's quitting had made you wonder if it might not be the perfect opportunity to do something about it?" He stopped again and gazed at Maeve, as if willing her to read his mind. But her face was set, frozen into a rehearsed-looking 'listening' expression, so he was forced to continue.

"When I was talking to Hazel at work, she mentioned that she gave up work after her youngest was born. What was his name again? I keep forgetting."

"Hugh," Maeve supplied tonelessly.

"Oh yeah, I never really liked that name, obnoxious kid too," Fintan continued. "Anyway, Hazel she said she had a real choice back then, her mortgage wasn't too high, her husband was earning decent money, and by the time they took account of tax, baby-sitters, commuting and whatever, they found they were almost as well off on one income as they had been on two."

He paused to take breath, unaware that Maeve had

given up all attempts to maintain a neutral expression, and that she now looked like a child about to check under its bed for a monster. All rational thought told her it didn't exist, but she was still terrified of what she would find lurking in the darkness.

"Hazel said that once she had got used to the idea of being at home she quite enjoyed it," Fintan announced proudly, "and their whole way of life as a family changed for the better. So I thought, as a fall-back position, if we shouldn't just consider that possibility!" Suddenly he noticed Maeve's strangled look. "Oh, you hate the idea, forget I spoke."

"You've started, so you may as well finish. I won't interrupt." Maeve needed to let him go on talking, if only to formulate her own reaction.

"Well . . ." Fintan spoke slowly now, aware that Maeve was staring at him with a look she normally reserved for politicians on the doorstep. "I haven't looked into it and I haven't mentioned it to anyone. I don't even know what the bank's policy is . . ."

He was interrupted by a quiet explosion of breath from across the table.

"The *bank*!" Maeve gasped. "I thought . . ." She was shaking her head in confusion.

Suddenly Fintan understood.

"You thought I was suggesting you should give up work?" he laughed. "But that's ridiculous. You earn more than me, even before you consider your shares. Why on earth did you jump to a conclusion like that?"

"I don't know," she sighed. "I suppose I'm a victim of my Irish upbringing."

"So I take it this discussion has come back to life?" Fintan asked, trying not to smile. "I'll pretend not to be offended that you think it's alright for me to slave away at home, but not for you."

"Oh Fintan, it's not that. I just misread you, that's all. The way you were saying Hazel had got used to being at home and had quite enjoyed it, blah blah blah. I thought you were wrapping me up in some sort of little housewifey package or something."

"But it's alright for me to be a housewife?" he teased.

"Stop it!" Maeve complained. "That's not fair. You came up with the idea in the first place. And we haven't discussed it yet so I haven't expressed an opinion one way or another."

"Right, let's discuss it then. Who starts?"

"Please, take the floor. You're way ahead of me on this one. I wouldn't know where to begin." She sat back and gestured with her hand for Fintan to continue.

"Well . . ." he began cautiously, "I thought I could apply to take some time off work to tide us over until we sorted out some more permanent childcare arrangements. It looks as though it will be a lot easier to find a place for Darragh in October, when he's one, and by then Ciaran will have started school." He looked to Maeve for a reaction.

She nodded in encouragement.

"So if we take the period from July to November,

that's four months without my salary. With tax, and what we were paying Sarah, we won't really be down too much on income. In fact, I worked out that if we take our holiday in Mum and Dad's place in Courtown this year instead of going abroad, we'd come out just about ahead."

He stopped and looked sheepishly at Maeve who knew he'd far rather spend two weeks in Courtown than in some Spanish hot spot.

"You really seem to have it worked out. And you're telling me this only came to you today?" she asked suspiciously.

"Honestly. I was working it all out in my head as I drove home. So what do you think in principle?"

"In principle, it sounds like a good idea . . . I guess," she admitted. Now that she was off the hook she couldn't understand her reluctance to embrace Fintan's idea with the enthusiasm it deserved. It seemed like the perfect solution, but it made her feel uneasy. Was she jealous that he could so easily give up his job for the sake of the family or was she afraid it would reflect poorly on her? Maeve told herself she was being ridiculous. If the positions were reversed no one would think it strange for her to stay home, so why should it be different for Fintan?

She tried to shrug off any negative thoughts. "I think we should still explore the possibility of a childminder before we jump into this," she said slowly. "Let's see what the newspaper ad brings. Don't say anything to anyone until we've thought about it properly. And are you sure you could cope at home all day with just the kids for company? Would you not miss work?"

"Plenty of parents manage it, Maeve. Just because most of them happen to be mothers doesn't mean a father couldn't manage it as well. Besides, to me, my job is just that. A job." Fintan shrugged. "I'm not as passionate about my work as you are. And if this problem had come up in November instead of July, I wouldn't be half as enthusiastic," he said, grinning. "The idea of being a kept man for the summer months has a lot of appeal to it."

"It wouldn't be any picnic being at home with the kids – you'd more than earn your status as kept man," Maeve said, only half joking. She remembered her maternity leave and how at one level she'd been relieved to go back to work.

"I know, but it would only be a temporary measure,' Fintan said, and then, uncannily mirroring her thoughts as he so often did, he added: "No longer than you were off work after Fiona was born."

They were both silent for a few minutes while they picked at the remains of their meal. Eventually Maeve was the first to speak.

"All right. I'll be honest. I do suddenly feel as if a weight's been lifted, and it's a relief to know that we've got more than one option now. I suppose there's no harm in your making some discreet enquiries at work about parental leave – but apart from that let's keep it between us for the moment." She shuddered at thought of her mother's likely reaction.

"Ooh yes, I never thought of that. Anna really would have a field day," Fintan laughed, as he guessed the reason for her unease. "'Maeve, how could you *possibly* consider letting your *husband* give up his career in order to do *your* job? Didn't *I* willingly drop all notion of a career to put *your* welfare first? You really should get your *priorities* right, young lady'." He mimicked his mother-in-law to perfection.

Fintan knew that Anna's reaction to his proposal would be crucial to its success. Even as a successful businesswoman and mother of three, Maeve constantly sought her own mother's approval, but rarely received it. Anna was unusually critical of her daughter, and although she claimed to be proud of her achievements, Fintan suspected she was jealous of them. He actually liked Anna who was amusing, witty and full of life; as a mother-in-law, he had no complaints about her. She was just a rather difficult person to have as a mother.

"I'll tell you what. If we do end up doing this," he promised, "we won't tell Anna till it's all arranged and too late to change. And I'll be the one to tell her. I'll go on about how lucky I am that you've agreed to let me take some time off, while you're working hard to support the family. She'll buy that."

"From you, probably," Maeve conceded with a snort. "After all, aren't you the best thing since sliced pan, the wonderful son she never had?"

They finished their meal and walked home in companionable silence. Fintan had his arm around Maeve's shoulders and she had her hand wedged into the back pocket of his jeans. As they walked, her mind was in turmoil. Maybe she felt uncomfortable with the idea that he was once again being called upon to sacrifice his job.

Six years ago, it had been his idea to give up the college job in favour of the bank, but at the time Maeve had wondered if she shouldn't have made more of a fuss, encouraged him to try harder to get the permanent post he craved. Was this some kind of a second chance; should she put him first this time around?

"Penny for your thoughts?" Fintan asked.

She hesitated: "I was just thinking how lucky I was to have you. How many other men would be willing to make the offer you did?" She pulled him closer.

"It's not just an offer, Maeve. I'm serious about this."

"I know and I love you."

CHAPTER 11

"Fintan," Maeve mumbled from under the duvet the next morning, "you should reconsider Danny's offer of a round of golf."

"I wouldn't mind a round of golf," he replied with a frown then put his hands together, bent forward and mimed a long drive at the end of the bed. "Did you pass on my brush-off to Danny?"

"I said I'd forgotten to tell you so he's going to book anyway. If you call him this morning I reckon you'll get the round."

"Okay," Fintan agreed, now putting towards an imaginary hole behind the laundry basket, "so long as you don't mind doing the garden tidy-up without me."

"You won't be gone all weekend, and your dad volunteered to help. He's dying to get his hands on your buddleias," Maeve reminded him.

"If you let him cut so much as an inch off my beloved butterfly-bushes," Fintan warned, "I'll file for divorce. Those bushes will flower again this year, just you wait and see."

Pruning was a gardening specialty father and son could argue about for days. Paul was a great believer in cutting back hard, but Fintan preferred to trim gently and artistically. Maeve tended to come down on her father-in-law's side, not out of any knowledge of horticulture but because she loved the neat appearance of the garden after he had wielded the shears. When Fintan pruned, the only difference was a few leaves littering the lawn.

But she was not about to get into further argument about it now. There were children to be fed, dressed and driven to Sarah's, and two adults who somehow had to find time to refuel themselves and get to work. Without great enthusiasm Maeve climbed out of bed.

Finally, nearly two hours after the electronic beeping of the alarm-clock had roused them, the Larkin family were ready for the road. Maeve left first with the kids while Fintan loaded and started the dishwasher before leaving himself.

As he drove he began for the first time in months to question their crazy routine. Apart from the time he and Maeve spent at work, a disproportionate amount of their day seemed to be tied up in the process of getting there and back. Not just the commute but the time spent getting ready, getting the children ready, dropping them off, picking them up, debriefing them about their day etc etc etc. He wondered if all the time were added up, how many days a year they sacrificed in this way. As a family they spent more time out of their home than they did in it. And during the week, the children only ate and slept at home.

His mobile phone interrupted his thoughts. He pressed the reply button and wedged it under his ear just before the lights changed to green.

"Hello?" he mumbled, trying to change gears.

"Hello? Hello? Is there anyone there?"

Fintan could hear a disjointed voice in his ear and realised his mouth was nowhere near the mouthpiece, so he tried again.

"Hello, Fintan Larkin here, can I help you?"

"Hello, Mr Larkin. My name is Joan Megan. I was ringing about the ad you put in the paper looking for a childminder?"

"Can I take your number and phone you back? I'm in the car at the moment."

"Would you prefer me to ring tonight?" the voice on the other end asked.

"Yes, that would be great. But give me your number just in case." He repeated the number she gave him, and keyed it into the phone. "We'll get back to you before the day's out."

When he got to the office Fintan rang Maeve who was already at her desk.

"You'll be glad to hear that there's at least one applicant for the childminding job," he said. "She sounds nice."

"Brilliant!" Maeve let out a sigh of relief. "I hope it's

the first of many calls. And I told Danny you were on for that round of golf. So he'll pick you up at half ten and bring you home afterwards. I told him to stay for a late lunch, early dinner, or whatever it turns out to be by the time you get back." She blew a kiss into the phone and hung up.

Fintan stared at the phone in his hand. He had agreed with Maeve when she said that she hoped it would be ringing all day with applicants for the childminder's job, but he didn't really mean it. Now that he had actually contemplated giving up work, he was dying to give it a go. He had no idea if he'd enjoy it or not, but it was a challenge. His childhood had been blissfully happy, normal and stable, and his parents had always encouraged him to believe he could be anything he set out to be. So what was wrong with a stay-at-home dad? If he did get to give it a try, he knew he'd do a damn good job of it.

Fintan grinned at his cockiness and forced a dose of reality into his musings. A childminder was their best option and if one turned up, he knew he'd jump at it.

Part of Fintan's training responsibilities was to produce a monthly newsletter-type synopsis of what was going on in the world of finance and that was what he started working on now – to take his mind of his cosy domestic fantasies. It wasn't particularly highbrow stuff, aimed mainly at those members of staff who couldn't be bothered to read the financial journals themselves, but it was Fintan's favourite part of the job. Since he had taken over producing it, it was achieving a far higher circulation amongst staff than before and most managers had taken to devoting a section of their filing cabinets to back issues. The next issue of *Money Matters* was due out in a fortnight and Fintan had very little prepared. He set to work with relish and highlighter pen and didn't notice until he was packing up in the evening that his phone had been silent all day and not buzzing with scores of applicants for the childminder's job.

As he drove home, he began to look forward to his promised round of golf the next day. Maeve was right, it was too long since he had gone out socially. A whole round of golf and a kid-free afternoon would be bliss. Then Fintan remembered that Maeve had said something about Cathy having dumped Danny. He must remember to ask her so he didn't put his foot in it. He hoped Danny wasn't too depressed – the last time he'd been upset about something, he'd lost the round without even taking their handicaps into account.

CHAPTER 12

Cathy Houlihan walked out into the evening air, unusually warm for this time of year. She had spent the past two hours shopping in Harvey Nichols, a pastime she found reminded her of how fabulous it was to be living in London. And, to her surprise, she needed reminding.

"I made the right decision," she muttered.

"I'm sure you did, ma'am," the doorman reassured her, but Cathy didn't hear him. She hadn't even heard herself speak out loud.

Coming to London was the right thing to do, she was sure of it. It was just more difficult than she had expected. Her father's influence was not as powerful here as in Dublin, and although he had helped her get the interview, she knew that now that she had got a job with the monthly glossy *Power Babe*, she would have to work hard to prove her worth. It had been reassuring in Dublin to know that she would have to be really awful for her boss to fire her and so risk losing Daddy's advertising budget. And Cathy hadn't abused her position. Not really.

But the move to London was the best thing to do. She needed to make a clean break from Danny and leaving the country was as clean a break as she could make. Five years ago, when she started going out with him, she never guessed that he would have such an effect on her. It had been fun to start with, but then Danny began to get under her skin, and she suspected had tunnelled a secret passageway that stopped just short of her heart. Cathy was really fond of him. She might even have loved him if she put her mind to it. But she couldn't handle his indecisiveness much longer. If he was going to marry her, he'd have asked by now.

She regretted the way she had broken it off. But she was a coward and she hated good-byes. And besides Danny was sure to get over a clean break a lot quicker, wasn't he?

She didn't really want to hurt him because, despite his many faults, she knew Danny was a decent guy. His annoying obsession with work was balanced by that most trendy of current credos, a social conscience. Only with Danny it was for real and not because it was trendy. He actually knew what he was talking about when he went on about decent wages and sustainable economies.

But 'fond' could only go so far. It wouldn't power a platinum credit card and it wouldn't buy a large house in town and another somewhere hot for holidays.

And Danny had never been interested in real holidays. He wanted to go on 'adventures'. Two weeks in Morocco living out of the back of a jeep, staying in hostels with no hot water and eating local food. Yeuch! So, Danny got boring and it was time to move on.

Of course he hadn't always been boring. When Cathy started going out with him, she loved the way he enthralled her friends with stories of his travels and fascinating jobs all over the world. He had travelled extensively in Eastern Europe, when it was still Eastern Europe, and he could entertain for hours on the subject of six weeks in the back of a truck touring central Africa with some insane Aussies. But then he ran out of interesting stories, and although he tried to get her interested in coming on some of those outlandish trips with him, did he honestly expect her to travel for two weeks without a guarantee of hot water and sensible food?

And that business of his! It just ate up more and more of his time. No, Cathy really couldn't afford to invest any more in Danny, so she had ended it. But now she was panicking – London wasn't as glamorous as expected and she hadn't made the connections she needed to make.

She was so lost in her own thoughts as she waved down a taxi, that she almost didn't notice that the person she was about to growl at for bumping into her, was her old school friend Jo. She hadn't seen Jo since her engagement and, as Jo had recently moved to London and was moving in circles far more exalted than Cathy's own, Cathy felt it prudent to bite her tongue and kiss the air somewhere to the right and left of Jo's cheeks.

Jo was so mercenary, Cathy sighed to herself, as she congratulated her on her engagement. Everyone knew the only reason she had got engaged to Karl Jacobbsen, the Dutch diamond dealer, was so that she could lord it over the rest of Dublin with the biggest diamond ring ever seen in the city. Cathy was sure she would break it off after a decent interval and not return the ring.

"Isn't it wonderful news about Danny?" Jo simpered in reply to Cathy's greeting. "I always knew he was a good catch!"

So good that Jo had tried to pinch him on at least two occasions, if memory served Cathy correctly. But she was intrigued as to what Danny's good news was, so she played along.

"Yes, well of course, I don't have all the details, but it is wonderful."

"Stop being so coy. Can't I see you're enjoying a huge spending spree in London in celebration?" Jo looked down at Cathy's rather small collection of bags.

Now Cathy was getting really worried, but still she said nothing. She let Jo prattle on and the whole sordid tale emerged. Danny was selling out part of his company to some American conglomerate, and was going to be a millionaire several times over on the proceeds!

(Not that being a millionaire meant as much today as it used to, Jo reminded her several times.)

"Are you alright, Cathy darling?" Jo asked, managing to sound at least as concerned as she was curious. "You've gone a funny colour. Wow! You're not pregnant, are you? What delightful timing!" Jo seemed torn between the urge to rush away to share this latest gossip and the opportunity of staying with Cathy to pick up some more.

Somehow Cathy escaped from Jo, returned to her flat and spent the next two hours trying to ring her sister. In between times she tried to figure out how she could have so royally screwed up. If only she had shown a bit more interest in Danny's business! Admittedly it was boring, but it was obviously more lucrative than she had realised. And Danny had always been so generous with money – she should have read something into that. She tried to remember exactly what Danny had told her about the 'merger' he was always talking about, but it was no good; she had always switched off as soon as he started talking about work.

She finally got through to her sister and was dismayed to hear that her instructions had been carried out. To the letter. All Danny's things had been returned to him – in his beloved office, in front of his loyal staff as she had instructed, so that there was no way that he would think there was any chance of them ever getting back together. The clean break theory in action.

There was no going back. Cathy went back over the details of her last year with Danny and began to work herself into a rage. It wasn't long before she needed a scapegoat – the bile rising in her throat had to be directed elsewhere, it was threatening to make her sick.

She began to concentrate. Whenever Danny talked about the merger, Maeve Larkin was there too. That short fat cow, who worked with Danny. The one who thought she was so great to be balancing career and motherhood. The one Cathy often suspected Danny of having a crush on. If she concentrated hard enough, Cathy could see that it was Maeve who always changed the subject away from work and the merger. Well, sometimes. Maybe most of the time.

And that had to be it. Maeve knew Danny half-fancied her and although she had a pukingly perfect husband at home, she wanted to have her cake and eat it. She didn't want anyone else to get Danny.

Cathy felt better now that she had it all worked out – it wasn't her fault she'd lost Danny's millions. And Danny himself of course.

Maeve must have poisoned Danny against her and Cathy, subconsciously detecting a cooling off in his attitude towards her, had done the only possible . . . the only decent thing in the circumstances . . . she had let him go.

Well, Maeve needn't think she was going to get away with it! Danny might be lost to Cathy, but she was going to hit Maeve where it hurt. The husband wasn't worth going after, so it had to be the job. She smiled as she thought of the perfect person to help her.

CHAPTER 13

When Fintan got home, Maeve was just getting Fiona ready for bed.

"Daddy coming, Daddy coming!" the toddler shrieked, her face lighting up with joy.

Fintan opened the stair-gate and, scooping his daughter up in his arms, raised her over his head in a death-defying twirl that terrified and thrilled her. She squealed with delight.

Then he installed himself in the armchair in her room and she curled up in his lap. He opened the book he had read last night, the night before and the night before that again, and began to read the words Fiona knew by heart. But neither father nor daughter had tired of the story yet, and soon Ciaran crept sleepily into the room to hear it too.

A while later, with both older children in bed, Fintan went downstairs to offer to help with dinner.

"Everything's under control," Maeve promised,

"but you could open some wine and lay the table while I ring that childminder."

There was a wonderful smell of duck in the kitchen where Maeve had braised the skin of the duck-breasts to almost burning point and then popped them into the oven to join the baby roast potatoes and roasting vegetables. Fintan watched her from the door.

"Mmm," he said then, sliding up to her and putting his arms around her, "it's a long time since we've had duck."

"It's a long time since we've cooked a proper dinner. I swear I saw cobwebs in the back of the oven!" Maeve put the frying pan under the cold tap and then jumped back in surprise as the mixture of hot fat and steam spat angrily at her.

"I'll do that," Fintan offered, taking the pan from her. "You go and ring Joan Megan."

Maeve surrendered the pan gladly and went to make the call.

"Well?" Fintan asked when she came back into the kitchen.

"She's going to come and see us on Saturday evening, at around seven."

"Did you get any information out of her on the phone?"

"Could I stop her talking, more like it! I could have had her whole family history if I wanted it." Maeve laughed. "She's working for a family in Bray at the moment, but they've decided they need a live-in nanny. They've got one starting at the beginning of June, so a

July start with us suits Joan down to the ground. She lives in Deansgrange, so she could walk here."

Maeve paused, added some sherry to the orange sauce she was making for the duck and looked at her husband with a happy grin.

"I get a good feeling about her, Fintan, and I'm looking forward to meeting her. I think she might be the one."

"Hang on now, let's be realistic," Fintan protested. "She might walk through the door with the words 'I Am an Axe Murderer' tattooed across her forehead."

"She could have it tattooed across her left buttock and we'd be none the wiser. What's your point?" Maeve turned her back on Fintan and attacked the orange sauce with a whisk.

"I don't want us to jump at the first person that comes along, that's all," Fintan said gently. "It's not as if we're desperate. We have another option now. If we don't get the right person, I'm serious about doing it myself."

He came up behind his wife and put his arms around her. Then he rested his chin on the top of her head. He was worried that Maeve would rush into something. He didn't like her permanent look of desperation since Sarah had given notice.

"Maeve, I get the distinct feeling, that you're not mad on the idea of my taking time off work. Any idea why?" He let go of her and hopped up onto the edge of the work-surface beside the cooker. He sat there, trying to catch her eye.

"Do I give that impression?" Maeve avoided looking straight at him, but frowned with concentration at her sauce. "Sorry, I don't mean to. It would be great if you spent some time with the kids over the summer. But I don't want to turn down a childminder if she turns out to be the perfect person." She rushed to take plates out of the oven. "Dinner is about to be served so please take a seat. This meal I've conjured up is supposed to take our minds off childminders, so let's not talk about it again all night."

"Mmm, this is definitely one of your best orange sauces to date," Fintan gushed a while later as they ate, "and the duck is done just as I like it, crispy on the outside and pink in the middle. Perfect!"

He always had to make a big fuss when Maeve cooked. She was insecure about her culinary skills because cooking was about the only domesticated thing her mother could manage. Anna could whip up a dinner party at an hour's notice and, because she was terrified of falling below her mother's standards, Maeve had never cooked before she got married. Since then, although she had mastered the basics and had learnt a few special meals like tonight's, she rarely cooked a special meal just for the two of them.

After dinner they watched *The Late Late Show* and Maeve went up to bed afterwards. By the time Fintan had given Darragh his bottle and checked on the other children she was fast asleep, so he stayed up for a while and began to read through the financial articles he had brought home. He usually made it a rule not to bring work home with him – Maeve did enough of that for both of them – but he reasoned that as long as he was interested in what he was reading it didn't really count as work.

He sat happily with his reading until the clock in the hall rang one o'clock. As a student he had often stayed up later, even working through the night at times, but that was before the advent of kids who demanded attention at daybreak.

The next morning Fintan set off with Danny for the golf course while his father set about organising the children into a gardening 'work gang'. As they worked, the sun was shining, which meant Maeve had to dig sun block out of the back of the kitchen press for the first time that year. As she put it on the children, she tried to persuade Paul to protect the thinning area on his scalp, but he was far too proud to admit he needed it. Maeve herself loved the feeling of the sun on her arms, even though the air itself was chilly. She was strictly a good-weather gardener who packed away her enthusiasm along with the garden furniture each autumn.

Soon it was lunch-time, but Maeve didn't eat. With all this labour she planned on losing a few pounds, and anyway she had prepared a meal for whenever Danny and Fintan reappeared. After lunch Ciaran persuaded everyone to abandon gardening in favour of football and they played until it was time for Paul to go home. He took Ciaran with him, promising to drop him back exhausted at eight.

The house was blissfully quiet with Darragh and

Fiona both asleep and Maeve thought of all the things that she should be doing. Then she did none of them. She decided that the laundry and the ironing could wait. The bathroom, while far from spotless, was harbouring no fatal diseases. The freezer needed to be defrosted, but if she left it much longer the door wouldn't close and it'd defrost itself. And as for work, hadn't she promised Fintan she wouldn't go near her laptop all weekend?

Instead, she poured a glass of wine from a bottle chilling in the fridge and curled up in her favourite armchair. She flicked aimlessly with the television remote control, not watching anything for more than a few minutes at a time. It was ages since she had so wantonly wasted time and it felt great, so she sat there until the golfers returned.

They ate lasagne together and talked about golf, but Maeve was glad when Danny finally got up to leave: he seemed to be deliberately avoiding talking about work so as not to upset Fintan, the subject of Cathy was limited to whatever Danny was willing to say and there were only so many times you could discuss Fintan's perfect tee shot on the eighteenth. So although it would be an exaggeration to say the conversation was awkward, it was certainly limited. Besides, Maeve was beginning to get nervous at the prospect of interviewing Joan, their potential childminder, and she wanted to get into the right frame of mind.

Joan Megan, when she arrived, looked younger than Maeve had expected. Although used to Sarah's almost teenage looks, she had imagined Joan, who had grown-up children of her own, to look something like Fintan's mother. Instead she was tall and willowy with a shock of bright red hair tumbling over skinny shoulders. Her eyes and mouth, with a smile playing across both, looked gentle but mischievous. She wore so much brightly coloured make-up it was impossible to guess her age and her clothes were long and flowing so could be original hippy or one of its many revivals. They took her into the living-room and offered her a drink. She refused at first and then agreed to have a cup of tea. For a moment Maeve and Fintan looked at each other, each waiting for the other to move, then Fintan scuttled into the kitchen, under his wife's threatening glare.

Suddenly Maeve realised she hadn't a clue how to conduct this interview. She had interviewed hundreds of people down the years for LBS, so she hadn't given a huge amount of thought as to how to approach Joan. She cursed herself for her inane opening comments about the weather, and after a few minutes of awkward non-conversation on the subject of global warming, was relieved to see Fintan come in with a tea tray. A plate of chocolate hobnobs and carefully sliced buttered tea-brack sat on top of a pile of smaller plates, and he had made the tea in a pot rather than with teabags in mugs as he claimed to prefer. He must be as nervous as she was. He launched straight into praise of the beautiful sunny day they had just enjoyed, and Maeve felt herself go red. Then she caught Joan's eye and realised the other woman was trying not to laugh.

"And I thought I was the one who was supposed to be nervous!" Joan joked. "Honestly, I promise not to ask any difficult questions." When she saw that Fintan and Maeve were still looking at each other in desperation she took the lead gently, asking: "So, are any of the children awake?"

"No." Maeve let out her breath in relief at being over the initial embarrassment. "The two youngest would always be in bed at this time, and Ciaran, who's four and a half, is with his grandparents. They'll be dropping him home at eight. Now, would you like to tell us a bit about where you're working at the moment?"

Fintan looked at Maeve in admiration and they both tried to look business-like. Joan picked up their signal, and began to talk in much more of an interviewee style. She told them about the O'Connell-Riordans, the family whose three children she was currently minding. Both parents worked long hours, she told them, and they had decided that a live-in nanny had become essential as they did so much travel with their work.

"And you'd be available to start in July, which coincides more or less exactly with when we need someone," Maeve confirmed and went on to explain their predicament.

She asked a few more questions about Joan's views on children, how she would feel about cooking for them and bringing them to school and how flexible she could be on her hours. They continued to chat in a friendly, comfortable way and Maeve was surprised when the doorbell rang to discover that it was eight and they had been talking for nearly an hour. Fintan's mother Niamh was outside with Ciaran and she came in for a few minutes, on Maeve's whispered insistence, so she could share her first impressions later.

"Ciaran," Maeve said, "come in and meet Joan, a friend of mummy and daddy's."

She brought him in to the living-room and immediately he hid behind his granny and peeped out at the stranger. Joan reached into her large bag and half-pulled out a fox puppet.

"Oh no! Ciaran, I think Johnny Fox is stuck in my bag! Will you help to pull him out?" Ciaran looked up at his mother and grandmother for reassurance, before going over to get a grip on the bushy tail. With a huge tug, the puppet broke free, and Joan, Ciaran and the cuddly toy ended up in a big heap on the floor. Joan's attention was now entirely on the small boy, and she seemed oblivious of the adults chatting about how he had got on during the afternoon with his grandparents. After a few minutes of play Johnny Fox got tired and shy and crawled back into his bag so Joan suggested that maybe Ciaran might be tired too, and might want to crawl into *his* bed. Niamh brought him upstairs.

Fintan and Maeve walked Joan to her car and promised to let her know one way or another within a week. They were still hoping to get a few more applicants for the job and the amount of money Joan was looking for was a lot more than they had been expecting.

She obviously caught sight of Ciaran sneaking a look at her out his curtains, because just as she was about to close the car door Johnny Fox escaped from her bag again and gave the small boy a last wave before she pulled away.

Maeve and Fintan came back inside. They looked at each other, and nodded.

"I liked her," they said at almost the same time and they were still laughing when Niamh joined them.

"I liked her too and she seems a natural with children," she said. "She had no trouble at all getting Ciaran to play with her although he was quite tired and very cranky before we left our house. How did the interview go?"

"Fine, apart from our discussion of the weather!" Fintan laughed. "And we were more nervous than she was."

"Well, I'm glad I never had to go through that." Niamh shook her head in bewilderment. "I wouldn't have had the first idea of how to interview someone to look after you lot. For all the talk of a brave new world I think I certainly had things a lot simpler, if not easier. I wouldn't like to be bringing up kids today."

"Thanks, Mum – is that supposed to cheer us up?" Fintan asked.

His mother, mortified, blushed puce.

"Joking, Mum! I know what you mean though, things were a lot easier when one parent stayed at home to look after the family."

Fintan shut up when he saw Maeve looking daggers at him and Niamh, seeing the look and assuming her son had strayed into forbidden territory, left quickly.

"What was all that about, Maeve?" Fintan asked when they were alone again.

"We agreed we weren't going to discuss you giving up work until we'd looked into it properly," Maeve snapped, unsure why she was so annoyed with him.

"I wasn't going to say anything. I was just agreeing with Mum when she said that in some ways she had it easier. She was forced to give up her job in the civil service when she got married and I know she resents that the choice wasn't hers to make. Now that we have kids, she's beginning to see what the alternative to staying at home is like, and she realises that the grass wasn't necessarily greener on the other side." Fintan scowled at Maeve, daring her to argue with him. "I just agreed with my mother to make her feel better, so don't jump down my throat for it."

"So you don't really feel that way?" Maeve tried to sound like she wasn't sulking.

"What are we arguing about?" Fintan felt they were backing themselves into a corner. "We've just interviewed someone to look after our kids while we're at work. She seems to be just what we're looking for, so it looks as though we have ourselves a childminder. We'll both stay on at work, keep the status quo and nothing will have changed. What's the problem?"

His vehemence surprised Maeve.

"Sorry, I wasn't trying to start a row." She kissed him gently on the nose. "Come on, let's put these cups away and watch the gardening programme we recorded last night."

They gathered up the tea things and Maeve ate the last of the biscuits.

"Fintan," she said as he went out of the room with the tea tray, "Fintan, you're not by any chance disappointed that Joan seems like such an ideal childminder, are you?"

"Disappointed?" he said, taken aback. "Why on earth would I be disappointed?"

"I don't know – maybe you had set your heart on taking time off to be with the kids."

She watched him closely.

"Don't be ridiculous," he replied, just a fraction too fast, and vanished into the kitchen. Maeve stared after him, an uncertain look on her face.

CHAPTER 14

On Monday and Tuesday of the following week Maeve had enough work to keep ten people busy. Although the merger was now in the hands of lawyers and accountants, she was constantly being called on to make last-minute decisions about the most minor of details. She wondered why they were paying exorbitant professional fees since she and Danny seemed to be doing most of the work.

And as news of the merger began to leak out she was inundated with calls from clients wondering how their contracts would be affected. She and Danny had prepared a detailed document for clients explaining their position, but it was obvious that very few of them had bothered to read it. As Maeve took yet another call, late on Tuesday afternoon, she forced herself to smile as though the client on the other end could see her. Colm, who was doing some filing in her office began to make funny faces to make her laugh so she flung a balled-up tissue at him then picked up a paperweight, threatening to let it follow. He disappeared through the door and a few minutes later spoke through her intercom.

"You've got Andrea holding on line three and Danny's just come back to the office. Do you want me to field as many of the client calls to him as possible?"

"Yes, please!" Maeve gasped in relief and punched a button on the phone. "Andrea? That is really you and not another client, is it? If I have to take another call from some blathering idiot who can't read, I swear I'll scream!"

"Excuse me, is that Maeve Larkin? I was on hold for Mrs Larkin about my maintenance contract," said a slightly strangled voice on the other end of the phone. Maeve nearly died of embarrassment until she heard the muffled giggling.

"Andrea, you cow!" she exploded. "You nearly had me there. I should hang up and make you go through the whole call-screening process again."

"Oh do! Then I'll have an excuse to chat up that gorgeous boy who works for you. Are you sure he's only twenty-five? And does it matter? Any port in a storm."

"You leave Colm well enough alone," Maeve warned. "I've seen what you do to men when you eat them up and spit them out. I need this particular man to continue functioning as a human being, thank you very much."

"That's not fair. It's years since my eating and spitting days. Besides I only ever did it to men who well and truly deserved it, remember?"

"I'm not so sure about that," snorted Maeve. "Remember Gary Kiely? He spent the whole of sixth year composing love poetry to you and then had to repeat his Leaving Cert. Now you can't say he deserved it, can you?"

"Gosh, you really had to trawl through history to find that one! But that was before you sat me down and reformed me. What I really rang to say, before I was so rudely interrupted, is that I can't make Thursday night this week after all, so could we switch our dinner to Wednesday?" She rushed on without waiting for Maeve to agree or disagree. "I checked with *El Nino* and they can fit us in, but at eight, instead of half seven. That means you could get home first. Or, if absolutely necessary, we could go boozing, and leave the cars in town."

"Tomorrow?" Maeve didn't need to check her organiser. "Yeah, that's fine. I thought we'd have loads of childminder interviews arranged for this week, but after the initial call, *nada*! I'm not going boozing though. I don't know how you manage it in the middle of the week. If I'm out late I'm shattered the next morning."

"I don't have three kids at home so I can hit the sack at two knowing that nothing is going to wake me before half eight," Andrea gloated. "So you're on for tomorrow then? Do you want to meet at the restaurant, or come here after work? I'll finish up at around seven."

"Tomorrow's fine, but I'll have to renege on buying you dinner and have you over to my place instead – Wednesday's Fintan's soccer night."

"No chance of a baby-sitter?" Andrea asked.

"I suppose I could ask Fintan's mum, or his sister . . ." Maeve hesitated, "but to be honest, I'd rather not. Wednesday's kind of sacred. Usually it's the one night I'm on my own with the kids and I had a business dinner last week . . ."

"We could leave going out till next week," Andrea offered.

"No, no, I didn't mean I don't want you! If you can handle being surrounded by the kids before we eat, I'm sure they'd love to see you."

"Fair enough, I'm limbering up my storytelling muscles as we speak. Can you give me a lift? Then I can have a few glasses of vino and get a taxi home."

"I'll meet you at the salon at quarter past six," Maeve said. "No later – I want to be home in time to do the kids' baths."

"Why do I get the feeling I'll be the one cooking that dinner?" Andrea wondered out loud.

"Hey!" Maeve objected. "Stressed I may be, but suicidal? I don't think so. It won't be cordon bleu. It might even be M&S, but I'll find time to cook dinner. Don't you worry."

She hung up before Andrea could indignantly defend her non-existent cooking skills and half-expected Colm to interrupt immediately with another call. But the phone remained quiet and she kept her head down and got some work done for the first time since Monday morning.

As she fed the children later that evening, Maeve kept

watching out for Fintan, wondering how he had got on with Hazel. Apart from Joan, they had had no other answers to their childminder advert and Maeve had reluctantly agreed that it would be wiser to sound Hazel out about taking time off. Maeve knew that Fintan had planned to meet Hazel at half four so she guessed that he would stay in work late to avoid the worst of the traffic. He would devote the spare hours to *Money Matters*, lose track of time and then bounce home glowing with enthusiasm, spouting on about the latest run of financial institution mergers, giving an in-depth analysis of the pros and cons of each.

Maeve loved to see him in one of those moods. It reminded her of when she knew him first and he used to stay up till three or four in the morning working on the book he never finished. He always joked that he had never had any intention of finishing it, but it saddened Maeve to think he had stopped writing it. For about a year after Fintan started with the bank, he made occasional forays into the spare room, to 'sort through his notes'. But after a while, the boxes began to gather dust and he lost interest.

At last, to her relief, Maeve heard him pull up outside. The car door slammed and she waited in vain for the sound of his key in the front door. Then she heard him chatting to Matt's father over the fence and she prickled with annoyance. She had been dealing with grumpy children all evening and all Fintan could do when he finally made it home was to chat to the neighbours! Somewhere deep inside her a little voice told her she was being unreasonable, but she ignored it; she was too tired and stressed to be rational. When Fintan eventually appeared, he was bemused by the fierce look Maeve gave him.

"I'm not that late, am I?" He looked anxiously at his watch. "I left earlier than usual, and the traffic wasn't that bad."

"Oh God, no, you're not late." Maeve took a deep breath, guiltily driving back her earlier irritation. "I'm just having a rough evening after an even rougher day. Ciaran is in a foul mood. Sorry for being awful."

She put down Darragh's bowl of baby cereal (most of which had so far been applied to his face and clothes) and gave Fintan a long kiss. "How did the meeting with Hazel go?"

"Fine. I'll fill you in later. Look, you go and sit down and I'll finish feeding this lot."

"I haven't done anything about our dinner yet," she said helplessly.

"We'll dig something out of the freezer later. Now go, you look exhausted." He turned his attention to the kids. "Who hasn't been eating their dinner for Mummy, then?"

Maeve sat in the study reading a business proposal until the kids' dinner was finished, then got up to help with bedtime. Darragh was exhausted and went down with no trouble at all, and Maeve felt cheated when Fiona fell asleep halfway through her story and before their customary cuddle under the little girl's quilt. She was tempted to join in on Ciaran's bedtime, but her son was in one of his testing moods and was fighting with his father. There was a real testosterone-fuelled battle for dominance in progress in the box room and although Maeve's instinct was to rush in and calm everything down, she knew from experience that Fintan wouldn't appreciate the interference and that in no time he'd have Ciaran eating from his hand. So she went back downstairs and did her best to ignore the screams of fury as her son refused to get into his pyjamas, then claimed he had already washed his teeth and finally objected to his father turning off the light.

When everything went quiet Maeve could hear Fintan telling one of his made-up stories. Ciaran loved these adventures, which involved brave heroes called Ciaran who found treasures, killed dragons and rescued princesses called Fiona. The only problem was that he asked for the same story again a week or so later and was livid when the details weren't identical.

Fintan came back downstairs and squeezed into the armchair beside Maeve.

"Wow, I can see what you meant about Ciaran being in a bad mood! What's eating him? You don't think Sarah's said anything to him, do you?"

"No, they were all like that before you came home, even Darragh – maybe they just wanted to torture me!" she said with a gloomy cackle. "Or maybe there's a full moon or Sarah was feeding them sweets all day. I've got rotten PMS, so maybe my mood's contagious." Maeve was pretty sure that she *was* projecting her tense mood onto her kids, but she also knew she couldn't entirely blame PMS.

"Thanks for the PMS warning!" Fintan hopped out of the chair in alarm. "I'll be very careful what I do and say for the next couple of days. Should we scrap dinner, and go straight to a chocolate dessert?"

"No, don't scrap dinner, let's have a chocolate starter, a chocolate main course *and* a chocolate dessert!" Maeve grinned and was about to launch into another speech.

"Yeah, yeah, I know," Fintan interrupted. "There's a rational biological explanation for chocolate craving at this time of the month. It's high in iron, blah, blah, blah. I wonder where you get these facts sometimes."

This particularly useful piece of information had come from Andrea, who had heard it from one of her beauty therapists. It was a lifesaver for Maeve after Fiona was born and she should have been trying to lose weight. Eating chocolate instead of taking iron tablets made her self-indulgence feel almost virtuous.

"But theoretically speaking, if you did feel like eating a normal meal, what would you fancy?" Fintan asked.

"I think there are a few Chicken Tikkas in the freezer."

"Okay, Chicken Tikka it is. Would you like something to drink with that? I think there's some red wine left from the weekend."

Maeve made a face. "Yeuch! I don't know how you can drink red wine with a curry. You're welcome to the wine."

Fintan put some rice on to boil and put the meals in

the microwave to defrost. Then he opened the double doors to the living-room.

"I'm going to be a couch potato and eat watching telly. Care to join me?"

"Don't get too tied up in watching something before you tell me how your meeting with Hazel went," Maeve reminded him.

"Of course, yes. Was that only a few hours ago? It feels like last week. Anyway, Hazel . . ." He stopped when the microwave beeped. "I'll tell you while we're eating."

He disappeared into the kitchen and reappeared a few minutes later with two steaming plates. From the depths of the freezer he had also resurrected two Naan breads, which perched precariously, one on each plate.

As they tucked in, Fintan began again.

"So, the meeting with Hazel. There's very little to tell really. She was very open to the idea of my taking parental leave and she didn't seem at all surprised. She agreed that I should keep it confidential until I've made a definite decision, but given all the new parental leave regulations and the bank's need to keep staff, she should be able to put it through fairly fast when the time comes. If the time comes," he corrected quickly. "As Hazel herself put it, the bank management can't really kick up a fuss about it. After all, if I resign, I only have to give a month's notice."

"It's not going to come to that!" Maeve nearly choked on her chicken.

"Of course not. Hazel was just illustrating a point,"

he mumbled through his naan bread. "If I resigned, in the current economic market, I could go back to them in six months and almost certainly get my job back. Or a better job somewhere else."

"She's doing a great job as personnel manager if she doesn't care whether you leave or not!"

"Hazel's pragmatic. She knows if she doesn't say it to me, someone else will."

"I suppose so. But it still feels weird to hear it said. When you think of all the trouble we had in getting jobs just because we wanted to stay in Ireland."

"Different times. Even five years ago, when I got the bank job, I felt lucky to be in the right place at the right time. But you had it even tougher, ten years ago. Six months waitressing, before Danny rescued you. Kids today just don't know how lucky they are."

"I know," Maeve agreed with a deadpan expression, "and they never had to walk ten miles, barefoot, to school through muddy fields like we did. And as for eating cold nettle soup, and being grateful for it . . ."

Fintan flung a cushion at her, and she grabbed it to throw back. She was an instant too late as he had a firm grip on it. They wrestled for control of the upholstery for a minute and then their wrestling became more intimate with the emphasis switching to gaining control of each other's clothing. Fintan stopped and put the half-eaten meals on the coffee table where they remained, untouched, until an hour later when, with their appetites hugely increased, they had to re-heat the congealed mass they had become.

CHAPTER 15

As she drove to meet Andrea the next day, Maeve tried to shake off the cloud of guilt that had hung over her since morning. When she was kissing Ciaran good-bye, he asked so matter-of-factly, "Will you be home tonight, Mummy?" that even though she was able to answer in the affirmative and he nodded and said he'd see her later so, Maeve felt an ache inside – certain that he would have been just as accepting if she had said no. He took it for granted that she often left the house before he was even dressed and that there were would be days when she wouldn't even be there to kiss him goodnight.

Maybe in some ways it was good that Ciaran was so independent, but who needed independence at his age? And she knew it was selfish, but she wished that he had shown just a little bit of regret in waving her off.

Andrea kept Maeve waiting as her last client suddenly developed an urgent need of a restyle. Maeve tried to relax and resisted the urge to open her briefcase and take out her laptop. Andrea had told her to wait in one of the treatment rooms and to try out a new electric massage-chair she had on trial. Maeve lay back with the remote control in her hand and discovered that the chair on its own was blissfully comfortable even without attempting to operate the electronic motor. Eventually she plucked up the courage to start the massaging action and fiddled with the buttons.

Mechanical fists pummelled her spine giving her a strange sensation – not unpleasant, but not massaging enough to be relaxing. So she gave the speed-and-intensity dials a good twist and leapt from the chair with a surprised yelp. Although the door to the treatment room was closed Maeve was sure the whole of Leeson Street must have heard her. Feeling foolish, she turned off the motor and lowered herself gingerly between the black leather arms again. Before she could persuade herself to try again, Andrea burst through the door grinning.

"I should have warned you about that, but I couldn't resist seeing if you'd succumb to the same temptation as everyone else. Here, let me show you how relaxing this contraption can really be." She took the control from her reluctant friend, and began to punch buttons. "Ready? Okay, here goes."

This time, Maeve really could feel the massaging effect of the chair. As she relaxed into it, she giggled.

"Phone out for a takeaway, would you? I could be here a while."

"Forget it. I only have one of these yokes and I'm not going to spend the night watching you get off with a leather settee."

"It's no worse than all the teenage nights I spent watching you get off with some spotty guy, while I waited to share a lift home. Hey! Spoilsport!" This last was added as Andrea pulled the plug on the chair, raising Maeve to a seated position in a movement faintly reminiscent of a dental chair. Maeve shivered, suddenly glad to be getting out of it.

"So do you think you'll keep it?" she asked.

"Not a chance," Andrea answered. "Imagine if I let my clients into that yoke? They might decide to buy their own and then how could I make a fortune by charging obscene amounts of money for a massage by one of my skilled therapists? These Frankensteins should be banned."

"Hear, hear!" Maeve cheered. "Send it right back tomorrow."

"Oh no," Andrea stroked the leather possessively, "I'd hate to upset the poor rep! I'll keep it for the full three months, but in my office – where I can carry out a proper evaluation of it!"

"You'll never change! Come on. I'm starving. That thing seems to have given me an appetite. Maybe you should promote it as a workout – it couldn't be any worse than toning tables."

"I keep telling you, toning tables are not intended as a workout." Andrea took on tones Maeve remembered from the head nun at school. "They just tone your muscles so that you can hold in all the fat that shouldn't be there!"

"Humph! That's not the way most of your clients see them. They pay to have a totally passive exercise experience."

"I can't help it if they won't listen to me. Besides they seem to work for some people. At least I don't go for that con-job of measuring a hundred and fifty-nine different dimensions, so that I can get a total loss of two inches after a forty-quid session."

"St Andrea of Leeson Street." Maeve held her hands up over Andrea's head in a halo shape. "Now, come on! I only paid for twenty minutes' parking and I don't want a clamp!"

Andrea locked up the building and they set off, arm in arm, towards Maeve's car.

Half an hour later, they were installed in Maeve's kitchen and she was shovelling food into Darragh who was eating it like he hadn't seen food since sometime the previous week. His mother was relieved that this was not going to be one of his one-hour dinner sessions.

"Red or white?" Andrea asked, holding up the two bottles of wine she had brought with her.

"Neither thanks. I'll just have water for the moment. I'll have some wine later, when we're eating and when the kids are in bed. If I start drinking now I'll be plastered before I start cooking your dinner."

"You, plastered? Ha! I can't remember the last time I saw you really pissed! "

"Last month – remember? At that new place in

Temple Bar? By the time we actually got food, we were *both* too plastered to eat!"

"If you remember it that well, you weren't really plastered. Oh come on, you're not going to watch me drink two bottles of wine on my own," Andrea pleaded.

"For God's sake, Andrea, it's a Wednesday night! Some of us have to earn a living tomorrow. And I said I'd have some with dinner." Maeve realised too late that she sounded snappish.

"Oooh, I *am* sorry. I really will have to grow up, won't I?" Andrea whined nasally in an ever-so-posh accent. "After all, I wouldn't want to offend your sensibilities by getting *tipsy* in your company!"

"Sorry," Maeve apologised. "I didn't mean to sound like that. I've had a bad day, and I'm jealous that I can't go on a real bender to cheer myself up." She thought wearily that she seemed to spend all her time saying sorry lately. She was just so worn out and cranky. "If you want to get plastered, be my guest. I'll even drive you home afterwards and pour you into your flat."

"Well, I suppose seeing as we're not likely to be hitting any nightclubs later and I'm going to end up in my bed alone," Andrea grinned and poured herself a small glass of white wine, "I may as well be temperate too. Will yours be sparkling or tap water?"

Soon, Darragh was turning his head away from the spoon and rubbing his eyes. Maeve brought him up to Fintan who was watching the older two children for the last few minutes of their bath. He took the baby to settle him for the night before going out to football, and left Maeve and Andrea in the bathroom.

Ciaran was holding a beaker of water in his hand as they came in and was wondering whether he would get away with pouring it over Fiona's head. But then he spotted Andrea and decided her moleskin skirt was a far more worthy target. Fortunately his aim was poor, but he managed to splash enough water in her direction to leave a few satisfactory-looking brown marks on the soft beige fabric.

"Ciaran Larkin!" Maeve exclaimed, trying not to laugh, "how dare you throw water all over Andrea like that. Say sorry at once."

Ciaran was nearly choking on his own laughter and both adults had a tough job pretending to be cross. Fiona, horrified, waited to see what would happen next. When no retribution seemed to be heading her brother's way, she banged an open palm down on the surface of the water and screamed with delight at the splash produced. Then she decided to repeat the action over and over with both hands.

"That's it!" Maeve ordered, wiping soap bubbles off her top, "everybody out!"

She reached for the plug before Ciaran could get to it first and sit on it.

"I can't remember the last time I had that much fun. Or that much exercise." Andrea laughed about an hour later, pretending to stumble downstairs with exhaustion. "Is it like that every night?"

The 'water fight' in the bathroom had escalated into full-scale warfare by the time Maeve and Andrea had managed to get Ciaran and Fiona dried. Fintan had stayed only for the time it took to get Darragh settled and then he left for football, warning Maeve that the kids were particularly 'hyper' this evening. It took the best part an hour's chasing them round the house to get the two children into their respective bedrooms.

"It only like this on the good nights!" Maeve answered with a grin. "And only when Fintan's not here. He doesn't believe in letting the kids get too wild before bedtime. Says I let them get away with murder."

Andrea followed Maeve into the kitchen to get the bedtime drinks.

"How's the hunt for childcare going, by the way?" she asked as she watched Maeve pour two beakers of milk.

"Don't ask," Maeve warned. "Or things could get ugly."

"That bad? Come on, tell Auntie Andrea all about it."

"Unfortunately, there's incredibly little to tell," Maeve said, her good mood suddenly draining away. "We've been round all the crèches and we have a possible place for Darragh when he turns ten. It's almost impossible to get a place for a baby. Any crèche that runs a baby room is booked up for years in advance."

"What about that ad you put in for a childminder? Surely you must have got some answers to that?"

Andrea was almost afraid of the answer. The

conversation had taken a definite turn towards depressing.

"As for childminders, once you exclude the axe-murderers, we're down to one possibility." Maeve brightened a little. "She, I mean Joan, is more than a possibility really. We both really liked her, and she got on well with Ciaran. But she's looking for *way* more money than we were paying Sarah. Nearly twice as much. I mean we can afford it, and even supposing we could get crèche places, we'd probably pay more for them, but it's a big commitment. Taking on all that extra expense, you really have to be sure it's what you want. It's scary. But just imagine if we weren't earning what we are! How do people on average salaries cope?"

Maeve fastened a sippy lid onto Fiona's beaker and handed Ciaran's beaker to Andrea as she had promised to read his bedtime story. They walked upstairs together and split up on the landing.

"He normally gets one story from his big blue storybook," Maeve told Andrea "If you read two, he'll think he's pulled a fast one and he'll be delighted with himself!" Then she took a deep breath. "Of course," she added quickly as Andrea was going into Ciaran's room, "on the childcare front we do have one other option – Fintan has offered to take a few months off over the summer to tide us over till Ciaran starts school and Darragh turns one."

She disappeared into her daughter's room as she said this and closed the door before Andrea could react, but when she came back downstairs, Andrea was waiting for her with a glass of wine ready to force into her hand.

"Don't think I didn't hear what you said about Fintan. Now come on, talk."

Maeve opened the fridge, took out some salad ingredients and laid them on the work-surface before answering.

"It's no big deal really," she said. "If we're really stuck, Fintan said he'd take some time off to look after the kids. Stop that! It's not that weird."

Maeve pretended to throw an iceberg lettuce at Andrea who had started humming the tune for *The Twilight Zone*.

"Of course it's not weird." Andrea's look was inscrutable.

"If we can't sort out childcare, then one of us will have to stay at home. At the moment, it just makes sense for that person to be Fintan." Maeve unwrapped the lettuce and sliced the head in two with a heavy downward blow from a chef's knife.

"You've obviously worked this out."

"If it was the other way around, no one would think it the slightest bit odd, if I were to pack in work for a while."

She hacked the leaves into bitesize pieces and gathering them up in both hands, emptied them into a wooden salad bowl.

"Not odd at all," Andrea agreed.

Maeve opened a punnet of baby tomatoes, rinsed them and picked off the stalks. She made as if to cut the first of them in half, then just picked them all up and dropped them on top of the lettuce.

"And this is the start of the new millennium," she said. "There must be thousands of men who stay at home to look after their children."

"Tens of thousands."

"And it's not as if it's a permanent thing – it'd only be for three or four months, five at most. And that's no longer than I took as maternity leave."

"Absolutely." Andrea's expression was still deadpan.

Maeve finished the salad by adding some chopped cucumber and spring onions, then took a bottle of low fat dressing from the fridge and put it on the table beside the salad bowl. She added a prepared garlic baguette to the lasagne already in the oven and collapsed into the chair opposite Andrea's.

"There's no way I can take time off at the moment," she said. "Besides, it would be unpaid leave, and I earn more than Fintan."

"There you have it."

"Oh stop that," Maeve growled. "Tell me what you really think."

"I'll show you mine if you'll show me yours." Andrea allowed herself a small smile.

"What's that supposed to mean?" Maeve asked.

"It means, I'll tell you what I think, when you tell me what you think," Andrea said brightly. She stood up and began to make her way expertly around Maeve's kitchen, opening cupboards and drawers, bringing plates, table-mats and cutlery to the table.

"I've just spent the last ten minutes telling you what I think," Maeve protested.

"No," Andrea countered, "*you* just spent ten minutes giving me the official Maeve Larkin position. You haven't told me what you feel."

"That is what I feel. What would you know anyway? You don't even have kids, let alone a husband to look after them."

"I'll let that slur pass, but you'll pay later. Now as for what I know . . ." Andrea paused, took a large slurp of wine and reached for the bottle to refill her glass.

"I know that if you were as thrilled about this idea as you claim to be, you wouldn't have taken so long to come out with it. I know that it wouldn't have been the last thing you mentioned in your litany of childcare woes. I know that you wouldn't still have that desperate, hunted look in your eyes. I know you wouldn't have spent the last ten minutes trying to sell the idea to me." Andrea snorted. "I mean when have you ever worried about what other people think, as long as you're convinced you're doing the right thing? And you've spent way too long rehearsing all the pros and none of the cons of this whole scheme. But now I'm starving and if you don't get that lasagne out of the oven, I'm going to start gnawing on the edge of the table. So what do you think?"

"Oh, yeah, the food! I'd completely forgotten about it."

For a few minutes Maeve busied herself with serving the lasagne supplied by her local deli. She cut two enormous portions and put them on plates then tipped the garlic bread straight from the silver foil into a breadbasket in the middle of the table. But not before helping herself to a big slice dripping with garlicky butter. Andrea tried a piece of lasagne but found it too hot, so helped herself to garlic bread as well.

Mmm," she enthused, "worth the wait. Now sit down and tell me what you really think about Fintan being a housewife."

"Oh God!" Maeve groaned, dropping her garlic bread onto the plate and resting her chin on one fist. "Fintan a housewife! I mean I'm thrilled he wants to spend more time with the kids of course. And it's the perfect solution, if Joan doesn't work out – but I can't be as enthusiastic about it as I should be and I have no idea why." She stared glumly at her plate and pushed steaming sheets of pasta and lumps of sauce around it. "I'm a modern woman; I can go with the flow. So why do I get the heebie-jeebies every time I imagine going off to work in the morning and kissing Fintan goodbye at the door?" Now Maeve looked truly miserable. "There's absolutely *no* logical reason why I shouldn't be jumping for joy at the thought of my children having a loving parent at home. Especially when that parent doesn't have to be me."

She looked across the table for answers.

"Will you allow me to hazard some guesses without interrupting if I hit a nerve?" Andrea asked.

Maeve just shrugged her shoulders.

"Well first," Andrea suggested carefully, "I think

you're afraid of change. You're comfortable with what you've got at the moment, and you're worried about rocking the boat."

"But that's just it, I'm *not* particularly happy with the way things are at the moment. I know there's room for improvement."

"I didn't say you were happy with the way things were, just comfortable. And you promised not to interrupt." Andrea paused to reframe her thoughts, then launched back into full flow: "You're used to a fairly balanced marriage, with both of you sharing all the roles: breadwinner, parent, and for God's sake you even share the housework – there must be millions of women who'd love to know how you pulled that one off. And now Fintan wants to upset the apple-cart and completely unbalance the division of labour. How am I doing so far?"

Andrea looked across the table for reaction. All she got was Maeve miming a zipping motion along her lips.

"Now I'm going to move onto a more delicate area, and I may talk complete crap. If I do, feel free to ignore me."

"I'm good at that. Ignoring crap, I mean."

"Not that you ever get it from me. Anyway, some women – and I'm not saying you're one of them – realise, when they're on maternity leave, that they would go absolutely barmy if they had to stay at home all day. In fact, they're dying to get back to work. Now imagine if one of those women were suddenly faced with the prospect of a husband staying home and maybe even enjoying it? Would it make her feel as if he had succeeded where she had failed?"

Andrea paused to let that sink in. She half-hoped that Maeve would choose to interrupt again but was disappointed. So she took a deep breath and went on.

"What if that woman loved her job and was afraid to admit that she would rather split her time between job and kids? And then her husband seems willing to make a sacrifice she isn't prepared to make – would it make her feel guilty? Despite her modern beliefs and the reality of their situation, might she feel as if he were usurping her role in some way?"

Maeve's silence was black and menacing and Andrea was afraid she might have overstepped the mark. In fact, the silence was making her skin crawl and she was glad when the washing-machine in the utility room next door chose that moment to begin a high-pitched final spin cycle, distracting both women for a moment. She almost wished she had kept her big mouth shut. But Maeve had been at a loss as to why she was feeling the way she was, and sometimes it took an outsider to see through the bullshit. Just as Andrea was about to do the only thing possible in a situation like this – change the subject – Maeve came out of her reverie.

"Thanks," she muttered almost inaudibly.

Andrea let out a quiet sigh of relief. "Don't mention it. You had me going though – I thought you were going to throw me out and never talk to me again."

"I should. You were quite vicious. It's a testament to

thirty years of friendship that you're still here." Maeve knocked back what remained of her glass of wine. She felt like getting well and truly plastered. She still couldn't meet Andrea's eyes, but stared fixedly at the half-eaten meal in front of her.

She stood up.

"I'd better take the laundry out of that machine," she announced, "or the kids will have nothing to wear tomorrow."

When she was out of sight, Andrea put her head between her hands, and let out a silent scream. When would she learn to keep her mouth shut?

In the utility room, Maeve sorted through damp clothes without much enthusiasm. She shoved some in the tumble-dryer and knew she should really hang the rest on the large radiator in the kitchen. But she couldn't go out there just yet. She was furious with Andrea, but just about honest enough with herself to admit that she might just be shooting the messenger. What her friend had said hurt. It struck at the very core of everything she believed about herself. But Maeve had the same nagging feeling inside her that she had since Fintan offered to take time off. What if Andrea was right? Not all down the line obviously, but what if she was even a fraction right on one of her points. What kind of a selfish, insecure bitch did that make Maeve?

She wasn't sure she wanted to explore this right now. Right now she had to go back out and face her best friend, who had been trying to help. What could she possibly say to her? She tried a few introductory statements, but they all sounded pathetic, so she decided to wing it.

"About what you were saying earlier," Maeve said as she sat down again. "I'm not sure I'm ready to talk about all this right now. I was stupid to bring it up. I really appreciate your trying to help, but it's hard to understand from outside. Let's just let it drop for the moment, can we?"

"Yeah, sure. Forget I said anything. It was probably the wine talking."

Andrea looked so dejected that Maeve felt as if she'd just killed her puppy.

"Oh look," she said, "you really hit a nerve with what you said. I get this awful feeling that you're closer to the mark than I'm willing to admit. But I just can't believe that I could possibly be guilty of half the crappy emotions you suspect me of."

"What's there to be guilty about?" Andrea asked, genuinely at a loss.

Maeve raised her eyebrows in cynical disbelief. "You virtually accused me of not wanting Fintan to spend time with the kids because I'm afraid he'll do a better job of it than I will. You said my job was more important to me than my children, and you implied that I thought I had failed as a mother. *And* you said I was jealous of Fintan for getting a chance to prove himself the better parent."

Although Maeve didn't quite lose her temper as she said this, her voice grew louder and her face looked dangerously flushed.

"I said that, did I?" Andrea asked caustically. "I must have been out of the room at the time. Come on, Maeve, if you heard that, it wasn't from me. It was you reinterpreting what I said to fit into your own massive guilt complex. There's no need to be ashamed of feeling that it would be wrong for you to stay at home full-time – what is wrong is that you won't admit that it might be right for Fintan. Or rather that you won't give him the chance to find out for himself. Who knows, by the end of day one, he might be climbing the walls. But if he wants to try, he deserves your support. End of lecture!" When Maeve didn't respond, she continued, "I really admire the way you organise your life. You're a successful businesswoman, a great mother, and you have one of the best marriages I've ever seen. In fact, I would go so far as to say you're what I want to be when I grow up. So stop being so damned scared that the whole thing will come tumbling down just because you make a few changes. Now I don't know about you, but I reckon that we should knock back what's left of the white wine, and open the red."

Maeve hesitated for a fraction of a second then said: "Oh what the hell! Here we go!" She threw back her remaining half glass as ordered, but put her hand out to stop Andrea opening the other bottle she had brought. "Hang on – I've a bottle of Chilean Sauvignon in the fridge. If we're going to drink too much, let's at least reduce the chance of a hangover by not mixing red and white!"

CHAPTER 16

An hour later, the second wine bottle had been drained of its last few drops and Maeve was in the process of opening a third. The two women had talked about everything except Maeve's childcare dilemmas. Finally, strengthened by more than her share of the wine, Maeve returned to the subject.

"You know, I've been thinking . . ." she said slowly.

"Really? I'd never have guessed," Andrea smiled sarcastically. "Apart from the smoke spiralling out of your ears, I've lost count of the number of times you've completely lost track of what we were talking about."

"Watch it, Egan! Don't forget you're on a yellow card," Maeve warned. "Anyway, as I was saying before you tried to ruin my train of thought, I'm beginning to see your point on some of the things you said earlier. It makes me wonder, though, if I've become a control freak. Do you really see me like that?"

"I didn't say you were a control freak," Andrea

protested, "just that you've got your life well organised. I'm dead jealous – I'd swap lives any day."

"Really? When you tell me all about the fabulous parties you go to, and all the fabulous and interesting people you've met, I'd give anything to be in your shoes for a few nights. I mean, it all sounds like such fun."

Maeve began to dream about the high life, then came back down to earth with a wry grin.

"Do you know, when Fintan and I went out for a meal last Thursday, it was the first time we had been out together on a week-night since Darragh was born?"

"But that's just it," Andrea said, referring back to Maeve's earlier comment.

"What?"

"You said you'd like to be in my shoes *for a few nights*. Any more than that and it gets boring. It's like your business dinners," she explained. "I go to see and be seen for the salon's sake. Or I do it because I don't know what else to do with my time. I haven't the staying power to do an evening class or to take up a serious hobby. And. . . I need to meet men. I still want to get married some day and have kids." She stared into her wineglass. "Who am I kidding with 'some day'? I want it now if I could find the right man!"

"Talking of which – Danny Breslin's single again," Maeve told her.

"What?" Andrea gasped. "We've been talking all evening and you wait till now to mention that? What kind of a friend *are* you?"

"But I thought you'd lost interest in him years ago."

Maeve was surprised at the eager look in her friend's eyes.

"I was going through a phase of losing interest in men who were married, or as good as," Andrea sniffed. "It felt like a nice, virtuous phase to go through."

"Danny's not married."

"Come on, can you honestly say you didn't expect Cathy to drag him up the aisle one of these days? After all, Daddy must be getting a little sick of financing that lifestyle of hers. He probably got her the job in the hope she'd settle down. Little did he realise that being a social columnist was the perfect licence for Cathy to spend three times her gross income. And rumour has it her income was rather gross – at least in comparison to some of the other writers on the magazine." Andrea giggled at her own joke. "Isn't it amazing what you can achieve when your daddy owns one of the biggest ad agencies in town, and no publication would dare get on the wrong side of him?"

"Oh Andrea, be fair!" Maeve protested. "Some of Cathy's articles really were quite funny – I'm sure she managed to *keep* the job on her own merits. Even if Daddy got it for her in the first place."

"Earth calling Maeve! Come in, Maeve!" Andrea waggled her finger over her head like an antenna. "She's not going out with your boss any more, and anyway he's not here, so you don't have to try and be nice about her. Speak your mind, woman! I know your flesh crept when you had to be polite to her in the office – let alone when you had to socialise with her."

"You're right – why am I defending that talentless bit of fluff? Do you know, I heard through the grapevine that Cathy's editor had to rewrite virtually all her articles? Apparently she could do bitchy but couldn't pull off humorous. Or even proper English for that matter."

"Atta girl! That's better. Now what about her dress sense?"

"Don't get me started!" Maeve warned. "With a fraction of what Cathy spent on clothes, the Queen Mother would have looked more stylish. Cathy came up with the novel concept that any two items of clothing would co-ordinate, as long as each was more expensive than the entire outfit of any one else in the room. And of course the whole effect would be lost if people didn't know what labels she was wearing, so she was always very considerate in pointing them out. *And* in telling me how lucky I was not to have to take the trouble to dress as fashionably as she did."

"She never said that, did she?" Andrea's expression was a mixture of shock and delight.

"Oh yes, frequently. So much so that I gave up trying to pretend to like what she was wearing. Not out of any personal sensibility, but I was afraid Fintan might clock her one – and Danny always looked so embarrassed."

"The mystery is – how did he put up with her so long? How did it take him till now to break it off?"

"He didn't break it off – she did."

"No way!"

"Yes way. By e-mail."

"You're joking!" Andrea could hardly believe her ears. How could Maeve possibly have kept this to herself? "When did all this happen?"

"The weekend before last, I think."

"And you kept it to yourself till now?" Andrea was incensed. "I've been talking to you at least five times since then!"

"I only heard the other day," Maeve said, crossing her fingers under the table. To be honest, she had been too caught up in her own troubles to pass on this delicious bit of gossip to Andrea. Besides, she hadn't realised her friend would be quite so interested.

"So how's he taking it?" Andrea asked, with a concerned face. "Is it too soon for him to need comforting?" She tapped her fingers on the table with concentration. "It's a delicate matter really. Rush in too soon, and you're the rebound woman, leave it too long and someone else gets in ahead of you. Especially now that he's about to join the ranks of Dublin's new techno-millionaires. He is, isn't he?"

"You know I can't officially tell you, but yes, several times over. Ofiscom is paying quite generously for their toehold on the European market."

"There's something wrong here." Andrea picked up her glass and twirled it around. "How could Cathy possibly have broken it off at a time like this? Has she dumped him for a mega-rich pop star or something?"

"I never thought of that – it is odd." Maeve frowned in concentration, and tried to remember exactly what Danny had told her. "No, as far as I know, there is no one else on

172

the scene – and I can't imagine she'd lie about that just to save Danny's feelings. Maybe she really doesn't understand the implications of the merger. She always made a point of how boring Danny's 'little business' was."

"No doubt one of her 'friends' will enlighten her before long." Andrea rubbed her hands together with glee. "I'd love to see her face when she realises she's chucked the golden goose!"

"It may be a while before she hears. She's working in London now," Maeve explained. "I wonder how long she'll last without someone rewriting her articles and Daddy threatening to pull the ad budget?"

"Long enough for her to get well settled in London, I hope," said Andrea. "We don't want her back here getting her claws into Danny again."

Maeve hadn't considered that Cathy might come sailing back to Danny, claiming she had 'missed him too much to stay away'. Now she was afraid he just might buy it.

"So, you're really interested in Danny now he's free again?" she asked. "You know, I always thought you two would be a perfect match. God knows I tried hard enough to set it up."

"Yeah well," Andrea shrugged, "the timing was never quite right. He spent most of the first three years after returning to Ireland pining after you. . ."

"He did not!"

"He did, but you're never going to believe me, so let's forget about it."

"Danny Breslin has always been a good friend as

well as my boss. But there was never more to our relationship than that."

"I know there wasn't, but that doesn't mean *he* didn't wish there was. I know a lovesick puppy when I see one. And I've seen plenty."

"You've got a vivid imagination."

"Okay." Andrea let it go. She knew she was right. For all she knew, Danny might still regret that he never made a move on Maeve. But she could understand why Maeve would be so reluctant to think about it. It could make their working relationship very difficult. "Anyway, back to me and Danny. When he got over you, I was going out with Tom. Then when I was free he was with Cathy."

"I never realised you were that serious about him. If you'd told me, I'm sure we could have worked harder on it."

"I suppose I didn't realise it myself until he suddenly started going out with Cathy. I had watched him. . ." Andrea held up her fingers to frame her next word in quotation-marks, "*not* pine over you for so long that I reckoned I just had to bide my time."

"What I never really figured out," Maeve mused, "why, out of all the women in Dublin, Danny chose Cathy."

"Well, he didn't exactly choose her," Andrea pointed out. "He reminded me more of a fly caught in a spider's web. He was one of the best-looking bachelors in Dublin and he was older than most of Cathy's set – so I suppose he gave her an air of maturity which she couldn't have pulled off on her own merits."

"Oooh! You make her sound *soooo* calculating!"

Maeve swirled the wine around in her glass before taking a slow sip.

"Do I? Thanks." Andrea grinned. "It's not always I can describe someone so accurately. But, really, I'm thrilled it's over between them, and not just for my own sake. I've sat back for the past five years and watched someone I cared about be used and abused in a horrible, callous way. And I was powerless to do anything – because in his own pig-headed way, Danny was loyal to the death to Cathy, and I wasn't going to risk losing his friendship. Even if it meant I had to sing at their wedding."

"I'm glad it didn't come to that. You'd have cleared the church!" Maeve looked thoughtfully at her friend. "You really have a thing for Danny, don't you? I've never heard you sound so mature and sensible. I often wondered how you could to be so tactful around Cathy when you hated her guts. If there's anything I can do, you'll let me know, won't you?"

Andrea looked at her in horror. "You wouldn't do anything, would you? Seriously, no offence but I'd really prefer to handle this my own way."

"Okay, I won't mention to Danny that you're free at the moment and dying to get permanently hooked up." Maeve watched Andrea go pale. "Only joking – I'm glad you have such a low opinion of my tact! When I think of the hundreds of guys – all of them losers I may add and not gorgeous rich bachelors like Danny – that you tried to hook me up with over the years!"

"That's a bit of an exaggeration. Besides, you were going out with James for years."

"That didn't stop you. You were always trying to persuade me to come on double dates with you, your current boyfriend, and his spotty mate. You couldn't understand that I was too principled to two-time."

"Two-timing James wouldn't have counted."

"What do you mean?"

"Oh nothing," Andrea answered rather too fast. "It's just that we were teenagers and no one was expected to be totally faithful."

"You weren't, you mean. I was never unfaithful to James, over the whole five years."

"Fat lot of good it did you. He didn't exactly turn out to be Mr Right, did he?"

"There was nothing wrong with James – we just grew apart. I suppose we wanted different things out of life or something."

"You could say that again," muttered Andrea under her breath.

"What did you say?"

"I agreed. James obviously did want different things from life. Look at you – married with three kids, and he's still living the single life in London. Not a care in the world."

"I know, I'm beginning to worry a bit about him – he never seems to last more than a few weeks in any relationship."

"Don't worry, he just hasn't found the right person yet," Andrea reassured her. "And I'm sure London is just the right place for him to do that."

"Oh, I don't agree with you there," Maeve said. "I

wish he'd come home and settle down. I don't know what you've got against him. The three of us were such close friends when we were younger. It wasn't until he started going out with me that you really began to have a thing against him. You didn't fancy him yourself, did you?" Maeve said this as a joke – she knew the answer.

"As if!" Andrea refused to rise to the bait. "No, best friends and all that though we all were, I just didn't feel he was right for you. Let's leave it at that."

It had always baffled Maeve why Andrea took such a violent objection to her relationship with James. The three of them had been inseparable since they had gone to playschool together – a friendship which had lasted right up to their teenage years. When Maeve and Andrea started going to discos and became obsessed with boys, James tagged along, but resisted their attempts to fix him up with one of their friends. As time went on Maeve and James had been pushed together as Andrea flitted from boyfriend to boyfriend, often neglecting the two of them as a result. Maeve would have loved to be as popular as Andrea and to have had even one boyfriend for every ten her friend seemed to attract, but she always felt like the gooseberry. When James suggested that they pair up for some disco or party it seemed like a good idea. She couldn't remember when exactly they had changed from being friends to being a couple. But she remembered exactly what happened when Andrea found out. The two girls had the worst row of their lives. Maeve accused Andrea of being jealous and Andrea had just kept saying James was wrong for her – and if she couldn't see that she was the biggest fool in Ireland.

For nearly a month the two girls hardly spoke to each other and then, for the first time in her life, Andrea was the first to say she was sorry. She said she still didn't believe James and Maeve made a good couple, but she didn't want to lose Maeve's friendship over it. The friendship between James and Andrea was lost. At best Maeve got them onto civil terms with each other and she knew they still had the odd argument out of her hearing.

Maeve and James stayed together for five years. During that time, Maeve occasionally asked herself if she was putting in the extra effort to prove Andrea wrong. Certainly James just drifted along, happy to let her make all the decisions. And at first this had suited her down to the ground. Then it began to annoy her that James never badgered her to sleep with him, like her friends' boyfriends seemed to spend their time doing. If she asked him about it, he told her not to be ridiculous, that of course he fancied her, but he respected her more than most men respected women. And Maeve assumed it was the influence of his very religious family.

"Earth to Maeve! Come in, Maeve!" Andrea was looking at her strangely. "What planet were you on?"

"Sorry, I think I must have almost fallen half-asleep. It must be the wine." She didn't want to raise the subject of James again. "If you get the Tiramisu out of the fridge and prise it loose of its plastic wrapper, I'll make coffee."

CHAPTER 17

It was after midnight when Andrea finally stood up to leave. Fintan, who had returned home and poked his head into the kitchen to find a four-portion pack of Tiramisu demolished, the coffee pot on the table and the third bottle of wine nearing its demise, had taken refuge in the study. He offered Andrea a lift home, but she insisted on calling a taxi.

"Had a good time?" he asked Maeve as he closed the door after walking Andrea to her taxi.

Maeve looked preoccupied and she blinked several times, then shook her head as if to clear it – a gesture she often made when troubled.

"Something wrong? You didn't have a row with Andrea, did you?" Fintan began to rub her shoulders.

"No," she said vaguely. Then more firmly: "No, we had a great evening. Too good in fact. I'm not sure the alcohol will have cleared my system in time to drive to work tomorrow!"

"If you like, we can all go together in my car in the morning. I'm taking a half day, remember, so I can come home here to pick up your car before collecting the kids. You don't need to be in especially early, do you?"

"No, not really. But I won't drag you to Donnybrook, it'll add ages onto your journey, and I'll be fine. I was only joking about the alcohol."

Fintan raised his eyes in amusement as Maeve swayed and fell against him as she said this.

"We'll see," he grinned. "But now I think, it's time for bed – you look knackered!"

"Is that supposed to be romantic?" Maeve giggled wickedly as she led Fintan towards the stairs. "Why don't you tell me I look wanton and uninhibited instead?"

"Well . . ." Fintan looked as if he was giving it serious consideration, "now that you mention it . . ."

About an hour later, Maeve wriggled free of his post-coital embrace. Her mind was working overtime and she wasn't sure if it was her thoughts or the coffee keeping her awake, but she knew if she stayed in bed much longer, she'd start tossing and turning and wake Fintan.

She wandered into the kitchen and began to clear the wreckage left behind from her meal with Andrea. As she worked, she began to wish she hadn't drunk so much – she needed to sort through some of the noise in her head, otherwise she'd be awake all night.

She kept hearing what Andrea had said about her

attitude to Fintan taking time off over the summer. There was no escaping it: Andrea was right. Maeve did like the way she and Fintan had organised their life, and she was afraid of the changes that the next few months would bring. She resolved to phone Joan this weekend to meet her again, and hopefully convince Fintan that she was worth the investment, but that still left her pacing the kitchen.

Eventually Maeve resorted to the box of medicines she kept on top of the kitchen cupboard. She knew from experience that the anti-histamines they brought with them on holidays for insect-bites could floor an elephant if the instructions to avoid alcohol were ignored so she took one of the small yellow tablets with a large glass of water and went upstairs to go back to bed.

Fintan hadn't moved since she left him. Maeve envied his ability to drop off so easily the way he had within minutes of their having had made love. If he wanted to sleep, he could, no matter where he was. On trains, buses, planes, wherever. All Fintan had to do was close his eyes, find somewhere to rest his head and he was gone. When she slipped in beside him, he rolled over, still asleep, and wrapped an arm around her. His breathing got slower and deeper, and as he pulled her close to enclose her in his large frame, his face relaxed into a half-smile. Maeve drifted into a drug-assisted sleep beside him.

When she woke, it was to the sharp beeping of two alarm-clocks. She groaned as she hit the off-switch on her clock, then reached over to nudge Fintan to get him to do the same with his. She wondered why he bothered with an alarm-clock, as he invariably slept through it. In the next room Darragh had already responded to the clocks that had so spectacularly failed to rouse his father. Eventually, as Maeve was climbing over Fintan, he woke with a start and grinned up at her as she tumbled over him.

"What a wonderful sight to wake up to. Are you doing some early morning gymnastics, or is that a none-too-subtle pass? Maybe you didn't get enough of me last night?"

"Shut up and turn off your bloody clock before I throw it against a wall," Maeve threatened. "I'm going to try and get another half hour's sleep, so take Darragh into the bathroom with you and try not to wake Fiona." She disappeared under the quilt and was asleep again in seconds.

Her second attempt at facing the morning was more successful. Although it was only twenty-five minutes later, she felt more rested. She still didn't feel quite up to facing the kids, so she listened at her bedroom door and as the only sounds she could hear were Fintan and Darragh in the kitchen, she made a run for the bathroom.

She got herself ready for work despite the anti-histamine-assisted hangover and soon the whole Larkin family was en-route to Sarah's house. After successfully offloading their offspring, Fintan and Maeve set off for Donnybrook.

"Don't leave work too late this evening. With the bank holiday, the traffic will be mad," Fintan said as he kissed her goodbye.

"Easter weekend already? I don't believe it," Maeve said and then groaned. "I haven't done any of the packing for Courtown. Will you try to make a start on it when you get home? Even a couple of loads through the washing-machine would be a help. I did some last night, but there's a mountain of it."

"Don't panic. We're not going down till Saturday morning, remember? Mum and Dad have some friends staying and they'll be there till Saturday."

Maeve knew that, even so, she would probably have to spend most of Friday getting organised to go down to her parents-in-law's holiday house. Although it was only for three days, they would still fill the car and the roof-box. It was their first trip of the year, so the kids' beach stuff, a spare portable cot, some bedding, wellies and waterproofs – all would have to be brought down for the summer. Maeve began to get a headache just thinking of it. And she still had to get a day's work done first. Why, oh why, despite all her good resolutions had she drunk that much wine last night?

"Even with a week to pack, we'd be cutting it fine," she complained, as she struggled out of the car. "I haven't a clue where anything is. We should keep all the Courtown stuff in a separate room, and then every year it'd be so easy to chuck in the car."

"That would be too easy," Fintan pointed out. "Besides it wouldn't work. Can you imagine poor Ciaran trying to fit into last year's raingear? To say nothing of Fiona – she's doubled in size since autumn. And she certainly won't be happy any more with Ciaran's hand-me-downs." He grinned, acknowledging that this was mainly his fault.

Fintan loved to see his daughter in pink, feminine clothes and Fiona was now quite the little Miss when it came to choosing outfits. Before she'd had children, if anyone had told Maeve that a two-year-old could be quite so particular about clothes and pig-headed about what she wore, she'd have thrown her eyes to heaven and said 'Blame the parents'. Of course she still threw her eyes to heaven whenever she could muster up enough of a sense of humour after one of Fiona's tantrums, but now she said 'Blame her father'.

"Will you be free at lunch-time?" Fintan asked. "Do you want to get a sandwich or even a proper lunch somewhere?"

"I'll make myself free," Maeve promised. "It would be great to go for lunch together. Like when you were working in UCD, and you used to shoot down on the bike to meet me."

"Well, if we're going down memory lane, it'll definitely have to be a sandwich. We were so broke then!" Fintan laughed.

"Hey, you don't get out of buying me lunch that easily, you cheapskate!" Maeve laughed, as she finally closed the door behind her. "See you anytime after one," she added through the open window. "I'll leave you to do all the planning!"

She bounced into work, feeling more like the girl who used to meet her boyfriend for lunch on a bench in Herbert Park than the hung-over mother of three who'd been woken twice in the night to screaming children.

And her mood remained good all morning. She was even bright and cheery with Peter when he came into her office at around eleven to say nothing much, other than to try to find out what she was working on. He really annoyed her with that habit. He pretended to be so interested with the day-to-day running of LBS when it was obvious that he'd scuttle back to Texas as soon as the ink was dry on the final deal. Maeve couldn't figure out why he spent so much time in her office. At first, to her horror, she had suspected that he might have some kind of a crush on her, but eventually she had decided that he needed to justify his existence in Dublin and, as she was doing most of the work on the merger, he merely hung around her to look busy. At least she hoped that was the explanation. Andrea joked that maybe he was writing secret reports to Ofiscom about everyone in the company and for a few days afterwards Maeve was paranoid. But she put it out of her mind when she realised that Peter wasn't spending nearly as much time nosing around everyone else.

By one o'clock Maeve was looking at her watch every couple of minutes. She had finished what she was doing, and didn't want to start anything fresh before meeting Fintan. When her phone rang she jumped on it in relief.

"Where are you?" she asked.

"I can't make it to your office –" he started.

"Oh no, Fintan! I was really looking forward to lunch! What happened?"

"Nothing happened. I'm just guarding our old bench here in the park. So get your skates on and meet me down here."

The line went dead – she wasn't sure if the signal on his mobile had been weak or if he had hung up. She was so relieved he hadn't cancelled, that she forgot to be disappointed that he wasn't taking her for a posh lunch in favour of a picnic. She tore out of the office and covered the distance to Herbert Park in record time. Fortunately the weather had taken a turn for the better and she felt comfortable in her summer-weight suit. She spotted Fintan before he saw her and gasped.

He was occupying their old bench alright: the whole bench, quite a long bench, a bench which could comfortably seat six. He was at one end and he had laid out an elaborate picnic along its length. So elaborate that he was attracting quite a few amused stares from the other park users. He had somehow managed to get hold of a picnic basket, a red and white checked cloth, and some real glasses. Maeve didn't know whether to rush towards him or disappear in embarrassment. Hunger decided her to brave it out.

"Guess who?" she asked, having managed to sneak up behind him and cover his eyes. Fintan didn't answer, but caught her hands, pulling her around to face him. Still without speaking, he continued to pull on her arms until their faces were almost touching, and then he smiled and kissed her slowly. Once again Maeve felt herself catapulted back in time, and her stomach began to flip in the same way as it had when they used to kiss all those years ago. Then she lost her balance and collapsed into his lap. Fintan made a grab for a glass about to topple off the checked cloth, and the spell was broken. They both laughed, then realised they were providing live entertainment for the rest of the lunch-time crowd.

"I think Madame might be more comfortable on the bench rather than in the picnic basket," Fintan suggested.

Maeve removed herself, sat down properly and spread a large red paper napkin across her lap.

"Where did you get all this?" she asked.

"It's not a real picnic basket; it's the basket we use to display the Easter egg for the raffle at work. Someone won the egg this morning, so before the basket got buried in stores, I borrowed it."

On closer inspection, the cloth turned out to be paper like the napkins, but the glasses were real. From the basket, Fintan produced two small bottles of sparkling wine to fill them.

"Imagine it's summer," he said, "and you're sipping champagne and munching on strawberries."

He produced a small punnet of the latter with a flourish. Maeve dug into the basket to see what else she could find. There was a selection of Marks and Spencer's goodies, and as she kept digging her mouth began to water.

"How many were you planning on feeding?" she

asked in delight, determined to put a good dent in the food. She'd never have bought this amount for herself, but as it was there, it would be a waste not to eat it and to hell with her latest diet. Besides, everyone knew that food eaten outdoors wasn't half as fattening.

"Well, I thought I had enough for both of us, but I can always go back for more, if you're that hungry," Fintan joked as Maeve opened packet after packet and began to pile food onto her large polystyrene plate.

"Oh, did you want some too?" she giggled and held out a sushi roll. He took her hand and ate it from her fingers, then licked off the remaining soy sauce. Maeve caught her breath.

"Woah!" she whispered, leaning in towards him "There are people around."

"Does that mean you won't disappear behind the bushes with me later and behave like a teenager?" Fintan took advantage of her proximity to blow gently into her ear as he whispered. He pushed a strand of hair back from her face then let his finger slowly follow the line of her jaw to her chin and up onto her lower lip which he traced gently backwards and forwards.

"Oh God, Fintan! Stop it!" Maeve said, wishing she didn't have to mean it. "I have to go back to work this afternoon. I won't be in a fit state to do anything." Her heart was racing, and a healthy flush coloured her cheeks. Fintan looked at her with longing. She so obviously wanted to rush home as much as he did.

"Any chance you can skive off for the afternoon?" he pleaded, his voice hoarse with desire.

"I wish . . ." She didn't trust her voice. But she knew it was impossible. As she had forgotten about the bank holiday; there were a million and one things she had to sort out. If there was any way she could have got out of them . . .

The expression on her face was enough to tell Fintan what he needed to know. He leaned away from her. "Oh well, it'll hold till tonight, I suppose."

He was still unable to banish from his mind the fantasy of going home now, in the middle of the day, to a child-free house. But that was the price to pay for being responsible grown-ups with a mortgage. At this precise moment in time, neither of them was sure it was a price worth paying.

One desire thwarted, they fell on the food with renewed vigour. For a while neither spoke, and then, reluctantly, they began to pack up the remains of their picnic, while they chatted about anything to take their minds off what they'd rather be doing.

CHAPTER 18

The next day Maeve had arranged for Joan to meet the other two children at home. Joan charmed Fiona in the same way as she had Ciaran. Even Darragh seemed to like her – in other words he fell asleep on her lap without first depositing the semi-digested contents of his last bottle all over her. They were more convinced than ever that they were doing the right thing by offering her the job. To their delight, she accepted straight away and for the rest of the day Maeve was on a high. She sang her way through ironing the pile of clothes they were bringing down to Courtown. As for any Irish holiday, Maeve had planned for every conceivable type of weather – so for one weekend she packed more clothes than she did for a two-week summer holiday. By half seven that evening, the hall was full of suitcases and black plastic bags, ready to be thrown into the car the next morning. As she still felt full of energy, Maeve refused Fintan's offer of a takeaway and decided to cook.

"We're going to get so much exercise all weekend, it would be a shame to have a horribly unhealthy, greasy meal," she announced. "I'll defrost a couple of nice lean steaks and make some mashed potatoes with scallions." It was one of his favourite meals.

She hugged Fintan, wanting him to share in her good humour. She sailed into the kitchen, turned on the stereo and began to prepare the meal. She would be careful not to use too much oil on the pan when frying the steaks and she would use low fat milk with no butter to make the mashed potatoes. Really, she thought, she would have to get herself properly in hand. It was so easy to make a good, healthy, non-fattening meal. And this weekend the whole family would get so much exercise that Maeve would return to Dublin at least two pounds lighter.

"Would you like wine with your steak, Fintan? I'll just have water," she called into the living-room, where he was watching a gardening programme. He appeared at the kitchen door and watched his wife from behind as she wiggled her hips in time to music, mixing the potatoes vigorously. He recognised that she was in one of her 'Top of the World' moods. When she was like this, she always went on a diet although Fintan wished she wouldn't. He loved the way she looked right now. He crept up behind her and whispered in her ear.

"Have a glass of wine. We're on holidays. I don't want to open a bottle just for myself – and it won't keep till Tuesday."

"No, I'm being good. I've been comfort-eating for the past two weeks, and now I need to lose all the weight I put on. I still haven't really got to grips with my post-Darragh diet." For a moment Maeve looked deflated, then cheered up as she remembered she could achieve anything she set her mind to. "I've a stone and a half to lose – starting right now. Plenty of long walks all weekend and nothing but healthy food." She spoke in a tone that brooked no argument from her husband.

"Maeve, right now you don't need to lose an ounce," he pleaded. "You look gorgeous, sexy and every man's dream. Please, please, relax for the evening, and share a bottle of wine with me."

For a moment, Maeve looked as if she might relent. "I love you, you know that." She leaned her head back so that it snuggled against Fintan's chest.

"I know, but I really mean it when I say I find you gorgeous and sexy. I'm not just saying that to make you feel good."

"I believe you. But believe it or not, most women don't diet for men. After all, unless you're as thin as Kate Moss, most men wouldn't notice the difference a few pounds here or there can make. Women diet for themselves, or more precisely, for other women. Only girls diet for the opposite sex."

"And you are very much woman," Fintan purred, burying his face in his wife's hair, breathing in the heady scent of perfume mixed with a busy day's work. They stood like that together until the empty frying-pan began to smoke.

"Quick, pass me the steaks," Maeve said, extricating herself from her husband's embrace.

Reluctantly he let go and watched while she quickly browned the meat on both sides, then turned down the heat to finish cooking it. They both liked their steaks rare, so he took the plates out of the oven where they were warming and put out the mashed potatoes. He opened a bottle of wine and poured a glass, waving it under Maeve's nose in a last-ditch effort to change her mind.

"Oh, go on then. One small glass. I can resist anything except temptation." Maeve turned the meat out on to the plates and swirled a little of the wine around the pan – a trick she'd picked up from Fintan's mum – before tipping the juices on top of the mash. She took a salad from the fridge and they carried their plates into the dining-room, as they both agreed the kitchen was too much of a disaster zone to eat a relaxed meal in.

They ate in silence until the edge had gone off their hunger, then Maeve asked Fintan, "We are doing the right thing aren't we?"

"With Joan?" He didn't need to ask what she was talking about. He had been thinking about it all day. "Yes, I think so. I know it's a lot of money, but it'll be worth it. The kids seem to like her."

"What about you?" Maeve asked.

"Yeah, I like her."

"I didn't mean if you liked her. Are you happy with our decision?"

Fintan didn't answer at first. Then finally he said: "Yes, I'm happy. I suppose I would have liked to have a crack at looking after the kids, and a summer off would have been great, but I'm glad we've made the decision we have." He was telling the truth. He hadn't seen Maeve looking this happy in a long time, and he knew it was thanks to the decision to employ Joan. "Stop looking for an excuse to keep worrying, things are going to be fine." And for the first time in two weeks he actually believed his own reassurances. "Now all we have to do is get this merger behind us, you back to working sociable hours and we'll be the luckiest couple in Dublin." He looked at her. "Do you realise it's at least a week since we discussed how we're going to spend all your lovely money?"

They spent a pleasant hour doing just that and then opted for an early night. When Maeve fell asleep as soon as her head touched the pillow, Fintan was surer than ever that they had made the right decision in employing Joan.

CHAPTER 19

The next morning they awoke to the sound of rain pelting on their bedroom window. Maeve groaned and felt like rolling over in bed and calling the whole weekend off. The idea of being stuck in a small cottage for three wet days with three small children, even three as wonderful as her own, fell just short of purgatory. She only agreed to emerge after Ciaran came in to jump on top of her and sing, "We're going to Courtown, we're going to Courtown!" over and over with such enthusiasm that she remembered why they all loved going down there so much. Ciaran loved the freedom, loved the beach, the harbour, the boats. In fact he would have happily moved down there to live – despite the lack of television. Fintan loved the fact that they were all away as a family and there was no interference from work. Maeve loved just spending time with the kids without feeling she should be 'doing' something with them. Because they were together all day, they could just enjoy each other. There was no such thing as 'wasted' time, 'quality' time, time for work or chores or time carefully set aside for stories or playtime. In Courtown Maeve never had to think too hard about what she should be doing at any time; she just found the children naturally set the pace of the adults' days.

Finally, when the rest of the city was waking up, looking out the window, turning over and going back to sleep, the Larkin family hit the road. They made good time, and arrived in the small seaside town just as it was waking up. It was full of holiday-home owners down to make the most of their first long weekend of the year. So despite the rain, there were already a few brave parents supervising the construction of sandcastles on the soggy beach.

At the house, Paul and Niamh were clearing up after a huge Irish breakfast, having just waved their friends goodbye. They put on another pot of tea and decreed that there was no point in unpacking the car yet as the rain wouldn't last much longer. Maeve deferred to Paul's greater meteorological knowledge, but she couldn't help glancing sceptically at the rolling, almost thunderous sky.

Finally the rain eased enough to make venturing outside sane, if not pleasant, and Niamh shooed Fintan and his father out with the two older children, and instructed them not to return for at least two hours. She helped Maeve with the unpacking, laughing at the number of bags they always brought.

"If the amount of stuff you lot bring goes on

increasing each year, we're going to have to build an extension." The two women stood in the middle of the small living-room which now looked like the baggage collection hall in Dublin Airport on the August weekend.

"I hope this is as bad as it will get. At least half of this stuff is Darragh's." Maeve pointed to the pile she had dumped in the kitchen. Apart from his cot, there was a bottle-steriliser, several bottles, cans of formula, baby food, and a bag of nappies. It looked like a small branch of Mothercare. "It can only get easier from here on in." She wasn't sure whether she believed this, but she had to pretend to, to preserve her sanity.

To say the two women then unpacked or tidied would be an exaggeration – they merely distributed the mess more evenly around the small house. Then Niamh took Darragh out for a stroll in his buggy with the rain-cover on and Maeve settled into the old armchair by the window and took out the novel she had been reading for the past few months. At the last minute Fintan had spotted her trying to smuggle her laptop into the car and had ejected it in favour of this book and the two others he had bought her at Christmas but that she had not yet got around to reading.

As she watched the rain trickle down the windows and scanned the horizon for a hint of brightening skies, Maeve began to appreciate the relative isolation of their holiday retreat. (Fintan had hidden her mobile phone before she could even consider packing it.) She found she was beginning to put work in perspective and gradually relax, and when she looked up again, she was surprised to realise that she had spent a whole hour reading without once worrying about who'd overhaul Joe O'Connell's computer payroll system. She dived back into her book.

After one, she was disturbed from her reading by a disconcerting craving for fish and chips. There was still no sign of the others and Maeve wondered if she should start to do something about lunch. The rain had nearly stopped so she decided to venture out to see if she could find them. She got as far as the town before she spotted Ciaran's bright yellow raincoat leading a 'singing train' made up of four grown men, one pink plastic little girl and a buggy-pushing granny. Maeve didn't know whether to laugh or flee in the opposite direction, but her curiosity got the better of her. She wondered who the two surplus males were. Although she was close enough, she couldn't see past the hooded Barbour jackets.

"There she is!" Fintan roared as he spotted her. "Quick, Ciaran, steer the train to the right."

Virtually every head in town turned in Maeve's direction and she knew she could no longer pretend she had nothing to do with the band of lunatics heading her way.

"Look who we found, Maeve, James and Tony!"

But before Maeve could respond, Fiona spotted her mother and wailed, "Mummy, mummy, bottle, please! Night, night!"

Two hours of walking, sand and fresh air had taken their toll on the exhausted toddler. Darragh, woken in his buggy by the racket, also spotted Maeve and tried to outdo his sister in the wailing stakes. Then the heavens opened again and the party retreated quickly and noisily to the cottage

"James, what on earth are you doing here?" Maeve asked when they got back and were stripping wet raincoats from wriggling children. "And how dare you be in Ireland without letting me know!"

James hugged her before answering. Or rather he enclosed her and Fiona in his arms briefly, having bent towards them from the waist to avoid trampling on Ciaran who was clinging to his mother's legs. "It was a spur of the moment decision," he explained. "Tony persuaded me to come. We needed to get out of London." He pointed to Fintan's cousin who was helping his Aunt Niamh collapse the buggy and return it to the boot of the car. "We weren't even sure we'd get on a ferry when we turned up at Fishguard. It was either a long weekend in Courtown or South Wales."

Fintan's Uncle Brian, Tony's father, had also bought a holiday house in Courtown, and he and Fintan's father had helped each other renovate the rundown cottages. Some of Fintan's happiest childhood memories had been the adventures he and his cousins had shared in the woods around Courtown.

"I didn't know you and Tony saw so much of each other in London," Maeve said to James.

James and Tony had been friends since a New Year's Eve party at Fintan and Maeve's a few years before. They were the only single, childless males present and they had fled in terror as soon as Maeve tried to fix them up with some of her single friends. She was horribly drunk that night and was still embarrassed about it. (She couldn't be absolutely certain, but she had a nasty feeling that she might even have tried to fix up James and Andrea, working on the principle that two people who had taken against each other so suddenly and so violently, must secretly be in love.)

"When Tony moved to London a few months ago," James explained as they went into the house, "it was around the time my bastard of a flatmate did a runner, owing me three months' rent. I was desperate for someone to come in and help pay the mortgage, so when Tony rang to say he was moving over and did I know of any cheap flats, it seemed like the ideal solution."

"Why don't you young folk go and get a pub lunch somewhere?" Niamh suggested, taking Fiona from Maeve. "We'll hold the fort here until you get back."

"Young folk!" Fintan was delighted. "I never thought I'd be glad to hear myself referred to as 'the young folk'. What is it about kids that you seem to age exponentially with each of them? With the first you age ten years, the second twenty –"

"Shut up and let's get down the pub before one of them wakes up and Auntie Niamh rescinds her offer," Tony joked.

The mere suggestion of this caused an urgent but quiet exodus by the 'young people', with Fintan and Maeve leading the charge.

"So how come you're returning to your roots,

Tony?" Fintan asked when they were finally ensconced in front of a blazing fire and waiting for food to arrive. "You haven't been down to Courtown for centuries. You 'grew out of the place' – as you were so fond of telling us."

Tony thanked James, who had just reappeared from the bar with their drinks, before answering, "I suppose London just began to get under my skin a bit, and seeing as the folks weren't using the place for Easter, I thought it might be nice to come down and blow away some of the cobwebs. I hadn't counted on getting a full spring-clean with a power-hose though." He pointed wryly at their wet jackets. "It never rained like this when we were young, did it?"

The food arrived and Maeve looked enviously at the steak and kidney pies with chips the others had ordered. Her sensible crab salad looked delicious, but not nearly comforting enough.

"So what have you been up to in London?" she asked James trying to keep her eyes off his plate and her fingers off Fintan's chips. "Any romance in the air?"

James had had a few girlfriends on and off in the past few years, but nothing serious by all accounts. Maeve was beginning to worry that he'd never settle down and it was always her first question.

"Maeve dearest," James answered theatrically, "as I never tire of telling you since we parted, no woman has ever matched you. And while I continue the search for perfection, every night I rue the day I let you go."

Maeve flushed to the roots of her hair, laughed out

loud and looked at Fintan who was amused at her ex's protestations of love. Tony however looked annoyed – still defending his younger cousin, Maeve thought. He obviously didn't know James well enough yet to realise that this was the kind of idiotic banter typical of him. And maybe Maeve was childish for letting it embarrass her each time – but it was nice to be flattered now and again, even if only by an idiot of an old boyfriend like James. She was suddenly glad she had stuck to her diet and she sucked in her tummy and sat up straight to minimise the bulge under her voluminous winter sweater.

The conversation continued in a light chatty tone as they had a few more drinks, and then eventually parted at the door of the pub. Tony and James decided to brave the weather and go for a long walk. Fintan and Maeve felt they ought to go back and rescue his parents from their grandchildren.

They wandered back along the country road in silence, and then Fintan wondered out loud: "Do you think James was being strictly honest when he said there was no one special at the moment? He seemed to be on some kind of a high, which I could hardly put down to the excitement of being on holidays in Courtown."

"I didn't notice anything," Maeve answered, a shade too fast. "Are you sure?"

She knew it was silly, but she still had a glow inside from James telling her that no woman could match up to her.

"No? Well, maybe I was just imagining it. James just seemed to change the subject rather too fast off the subject of women, that's all. He usually gives us a list of his latest conquests and their shortcomings. But maybe we're seeing a new mature James." Then Fintan laughed. "Now if that's not a classic example of an oxymoron, I don't know what is: 'mature, James'! Ha, ha!"

The children were awake when they got back and the sky had finally cleared, making way for a walk on the beach. So they all set off with Darragh bouncing happily in the carry-frame on his father's back and the two older children walking as fast as their legs would take them.

"I wan' my straps *off*!" Fiona roared angrily, struggling in the safety-reins she had been strapped into for the walk to the strand. She could see Ciaran racing down the beach and she was sure that if she didn't get free soon, there was a real danger that her brother would use up all the sand. "Off, *now!*" she yelled again.

Finally released, the toddler took off down the beach screeching happily, tumbling over minor obstacles in her way, but too engrossed in the joy of outdoors to worry about the mouthfuls of sand she consumed every time she fell.

"Nothing bothers her, does it?" Niamh marvelled. "She's just like Orla at the same age. A huge capacity for joy – always happy and expecting to be. The boys were a lot more cautious and had to have every bump kissed better before they went on their way again."

"Like Ciaran," Maeve agreed. "He can't bear to waste

an opportunity for drama. He plans every activity with military precision, and if any small thing goes wrong, it's the end of the world."

As Niamh sprinted to the water's edge to stop Fiona playing with the waves, Maeve thought about the differences in temperament between her two eldest children and couldn't help thinking that the same differences existed between herself and Fintan. While Maeve worked at happiness and was too busy looking over her shoulder to really enjoy it when it came, Fintan took happiness for granted. In fact if he had to work too hard at it he probably wouldn't believe it was real happiness. Maeve wondered what would happen if things got tough and Fintan found the going harder than he expected – would she have to take on the responsibility for the whole family's happiness? She wasn't sure it was a burden she wanted to shoulder, having always relied on Fintan's feedback to let her know that all was right in their world.

"Fiona, if you go near the water again I'll have to get the buggy," Maeve warned her daughter and tried not to laugh as Niamh led her reluctant granddaughter back up the beach. "Do you want to go in the buggy, or walk?"

"No buggy!" The toddler was emphatic – and ever so slightly subdued. She kissed her mother in apology and then, looking back over her shoulder cheekily, raced to the water's edge again.

"I'm going to get the buggy!" Maeve shouted.

"*Nooo!*" Fiona wailed, and ran from the edge of the waves as fast as her chubby little legs would carry her.

"I think she's going to be good now – aren't you, love?" Niamh asked the little girl clinging to her legs who nodded furiously in reply.

They caught up with the others and then the grown-ups almost had trouble keeping up with the children's impressive speed through the soft sand. But soon their shorter legs and lower energy reserves began to tell and no amount of cajoling could prevent them from lagging behind. Maeve thought it would be a good time to produce a packet of chocolate biscuits from her bottomless pockets and they munched their way happily home.

CHAPTER 20

The next day, in typical Irish style, the weather changed mood without warning and made up for its previous sulky behaviour by throwing a glorious party of a day. Although the air outside was still cool, the small enclosed back garden was a suntrap and by mid-morning Maeve was searching for the children's T-shirts and sun-hats. They played happily in the sandpit while their parents indulged in a second breakfast on the patio.

"How does your mother *make* pastry like this?" Maeve enthused, with a mouthful of apple heaven. "Even my mother, who was always known for her pies, stopped making them after she tried one of these. You know Mum – if you can't be the best at something, don't bother."

"You're the same, honey. That's why you never bake either!" Fintan grinned.

"Ha, bloody ha!" Maeve grunted, and tipped the crumbs from her paper napkin all over him.

"Bloody, bloody, bloody!" Ciaran sang, "Mummy's saying bloody!"

Maeve went puce and Fiona did her best to join her brother's refrain.

"Buddy mummy, buddy mummy."

Fintan tried not to laugh while Maeve looked as if she could happily strangle her offspring. She longed to tell Ciaran to stop, but knew that it would only make him worse. So she picked up her book and ignored him. Sure enough he got bored after a few minutes and started singing 'Ten Little Ducks' instead. He sang as loud as he could, almost shouting, trying to get a reaction from his parents by waking Darragh in his pram in the shade.

Maeve decided to abandon Fintan to his fate.

"I'm going up to the pay-phone to check for messages. I shouldn't be too long," she said. "Think you can manage here on your own for a while?"

"Yeah, no problem. Say hello to the answering machine for me."

Fintan didn't even open his eyes. He was getting into the spirit of ignoring Ciaran's singing.

Maeve sauntered off, phone-card in hand, determined to spend as long as possible to punish Fintan for banning phones. He did it every year, but she never put up much of a fight to bring the blasted thing. She was glad to escape from its tyranny of constant availability. Ten years ago when she started with LBS, hardly anyone had a mobile phone and although the business was at a much more vulnerable stage of expansion, they got along fine. Now if you didn't carry a mobile, your competitors did, and you lost business as a result.

When she returned, Fintan and the two older children were constructing elaborate sandcastles in the damp sandpit while Darragh watched from his buggy.

"House still there?" Fintan asked, hardly looking up as he eased another turret onto his son's fortifications. When it was securely in place he stood up, leaving Ciaran to his building.

"Maeve, what's wrong?" he asked when he saw her expression.

"I don't know, probably nothing." Maeve waved her hands about and tried to clear the worried look from her face. "It's just that Joan left two messages. One on our home phone and one on my mobile. She wants us to ring her."

"Did you?"

"I tried, but there was no answer. I left a message – there wasn't much else I could do."

"Exactly, so what's the problem?" Fintan asked, although he knew that for Maeve any uncertainty was as worrying as it got.

"I don't know. I just can't figure out why Joan would need to call us when we spoke to her only two days ago. She knew we were going away."

"She probably just thought of something else she wanted to ask us. You're not going to spend the rest of the weekend worrying about this, are you?" Fintan asked, knowing she would.

"No, of course not," Maeve lied brightly. "I was just curious, that's all."

For the rest of the morning they both pretended nothing was wrong, but a cloud had darkened the otherwise perfect April day. After lunch, Fintan cracked first.

"Do you want to try ringing her again?" He didn't need to say who he was talking about.

"Will I go, or do you want to?" Maeve pulled the phone-card from her pocket.

"I've a confession to make," Fintan said sheepishly. "I brought my phone, so we can call from here."

"And you let me walk all the way up to the town to use the pay-phone earlier?"

Maeve pretended to be indignant. She knew that Fintan would never leave them without a phone for emergencies, and even knew that he hid it in the bottom left pocket of his bag.

"Well, go and call her then," Maeve ordered. "I couldn't face that cheery message on her answering machine again."

Fintan discovered what Maeve meant by the message on the machine. It was in rhyme and sung by the whole family. He hung up before the beep, not wanting to leave another message and seem too anxious.

"Any luck?" Maeve looked up from the book she was pretending to read.

"No, but I see what you mean about the answering-machine recording. I wonder if we'll be able to persuade Ciaran and Fiona to do that when they're teenagers?"

They both shook their heads doubtfully.

"By then landlines will probably be obsolete," mused Fintan, "and the debate will be, not whether we supply them with their own phone, but whether we get them a portable model, or get it implanted into their heads."

"Yeugh, that's gruesome." Maeve made a face at her husband. "How do you come up with ideas like that?"

"It's the next logical step, when you think about it. Phones are going to get so small that you won't be able to carry them without losing them. Some people already can't," he teased. "'Where is it? I can hear it ringing. It's in here somewhere!'" He mimed Maeve frantically searching through her handbag. "'Here it is . . . oh, they've hung up . . .'"

"You could get a job as a stand-up comic, you could," Maeve sniffed, pretending to be insulted. She had a habit of losing her phone at the bottom of her bag. Danny thought she left the phone ringing for ages to give the impression of being too busy to take the call, so that when she finally did, the client felt grateful to be granted an audience. She didn't disillusion him.

"Mum, is it time for Fiona to wake up yet?" Ciaran whispered a while later. He had been promised that the Easter egg hunt could begin as soon as she was there to join in, but he'd been warned that if he woke her deliberately, the Easter Bunny would magic the eggs away till next year.

Maeve looked at her watch and decided that it was time to wake her up gently.

They opened the bedroom door and Fiona lifted her head sleepily. Then she remembered she was on holidays, scrambled her way upright and almost fell off the lower bunk.

"Go water, go water!" she commanded, pointing in the general direction of the beach. Her parents were able to distract her for just long enough to get the egg-hunt started. Five minutes later they were both in fits of laughter as they watched the two children rip the small living-room to pieces as they hunted for chocolate-filled candy eggs.

"Amazing the fun you can get from a one euro bag of sweets!" Maeve laughed as she was evicted from her armchair for the fourth time, just in case Ciaran had overlooked an egg under the cushion. Fiona hadn't quite grasped the concept. She followed her brother round, lifting each object after he did, and then looked annoyed when her pile of chocolate wasn't growing at the same rate as his. She was about to sit down and wail when Fintan intervened and explained to Ciaran that he had to share. Grudgingly, he parted with some of his treasures. Then they heard Darragh beginning to stir in the other bedroom.

"Darragh's too small to eat Easter eggs, Daddy, isn't he?" Ciaran asked in a worried tone. Fiona, less subtle, began to cram the eggs into her mouth as fast as her cheeks would stretch to accommodate them.

While they were laughing and cleaning chocolate off

Fiona's face, hands, clothes and hair, Fintan's phone chirped and rattled in the kitchen.

"I forgot to switch it off again," he said guiltily, and picked it up off the work surface.

"Joan," he mouthed silently to Maeve as he answered. He said very little, just the occasional "Yes, yes," and, "I understand".

Maeve felt sick. 'I understand' usually meant bad news. She felt guilty for wishing Joan were announcing some catastrophe, even a death in the family, just nothing to do with their childminding agreement.

"Do you want the good news or the bad news?" Fintan asked when he hung up.

"Good, please."

"Well, Joan still definitely wants to work for us."

"But?"

Fintan took a deep breath then spoke quickly. "The nanny who is due to take over from her has broken her shoulder and won't be fit to start the job until October."

Maeve who had been holding her breath let it out in a loud explosion. "Surely that's not our problem – Joan agreed to start with us in July."

But she knew she was clutching at straws. Fintan said nothing in reply and Maeve gathered the tissues she had been using to clean Fiona and flung them in the bin in the kitchen. She slammed the lid, then leaned against the sink as if to steady herself.

"I suppose the O'Connell-whatever-they-weres have asked her to stay and she feels she can't refuse?" Maeve asked.

"She hadn't formally been given notice there, and she hadn't given them notice," Fintan explained. "The O'Connell-Riordans had even been willing to keep her on for as much as a couple of months after the new nanny started if she hadn't found something else."

"How magnanimous of them!" Maeve sniffed. "It was a fairly safe bet that she was going to find another family desperate for her. But they obviously have enough money to make an offer like that." Maeve knew she was being unfair, but she had to hit out at someone.

"Joan said that it's mainly for their kids' sake she couldn't say no. She knows the family could get by on a series of temporary or agency nannies, but that she didn't feel it was fair on the kids. After all, they spend a lot more time with her than they do with their parents."

"Well, if they have so much money, why don't they go and get themselves another nanny, instead of the one with the broken shoulder? And leave our Joan alone?"

"Apparently this girl's been recommended by so many of their friends, and she got on so well with them when they all met up for a weekend in Disneyland Paris . . ." Fintan grinned despite himself.

"You mean they interviewed their new nanny in Disneyland?" Maeve asked in disbelief, and then shrugged her shoulders, conceding defeat. "If we're up against that, we didn't stand a chance. So did Joan have any suggestions as to what *we* should do?" She opened a cupboard door and slammed it for no reason.

"Mummy, do you not like Joan any more?" Ciaran

asked, looking worried. Maeve suddenly realised that he and Fiona were standing between their parents, and watching the exchange with awestruck faces. She forced herself to smile, but found she couldn't speak so Fintan took over.

"Of course we still like Joan. Do you?"

"Joan's *my* friend," Ciaran answered looking at his sister, daring her to challenge his claim.

"Do you think Fiona likes her?"

"Yes. I think so, but not as much as me. Joan's my best friend," he said proudly.

Fintan produced the last few chocolate eggs from behind a book on the bookcase and handed them to his son. "You share these with Fiona. Me and Mummy have to go in the garden for a few minutes with Darragh to see what the weather's like. If it looks okay, we might go down to the beach for a while."

He scooped up the baby and a play-mat and marched out onto the patio. Maeve followed, but not before grabbing the remains of a packet of chocolate biscuits from the cupboard.

"These aren't fattening," she said to Fintan. "They're medicinal."

"In that case give me three."

"You'll have to fight me for them."

For a minute or two they munched in silence, then looked through the window at the two children who had eaten so much chocolate that they were only arguing about the last few eggs as a matter of principle.

"I keep forgetting how much he takes in," Fintan said.

"I know, and Fiona's not that far behind him," Maeve agreed. "We have to be more careful what we say in front of him. So where do we stand?"

"Joan still wants to work for us, but understands that we need someone in July. She won't go looking for anything else for the moment, so if we can persuade Sarah to stay on until October, she'll start with us then."

"I don't think there's much chance of that. Even if we could persuade her not to do the returning-to-study course, she'd still need to start school in September. Besides, holding out for Joan till October kinds of defeats the purpose. We can get a crèche place then. You did say that to her, didn't you? If she really wants to work so close to home, that might sway her."

"I didn't say anything else other than 'Yes, no, maybe and I understand,'" Fintan said carefully. "I didn't want to land us in anything, or burn any bridges."

"We're not the ones holding matches," Maeve snapped, bitter again. "You're always so considerate of how everyone else is feeling – what about us? At least think of me if you don't care about yourself."

As soon as the words were out of her mouth, Maeve regretted them. All the more guiltily because Fintan didn't react angrily, or rise to her challenge. He just pulled her towards him and tried to console her with a hug. She stayed in his embrace although the tension which suddenly swept through her body threatened to make it rigid and made her want to pull away from Fintan – despite her longing to be able to respond to the comfort he was offering.

She was floundering around helplessly and she wasn't used to being helpless – she who was always so in control of everything in her life. For a few weeks things had spun out of control then she beat the odds and got her life sorted again. Now fate was playing silly buggers and Maeve was pissed off.

"Let's wait and cool off a little before we continue this conversation," Fintan suggested. He recognised the signs and knew they were getting nowhere. He also knew it was only a matter of time before everything was somehow his fault.

"You're right, I'm sorry," Maeve said. "But it's just so unfair."

They stood there for a while, each waiting for the other to say something.

"I'm just going to check my face, then take Darragh for a walk," Maeve said at last. She was aware that tears had been threatening to spill from her eyes and she wanted to assess the damage before venturing forth. Not that she was likely to meet anyone she knew in Courtown at this time of year.

In Dublin someone else was hoping to avoid being seen. Although there were plenty of people she could have arranged to meet, and plenty of hospitality she could have taken full advantage of, Cathy had told no one, not even her parents, that she would be in Dublin for Easter. She had chosen to stay in a rather second-rate hotel near the airport because she was certain that no one she knew, or rather no one she would like to be seen to know, would come within a hundred feet of the place.

The other reason for her rather eccentric choice of accommodation was that it was only a short distance from the Aer Lingus sports grounds where on Easter Saturday a one-day American football league was to be played for charity. It was to feature teams from businesses all over Ireland and even a few from London. Cathy was pretty sure Danny's colleague Peter would be there, and she planned to 'bump into him', telling him she was planning to write a feature on how American football was the new rugby – only for Real Men. He'd love that! Unfortunately it meant that Cathy had to do some actual research on the subject of American football, but that was just one of the downsides of being a journalist and using your job as cover.

On the day itself, once she had established that Peter was in fact at the event, and had managed to get himself picked for a team that stood a good chance of progressing beyond the preliminary rounds, Cathy returned to her hotel and changed into a sprayed-on pair of jeans, knee-high high-heeled boots and a low-cut white top that left very little to the imagination. The fabric was so clingy that Cathy worried for one brief moment that it might even show up goose pimples – she wasn't used to walking around outdoors anywhere north of Malaga. But clingy was good. Clingy showed off Cathy's perfect figure. (How dare that cow Jo ask Cathy in London if she was pregnant? If anything Jo was the one who looked pregnant – she must be tipping the scales at *well* over eight stone!)

Cathy wandered round the sports grounds asking what she hoped were intelligent questions and pretending to write copious notes. She avoided Peter all afternoon so that he felt very clever indeed when he cornered her and persuaded her to let him take her out to dinner that night.

"I really should make sure that you have all the facts you need to present American football in the best possible light," he explained. "Do you have a photographer here?" He looked around eagerly, smoothing down his hair with his fingers.

"No photographer this time, Peter. I'm just getting a background feel for the sport. I'm not even convinced my editor is fully sold on the idea." Cathy smiled a seductive smile, which she hoped implied that Peter's chance of appearing as a centrefold depended entirely on the success of their dinner that night.

It seemed to work. He pulled in his stomach, stuck out his chest and held his head at a more flattering angle – a display of preening that would have done a peacock proud.

"Well, I guess it's up to li'l ol' me to convince you then."

"Oh, *I* don't need convincing, Peter! What I've seen here today is more that enough to convince me that it's a sport for real men."

His chest expanded to bursting point. "Dinner, then. Eight, at your hotel?"

Cathy agreed and tried to escape, but not before Peter could assure her that he understood she might feel awkward being seen in his company so soon after breaking up with Danny and he promised that he wouldn't mention it to the other man.

"I can well believe that you'd hate me to go back into work next week, talking all about how I met you. Rubbing salt in Danny's wounds, so to speak. But I promise you – Peter Fisch is not the bragging kind. And I never hit a man when he's down."

Cathy wasn't exactly sure what Peter was hoping he'd have to brag about, although she could guess, and knew that he must have his own reasons for wanting to cosy up to her. But that suited her fine. In fact, it amused her to watch him trying to be subtle with her.

"Oh Gosh!" Peter drawled over dessert that evening. "I keep talking about work, and about Danny 'n' all . . . I keep forgetting that he and you . . ."

"It's quite alright, Peter . . ."

Cathy reached across the table and placed her hand over his to forestall the rest of his apology. It was true that the main topic of conversation had been Danny and LBS, and she was glad that Peter hadn't noticed that it was she who kept bringing the subject back there. In fact, she had gathered enough information to formulate a plan. All that remained was to get Peter on side, whether he realised it or not.

Still holding his hand she continued: "Although it must seem like no time at all since I broke it off with Danny," (she managed to emphasise the 'I' without quite speaking in italics) "things hadn't been going well between us for quite some time." She looked down at the table and sighed. "I did my best to make it work, but . . ." another sigh, "there's only so much a woman can be expected to put up with. And of course the age gap didn't help. Danny's quite a bit older than me . . ."

Her gaze remained fixed on the tablecloth for about half a minute, then she looked up at Peter and stared longingly at him. Not even the most obtuse of men could fail to realise that if he could satisfy Cathy, in ways that she had never *quite* said Danny couldn't, he would have plenty to brag about.

Peter wasn't that obtuse. Refusing the waiter's offer of coffee he asked for the check.

CHAPTER 21

It took Maeve half an hour of brisk walking to admit to herself that the reason she was out walking and not back at the house talking to Fintan was to stop him raising the subject of what they were going to do now.

"If I can't come up with a good reason why Fintan shouldn't take time off over the summer by the time I reach the next corner, I'll go straight back and tell him that's what we're going to do," Maeve promised herself. She knew he'd agree immediately and she felt guilty, and furious with herself, for not having suggested it already.

"Blast Joan, blast the O'Connell-what's-their-names and blast that bloody English nanny who was careless enough to break her bloody shoulder."

Maeve spoke out loud and kicked savagely at a stone on the road. She looked around to see if there was anyone listening, but the road was deserted.

"Bloody, bloody, bloody! Shit, shit, shit," she muttered, but didn't feel any better. She hadn't taken any notice of where she was walking and realised she was at the track that led to Tony's parents' house. She hesitated, then took a few steps up the lane. The house was much bigger than Paul and Niamh's, although both cottages had started out around the same size. Fintan's aunt and uncle had put on at least three extensions over the years and now the house had none of the charm of the original building.

Maeve could see lights in the windows, but no car parked in front. She knew Tony had driven over, so if anyone was home it was probably James.

She struggled with the buggy over the rough track and was relieved when the rhythmic jolting caused Darragh to give up his struggle with sleep. It would take a brass band to wake him now, she knew.

Nonetheless, she left the buggy well back from the door when she knocked so that when James opened it and greeted her noisily, she was able to point to it and shush him.

"Maeve," he whispered enthusiastically, "I was just thinking about you. Come in. Is Fintan not with you?"

"No. He had to take the other two to the beach. The buggy's a disaster on the sand, so I took Darragh for a walk instead. I wouldn't have called in on you at all," Maeve quipped, "only Darragh fell asleep, so I'll have to make do with your company instead."

"Well, if I drift off while you're talking, at least I'll have the comfort of knowing you can't blame me as I'm the second man you've put to sleep today."

They fell easily back into their old banter and James

helped her lift the buggy up the two steps into the house. They wheeled it into the unlit front room.

"Is Tony out?" Maeve asked.

"He's gone to Carlow to visit a cousin who's just had a baby," James answered.

"Which cousin?"

Maeve racked her brain for any cousin that Tony and Fintan might share. It would be just like Fintan to hear about the baby and not say anything, never thinking to go get a card or a present.

"On his mother's side. It's okay, you haven't mortally insulted someone by ignoring the birth in the family," James said, guessing the reason for her cautious look. "Tea or coffee?" He held the kettle over the two mugs. They both had tea, so he stirred the teabags in the mug, squeezed them out and threw them in the sink.

"Tiny drop of milk, no sugar?" he asked.

"No change there," Maeve confirmed, touched that he remembered.

They took their mugs into the conservatory that Fintan's Aunt Olwen had insisted on three summers ago. Of all the extensions, it was the best. It faced east towards the sea and, while the view was great right now, Maeve knew it must be spectacular to have breakfast here and watch the sun rise. If you could get up that early.

"Tony probably won't get back till later tonight, but would you and Fintan like to come out for a drink?" James asked.

"I'm afraid Paul and Niamh went home this

morning, so we've no baby-sitter. But if you bring a bottle, or two or three, you're welcome to join us for dinner," Maeve answered. "I brought a leg of lamb from Dublin and it's way too big for the two of us – I wasn't sure if Fintan's parents would change their minds and stay."

Maeve knew that if James and Tony joined them for dinner, it would delay the discussion over who was going to look after the kids for the summer.

"That is, of course, unless you two bachelors had other plans for the night," she added. "Were you planning on hitting the fleshpots of Courtown to see if you'd get lucky?"

"Hmm, let's see, the fleshpots of Courtown versus Maeve's cooking?" James rubbed his chin and pretended to give it real consideration. "I think I'll go for the fleshpots. No, seriously, I'd love to join you for dinner. I'll let Tony know and he can join us when he gets back."

They sat in silence for a while, admiring the view. It was a bright, calm day – the rain of the day before had cleared the air and you could see forever out to sea.

"So how are you and Tony getting on together now you're sharing a flat in London?" Maeve asked.

It seemed strange to her that she hadn't heard about Tony and James sharing a flat. Maybe Fintan had heard and forgotten to tell her. Or he had told her and she'd lost it in the hormonal haze around the time of Darragh's birth.

"Oh, you know Tony," James said, getting up

suddenly to make another mug of tea. "He's easy enough to get along with. We don't rub each other up the wrong way or anything."

"Has he tried to fix you up yet?" Maeve called through to the kitchen. "He was always passing his reject girlfriends off on Fintan when they were younger."

"No, he must be too busy with the new job for any serious womanising. But enough of Tony, let's talk about you. It's ages since we've had a chance to talk, just the two of us." James sat down, and moved his chair closer to hers. "It's about time we had a long heart-to-heart. There's something I've been meaning to talk to you about for ages."

Maeve was intrigued, but somehow then found herself telling him all about Sarah, the problem with Joan and the solution Fintan had come up with. It was so easy to talk to James – he had known her forever and never judged her. When she said she was scared that Fintan staying at home would change things between them, he accepted that fear and didn't try to analyse it. When she told him about all the things Andrea had said, he didn't agree or disagree, but just asked her how she felt about them. And when she said she hadn't a clue how she felt but that she just had a sense of uneasiness, he accepted that and gave her the only piece of advice she ever remembered him offering in all the years she had known him.

"Stop trying to take advance responsibility for whatever happens in the next few months. It's not as if you have any real choices left – you've explored all the options and come up blank. Fintan minding the kids is the only choice left, so stop trying to figure out if it's the right choice or the wrong choice." He shrugged. "And may all your difficult decisions be as uncomplicated."

James looked distant as he added this as if he was thinking of something else and then he looked up horrified.

"Oh God, Maeve, don't think I'm trying to trivialise your problem."

He was terrified he might have upset her, but she took pity and laughed.

"Don't panic, I'm not mortally offended. And thanks for the advice. But now I think I'd better get back to my horde of barbarians – after all I wouldn't want Fintan to realise what he was letting himself in for until it's all signed, sealed and delivered."

Suddenly Maeve realised she had been getting herself into a state about nothing. As James put it so clearly, they had no other choice, and she couldn't keep trying to take responsibility for events beyond her control. Why was he always able to help her see things so clearly?

She got up and discovered that it was later than she thought. She would have to hurry to get the dinner on if they were going to eat this side of midnight. The leg of lamb she had brought from Dublin was huge, in fact possibly too big to be this season's, as promised by the butcher, and she'd forgotten to check a cookbook to see how long it needed in the oven. It was a good thing Fintan had his phone so she could ring her mother.

Maeve could just imagine the mileage Anna would get out of her daughter not knowing how to cook a joint of meat after eight years' marriage, but she could just about handle it at this distance.

"Do you want to come down to the house with me now or follow on later after the kids have gone to bed?" Maeve asked James.

"I may as well walk down with you. I'll put Ciaran to bed if you like, and give Fintan a break."

He picked up their two coats and helped Maeve into hers. It was one of the things she had always liked about James. He was effortlessly courteous. He could hold open a door, remain standing until you were seated, walk on the outside of the footpath and not even the most militant feminist could take offence. He did it naturally, without noticing that he was doing anything special at all.

Darragh woke up when she was tucking the blanket around him. He was about to scream in protest until he realised he was still in his pram and about to go out for another walk. Holidays were great! He chewed happily on the heel of bread Maeve had robbed from the bread-bin to tide him over till he got home.

Where the track up to the house met the road, the front wheel of the pram got stuck in a pothole and Maeve nearly tipped her youngest son onto the tarmac.

"Women drivers!" James snorted. "Here, let me."

He expertly steered past the obstruction and continued to push the light buggy along the road. Walking beside James, watching as he pointed out clouds and birds to

Darragh, Maeve got a brief flash of how things might have been. Then she shook her head as if to clear it of such a treacherous thought. She and James would never have got this far. They were good friends now, but would never have made it much further than they had as a couple. Besides, she and Fintan were perfect.

She tried to get James to talk about himself again: "You said it was time we had a heart-to-heart."

"I thought we just had one."

"But did you not say you needed to talk to me about something?"

"Did I say that?" James looked intently at Darragh in the buggy as if he was avoiding looking at Maeve. "I don't remember; it must just have been a figure of speech."

Maeve knew he was lying, that he had been about to tell her something, but had changed his mind. She decided to probe further. "You know, if you had found someone in England, I'd love to hear about it," she prompted gently. "I'm not going to take offence or anything."

James stopped walking and looked at her in disbelief. "Maeve, it's over ten years since we broke up. What makes you think I would give a second's thought to you before getting involved with someone else? You have an exaggerated sense of your own importance!"

He walked on rapidly forcing Maeve, who had stopped alongside him, to run and catch up. She caught his arm and forced him to turn and face her to take the full onslaught of her indignation.

"What do you mean?" she raged. "You're the one so fond of saying you've never got over me, that you compared every woman past and future to me and that they all came up lacking. Flattering though it may be, I've always been left feeling guilty for finding someone else so soon after we broke up, while you're still looking!"

"Sorry, that was a bit harsh." James gave her arm a conciliatory squeeze and then started pushing the buggy towards town again. "And sorry if I ever made you feel bad in any way about finding Fintan. I'm really happy for you guys." He paused. "I suppose I'm just fed up of everyone trying to sort poor James' life out for him. I'm a big boy now and I can look after myself." He smiled shyly. "And to use your phrase, I'm not still looking."

"You mean there is some –" Maeve stopped when she saw his warning expression. "OK . . . sorry . . . none of my business. But James, you know I still care about you and I'd love to know you're happy. Are you?"

He didn't answer for what seemed like forever, and then sighed. "I'm more content than I've ever been before. And everything feels right at the moment. But am I happy? I don't know . . . at times, yes, very happy. But then something always seems to get in the way."

"What?"

"Oh nothing in particular, just things." He withdrew into himself, and Maeve knew she would get no more from him. Then he seemed to brighten. "Stop worrying about me, Maeve. I am happy, or as happy as I could be at the moment. Now will you look after this young man while I pop into this off-licence so I don't arrive to dinner with one arm as long as the other."

He dashed through the door before she could object. She looked around the small town, and tried to remember if there was anything she needed to buy for the dinner. She decided they needed cream for Niamh's apple-tart. If it was just herself and Fintan, Maeve would have stuck to her diet, but if they were going to have a guest . . .

She stuck her head round the door of the off-licence to tell James she was going across to the convenience store, and manoeuvred the buggy down the steep kerb.

Fintan had already started on the dinner when they arrived back. The potatoes were peeled, the carrots chopped, and the oven was pre-heated and waiting for the lamb. Maeve felt so guilty that she'd left him to do all the work that she completely forgot the little speech she had rehearsed about how wonderful it was to have James and Tony to dinner.

James stepped into the breach.

"Sorry about the intrusion, Fintan," he smiled ruefully, "but Maeve insisted I come to dinner because your cousin abandoned me to go and pay homage to a baby. But I intend to work for my keep. Where are the monsters? I'll get them ready for bed while you sit down and test the wine – just to check it's of sufficient quality to accompany Maeve's lamb."

He thrust a bag with two bottles in it at Fintan who managed to hide his annoyance that he wouldn't be able to talk to Maeve over a long, romantic dinner as he had planned. It was much easier to hide his annoyance when he examined the contents of the bag.

"James, you shouldn't have! Maeve's lamb has a lot to live up to." He was impressed with James' choice of wine – two bottles of a well-aged red Côtes du Rhone.

"May I remind everyone it's the butcher's lamb?" Maeve's voice came from the bedroom where she was changing Darragh into his nightclothes. "If it's good I'll take full credit for the quality of the cooking, if it's not, remember I had reservations about it from the start."

"Does it not need to go in the oven yet, honey," Fintan asked innocently, "or had you some other cooking method in mind?"

Maeve appeared panic-stricken in the kitchen and almost threw Darragh at him.

"You deal with him and give me your mobile. I need to check with Mum how long it will take to cook."

"I thought we'd banned phones."

Maeve held up the lamb by the leg-bone, threatening him with it. "Do you want to eat?"

"Okay, okay, I know when I'm beaten." Fintan retreated to get the phone.

Ciaran meanwhile had realised that James was available to tell stories and intended to make the most of it.

"Uncle James, will you read me my story tonight?"

"Unc, Jay, tory," Fiona agreed, nodding wisely.

"Oh, I don't know," James said gravely. "Did you eat all your dinner?"

"Nearly all, then I was full, and Daddy said I could have my yoghurt."

"Yoghurt!" James nodded knowingly. "I could tell you'd eaten yoghurt. Now let's see what else you had for tea."

He glanced at the telltale remains on the kitchen draining-board while Ciaran held up his pyjamas. James examined his stomach, prodding gently.

"Sausages, definitely sausages. And let's see, what's this, potatoes? No, mashed potatoes! And carrots! No wonder you're bigger than you were yesterday. If I'd eaten all that I wouldn't get through the door."

James led an awestruck Ciaran into the bedroom, book in hand. Fiona had to be persuaded that it was safe to be tucked in by this exhilarating stranger so Ciaran snuggled in beside her on the lower bunk.

Meanwhile Maeve was in the kitchen on the phone to her mother. She had received her instructions on how to roast the leg of lamb, and to prevent any discussion of how she should know this by now she told her about Joan's phone call.

"Oh no, Maeve!" Anna was genuinely distraught. "What are you going to do? You were relying on her." She paused, and then said hesitantly: "Look, if you're really stuck, I do have a few weeks' holidays owed to me . . ."

Maeve whispered this to Fintan who was sitting at the kitchen table, obeying James's instructions to carry out quality control on the wine. He shook his head and waved his hand in the negative, almost choking on his wine.

"No, Mum. Thanks for the offer, but I think we're just going to have to rely on our fall-back position."

Anna's relief was almost audible. "Fall-back position? I didn't know you had one. That's wonderful, darling, what is it?"

Maeve was aware that Fintan's hand was frozen in mid-air, his glass suspended in the act of delivering wine to his mouth. "Fintan will take some time off over the summer and look after the kids himself. Just until Joan can take over."

The silence at the other end of the phone was deafening. It was echoed by the silence in the kitchen. James's story filled the whole house.

"Well, I'm sure the two of you have discussed this . . . that you know what you're doing . . ." It was with great effort that Anna spoke calmly.

"Yes, Mum, we're both convinced this is the right thing." Maeve said steadily, finally managing to meet her husband's gaze.

"Well, don't rush into anything," Anna could be heard saying slowly on the other end of the phone. "You never know what the next few weeks –"

"Mum, I've got to go and put the lamb on. I'll call you when we get back."

Maeve hung up and stood staring at Fintan. He said nothing but took a wineglass from the table and filled it for her. Then he raised his own.

"The summer!" he toasted.

"The summer," Maeve agreed, touching her glass against his.

"And whatever it brings?"

"And whatever it brings," she agreed, trying not to sound nervous.

Fintan took a few sips of wine and watched Maeve as she seasoned the meat. He couldn't help thinking that James had something to do with her sudden change of heart. He knew he should feel grateful and not care how Maeve had come to agree with him, but to his surprise he was jealous that James might have been the one to swing things in his favour.

CHAPTER 22

The lamb got shoved in the oven and 'Uncle' James began to wind up his story in the bedroom. "And after their story, the children all looked up, and there were their mummies, and daddies, and childminders waiting to collect them! The End." He was reading a book Anna had bought Ciaran about a boy going to school for the first time.

"For fuck's sake!" James said in exasperation as he emerged. "Oops, sorry, I don't think anyone heard that. But honestly, do you have to have a degree in political correctness to write children's books these days? That class had a black kid, a white kid, a yellow kid, a kid in a wheelchair, and two teachers: one black male and one yellow female. The female wore glasses, oh, and the guy was bald. One kid, smaller than all the others, was crying. And instead of beating the shit out of him like we'd have done in our day, Daniel, our hero, became best friends with him – 'because it's nice that everyone's different'. That's such an unrealistic fantasy he's going to get a rude awakening when he joins the real world. How can you pollute your children's minds with that kind of crap?"

"Sssh!" Maeve spluttered, trying not to laugh. "Mum bought it for him."

"That figures! Anna always did live in a different world from the rest of us," James snorted. "A world full of shiny happy people holding hands. Attending the right charity functions in perfect outfits with matching hats and gloves. How is your dear mother anyway?"

"A lot easier to live with since she got a job."

"A job!" James shook his head. "I could never get over that one. Imagine . . . Anna, doing a job . . . a real job! So what's she up to now?"

"She's working in a PR firm," Maeve explained. "Secretary to the boss's personal assistant or something. Her job description seems to be to run the company single-handedly if she's to be believed."

"PR, that figures. I'd love to say that's not a real job, but I was in PR for too long myself." James paused. "Hell, that just qualifies me to say it convincingly: that's not a real job! But it would suit Anna. Imagine – all those years of socialising finally put to good use."

"That's exactly what she said herself."

Maeve uncurled herself from her armchair and stood up to go into the kitchen and look as if she was doing something about dinner. James followed her through to help himself to more wine. Then he stood in the doorway between the kitchen and living-room so that he could talk to Fintan and Maeve at the same time.

"Andrea heard of the job through one of her clients," Maeve continued, "and when she heard what it entailed, she thought it would be ideal for mum, and set up an interview."

"I didn't know Egan had set up as a rival to me in the recruitment business." James' own recruitment company in London was doing so well that there was talk of expanding back into Dublin, but he never seemed to get around to it.

"All the more reason not to bother entering the Irish market," Fintan said wryly.

James laughed.

Maeve checked the lamb and was opening the second bottle of wine when a phone began to sing from the porch.

"That'll be Tony," James said, and he went out to root through his pockets then stayed in the porch to talk.

"He's already managed to escape," he announced with a grin, as he reappeared, "and he's on his way. I told him he wouldn't be allowed to drink anything unless he helped us eat the lamb."

"Good thinking. But if he's already had dinner, he's not allowed any roast potatoes. I'm not peeling any more," Fintan said firmly. "By the way, you don't happen to know what baby he was visiting, do you?"

It had just dawned on Fintan that he shared cousins with Tony, and he hoped he wasn't in the bad books for neglecting a new arrival. James and Maeve laughed together.

"Don't worry, your good lady wife already had that one covered. It's okay, it was someone called Alison, wife of a cousin on his mum's side of the family."

Rather too soon, given the speed limits he should have been observing, Tony appeared at the door. The others had just sat down to eat so James jumped up and began to pile food on a plate for him.

"Sit down, you must be knackered after the drive." He handed him a glass of wine. "Get that down you."

When they were all seated again, Tony began to describe the nightmare of a day he had had.

"I thought I'd get away with just dropping in unannounced on Mike and Alison, but of course Mike wasn't there. Grace – my aunt from hell, Mike's mum – was there, and Alison begged me, almost in tears, not to leave until Mike came back. Then Grace insisted I come for dinner . . . I swear, if there were ever two sisters more different than my mum and Grace . . . how on earth does Mum put up with her?"

He lapsed into silence and Maeve caught Fintan's eye – he was trying not to smile. Although Maeve had never met Grace she had met Tony's mother Olwen far too often, and by all accounts, one was as bad as the other.

"You know, today just confirmed my decision never to get married and have kids. There are some dodgy genes in our family which should be left die off."

"Oh, come on, Tony! You're great with kids," Fintan protested. "How can you be sure you'll never want any of your own? Besides, how can you decide not to get married, before you even know if you'll ever be able to persuade some poor unfortunate woman to take you?"

"Other peoples' kids are fine," Tony grunted. "You don't have the responsibility of wondering what you've unleashed on the world."

"Tony, what you going on about?" James refilled his glass. "You're full of crap sometimes. Was the car radio acting up again, making you do too much thinking on the way down?" Then changing the subject, he turned to Fintan: "Did you know your cousin's been promoted *again*?"

"Tony? You never mentioned it. You really will have to learn to blow your own trumpet a bit more. I'd have thought after living with James for six months, some of his trumpeting ability would have rubbed off." Maeve laughed. "Every time James visits us, he's full of how brilliantly his agency's doing and how he's now placed executives in well over half of the 'fortune one hundred companies', whatever they are. So Tony," she went on quickly, aware that James was about to interrupt, whether to correct her or do a bit of trumpeting she couldn't tell, "tell us all about this new promotion."

"It was nothing really," Tony said modestly. "I was just in the right place at the right time. The manager I work for just made partner, so there was a gap at manager level. I got the job." He shrugged.

"Don't be so modest, it's sickening," said James. "You're the youngest at that level and there were three others more senior to you after the job." He raised his glass. "To your genius of a cousin who, I'm reliably informed, will probably make partner before he's forty. If he does, I'm raising his rent."

"If I do, I'll be able to afford my own place."

"God, I hadn't thought of that. I'd have to find another tenant who's willing to take all the abuse I dish out." James raised his glass again. "Here's to Tony being a long way off forty and may he continue to look youthful so they'll be embarrassed to promote him too soon."

"Okay, I'll drink to the youthful bit so long as I get to keep my hair," Tony laughed, and raised his glass.

"Ooh . . . nasty!" Maeve giggled, at James who had begun to massage his challenged follicles.

"You just wait, Tony," James warned. "Your grandfather's bald as a coot, and they say it skips a generation! That's a family inheritance you won't escape!"

"Apple-pie and coffee, anyone?" Maeve vanished into the kitchen.

"How much longer are you guys staying in Ireland?" Fintan asked.

"Only till Tuesday," Tony answered. "We'd have gone back on Monday, but with it being a bank holiday and not having booked, we couldn't get a ferry crossing."

"Are you staying down here or going up to see the folks?"

"My parents are away," Tony said and turned to James to allow him answer the question for himself.

"I haven't told anyone I'm in Ireland," James answered with a guilty expression. "So I'd appreciate if you didn't mention to my parents that you happened to see me down here. They'd be livid if they thought I was this close and hadn't called up. I just couldn't face it somehow."

"Have you had some kind of a row?" Maeve asked, as she returned with the apple-pie.

"No, but I suppose I just wanted a weekend off, relaxing, without having to make the compulsory visits to the aunts and uncles and everyone. And it wasn't as if we'd planned to come to Ireland. It was a spur of the moment decision."

"Oh well, I'm unlikely to run into your parents, but I won't let the cat out of the bag," Maeve promised. "I suppose I'd better not tell Mum though – she often runs into your Mum in Dalkey."

She didn't add that James was often held up as an example of the perfect child in his observance of his duty towards his parents. Once Anna had gone so far as to suggest that his parents received more visits from James since he moved to London than Anna did since Maeve moved to Blackrock. Maeve didn't like to point out to her that James didn't have three small children who made every visit home an ordeal. Anna seemed to have no concept of the damage thirty little fingers could do to her treasures and made no attempt to make the house more child-friendly. Every time they visited, Maeve spent the first ten minutes moving things out of reach and the rest of the time watching and worrying, wondering would the children wreck the house or would the house make a pre-emptive strike. It certainly had the means. Unguarded sockets, heavy lamps with enticingly coiled wires and a steep spiral staircase over a tiled floor; all waited for their chance to tempt an over-curious child to almost certain injury.

The house hadn't always been like that. The house Maeve had grown up in was a warm, friendly place. But a year after her father's death Maeve watched her mother begin to slowly transform their home into a centrefold from *Homes and Gardens*. It was as if she wanted to extinguish all signs of family life and embrace her new role of glamorous widow. And to be fair, Maeve was relieved that Anna had at last found an outlet for the nervous energy built up since her bereavement. But she was saddened to watch her memories retreat upstairs and finally find refuge only in her own childish bedroom, a room unchanged since she was twelve.

A few weeks before his fatal heart attack, her father had sat on her bed and together they had planned the redecoration of Maeve's room. He wanted to give her a more grown-up refuge, somewhere she could bring friends, to study and laugh together. Those plans remained untouched in the bottom drawer of her dresser and sometimes, even now as an adult, Maeve would take them out and touch the pages covered with her father's fluid bank-manager's script. He had penned lists, drawn plans and invented timetables, unaware that his own treacherous heart had already finalised its own deadly schedule.

It would have happened whether or not they had

chosen to go to Brittas for the first swim of the year on that warm June day. The doctors told Maeve and Anna that the weak vessel in his heart, waiting to betray him, could just as easily have given way as he climbed the stairs to bed. It didn't really help the distraught teenager and her mother, whose last memory was of him getting out of the sea uncharacteristically soon, retreating up the beach to lie in the sun, ignoring their taunts. When Maeve joined him a while later, her father was already dead.

"Maeve? Hello? Anyone home?"

Maeve looked up, startled, suddenly aware that they were all looking at her. She blinked rapidly, afraid that her eyes had moistened.

"More coffee?" Fintan held the pot over her half-full mug.

"No, thanks. It'll keep me awake. I think I'll get a drink of water." She went into the kitchen, and poured the dregs of her coffee down the sink. She looked for a clean glass, but then just filled her mug with water and swallowed it down fast. As she refilled it, Fintan came into the kitchen.

"Are you okay, love?" he asked gently. "You looked a bit funny in there."

"Fine. I'm just tired – you know what Darragh was like last night. Or rather you don't, do you? You slept right through it." She tried to laugh to reassure him. "I think I've drunk too much wine, I nearly fell asleep at the table."

When they returned, James and Tony were getting up to leave.

"We've kept you up far too late already," James apologised, "but I promise we'll be thinking of you in the morning when we turn over and go back to sleep, knowing you'll have no such luxury."

"Save your sympathy for Fintan. I'm not emerging before ten." Maeve stared at her husband, daring him to challenge her. He threw up his hands in silent surrender.

"Ten? How horrible! Is the sun up that early at the weekend?" James asked. He stumbled as he went out the door, and would have fallen if Tony hadn't caught him.

"Looks like I'm going to have to carry you home," he said to James and then added to Fintan, "I've left the car in front of the house. I'll come down and collect it in the morning."

"Come on, Tony, home to bed, and leave these poor folk in peace," James ordered dramatically and staggered again, grabbing onto Tony briefly to stop himself from falling. They wandered off into the night with Tony occasionally reaching out to stop his companion tripping on some unseen obstacle.

"I didn't think he'd drunk that much," Fintan said as they watched the two of them disappear into the darkness.

"He didn't, not really," Maeve said. "I think there was an element of play-acting. Maybe he felt they'd stayed too late and he was covering up his embarrassment. My falling asleep at the table probably made them feel bad."

But she was glad they were gone. She was genuinely

tired and the sudden memories of her father, coming out of nowhere, had surprised and upset her.

"*To sleep, perchance to dream?* You looked like you were in another world." Fintan probed gently.

"What? Oh." Maeve didn't want to talk about her memories of her father right now. "No, no dreams. And goodnight! If I don't get to bed soon you'll have to carry me in and undress me yourself."

"Now there's an offer I couldn't refuse." Fintan wrapped his arms around her. "Do I have to wait for you to fall asleep?"

"Tired. Sleep. Bed. Now!" Maeve said firmly, disentangling herself and making for the bedroom.

"Oh well, can't blame a bloke for trying."

CHAPTER 22

A few weeks later, on a Sunday morning, Maeve's mother Anna 'was just passing' and called in on her daughter. It was almost unheard of for Anna to drop by unannounced so Maeve was sure she was in for an earful. Fintan had taken the kids to his parents' house to test a new swing Granddad Paul had installed in the garden for them, and when Maeve opened the door to her mother she was tempted to shut it straight over again. She wasn't sure she could face the discussion her mother had come to have without Fintan to back her up.

"Mum, come in. Excuse the state of the place," she waved her arm about helplessly.

Anna's eyes drifted over the hall which was strewn with toys and looked like it hadn't been vacuumed in a week – although Maeve had run the Hoover over it quickly the night before.

"I'm in the middle of writing an important paper for

the Ofiscom board," she told her mother hoping she would take the hint and not stay too long. "Fintan's taken the kids out so that I can get some peace and quiet to do it."

"There's not many husbands would be as tolerant as Fintan, giving up his weekend just because you've left everything to the last minute," Anna sniffed, warming to her theme.

"We don't call it tolerant these days, Mum. We call it supportive," Maeve said slowly through gritted teeth. "And I didn't leave everything to the last minute – the paper's written, I only need to slot in some diagrams of data I only received yesterday."

"No need to take that tone, I was only commenting. And if everything's nearly done you'll have time to offer me a cup of coffee so we can have a little chat."

Anna made her way towards the living-room.

"No, Mum, come into the study with me, we can talk in there." Maeve moved quickly. If the hall was untidy, the living-room was a disaster zone. It was clean but messy – decorated with toys and the remains of Ciaran's breakfast. Besides, if Anna came into the study, she might realise that Maeve really was busy, and leave sooner.

The study, beside the kitchen, had been the breakfast room of the original house. The previous owners had enlarged the kitchen back into the garden by adding a bright, light-filled extension and normally Maeve would have brought her mother in there to sit at the kitchen table. Today she wanted to make a point so she led the way into her small, dark study.

"Sit down there, Mum, and I'll put the coffee on."

She pointed to the settee under the window, the only place in the whole room not covered with printouts of her presentation.

From the kitchen, Maeve could hear her mother wander around picking up bits of paper then putting them down again. She itched to tell her to leave things as they were. But maybe Anna would read something which would convince her that Maeve was a real businesswoman and not a little girl playing at having a job.

Maeve could delay no longer in the kitchen, so she brought in two steaming mugs of coffee, already milked. She knew her mother liked to pour her own milk, but as she couldn't find a clean jug she calculated that giving her white coffee would be preferable to presenting her with a milk carton, which would really convince her that Maeve had gone to hell in a handbasket.

Anna sat on the settee as she took her coffee. Maeve sat at the desk and swivelled her chair around to face her mother. It was where she had been sitting before she was interrupted, but it crossed her mind that she might unconsciously have chosen to sit at the higher level to boost her confidence.

"How are the children?" Anna asked awkwardly. Now she was here she wasn't sure how to raise the subject she had come to discuss.

"The kids are fine, Mum, pity you missed them. They'll be disappointed they missed their Ganna."

Fiona couldn't pronounce 'Granny Anna'; there were

just too many N's, so she condensed it down, and now the whole family used her version.

Maeve decided to launch straight into the subject she had no doubt her mother was here to raise and save herself half an hour's pussyfooting around it. "By the way, don't mention to them, will you, that there's going to be a change in arrangements. We're not going to tell them until closer the date. If they hear now that Fintan will be minding them for the summer, they might ask why he can't start straight away and then give poor Sarah a hard time."

"That's what I wanted to talk to you about, Maeve." Anna cleared a space on the desk and placed her coffee mug down carefully. She joined her hands together in her lap and looked at Maeve, assuming the facial expression she used when Maeve was a child and she was about to preface a telling-off with the words: 'I really want to treat you more like an adult, Maeve darling, so why don't we begin by both acting like grown-ups.'

Maeve steeled herself for an updated version of the speech.

"I really wish you would think about all this again before you rush into anything and do something you may both end up regretting," Anna said carefully.

"We've been thinking about nothing else since Sarah quit, Mum." Maeve tried to hide her exasperation. "The only suitable childminder we found is Joan, so we're prepared to wait for her."

"But at what cost, Maeve?" Anna was almost

pleading. "You expect Fintan to stay at home over the summer, putting his job on hold –"

"Let's get something straight, Mum. I didn't expect anything of Fintan. He was the one who came up with the idea and he was the one who talked me into it . . ." As soon as Maeve said this, she regretted her wording.

"He talked you into it?" Anna jumped at the first chink in the armour. She allowed herself a sad smile. "So you'll admit you had reservations. But you didn't put up too much of a fight, did you? It must have seemed like the ideal way to hang onto that precious job of yours. And why were you not the one to make the offer? What do you think it'll do to your marriage in the long term when Fintan is at home and you out at work?"

These questions came so close to Maeve's own fears that she didn't know how to answer them. She went on the offensive.

"Mum, I didn't have reservations, so much as prejudices. Prejudices I may add that I probably picked up from you." She ignored her mother's wildly flapping mouth, and forged ahead. "Fintan was able to show me those prejudices for what they were, and helped me put them aside. Besides, he really wants to spend more time with the children, and there's no point in worrying about the long term because it's only for four months, no longer than I took off on maternity leave."

"That's completely different, and you know it. Besides it's more natural for a mother to bring up her children than a father. Maybe that's old-fashioned, but it's what

I believe." If Anna was challenging Maeve to contradict her, she was disappointed. Maeve sat with her arms folded, waiting for her mother to continue.

"Well, I've had my say," Anna said, "though I know you'll go and do exactly what you want to anyway. You never take the blindest bit of notice of what I think."

She was warming up to the theme of martyr so Maeve cut her off. The one thing Maeve couldn't handle right now was Anna's revisionist version of the past. A version in which Anna had spent every waking hour with Maeve rather than dropping her with baby-sitters and grandparents at every opportunity. Maeve's only memories of 'family time' featured her father in the starring role.

"I know you'll find this hard to come to terms with, but we believe it's the best option, and if we're wrong . . . well we all have to make our own mistakes." Maeve didn't add that Anna would then be able to say 'I told you so'. Anna was very good at saying 'I told you so' without ever uttering the words.

"Things have changed, Mum. There's hardly a family in the country who don't have to make some kind of a compromise, and we're lucky that this is the first time we've been faced with it."

"Well . . . you know *I* think your whole way of *life* is a compromise. Can you imagine what things would have been like for you if I had decided to go off and get a job instead of honouring my commitment to you? You can't expect to have your cake and eat it, Maeve."

Anna had run out of steam at that point and maybe,

just maybe, she had noticed the fleeting look of exasperation that had crossed Maeve's face as she made her last little speech. If Maeve didn't want to challenge Anna's version of the past, neither did Anna want it challenged and she knew there was a limit to how far she could push her daughter. So she finished her coffee quickly and told Maeve she would let her get back to work. Then at least, when Fintan came home, she could have a meal ready instead of hiding in the study for the rest of the day.

In town, Cathy pushed open the door of Habitat on St Stephen's Green and made her way towards the stairs up to the café. She was quite pleased with her choice of meeting place. It was bright and airy, there was a view over the Green and the prices were reasonable. Aoife would appreciate being invited here. Cathy was only in Dublin for a long weekend and she had so much to fit in, so many people to see, that picking a time to meet Aoife had caused her a few headaches. It was important that she meet the blasted girl, but not so important that Cathy was prepared to give up a Friday or Saturday night for it and Saturday afternoon had been devoted to a shopping trip with her good friend Antonia. Cathy had enjoyed *that* immensely. She hadn't bought much of course – the shops in London were *so* much more fabulous. Besides, it was important to impress on Antonia, and by extension the rest of her set, that Cathy was well above shopping on Dublin's *pedestrian* Grafton Street.

But a few days before she flew in from London, her parents had suggested a family Sunday lunch and that made up Cathy's mind – Sunday lunchtime would be the perfect time to meet Aoife.

"Aoife, over here!" Cathy stood up and waved at a tallish young woman wearing very little make-up, who wore her plain reddish-brown hair swept off her face into a simple ponytail. Aoife looked around uncertainly to see where the call was coming from, spotted Cathy and made her way nervously across the crowded café. A large leather handbag swung from one shoulder, wreaking havoc in its wake.

"Oh, I'm sorry. . . excuse me . . . here – let me pick that up for you."

By the time she reached Cathy's window table, Aoife's face was redder than the soft red leather boots that peeped out from the ends of her jeans. Cathy took a surreptitious look around to make sure she didn't recognise anyone, before kissing Aoife on both cheeks.

"Aoife, you look great!" Cathy sounded surprised. She had been prepared to flatter, but Aoife really did look good. In a simple girl-next-door kind of way. Not in a million years would Cathy have chosen Aoife's outfit for her, but now that she looked at it, it was actually perfect for what she had in mind. The long-sleeved cream top and brown jeans were inexpensive and simple, but they suited Aoife. And they suited an image of Aoife that Cathy was very comfortable with.

"I couldn't believe it when you called!" Aoife said

breathlessly as she sat down. "I'd have thought you were much too busy . . ."

"Nonsense! It's ages since I've seen you. You must have loads of news for me."

"Nothing as exciting as your move to London, I'm afraid. But I have one piece of news – I have a chance at your old job!"

"Really?" Cathy's smile thinned somewhat. "You'll have to tell me all about it. But let's order first."

They opened their menus and both ordered salads. Cathy asked the waitress to leave off the croutons and bacon and to serve the dressing to the side of her salad; while Aoife ordered a goat's cheese panini to go with hers.

"Well, you know how when you left the magazine, you didn't give them much notice," Aoife began, "and they were stuck for a few pieces that they thought you were going to do?"

Cathy wondered if this was a subtle dig, but then decided Aoife was too straightforward for that, so she smiled graciously and listened to the story of articles submitted on spec, their rapturous reception and the promise of an interview for Cathy's old job.

"It will be such a relief to get away from covering church fêtes, politicians kissing babies while opening supermarkets and – "

Aoife was interrupted by Cathy jumping to her feet, then sitting down again to say: "Sorry, I didn't catch that, I thought I saw someone I knew."

Before Aoife could re-start her tale, the two women

were interrupted by the appearance of what seemed to Aoife one of the best-looking men she had ever seen up close. He seemed as perfect as a shop-window mannequin, right down to the plastic half-smile.

"Cathy!" Peter said in his slight American drawl, "I thought it was you. Why, I haven't seen you in . . . how long is it?"

About four hours, Cathy was tempted to say, remembering the previous night with pleasure, but instead she smiled sweetly and simpered: "Much too long, Peter. I should have kept in touch, but since I broke up with Danny . . ."

"I understand, Cathy, it would have been awkward. And this is . . ." He turned towards Aoife.

"Excuse my appalling manners! Peter, this is Aoife. Aoife . . . Peter. Peter used to work with Danny," she added as explanation.

"I still do. Or at least I did last time I checked." Peter pulled up a chair without waiting to be invited to join them and flagged down a waitress to ask for a menu.

"And what do you do, Aoife? What a lovely name – Aoife. Is that a Gaelic name?"

Peter studied her as she told him about her job as a journalist in a small local newspaper. Cathy had sold Aoife short, he decided. He hadn't expected her to be this pretty. A bit quiet maybe – Cathy had described her as terminally shy. He still wasn't sure he completely understood Cathy's reasons for wanting him to date Aoife, but it seemed to be one of the conditions she had attached to helping him get further with Danny. And he desperately needed to make some headway there. So far Danny was closing him out completely and although Peter hadn't decided yet what he wanted from LBS after the merger, he knew that having Danny's confidence was essential.

"I'd far rather date you," he'd told Cathy last night as she explained what she wanted him to do.

"Well, if you're a good boy, and do what you're told. . ."

He remembered this now and paid attention to Aoife, asking enough questions to sound interested in what she was saying, but paying enough attention to Cathy as well in case she might get jealous.

Finally as per their plan, Cathy got up to leave. She insisted that Aoife stay and keep Peter company: "He's only just ordered dessert, Aoife. And you haven't anything more important planned, have you? Whereas I have a plane to catch . . ."

CHAPTER 24

Little changed over the next couple of months. Maeve was snowed under with work and took the news that Fintan's leave from work was approved, with relief. Not so much because she had fully accepted that they were making the right decision – she still had secret reservations – but once it was sorted out, it was out of her hands and she could stop feeling guilty.

LBS was working at full capacity at the moment and Maeve was working out ways for some staff to work from home. What had seemed like a sensible suggestion at a staff meeting was turning into a tactical nightmare and Danny and Peter seemed to have left it all to her to sort out. In fact, they seemed to spend most of their time huddled in Danny's office discussing God knows what. Probably golf handicaps. Since the advent of the good weather, Peter had suddenly developed an interest in the sport and Danny was more than willing to act as coach.

When Maeve went into the building one morning at the end of June, an air of tension hit her. As she strode into reception she saw an unusually large number of people for this time of morning congregated there. Surely all these people should be out with clients, she thought in annoyance, but then she caught Colm's eye. He made a face and glanced towards her office. She trusted his judgement and fled there, aware of several pairs of eyes following her retreat. Colm followed seconds later and theatrically checked that he hadn't been followed before shutting the door.

"What on earth's going on out there, Colm?" Maeve asked. "There are at least three technicians and a couple of programmers who should be miles from here right now. Has someone called a meeting and forgotten to tell me? We'll have furious clients on the phone in no time. And don't tell me Fiona's managed to sort out Joe O'Connell's invoicing in one afternoon. If that isn't running perfectly when he gets in this morning, he'll be on to me, threatening to pull the contract." Maeve was getting more and more agitated. She thought that now, with everything out in the open about the merger, everyone should have settled back to the old routine. The company couldn't afford this much down-time.

"Well, boss, everyone's kind of wondering what's going on. Is there something you guys at the top haven't been telling us?" Colm wore an unusually aggressive expression, but Maeve had no idea what he was talking about. He continued. "It seems that now Ofiscom's taking over they may be downsizing the company. Is that true?"

He now wore an expression that reminded Maeve of a puppy kicked for the first time by its beloved owner. She was more confused than ever.

"I have no idea what you're talking about."

"It's okay if you can't tell me. I understand. I just thought you ought to know what's been going on. There are a lot of very pissed-off people out there."

Maeve knew she had to control her irritation if she was going to get any information out of Colm. She told him to take a seat and was relieved to see that he must have already put the coffee on before getting so upset, so she poured them both a cup. He seemed slightly mollified to have his boss serve him and relaxed back into the chair, taking a long swig of coffee before talking.

"It's about the new office in Sandyford," he began, then caught Maeve's look of surprise before she rapidly resumed a neutral expression. "You knew about this, didn't you?"

"What did I know about, Colm?" She was damned if she was going to feed him any information he didn't already have, despite her policy of keeping everyone informed.

"One of the guys, coming out of a client's building, saw Danny and Peter in hard hats in a new office block in Sandyford. After they left he got talking to the site foreman, and it seems that Peter was adamant that they didn't need an office which could hold more than twenty-five or thirty people. We're already packed in like sardines here and you keep talking about recruiting more people once the merger's complete. So who's going to get the chop when we move offices?" Colm had built himself into a lather of righteous indignation.

"Well, Colm, you know I could never survive without you," Maeve felt it wise to soothe the younger man's anxieties and boost his ego, "but we have no plans to shed any personnel. Did it occur to anyone to ask Danny or Peter what was going on?"

"That was the plan. But they've been hiding in Danny's office all morning. In conference call to Texas," he added ominously.

Maeve could see why this should cause anxiety. For Danny to lock himself into an office for that long with only Peter for company was worrying.

"Are they still there now?" she asked Colm.

"I think so. They said they didn't want to be disturbed," he added in warning.

"Well, I'm going to disturb them."

Maeve left her office, ignoring the curious looks from the mob now gathered at reception, and marched towards Danny's office. She burst in without knocking, mainly to impress the watching crowd. After she closed the door behind her, she relaxed somewhat. Danny looked up curiously and Peter looked as if he was about to explode when he noticed Maeve, but then turned on the charm offensive instead. Or rather he would have, if he wasn't in the middle of a call to his immediate boss in Texas. He beamed at Maeve and pointed to the phone, waving her towards the armchair in the corner. Maeve, indignant on Danny's behalf that Peter was offering her a seat in his office, remained standing.

"Danny, I need to see you about something important," she whispered. "Now, please. Perhaps the boardroom, if Peter's tied up here?"

On hearing this Peter panicked, hating the thought of missing something Maeve considered this important. He ended the call to Texas without his usual dose of sucking up to his boss.

"That's alright, I'd just finished. What did you want, Maeve?"

Danny still hadn't spoken, and Maeve felt her resentment mount as the Texan seemed to assume he was in charge. This was Danny's office, for God's sake. He owned the company. Fisch was just some lackey sent over from the soon-to-be mother company. Why did her boss let this little twerp treat him like this? Danny seemed oblivious however and looked to Maeve for an answer to Peter's question.

"We've got a problem, Danny," she said. "News of the new office has leaked out and two and two has been added up to make a hundred. There are rumours of redundancies and backstabbing all over the place." She waited for Danny's reaction, but Peter exploded first.

"How the hell did that get out? That was supposed to be confidential." He seemed unreasonably angry. "The only people who knew about it are standing here in this room right now. Even Texas knows very little – I was just filling them in on some of the final details before you came in. I demand to know how this leaked out!" He glared at Maeve.

"You were seen in Sandyford looking at office space,"

she said icily. "The foreman on the site was able to share a lot of the information you had given him. It seems that you were more forthcoming with him than with the staff here."

Peter had the good grace to back down. "Naturally, Maeve, I wasn't trying to imply . . ." He withered under her gaze.

"Well, if you'll excuse us, Peter," she looked murderously at him, "Danny and I have to decide what to do about this."

She held the door for him. He was about to protest and looked to Danny for support, but the other man was looking out the window. Peter picked up a bundle of files and tried to exit the room without looking as if he'd just been thrown out. Maeve, who was just short of slamming the door behind him, redirected her anger towards Danny.

"Thanks for the support, boss!"

Danny turned around slowly and spoke for the first time since she had entered his office a few minutes earlier.

"You barge into my office without knocking. You force Peter to break off an important call to the States." Danny was counting off points on his fingers, something Maeve had seen him do only rarely – a mechanism he used to control anger. "You let your dislike for Peter cloud your judgement so much that you end up almost in a shouting match with him. You virtually throw him out of my office. *My* office. You seem to have things covered, Maeve, what do you need my support for?"

Maeve stood with her mouth hanging open. Danny had never spoken to her like this. She could feel treacherous tears moistening her eyes like they always did when she was angry. It was a physiological reaction she hated; it made her feel like some kind of weak woman, crying at the first sign of discord. Right now, she wanted to shout not cry. She blinked hard and gritted her teeth, waiting for whatever Danny was going to say next.

He sat down and seemed to be arranging some notes on his desk. When he looked up again his face was clear with no trace of the outburst of a few seconds before. He looked at Maeve expectantly. Should she just behave as if he had said nothing? She decided she couldn't just let it go. She had a feeling that there was something going on here that she didn't like.

"To start with, Danny, I wasn't the one that got aggressive. Peter as good as accused me of leaking the possibility of a second office to the rest of the staff. But how could I have? I don't seem to have as much information as you or Peter." She paused to allow Danny to offer an explanation, but when he remained silent she continued. "Last time I spoke to you about new office space, it was all still up in the air. Since when have you got to the stage of actually reserving space in the building? Did you forget to tell me about it?"

Maeve waited for an answer and felt a jolt of cold fear when she realised Danny couldn't look her in the eye.

"You were under a lot of pressure," he said, speaking

into the open file in front of him. "You had all that hassle with your childminding arrangements, you were working day and night on the merger and I just didn't want to bother you with anything else at the time. Then it just slipped my mind."

Maeve wasn't convinced, but decided to come back to it later. She was uncomfortable with what he had just said. Was he suggesting that her preoccupation with her children was getting in the way of her job? Or was he saying that he was such an understanding boss that he was helping her out without even discussing it with her first? She wasn't sure which was worse.

"And what's all this about my dislike of Peter clouding my judgement?" she asked. "Since when have you become all buddy-buddy with him? Last I heard you hated his guts and I was always keeping the peace between you. Pity you never told me how you really felt about him – it would have saved me a lot of hassle."

"We've all got to work with Peter. He's Ofiscom's representative, so let's leave it at that." Danny closed the file in front of him and Maeve knew he wanted no more discussion of what had happened in the past few minutes. She bit her lip and waited for him to continue.

"The reason you burst in here on top of us was to sort out a staff rebellion about this new office. So what do you suggest we do about it?" Danny asked.

"Well, I think we have to tell people exactly what's going on, or the rumours will spread out of control."

"Okay, draft a memo." Danny looked back down at his desk as if dismissing her so Maeve hovered in front of him, forcing him to look up again. "Was there anything else?"

She wanted to throttle him. She couldn't remember a time she'd felt angrier. Where had their cosy working relationship gone? She'd bet a month's salary that it had something to do with The Fish. She longed to storm out, but her professionalism stopped her.

"The thing is, Danny," Maeve hated to admit it, "I'm not sure myself what to write in this memo. All I know is that a couple of months ago Ofiscom suggested a second office might be necessary. You said you'd look into it, I suggested Sandyford and I haven't heard anything since."

As well as angry, she was hurt. This was the first time in ten years that she had not been involved in a significant decision in the company. Even when she was on maternity leave, Danny used to call her at least once a week to ask her advice or to keep her informed.

"I don't know what you're getting on your high horse about, Maeve," he replied. "You suggested Sandyford as a possible site for a new office. I happened to agree with you and so did Peter. We signed a lease six weeks ago and we should be ready to put people in by Christmas. As yet there's been no decision as to who's moving and who's staying. Will that do it?"

"I'll write a memo and let you have it before I leave the office for my meeting," Maeve barked and turned towards the door.

She left Danny's office and made straight for the ladies' toilets. She stared at herself in the mirror and saw her face was flushed and her eyes glistened angrily. Without make-up there was very little she could do apart from force herself to breathe slowly, and splash some water on her neck and wrists. She tried to visualise something pleasant to calm herself down. She focused on her children – that could always bring a smile to her face.

Unbidden, a memory of Fiona's christening came to mind. The glorious early summer day, all her friends and family gathered in the garden after the ceremony. She began to smile as she remembered how Fintan's mother had fussed around Danny. Although he was a friend of the family, Niamh could never forget that Danny was also Maeve's boss. Maeve wondered if that was what was behind his behaviour today. Had she been taking advantage of their friendship? Had their easy, friendly working relationship begun to annoy Danny? Would he prefer to keep to a more professional relationship? If that's what he wanted, that's what he was going to get. It would be strictly business from now on.

Finally Maeve felt sufficiently composed to leave the sanctuary of the ladies'. As she made her way down the corridor, Danny's door opened and they nearly bumped into each other. He stood back to let her pass along the narrow corridor. She acknowledged him with a nod and a tightening of the lips she hoped would pass for a businesslike smile. Just before she made it to the large communal office he called after her retreating back.

"Maeve, I need to talk to you!"

"Again, so soon?"

She turned slowly to face him. He looked vaguely embarrassed, a confused expression on his face. He looked more like the Danny she was used to. She nearly softened, but at the last minute kept to her resolve to keep things businesslike.

"I need to get this memo written and then I've got to meet a client in Dundrum," she said. "That will take up most of the rest of the morning. But most of my afternoon is okay. Get Amanda to fix a time with Colm."

She was about to stalk off again.

"I'm out of the office this afternoon," he said. "Hell! And most of tomorrow."

"Well, I'm sure Amanda and Colm can find a slot if they exert themselves."

This time Maeve did manage to get away and the curious glances of a crowd of interested onlookers who witnessed this final exchange prevented Danny from following her. Maeve cursed her own childishness, but pride prevented her from turning back to him. She made it to her office and closed herself inside. She was relieved that Colm had not obeyed her instructions to stay put.

Half an hour later she buzzed her intercom to call him. He appeared before her, genie-like, so fast that he had to have been waiting outside. She handed him the newly written memo and told him she would be out for the rest of the morning.

"What did you do to the boss, Maeve?" Colm couldn't resist asking. "He looked devastated after you left him. He stood in the corridor outside his office for about a week – looking at your closed door and scratching his head. Then he retreated into his own den, shut the door and no one's seen him since."

"I didn't do anything that I can think of that might have upset him, Colm. We just had a civilised discussion on the subject of the new office space. Maybe he's feeling guilty that he didn't let everyone know about it sooner." She could see Colm's eyes scanning the memo in his hands, unable to wait even until he got to his own desk to read it.

"Good on you, Maeve – you let him know how we feel about being left in the dark, did you?"

"I did no such thing, Colm," Maeve said emphatically, feeling guilty that that's how he'd report it to the rest of the staff anyway. "Now I have a call to make . . ."

She looked pointedly at the door and Colm took the hint.

CHAPTER 25

Maeve got through her meeting with her usual efficient haste. It was just one of the annual 'How are things?' get-togethers that she tried to arrange with all the clients she had brought in personally. In this way she had never lost a client while some of Danny's had fallen by the wayside – especially the female ones who couldn't be softened up with tickets for the rugby or a round of golf. Then, instead of going back to the office, she decided to call to couple of potential clients she had been wooing for a few months. Although LBS was busy, they still couldn't afford to get complacent, and soon Ofiscom would be looking over their shoulders to make sure their dollars were being well spent.

It was almost four when she finished up and she was very tempted to go straight home. But she knew she would go crazy if she didn't go back and try to pick up some hints as to what lay behind Danny's earlier behaviour.

She got into her car and switched on her phone to collect her messages. Before she had a chance to, the phone rang.

"Maeve, where have you been? I've been trying to reach you for over two hours!" Colm sounded frantic.

"You know where I've been," she answered patiently. "I rang you to let you know."

"Yes, but I've been calling you non-stop all afternoon!"

"So what kind of crisis is there that no one in the office could sort out?"

"Not a crisis exactly. The Big Boss has been looking for you. He cancelled whatever he had on this afternoon, and he's asked me about ten times if you're back yet."

"Shit!"

"What?" Colm wasn't used to his boss cursing at him.

"Sorry, I wasn't talking to you. I just missed a green light," Maeve lied. "And don't refer to Danny as the Big Boss," she added automatically. "He'd go livid if he heard you."

"Very well, Mrs Larkin." Colm repeated his message in an artificially formal voice: "Mr Breslin is enquiring as to your whereabouts. What would you like me to tell him?"

Maeve laughed in spite of herself. Everyone used first names in the company and Colm's formality raised visions of Danny's late father looking for Fintan's mother.

"Tell him nothing. Say that you still can't reach me, that my phone's still off."

She hung up before he could object. Colm would do anything for her, but he was a lousy liar and Maeve imagined him hiding from Danny until she returned to the office.

When she arrived back, she waltzed in, determined not to look as worried as she felt. She stopped in the main office on her way in and chatted casually with the few staff there.

"Maeve!" Danny's voice rang out. "Colm wasn't sure if you'd be back today. Did he tell you I was looking for you?"

"I'm only just in the door, I haven't seen him yet."

"Have you got a few minutes now?"

"I'll check in with Colm, just in case anything urgent's cropped up while I was out, then I'll be right with you," Maeve promised. "Your office?"

"Fine, I'll meet you there. Coffee?"

"No, thanks. I'm tying to cut out coffee after lunch."

This was complete fiction, but Maeve didn't want to give Danny the impression they were in for a cosy chat over a cup of coffee. Besides, she had always intended to reduce her coffee intake, so maybe this would be a good time to start. She disappeared into her office, signalling to Colm, who was at the photocopier, to follow her. He knocked and came in, looking puzzled.

"Are you not going to meet Danny?" No matter how long he worked for the company, he would never be able to look at Danny as anything other than 'The Boss'. And he couldn't understand why Maeve was deliberately keeping him waiting.

"Of course I am. As soon as I've checked with you that there's nothing urgent waiting for me."

"No, nothing's cropped up since I spoke to you on the phone," Colm assured her, *"half an hour ago.'*

"Thank you, Colm. Now could I get you to call these two numbers, and set up a couple of meetings for me? They're expecting me." If Danny and Fisch were going to play little games all day in the office, someone had to keep the work coming in. "I'll be in Danny's office if you're looking for me."

She ignored Colm's look of bafflement. He wasn't used to Maeve stating the obvious.

She knocked on Danny's door and waited till he called her in. Then she stood at the door.

"For God's sake, Maeve, come in."

She did, but left the door open and remained standing. Danny looked at her, exasperated – she obviously wasn't going to make this any easier for him than she had to.

"Come in, Maeve, sit down," he sighed, and waved at the leather armchairs by the window. She sat upright, leaning away from the other chair slightly, and snapped open her laptop computer and diary on the coffee table. A sort of business barrier between them. Danny looked at them wearily.

"To start with, Maeve, I owe you an apology," he began, looking to her for support.

She smiled benignly. He was on his own.

"I haven't been completely honest with you, Maeve, and I should have told you about the Sandyford project sooner. I said I didn't want to bother you because you had too much on your plate and that wasn't exactly true. I didn't discuss it with you because I wasn't exactly sure what was involved, and partly because Texas asked me not to. Not that that would have stopped me if I wanted to!" he added hastily.

"What do you mean Texas asked you not to?" Maeve asked carefully. "What's so hush-hush about new office space? We've been talking about it for ages – though it's only since Ofiscom came along that the idea of splitting operations between two sites came up."

"Well, they were worried that if we made public our expansion plans, other players might try to muscle in on the action."

"Oh come on, isn't that a bit paranoid?"

"I intended letting you know as soon as there was anything to discuss," Danny continued quickly as if he hadn't heard her. "I just never got around to it, and the longer I left it . . . the harder it would have been to explain why I hadn't said anything earlier."

"So, Peter specifically didn't want me to know about what was happening with the Sandyford office? Why?" Maeve's earlier feeling that something was wrong, that Peter was up to something, got stronger. She felt the soft hairs at the back of her neck prickle as they stood on end.

"Oh no, Maeve, I don't think it was anything to do with you personally, I just think he was really paranoid as you put it. You know what these Yanks are like in business – everything has to be so secret."

Maeve wasn't sure if Danny was terribly naïve or hiding something. She decided to tackle him head on. "Danny, I don't want to change the subject or anything, but what exactly happened between us earlier today?"

She watched him closely. She had known Danny long enough and could read him like a book – he wouldn't be able to lie without her detecting it. His face collapsed into an expression of misery at her question. He began to massage his right temple with his left hand – something he did when he was stressed or had something unpleasant to say. Maeve kept watching. If he kept his hand up, covering his face, she'd know he was lying to her – or at best hiding some of the truth.

Danny's hand dropped and he began to fiddle with a pen on the table in front of him. Still his eyes hadn't met hers. Then he looked up, straight at her.

"I don't really know where to begin. This is really difficult." His eyes fell to the pen again. He was dismantling it and putting it back together with an enthusiasm usually only shown by an infantryman for his rifle. Maeve closed her computer and diary and pushed them to one side. As she resumed her position, she leaned imperceptibly towards Danny.

"Was it something I did, or said?" she asked. It was enough to break the ice.

"No, God, no, Maeve. It wasn't your fault at all. It was just, that . . . well . . . I'm supposed to be distancing myself from the running of things."

"Why?"

Danny looked shifty. "It's Ofiscom's idea. Peter has been trying to take on more responsibility."

"But I thought he was going back to the States when the merger finally goes through?" Maeve was worried;

the thought of putting up with Peter for any longer than she had to was more than she could take.

"Well, nothing's definite and Peter hasn't said anything exactly . . . but I get the impression he's being left over a little longer to smooth over the transition from our management style to Ofiscom's."

"And what's wrong with our 'management style?'" To Maeve this sounded like pure Peter bullshit.

"He says that Texas feels I ought to have a more professional relationship with you, Brian and Matthew."

Brian and Matthew were team leaders of the programmers and technicians respectively.

"What does he say is wrong with the way you work with us at present?" Maeve asked gently, careful not to spook him. Whatever Peter had said, she knew it applied only to the way Danny worked with her. To bring Brian and Matthew into it was a smokescreen – Danny could go a fortnight without talking to either of them.

"I can't actually pin him down on it. I think he reckons I should play my cards a little closer to my chest or something. Maybe he feels I rely too much on you, always go looking to you for advice before making decisions."

"And have you discussed this with anyone in Texas?" Maeve felt with a chilling certainty that she had badly underestimated Peter Fisch.

"No, he was adamant that we keep it between the two of us," Danny laughed. "He'd totally freak if he knew we were having this discussion at all. He came back to me this morning to emphasise that this morning's scene was just the type of thing he was warning me about. He says I need to keep my distance a bit if the company's going to adapt to –" He looked as if he was about to say something, then stopped suddenly, and looked for a different wording "any changes, I suppose."

"What kind of changes?" Maeve knew he was leaving something unsaid.

"Well, we're going to have to convert from being a family-run company to part of a big conglomerate, for one." Danny looked around guiltily. "Look, I may as well tell you this. Peter has told me that he hopes to be staying over here beyond September. Possibly for as long as a year. So you'll have to get used to working with him. He has the ear of the board in Texas, so don't go making an enemy out of him."

"Don't worry, Danny, I'm sure I can handle him. I have up to now. Once the merger's through, and the company goes on making money and even expands, they'll be glad to give us back control. And Peter can go home again. And there's plenty of scope for expansion once we have that extra office space." She updated him about some new contacts she had made and two big contracts she was chasing.

He brightened visibly. "You're right. This company has done brilliantly for the last ten years, why should that change just because it's bought out?" He was beginning to look like the old, sometimes childishly belligerent Danny.

Maeve made moves to leave. She arranged the time for her next formal meeting with Danny, and gathered up her things.

"Don't worry, Danny, he's not going to push you out as boss!" she joked.

"Oh, I'm not worried about . . ." Again Danny looked as if he were about to say the wrong thing but just stopped himself in time. "You're right; I'm not worried about that." He got up and held the door open for Maeve.

Maeve paced up and down in the confined space that was her office. She didn't know what Fisch was up to, but she knew she'd have to keep a much closer eye on him.

She had planned to work late this evening, but now her concentration was shot. She was tempted to phone Andrea, but the thought of confiding in her best friend who was just recently beginning to get somewhere with Danny, seemed unfair. If she knew about Maeve's difficulties, she would probably use her relationship with Danny to storm in and insist he put things right. No, Maeve realised that until she knew exactly what Peter was up to, she would have to go it alone.

Finally she decided to leave for home. Although it was about the worse time of evening to hit Dublin's roads, she wasn't achieving anything here, and she'd feel less guilty doing nothing in traffic, than doing nothing in her office where she was being paid to work. Before she left, she rang Orla.

She longed to go for a walk on Killiney Hill with Fintan and the kids, to take advantage of the bright summer night, and then the whole family could go for a late supper somewhere. It would be like a celebration of Fintan's last week at work. Knowing that Darragh probably wouldn't stick the pace, and would ruin the evening for the older two, she had decided to ask Orla if she would baby-sit.

"Maeve, hi!" Orla finally picked up her phone. "Sorry I took so long to answer, I could hear the blasted thing ringing, but I couldn't find it in the bottom of my sports bag. I need to get a string or something to attach to my phone. Or maybe a hands free-set, what do you think? Would I look cool with a wire hanging from my ear? Even I'd have trouble losing that. But what can I do for you?" As usual, Maeve had to wait for Orla to stop and draw breath before she could get a word in edgewise.

"I was going to ask you if you wouldn't mind watching Darragh for a few hours." she asked hesitantly. "I know this is your last week in Dublin before you head off to London, but we won't be gone long."

"Would I miss the last opportunity to see my adorable nephew? I'd love to baby-sit for him, but you'd better not have put him to bed. I'm going to have that kid crawling before I leave if it's the last thing I do."

Orla had been there the first time both Fiona and Ciaran had taken their first steps, and she was devastated that she would probably miss Darragh's first attempts at self-propulsion. Both of the others had been early movers, but as soon as Darragh had learned to sit, he quickly discovered that a loud scream and a finger pointed at whatever he wanted was a very efficient way of getting the Mountain to come to Mohammed. Although with his lack of activity and increased appetite, it was increasingly a case of the mountain coming to Buddha.

"Please don't let's have him crawling any sooner than we have to," Maeve pleaded much to her own amusement – she had been full of encouragement for the older two. But Fiona had got going so young and wreaked such havoc on their home that she looked fondly at Darragh's contemplative refusal to budge.

She chatted for a while longer with Orla, or rather she listened while her sister-in-law babbled on, and when she finally left the office, she was in a much better mood. So as she drove home, instead of worrying about Danny and Peter Fisch, she was planning the evening ahead with all the bubbling anticipation of a special treat.

Two hours later, Maeve and Fintan were sharing a rock on the top of Killiney hill, while the children scrambled around happily within eyesight, occasionally bringing back 'treasures' for their parents to admire. There were so many lovely walks within such a short drive of where they lived that they were spoiled for choice, but Killiney Hill was always Maeve's favourite. She had come here so often with her father that the place still seemed to hold some essence of him that went beyond mere memory. When she felt particularly emotionally battered, as she did today, the woods, the views of the sea and the stillness of dusk always left her feeling comforted.

"So, are you going to tell me what's wrong, or am I going to have to play twenty questions?" Fintan asked at last, as Maeve absentmindedly stroked a smooth, startlingly striped pink and grey stone that Fiona had given her with the instruction, 'Mummy mind'.

"That obvious?" Maeve sighed, dropping the stone from one palm to the other. "On days like this I wish it was me taking the four months off next week instead of you."

"No, you don't, not really." Her husband knew her too well. "But it must be pretty bad to even get you thinking along those lines."

Maeve looked out to sea and leaned back against Fintan. It was said that on a good day Killiney Bay resembled the Bay of Naples and if that was true, Maeve thought, Italy might well be worth the trip.

She tried to explain all that had happened that afternoon to Fintan, as the hoard of stones, feathers and small sticks in their pockets grew, courtesy of Fiona and Ciaran trying to outdo each other in the interesting finds stakes.

"I didn't think we had office politics in LBS," she said at last. "At least not real politics, you know – back-stabbing, blood on the boardroom carpet and all that – but now I'm not so sure."

"I think you're being paranoid, honey, and even if you're right, and Peter is up to something fishy (excuse the pun), you're on to him now, and he's not going to get anything past you. Keep an eye on him, but don't get obsessed. As you say, he'll be gone in six months or a year."

"I suppose you're right," Maeve agreed reluctantly.

As she looked out over the bay, she was glad they had come up here. As usual, the beauty of the place had the ability to reduce her problems to manageable proportions. She *could* handle whatever Peter threw at her, and eventually send him packing back to whence he came.

"Come on, you guys," she called out, "let's race back to the car, girls against boys, and then let's go and get fish and chips!"

Hand in hand Fiona and Maeve took their customary head start, and by judicious delaying, Fintan ensured that the race was neck and neck all the way down, resulting in a draw at the bottom of the hill.

Then they stopped on the way home and bought fish and chips in Dalkey village and they ate them in the car in the church carpark. Both Fiona and Ciaran had to be carried into bed when they finally got home, and later Maeve slept better than she had a right to expect – considering the world of worries she had on her shoulders.

CHAPTER 26

On Monday morning, Fintan was up even before the children – so keen was he to start on his new, if temporary, way of life. He awoke to a blazing sunny day, which reminded him how lucky he was to be off work for the summer. He warned himself not to expect every day to be this bright and that he wasn't on some type of an extended holiday, but even that failed to put a dent in his good mood. He showered, shaved and dressed before Maeve's alarm-clock roused her fully – although she did throw him a few dirty looks as he clattered about the bedroom. He delighted in pulling on shorts and a T-shirt, especially when he saw his wife's neatly pressed suit hanging on the back of the wardrobe door.

As soon as he heard movement around the house, Ciaran was up in a flash. Fiona and Darragh quickly latched onto the holiday mood and in much less time than usual, Fintan had them all downstairs eating breakfast. Maeve, who felt excluded from the shared mood of excitement, stuck to her usual routine, and eventually emerged downstairs to find Ciaran and Fiona arguing over what to watch on television.

Fintan and Maeve sat down to an unbelievably leisurely breakfast for a Monday and Darragh, still in his pyjamas, cooed in wonder at them as he ate scraps of toast. He couldn't figure out why Mummy was in her work clothes, but everyone else was dressed for staying at home.

"Don't try to do too much today, will you, Fintan?" Maeve said, worried by his ebullient mood. "Save your energy for when the kids get cranky towards the end of the day."

She longed to give him a list of instructions and advice to ensure he survived his first day at home, but she bit her tongue and remained silent. The manager in her felt he should have some plan, some list of activities with which to occupy the two older children, built around nap times. But when she had suggested it last night, Fintan laughed and said the children had lived according to their parent's routine for their whole lives, and now it was their turn to call the shots.

He switched on the radio after Maeve left and decided to have a leisurely cup of coffee, and listen to the news before tackling tidying the kitchen or dressing the children.

"Daddy, Daddy. . . *Daddy!*" Ciaran screamed from the living-room, before the cup touched his lips. Fintan tried to ignore his son's insistent commands to "*Come here now!"* until Fiona's squeal of distress made it clear he would have to intervene.

He sorted out the argument only to return to the kitchen to find Darragh happily sprinkling the contents of his upturned beaker all over his head, the few remaining fingers of toast having already been mashed skilfully into his hair. Fintan cleaned off his son, threw his sodden sleepsuit into the utility room and took him upstairs to change. As he searched through the drawers of Darragh's boxroom, he realised that he would have to run a load of laundry as a matter of urgency – Darragh was down to his last outfit. Fintan dumped Darragh on the kitchen floor with a box of toys and began to sort through the dirty clothes.

Within seconds Ciaran arrived to help him and Fintan got a warm glow as he stood with his son in the utility room, sorting clothes into two piles. Not to be left out, Fiona appeared and added her own method of working – which was to remove clothes out of whichever basket took her fancy and stuff them into the machine her father had unwisely left open. Fintan was just about to undo Fiona's contribution when the phone rang.

"Don't move!" he told Darragh rather unnecessarily, and made a rush for the hall. For some reason he reckoned Fiona and Ciaran were safe in the utility room on their own for a few moments.

"Hello?" he gasped into the phone.

"It's only me! How are you coping?" Maeve asked.

"Fine, we're just about to start into the laundry," Fintan answered cheerfully.

"Don't bother with that, I can do a couple of loads when I come home this evening." Maeve was worried that he was already ignoring her advice not to do too much.

"It's no problem, honestly. I mean how long can it take me to shove some clothes in a machine? Don't worry, I won't tackle the ironing. I know how territorial you are about that!" This was an old joke; they both hated ironing.

"I suppose I'd better get back to work," Maeve said reluctantly. "See you this evening, about half six or seven."

Fintan returned to the utility room.

Fiona was tossing piles of clothes in the air in a scene reminiscent of a snow-fight. Ciaran had the detergent drawer of the machine open and he was hanging from it, trying to pull it open further. The whole room was liberally dusted with a layer of washing-powder.

Fintan let out a roar: *"What the . . . what on earth is going on here?"*

For a moment Fiona stopped throwing the clothes about, but resumed nonchalantly as she decided that the yell couldn't possibly be directed at her. Ciaran let go of the detergent drawer and stood ready to deliver a rational explanation.

"I was helping, but Fiona spilled the powder. She thinks it's snow," he added helpfully.

Their father let out a sigh, realising it was his fault for leaving them alone for more than ten seconds. He gathered them up, shook the detergent from their hair before it could get into their eyes and removed their pyjamas. He took them upstairs to get dressed, but not before putting up the playpen in the living-room and dumping Darragh in it. He wasn't going to get caught out twice. He turned the two older children out into the back garden and returned to the scene of destruction.

He had barely begun to sweep up when Darragh began to wail, indignant at his prolonged incarceration. He rescued the baby and brought him into the kitchen, where he could talk to him as he worked.

"Daddy," Ciaran was standing nervously at the back door. "Please can we have our bikes?"

"Bike pees," agreed Fiona.

Fintan toyed with the idea of yelling at the two of them to get out of his sight, but realised they had made a reasonable request. He trudged down to the shed at the end of the garden and disentangled Ciaran's bike, whose stabilising wheels were involved in an obscure mating ritual with the barbecue. Fiona's tricycle was nowhere to be seen. When she saw her brother on his bike, she began to wail.

"Bike, I want bike! Peeeees, bike!" she wept, and then just in case the message hadn't got through she added, with her voice rising in a high-pitched scream of anguish: "Bike *now*, Daddy, peeese!"

Fintan remembered that they last had the little ride-along trike at the park and prayed it wasn't in the boot of Maeve's car. He was in luck – it was in his own car.

When he returned to the kitchen, Darragh was playing happily with his blocks but, as soon as he spotted his father, he began to cry and rub his eyes. Surely it was too early for his nap?

"Daddy, I'm hungry. I want crisps." Ciaran was waiting for his father when he got back downstairs after settling the baby.

"It's too early for a snack, Ciaran – you should have eaten a bigger breakfast," Fintan tried to reason with his son.

"But I'm starving, Daddy."

"Okay, if you're that hungry, you can have some bread and butter. Go back out in the garden, and I'll bring it out. It'll be like a picnic."

Anything to get him out from under his feet for ten minutes while he cleaned the utility room.

"I'm hungry for toast, Daddy, not bread. Toast with chocolate." The boy looked at his father, guessing he was near breaking-point. "I'll share with Fiona," he added with a winning smile.

It worked. Fintan appeared in the garden a few minutes later with fingers of toast sandwiched together with a thin scrape of chocolate spread. He spread a waterproof play-sheet on the grass, and put the two plates at opposite corners. Ciaran inspected them, trying to figure out which was bigger, while Fintan fled indoors, leaving the door open so he could monitor what was going on in the garden. It was blissfully quiet as the two children ate and Fintan finally got the last of the washing-powder swept up.

He loaded the first lot of whites and then looked blankly at the dials. The control panel was completely foreign to him. He realised with shame that he hadn't run a single load of laundry since they had replaced the machine just over a year ago – how had he not noticed that Maeve did all the laundry? If anything she worked longer hours than he did. He guiltily remembered all the times she would put on a wash just before breakfast, at the weekend or during the ads while watching television – and always seemed to know just the right time to jump up and take the wet clothes out. Well, now Fintan would make up for that. He watched with satisfaction as soapy water filled the drum and then he went out, locking the door of the utility room this time.

With Ciaran and Fiona playing happily in the garden, Darragh asleep and the washing machine doing its stuff, Fintan finally returned to his coffee in the kitchen. It was stone cold. He took a clean mug and poured a fresh cup, but swallowed it quickly, making a face as the bitter liquid, sitting for hours on the hot plate, hit the back of his throat.

When he began to unpack the dishwasher, Fiona, who could hear the dishwasher being opened from a block away, ran in from the garden.

"Me help," she announced cheerfully and reached for the top rack – full of glasses.

"Not now, Fiona," her father sighed. "Look . . . Ciaran's still in the garden, why don't you go out on your bike with him?"

"Me help!" Fiona was firmer now and had an iron-like grip on a delicate wineglass.

"Oh, all right – here, put this in that cupboard." Fintan handed her a brightly coloured plastic plate and pointed to the bottom press. She released her hold on the glass and toddled off happily with the plate while the rest of the glasses vanished rapidly into the wall press. Next she decided on the cutlery basket. Fintan turned to see her contemplatively chewing a steak knife. Blade first.

"Fiona," he said gently, so as not to startle her or make her jump, "Daddy wants the knife now." He knelt in front of the toddler and tried to get her to open her mouth. Her jaws remained clamped shut.

"Would you like a biscuit?"

The child nodded vigorously and Fintan felt his heart-rate accelerate off the scale.

"Well, give Daddy the knife, and I'll see if I can find a nice chocolate biscuit for you." Fiona thought about it for a moment then removed the piece of cutlery from her mouth and jabbed it in her father's direction, forcing Fintan to swerve to avoid losing an eye.

A minute later he released his daughter, with her biscuit, into the garden and sat down for a minute until his heart-rate dropped. He imagined calling Maeve from Crumlin hospital, explaining that on his first day as a stay-at-home Dad he had let their daughter swallow a steak knife.

Then the phone rang, making him jump guiltily.

"Hello," he said weakly, carrying the phone into the kitchen so that he could watch the kids.

"Hi, Fintan, it's Hazel. How are things going?"

"Great! Exhausting!" Fintan tried not to sound as terrified as he felt.

"Oh well, you're nearly halfway through your first day now."

What was the woman talking about, halfway through? Fintan looked at the kitchen clock and realised she was right. Where had the morning gone?

"Everything's going great, Hazel." For some reason, although he wasn't at work, Fintan felt he should be reporting to her. "Fiona and Ciaran are in the garden, Darragh's having a nap, and I'm just about to get their lunches." He spoke with a cheerful resolve he didn't feel.

"You mean everything's going okay?" Hazel repeated – she sounded almost disappointed. Then she brightened up. "I think I hate you, for making me feel so inadequate. My first day at home – I can still remember it all these years later – was hell on wheels. By mid-morning I wanted to book myself in for a nervous breakdown, and by lunch-time – well, I'm still not convinced I didn't have one but I was too busy to notice. A nervous breakdown, I mean," she added in case he hadn't followed her mile-a-minute rhetoric.

Fintan let out a sigh of relief. "Well, it hasn't all been plain sailing, actually."

"You're just saying that to make me feel better."

"No, honestly . . ." He explained about the scene in the utility room. Before long he was laughing and even admitted to his scare with the knife. Hazel shared some of her domestic disasters with him and he began to feel a lot better. She also had a few work-related questions for him and he was glad she had phoned. Before she said good-bye however, she gave him a warning.

"I wouldn't tell Maeve about the knife thing," she said. "It sounds an awful lot worse that it probably was."

"You really think I shouldn't?" Fintan was having crisis of conscience over that and would undoubtedly have ended up spilling the whole story.

"Definitely!" Hazel was firm. "There was no harm done, a lesson learned. And I certainly know I wouldn't have wanted to know."

After lunch, Fiona went down for her nap and Ciaran insisted that he was always allowed watch *Rugrats* if he cleared his plate. Fintan could understand Sarah's logic. Not only did his son finish his meal in a time very close to his personal best but the coffee machine was gurgling seductively and the promise of a quiet half-hour with the kitchen to himself seemed like bliss.

Fintan realised he had never valued his lunch-break this much when he was working. He switched on the radio in the hope of catching the news. As a news junkie he was in serious withdrawal. He had barely caught a few lines of the morning bulletins and he hadn't even got out to buy a paper. Maybe Maeve was right – he really ought to plan his days around some kind of a routine. If not for the children's sake, then for his own sanity. He had assumed that at some stage during the morning, he would load the two younger children into the buggy and he and Ciaran would enjoy a leisurely walk together to the newsagent's. The possibility that he would be left with virtually no free time at all simply hadn't occurred to him. His analytical mind couldn't resist trying to work out where he had gone 'wrong' this morning.

Then with a sinking feeling he remembered the laundry in the machine. Should he jump up and hang it out straight away, or forget about it again until he had finished his cup of coffee? Resigned, Fintan got up and extracted the bundle of wet clothes. Of course *Rugrats* was over, and Darragh was awake, hungry and screaming by the time the last of the white towels was swaying in the scorching summer breeze. For the second time that day, Fintan looked with regret at his cup of coffee and wondered if the children were conspiring to make him live longer by reducing his caffeine intake.

By six o'clock, when Maeve burst through the door earlier than expected, Fintan felt he had run a marathon. While they both fell into the familiar routine of feeding, bathing and putting the children to bed, all he wanted to do was escape for an hour, half an hour, ten minutes even, and do nothing. But he forced on a smile and in response to Maeve's questions, assured her that the day had gone brilliantly and that he was glad they had taken the decision they had.

With the house finally quiet and as they sat relaxing in the garden over a pasta salad and a bottle of wine, Fintan asked Maeve about her day. She described it at length – especially the difficulty she was having trying to organise the official launch party for the new, merged LBS.

Then Fintan began to tell a story about one of the prize pieces of descriptive conversation Fiona had come up with during the afternoon and was surprised at the mild resentment he felt when Maeve seemed irritated by the interruption. Suddenly their cosy intimacy was lost and she retired to the living-room to look over some papers she had brought home, while Fintan settled into an armchair with a large book.

But he couldn't concentrate on it – he had been so busy all day that he was left with the nagging feeling that there must be something left undone. Or that there was something he should be doing now so as to prepare for tomorrow. After several unsuccessful attempts to get interested in his chapter, Fintan gave in to his restlessness and closed the book. He brought it into the study where he could place it high on a bookshelf out of the reach of little fingers, but the room suddenly looked horribly overfull to him. There were too many volumes filling the slim bookcase and they had spilled over onto the floor. There was a pile of 'to be kept' newspapers, waiting for him to tear out some relevant page. In the main it was book reviews that had caught his eye, or sections of the business reports that he thought might make it into *Money Matters*. Another toppling pile was made up of back issues of *Money Matters* and of journals he had dredged through for the material. He knew he should really return those to the 'library' at work, although he suspected he was the only one who made use of them. And as he looked at them, Fintan realised he would miss his access to all the financial press. There was no way he could afford to buy all the titles himself.

The only oasis of calm in the whole room was Maeve's area. Although she had trained herself to ignore Fintan's clutter, she couldn't work at an untidy desk. Her laptop sat in the middle of the desk and around it, arranged with geometric precision, sat a pen holder and notepad, a locked disk case and the file that no doubt had held the papers she was working on at the moment. Fintan decided that before the end of the week he would tidy the rest of the small room – then she couldn't fail to notice how industrious he had been!

CHAPTER 27

About ten days later, Fintan phoned Maeve at work.

"Are you free for lunch today?" he asked when he finally got through to her. "No?"

Fintan tried not to sound too disappointed. He had come up with a great idea to ensure the kids saw more of Maeve, despite the hours she seemed to be putting in since he gave up work. He would bring them in to meet her for lunch. He wouldn't tell them where they were going so it'd be a surprise – and because he was afraid that she might cancel at the last moment.

"How about tomorrow then?" he asked. "Okay, well, make that a firm date – book us into your diary. What? A surprise, you'll have to wait and see. See you this evening then."

Of course Maeve guessed what his 'surprise' was and when she eventually got home that evening, they planned lunch the next day. If the weather allowed, they agreed a picnic would be the ideal solution – the kids could run riot around the park and they wouldn't have to worry about them swinging out of the other diners' chairs in a restaurant.

"And if it rains, we can always relocate the picnic to your office," Fintan joked.

"Ha, ha, very funny! Not! Can you imagine the amount of disruption our bunch could produce in the office? We're short enough of space as it is without a whirlwind decimating the place."

"Oh, with all the hours you've been putting in lately, the least Danny could do is allow your kids in to see you now and again. He can write off any destruction against tax." Fintan was still joking.

"It's not on Danny's account I'm putting in all these hours. You know that!" Maeve snapped, not appreciating his humour. "I'm building up a firm client base for myself so that if we do split operations between the town and Sandyford sites, I'll be in a much stronger position to chose where I want to work."

"You virtually run the place," Fintan soothed. "I'm sure you'll be able to work wherever you like when the time comes. Danny's not going to stand in the way of what you want, is he?"

"I'm not so sure. Besides, anything could happen once Ofiscom take over. And Peter's staying longer than expected," she reminded him ominously.

Fintan was surprised how tense Maeve had suddenly become. He remembered her raising the subject a few days ago, but hadn't realised she was this worried. She was pacing up and down the kitchen – she hadn't changed out of her work suit so she looked every inch the stressed executive. Fintan waited till her next hurried pass, then reached out and grabbed her, pulling her firmly on his lap.

"Stop panicking. If Ofiscom really wanted to change the way you do things, do you not think they'd have sent over someone more senior and with a few more brains than The Fish? Besides, what's the worst-case scenario?"

"I don't know – that's why I'm so edgy. I've never worked anywhere else and I really don't know what I'd do if things got so awful that I hated working in LBS." Maeve leaned towards him, stretching her neck, enjoying the feel of his strong fingers massaging out knots in her muscles.

"If you hated working there you'd leave," he said, as if it was obvious. "You'd have no problem getting another job. In fact, I'm sure a few of your own clients would jump at the chance of employing you if they knew you were in the market."

"But what about the shares? If I don't stay three years I'll lose out on the extra allocation."

"And when those three years are up you'll get more and more share options in an attempt to get you to stay. The bank works the same way. But when the time comes to leave you have to make a decision to turn your back on future shares. There's no point being unhappy for years for the sake of a bit more money. It's all about quality of life these days. We are going to have to get into a whole new mindset – you won't find any of the twenty-somethings locking themselves into a job for life."

Fintan stopped, embarrassed at his lecturing tone.

"Speech over?" Maeve asked, laughing. "And don't get too excited about the prospect of paying off the mortgage. Ofiscom shares dipped last week." Everyone in LBS had been dismayed to see a couple of percentage points knocked off their early Christmas present.

"Temporary setback," Fintan reassured her. "Besides, if the euro continues to take the hammering it's been suffering for the past few months, any shares held in dollars are worth more to us."

"I hadn't thought of that. Aren't I lucky to be married to an economist? I leave the timing of the sale entirely in your hands," Maeve said, with no small measure of relief.

"Well, there's a lot to be considered," Fintan began with enthusiasm. "The value of the dollar v. the euro is only one factor. We have to think about the future value of the shares and what might happen to mortgage interest rates." He continued his analysis of their financial situation while massaging Maeve's neck and shoulders. Soon he became aware that her head was nodding against his shoulder.

"So, do you think we should trade for equity in Mickey Mouse?" he asked loudly.

"What? Oh, yes of course, if you think that would be for the best," Maeve answered with a start. "You know I always trust you on these complex financial thingummies."

"And I think it's time you went to bed! We'll discuss Mickey Mouse another time." Laughing, Fintan pushed her off his lap, handed her her shoes and propelled her towards the door.

"Mickey Mouse? What are you on about?" Maeve asked sleepily, not sure what she had missed. She didn't really care, 'bed' being the only word which had registered through her haze of exhaustion.

The next day, the sun put in an appearance and Fintan managed to get everyone to the park in time to meet Mum for lunch. Just as Maeve and Fintan sat down to eat, with Ciaran and Fiona tearing around them and Darragh playing happily on a mat in the one bit of shade they could find, Andrea appeared. At first Maeve looked mildly annoyed – although she had mentioned that she would be meeting the rest of the family she hadn't expected Andrea to put in a surprise appearance. But the two older children were so genuinely delighted to see their 'Auntie' Andrea that Maeve gave in gracefully. Besides, they climbed all over Andrea, allowing their parents to eat in peace – an almost unheard-of occurrence.

"So how are you finding it at home?" Andrea asked Fintan between bouts of chasing Ciaran and Fiona around the park bench.

"Great, so far. But the weather's been good. Wait until the real Irish summer starts! According to the doom and gloom merchants at Met Eireann, that could be anytime this weekend."

"Oh don't say that! I'm supposed to be having a big

girlie barbecue this weekend at my parents' house. Of course I didn't do anything as sensible as checking the weather forecast. Looks like we'll be toasting sausages in the fireplace," she added to Maeve.

Fintan fired a glance at his wife, then looked away. She hadn't mentioned going out this weekend. He had hoped they could actually spend some time together as she'd been home late all week. Maeve went pink and changed the subject.

"Fintan's dying to know how you're getting on with Danny," she said.

By now it was no secret that Andrea was in pursuit.

"I never . . ." Fintan objected, but curiosity got the better of him. "Well?"

"Zip, *nada*, nothing to report apart from a few outings as 'friends'!" Andrea answered with a disgusted snort. "Either the guy's running scared of all things female since Cathy, and I can't say I blame him, or he's taken a vow of chastity. The other possibility is that he's immune to my charms, but that's not really a realistic scenario, as it's never happened yet. Hey! I'll get you back for that!"

The last comment was directed at Ciaran and Fiona who had thrown grass clippings all over her. Andrea kicked off her high heels and chased them across the manicured lawn of the park. They fled, screaming with delight.

"I would have told you about the barbecue," Maeve apologised, "but I forgot. I haven't even decided yet whether or not to go."

"Why wouldn't you go?" Fintan's smile barely touched his eyes. "Go on, you let your hair down with the girls. When is it on anyway?"

"She's planning on having everyone there late afternoon, so that we can eat before the sun dies down. If there is any sun."

Fintan groaned inwardly. That would mean he'd have the whole evening on his own with the kids. Dinner, baths, stories. He'd been hoping to go through all the books in the study at the weekend – part of his big tidy-up. Not a particularly important or thrilling task, but he'd been looking forward to it in a strange kind of way. He forced himself to sound cheerful.

"That sounds like some session she has planned. No doubt you'll be drinking till the small hours of the morning, once such nuisance factors as food are out of the way." Too late he realised he sounded disapproving.

"I don't plan to stay that long. I can't drink like I used to and I can't afford to be off-form at work on Monday. Every day counts at the moment."

And I thought you might be planning on being in good form on Sunday with your family, Fintan thought wryly. He'd be glad when this bloody merger was finally through and he got his wife back.

"Ciaran, Fiona, come here and kiss Mummy good-bye. She's got to go back to work," he called to the children, as Maeve put on her jacket and brushed crumbs off her trousers. Then he said to Maeve: "I don't know how you can put that jacket back on in this heat."

"I have a meeting with a client when I get back. Imagine if he arrived just as I walked in, looking like I'd come back from a walk in the country." She kissed Fintan quickly and gave the children a hug. "And how can I fool everyone into thinking I'm a successful businesswoman, if I'm dressed like a teenager?"

Fintan couldn't understand why her explanation annoyed him so much.

"See you later, love," Maeve said, and to the kids she added: "Be good for Daddy now. Off to bed with no fuss and I'll see you in the morning."

"Will you do me a phone story?" Ciaran begged.

"I'll do my best." Maeve hugged him and walked away briskly. As Fintan followed her with his eyes, she looked at her watch and increased her pace until she was almost running. She didn't look back.

"She's working too hard."

Fintan jumped – he'd forgotten about Andrea. She was struggling to put on her sandals without first unfastening the straps.

"Hopefully not for too much longer," he answered without conviction. "Once the merger's finally through, everything should go back to normal."

"Do you want me to give you a hand getting this lot back to the car?" Andrea asked. She swept her arm around in a gesture taking in the remains of the picnic, the buggy, an assortment of toys and the children.

"That would be brilliant," Fintan answered, suddenly feeling exhausted. "Are you sure I won't be delaying you?"

"One of the joys of being your own boss. Where are you parked?"

He described it to her, and she took his keys and began to march Ciaran and Fiona back. They both behaved impeccably for Andrea, and Fiona didn't even scream when her harness was put on. Fintan followed with a dozing baby in one seat of the double buggy, and a pile of junk in the other. He loaded everything into the boot and turned to Andrea.

"Thanks for the help. Have a good party on Saturday and good luck with Danny. Maybe next time I see you, you'll be all fixed up."

"Next time I see you will be at that charity dinner on Saturday fortnight. Don't think you're getting out of that one! Maeve told me your parents are taking the kids to Courtown for the weekend."

Fintan groaned. He had forgotten about the dinner which Danny had been bullied into buying a table at before he split up with Cathy. Maeve, Peter and a few others were being frog-marched along to make up numbers.

"Right, so. See you then," he said glumly.

"Don't look so enthusiastic!" Andrea teased.

Fintan turned pink. "I didn't mean . . ."

"I know what you meant!" Andrea was laughing. "And I sympathise. It's bound to be a total bore. Although if Cathy's there, supporting Mummy Darling's favourite charity, maybe a few sparks will fly. That might brighten the evening up somewhat."

"Is she likely to be there? I thought she was in

London. Besides, I can't see Danny stooping to getting involved in a row with her." Fintan strapped Darragh into the baby seat.

"I suppose not," Andrea shrugged. "What a shame. That could have been fun – as Danny's partner for the night, I'd be guaranteed a ringside seat."

"His partner for the night? And I thought you were getting nowhere?"

"I'm not. So take that gossipy look off your face – it doesn't suit you. I'm just going along as a favour. As I have hundreds of times before. Just good friends and all that."

"Yeah right." Fintan's tone matched his raised left eyebrow. "See you Saturday fortnight then."

Darragh slept all the way home and he transferred to his cot asleep. He must have overdosed on fresh air, Fintan thought; he never used to sleep this well for Sarah. He was sleeping a lot better at night too. Fintan would have loved to believe it was because he was more secure in a home environment, but was forced to admit that Darragh was probably just growing out of restless nights.

Just as he was setting up the goals for Ciaran to play football in the back garden, Fintan heard the phone inside. Before he got to it, the answering machine picked up and he heard his mother's voice as she tried to leave a message. From the flashing number on the display, it wasn't her first attempt so Fintan took pity and lifted the receiver.

"Fintan," his mother said breathlessly, "I can't stay on long, I'm on the mobile."

He smiled. His mother had been secretly thrilled when he bought her a mobile for her birthday a few weeks ago, but she regarded using it as an extravagance.

"Fintan, I was wondering if you would all like to come down here for the weekend. You could come down on Friday evening if Maeve gets home in time from work. Your father tells me that this could be the last good weather for a while. You know he actually believes the weather forecasters. So what do you think? Ring me back later if you need to decide. I'm going to switch the phone off now to save the battery, but I'll switch it on again at some pre-arranged time if you like."

"Mum," Fintan laughed – he'd had this conversation several times already, "the battery's rechargeable – all you have to do is plug it in. You can even use it while it's plugged in. What's the point of giving the number to all your friends if you keep the thing switched off all the time?"

"Everyone knows they can reach me between eight and nine in the morning, and five and six in the evening. It's only you young folk who can't manage a concept like that."

"What if someone just wants to ring you for a chat? They might think of you at three and be busy again at five."

"Fintan Larkin. This is a mobile phone, it's not for chats. Do you know what it costs to ring one of these things?"

"Okay, Mum." Fintan knew an unwinnable argument

when he heard it. "I'd love to be able to come down this weekend, but Andrea's throwing a party on Saturday and Maeve said she'd like to go. Although, maybe I could bring the kids down, I'm sure she wouldn't mind."

"Fintan," his mother scolded, "only yesterday you were complaining that they'd hardly seen her all week, and now you're talking about whisking them away for the weekend. No, you stay there with Maeve for the weekend; you can always come down another time." Niamh was breathless as she always spoke at triple her usual speed on the mobile.

"I suppose you're right, Mum," Fintan agreed somewhat reluctantly. As he put the phone down, he realised that he would have enjoyed a couple of days in Courtown. Not only for the sake of the sea, sand and fun for the kids, but for the extra help his parents would have given him with them. He had a feeling Maeve wouldn't be of much use this weekend. And now it looked as if they were going to get the best of the weather for Andrea's party; no doubt whenever Fintan did manage to get down to Courtown it would be cold and wet.

CHAPTER 28

But when Maeve came home from the barbeque on Saturday night, she was in such a good mood and so full of stories after catching up with old school friends, that Fintan felt guilty that he had begrudged her the night out. So next morning he decided to be magnanimous and took the children off to the zoo so that she could have a lie-in in peace.

"How did it go?" Maeve asked when they finally got home. She was dressed in shorts and a loose T-shirt, her hair tied back with a scrunchie, leaving a few wisps across her face. And she had obviously spent some time in the sun – freckles were beginning to appear beneath the shiny red flush on her face. She leaned back against the sink and sipped the water she had been pouring when they burst through the door moments earlier.

"We had a great time." Fintan put Darragh on the floor where he chewed happily on the neck of a small stuffed giraffe, then leaned forward to kiss Maeve. "Fiona, tell Mummy about the monkeys."

"Mukkies, mukkies in a tree," declared the toddler with excitement. "Lots of mukkies. I seed mukkies."

"We had to drag her away from the primate area. Poor Ciaran was dying to see the demented polar bear, poor creature."

"Oh God, yeah. That's the one animal that makes me feel guiltiest about the whole zoo." Maeve shuddered. "Was he doing his usual circuit?" On previous trips to the zoo, Ciaran had watched, fascinated, as the polar bear got in and out of the water, like an automaton in a psychotic craze.

"No, the heat was too much for him. He was lying in the shade, completely crashed out. The new big cats' enclosure was great though. It even made up for not stopping at the monkeys again."

"Mukkies, I seed lots mukkies!" the toddler reminded them.

"Did you have lunch?" Maeve asked as they moved out into the garden where she had been sitting before they came home.

"The kids had some chips, but the smell of grease in the cafeteria put me off eating."

"I'll just finish up here, and I'll throw something together." Maeve pointed to the laptop and papers strewn across the patio table.

"You finish what you're doing," Fintan said, hiding his irritation at seeing her working on a Sunday. "I'll just put Darragh to bed first. Fiona, honey, would you like a drink of milk in bed?" The little girl collapsed in relief at his feet, and nodded.

"Fi wan mik, wan mik *now!*" Urgency crept in when she spotted her father picking up her baby brother, to attend to him first. She wailed at his retreating back, got up, chased him towards the kitchen and threw herself at his legs. "Wan bokkle, now, plees, Daddy!" She metamorphosed from happy, excited child to exhausted, demanding toddler in a split second.

"Come on, Fiona, I'll get your bottle." Maeve picked her up, and tried to give her a cuddle. Her daughter resisted for a moment, then her eyes darted between her two parents, and with a look of fierce concentration she came to the conclusion that as Mummy wasn't there as much as Daddy she had a rarity value. So she snuggled up to Maeve, burying her face in her mother's neck, and refused to look at Fintan. They both tried not to laugh.

"What are you working on?" Fintan asked when he came out onto the patio a while later. He was carrying a tray with a loaf of bread, some salad and some cold meats and cheese to make sandwiches. "It's self-service, I'm afraid," he said putting down the tray on the edge of the table, waiting for Maeve to clear a space.

"We've another couple of meetings with Texas this week. Teleconferences," she added as if he might be worried that she would be flying out there.

"Does that mean another couple of late nights?" Fintan tried to keep an even tone.

"I'm afraid so. The time difference is a real pain in the neck."

Fintan felt like he was about to explode, but instead he took a few deep breaths and spoke to Ciaran.

"Ciaran, you've spent enough time in the sun. Come into the kitchen and draw Mummy a picture of the animals in the zoo." He marched his son inside and switched on a tape of nursery rhyme songs. Then he closed the door as he came back out onto the patio.

"How much more of this, Maeve?"

"I don't know, honestly. I didn't realise how much communication we'd have to have with them. We're supposed to be running things much as before."

"It's not just the merger though, is it? You're putting in much longer hours than you ever used to before, and most of last week you were with Irish clients. You can't blame Texas for that. You seem to have got into some kind of absurd pissing competition with Peter and even with Danny. I can't believe your job's in any danger, so what the hell are you at?"

"I . . ." Maeve looked at him in despair. "I'm not really sure what's going on. I just keep getting the feeling that I need to shore up my position, secure myself somehow. I mean why in God's name are they keeping Peter over here? We don't have room for another manager at this level and I can't see him working under me, whatever about Danny. What if they decide to put him in charge? I couldn't bear the thought of working for him."

"You won't have to; we've talked about this before. If you're unhappy, you walk." Fintan felt that they had had this discussion too many times already and he tried not to lose his patience.

"It's not that simple," she snapped back. "I've put too much of my life into this job."

"But that's all it is, a job. And it's got to be that simple. Or at least you've got to make Ofiscom believe that. We both know they can't afford to lose you." Fintan smiled, as if to atone for his earlier aggression. "Even if you have no intention of walking out you've got to let them believe you would. And all this staying-in-late-to-impress-teacher behaviour doesn't exactly give the impression of someone who feels secure in her position, does it?"

"But the more clients I have who rely on me totally, the stronger a position I'll be in. No company can afford to lose clients and I know some would follow me." She paused and picked up a sheet of paper, looked at it briefly, then screwed it onto a tight ball which she rolled between her palms as she went on talking. "But I don't want to leave. I've given ten years to getting this company to where it is today. The next few years of expansion are going to be exciting and I want to be there to see it. And benefit from it." Now Maeve looked fierce rather than indecisively miserable.

"Look, I can't help getting the feeling you're blowing this out of all proportion," Fintan said impatiently. "There's no point in worrying about something that might never happen."

But as soon as the words were out of his mouth, Fintan knew they sounded lame and, worse, condescending. Maeve looked at him in exasperation and opened her mouth to let fly.

"Look," he interrupted quickly, "I know things are difficult for you at the moment, and I'll support you in any way I can. Just let's not lose sight of the important things in life, like each other, the kids and everything."

He knew he still hadn't said the right thing, but was saved from a sharp retort by Ciaran coming out onto the patio clutching a drawing.

"Look, Mummy. I drawed you a picture of the lion. And the tiger." He held it out proudly.

"You *drew* me a picture," Maeve corrected automatically, forcing a smile onto her face. "Let's see. A lion, wow! That's a huge lion. And the tiger – is he going climb up the tree to hide from the lion?"

She turned her shoulder ever so slightly towards her son, effectively turning her back on Fintan. He sighed and went indoors, grateful at least that she was spending time with Ciaran.

He remembered his mother's invitation to come down to Courtown for the weekend and wondered if, now that Maeve was going to be working late all week, he should bring the kids down for a few days. They could hardly see much less of her than they had in the past week. Then maybe Maeve could join them for the weekend and get away from Dublin altogether.

CHAPTER 29

Three days later, Fintan arrived at his parents' holiday house in the rain. It had rained solidly for two days in Dublin and he was going crazy cooped up at home. At least down here there was no television – one less thing for Ciaran and Fiona to argue about. They were dying to see their grandparents, and Fintan hoped his parents had missed them so much that they would insist on spending every hour of the day with them. He needed some time to himself.

Maeve waved them off as they left, and although Fintan was sad to be leaving without her (this was the first time either of them had taken the kids away on their own), mostly what he felt during the drive down was resentment, which stewed in his mind as he remembered Maeve's reaction when he proposed the trip. She had tried to hide it, but she looked relieved. Relieved to be rid of her husband and children for a few days to concentrate on work. But it was only for a few days, Fintan rationalised, and Maeve had promised she would join them on Friday night.

Niamh opened the door just as the engine stopped. She rushed to the car in waterproofs, carrying a green golf umbrella.

"Let's get the kids in – we'll worry about the luggage later," she said as Fintan clambered out. Then, looking into the car at her grandchildren, she added in the 'grown-up' voice that adults reserve for children, "Look at you, Ciaran! You've grown to be a giant since I saw you last! And Fiona, you look like a baby giant!"

"Don't worry, Mum, there's not too much luggage – I did the packing!" Fintan laughed, delighted to see Ciaran and Fiona launch themselves at their grandmother with obvious joy. She scooped up the little girl, and let her grandson run alongside her as she tried to hold the umbrella over them. Paul stood waiting for them with towels and he whisked Ciaran up to remove his shoes before he could bring half the mud from the path into the house.

"I think you need a few more bags of gravel for that path," Fintan commented as he shook himself dry in the porch.

"I was waiting for that daughter of yours to get over the habit of eating it," Paul laughed. As well as chewing gravel, Fiona hoarded it in her pockets, pushed it down the side of couches and created stashes all over the house for later consumption.

"If the weather improves, you can help your dad lay the new path." Niamh said. "He's been looking all over for the right stones, and last week he finally bought some lovely, used slate slabs. They're out on the patio if you want to have a look at them."

"So that's why you were so keen to get me down here!" Fintan pretended to be indignant.

They all poured into the kitchen laughing and fell on the apple-pie, tea and orange squash that Niamh had prepared. It was amazing how hungry they all were despite sitting in the car since breakfast. The sea air was already kicking in.

The next days flew by. The weather improved enough for walks and sandcastles on the beach and for Paul and Fintan to start on the path. Father and son worked together digging out the old path, adding drainage trenches into which they raked the remaining gravel and spreading the sand, to bed slabs of stone on. Fintan fell gratefully into bed each night, surprised at how much he enjoyed the exhausting physical labour – and the fact that his mother took on responsibility for some of the day-to-to-day care of the children while he worked.

Maeve was delayed until Saturday and Fintan's parents announced they would go up to Dublin for the weekend to check on the house and mow the lawn. On Friday night they all sat finishing a bottle of wine after a late dinner, with the children asleep.

"Give her the time she needs to sort out whatever problems she has at work, love," Niamh said gently, when Fintan went silent after explaining why Maeve hadn't made it down.

"How long, Mum?" he asked, not expecting an answer. "She's totally obsessed at the moment. I thought the whole idea of my giving up work was for the kids' sake, but any extra time I generate gets swallowed up by her job. I feel as if I'm looking after her job rather than the kids."

"And would supporting her in her job be such a bad thing?"

"That's not what I meant. I just thought . . . well, I just thought it would be different that's all. I suppose I had rosy visions of us all sitting down to dinner together each evening, no commuting to do, all that extra time for ourselves. And now I actually see less of Maeve than I did when we were both working full-time. At least then she had to arrange to finish on time two or three days a week to collect the kids, and we were all home together."

They went quiet for a while. Then Niamh spoke.

"If you were a woman in this situation, you'd probably feel the same way, but you might be afraid to admit it or speak out. What you've described is how thousands of women feel when they give up work." She hurried on, aware that Paul's head had shot up and he was giving her a funny look. "At least you have a choice. You've chosen this, and if you can't make it work then you'll be going back to the old arrangement in November. It's difficult, but I can't see you giving up this easily. And I can't give you any answers – this is between you and Maeve."

Niamh got up quickly and began to tidy the kitchen

while Paul said he'd go for a short walk to get some fresh air before bedtime.

"Mum," Fintan said gently as he began to dry the dishes, "you had to give up work when you got married. How did you find it?"

She didn't answer at first, just scrubbed savagely at the roasting tin.

"I loved that job," she said at last. "I was never going to get married. I was saving up to go to college at night to get a degree and to move up through the grades in the civil service." She went quiet again.

"So what happened?" Fintan asked.

"I met your father," Niamh answered. "I hadn't counted on that. Falling in love, I mean. I resisted at first, gave him a real hard time. Any other man, less stubborn or pig-headed than him, would have given up. But he kept at me, and eventually I agreed to go to a dance with him, then a walk on a Sunday, then a meal. And the rest, as they say, is history."

She clattered the saucepans, trying to end the conversation.

"You gave up work?" Fintan wouldn't give up that easily.

"I had no choice." Niamh shrugged her shoulders as if to convey indifference, but the anger sparkling in her eyes betrayed her. "In those days, if you got married, you lost your job in the civil service. The Marriage Bar, it was called. They wrote to me a few months after I got married, asking if I wanted to come in part-time. No pension, no rights, just doing the same work for a fraction of the money. I was so angry I tore the letter up. I couldn't tear the pieces small enough. I broke two fingernails as I ripped each tiny piece into smaller and smaller fragments, and then I felt better. They needed me, and they could go to hell." ·

Fintan had never heard his mother talk like this.

"Then your brothers were born, and you, and Orla, and I knew it was all for the best. I was a lot happier than I could ever have been no matter how high I had risen, or how important I had got to be. I realised that I loved being a mother, and in those days it was no crime to admit that. But I still resent the fact that I wasn't offered the option of doing both. And that the choice hadn't been mine to make. And I keep asking myself – what if your father hadn't been so persistent?" She shivered as she imagined life without her family. "I should have been allowed to follow my heart with him much sooner, and not have been forced to choose between him and my job."

Paul returned from his walk and shattered the intimacy between them. Somehow Fintan knew that his mother had never told his father what she had shared with him. And he knew she didn't have to. Suddenly he understood his family's happiness had been based on his mother's sacrifice and he felt ashamed of his earlier griping.

CHAPTER 30

The weekend was a great success. Maeve made an effort not to mention work at all, and Fintan enjoyed having the whole family together with no interruptions for two days. Maeve brought a message down with her from Hazel who wanted Fintan to ring her at the office. He decided not to think about it until Monday, and to Maeve's surprise that was the end of it. In his position, she would have been itching to get to the phone, and not being able to get an answer for two whole days would have her burnt up with curiosity, or anxiety.

They all returned to Dublin on Sunday night and on the way back they decided that Fintan would come back down to Courtown on Thursday. The previous week had gone so well that Niamh was determined to make a regular event of it, and anyway she had promised to take the children for the weekend so that Fintan and Maeve could relax and enjoy Danny's charity dinner. She was also determined that Fintan help his father to finish laying the front path.

Fintan rang Hazel on Monday morning to discover she had a proposition for him. The other managers in the company were dismayed when they realised that Fintan's leave of absence meant a temporary non-appearance of his monthly newsletter, so they wanted her to persuade Fintan to go on producing the newsletter at home on a freelance basis. He agreed to come in on Friday to talk to her about it and asked his mother if she wouldn't mind him sloping off to Dublin a day earlier than planned.

All week he was excited at the prospect of restarting *Money Matters*. He knew it would have no impact on the work he was doing at home, as he had always tended to read the material for it late at night – the only thing to suffer would be his television-watching. He scribbled down some ideas on how he could develop the newsletter although he knew that if the managers were so keen to get the in-house publication back, they might not take kindly to his tinkering with its format.

On Friday morning, having left the children with his parents, he drove to Dublin, rehearsing what he was going to say. He was looking forward to working on the first edition and Hazel had promised that she would collect all financial journals and back issues of the *Financial Times* for him. He found parking with difficulty, and arrived breathless into Hazel's office.

"Calm down, Fintan! This isn't a job interview," she said. "We just need to decide exactly what we're going to pay you for this. Oh, and we wondered was there any chance that you could stretch to two issues a month with maybe the odd in-depth article? It would be a good way to provide informal training."

Fintan didn't know what to say because he had spent so long rehearsing the arguments in favour of such an approach. Hazel took his silence for reluctance.

"Of course, I did point out to everyone that this wasn't exactly what you had in mind when you took leave," she said slowly.

"It's not that. I always thought we should produce *Money Matters* once a fortnight, but it would have been such a time commitment on top of the rest of the job . . ."

"Of course, and I understand that you might be reluctant to take on such a commitment, now of all times, but would you at least consider it?" Hazel slid an envelope across the table. "These are the terms the company would be prepared to offer while you're on leave. There's an offer for both the one issue a month and the two issues option with the in-depth review. You'll notice we've put in a contract for two years, just in case you decide not to come back to us full-time in November." She smiled, trying to make a joke of it. "I don't want to put pressure on you now. Read it when you get home, talk to Maeve, and let me know as soon as possible. I know it may be a tall order, but it would be great to have something out at the end of the month."

They gossiped for a while longer about people in the

company and how Fintan was getting on at home. He found it impossible not to keep staring at the envelope on the desk, wondering what was in it. Eventually curiosity got the better of him and he got up and left although he was quite enjoying their chat. He hadn't realised how pleasant office gossip could be, especially now that he no longer had the opportunity to indulge in it.

He tried to ring Maeve, but she was in a meeting so he decided to go straight to her office and surprise her. As soon as he sat into the car, he ripped open Hazel's white envelope and began to read. He went straight to the option involving an issue per fortnight and let out a small whistle while a childish grin lit up his face. He hadn't won the lottery, but the offer was better than expected. A quick calculation told him that by the time he took into account the tax, childcare and petrol he was saving, writing *Money Matters* at home would leave him only marginally worse off than when he was working full-time. And he'd be doing the part of the job he liked best.

The document had clearly not been drawn up with only a few months in mind and Fintan recognised Hazel's hand in that. He wondered at what stage she had decided that his four months leave might stretch beyond what was originally agreed. For the first time he let himself explore the possibility, and then put the thought out of his mind. He was only four weeks into this experiment, and although it was nice to know that he now had the means to stick with it if it all worked out, it was not part of the original plan. And he was afraid of Maeve's reaction if he so much as mentioned the possibility.

He reached her office in Donnybrook just in time to see her car pull out of the car park. She would already have the stereo on full blast so, even if he had the nerve to, there was no point in blasting the horn at her. He tried to follow her, dialling her mobile number as he drove, but lost her at the first set of lights. She turned down towards Ballsbridge.

Fintan fumed as his call was redirected to voice mail so he tried Colm in the office instead. He was no help. Maeve had taken a call mid-morning, Colm said, and cancelled her afternoon meeting, saying she had some urgent business to attend to. Something about a new client. Colm gave the distinct impression of being peeved at not being given all the details; Fintan would have to warn Maeve that all this cloak and dagger stuff was rubbing her assistant up the wrong way.

He drove down the same road as Maeve, in the vain hope of catching her further down, but gave up and began to drive towards home, his mood slightly dented. Then he spotted her car pulling into Bewley's Hotel. He followed her into the carpark, but her car was empty by the time he located it. He tried her mobile again and got the same annoying message. He should really go home; he knew it wouldn't look good if she arrived at a business meeting with her husband following her around. But if it was a new contact, what was the chance of his being recognised? It would do no harm to wander into the lobby and if Maeve was alone, still waiting for whoever she had to meet, he could share his good news with her and leave quickly.

He bounced up the steps, through the automatic door and into the lobby. He looked around and stopped dead. Maeve was going through a door labelled *Resident's Rooms Only*, followed by James whose hand was on her waist as he guided her past the swinging door. At least it looked like James. But Fintan couldn't figure out why Maeve would be meeting her ex. James was hardly in the market for LBS's expertise. Was he trying to headhunt Maeve for another company? Surely she wouldn't even entertain the possibility of that at the moment?

The only explanation, Fintan decided, was that it wasn't James but someone who looked like him and that there were meeting rooms on one of the other floors. Suddenly Fintan realised that he was attracting some odd looks from the receptionists. He was standing, blocking the door, staring across an empty lobby. He strode over to the desk and picked up one of the hotel leaflets, then walked out to the car.

He sat for a long time, phone in hand, staring at nothing in particular. Then he dialled the hotel's number and asked if they had a James Kirby staying. A few finger-clicks of a keyboard later, Fintan was asked if he wanted to be put through to James's room. He didn't recall saying yes, but he must have, because the receptionist apologised and said she was sorry, but Mr Kirby was carrying out an interview at the moment and had asked not to be disturbed. Would Fintan like to leave a message?

He drove home, with the lunch-time news playing loud in the car. He didn't want to think. He rang Colm when he got back and asked to have Maeve ring him as soon as she returned. Sulkily, Colm announced that Maeve had just rung to say she wouldn't be back for the rest of the afternoon.

Fintan mowed the lawn – it was amazing how fast the grass seemed to be growing with the combination of wet and warm weather. It needed two cuts a week at the moment. He piled the clippings onto the compost heap and decided that it could do with being turned and well mixed. He stabbed at the pile of rotting vegetation with his garden fork until he had the whole heap turned over. If there was one thing he did know about organic gardening, it was how to make good compost. When he finished that, he hacked at the privet hedge, which was threatening to block the path. Then he heard a car pull into the driveway.

That would be Maeve now, Fintan realised with relief.

She would tell him all about her meeting with James. No doubt she was trying to recruit some new staff. Or maybe it was a chance encounter – James was staying at the hotel to do some interviews and Maeve had run into him in the lobby, early for her own meeting. Fintan opened the door for his wife, a welcoming smile on his face.

CHAPTER 31

Maeve pulled into the drive, switched off the ignition and sat for a few seconds without moving. She noticed Fintan's car parked on the road and cursed. She didn't feel like talking just now. But he must have heard her coming, because he opened the front door and stood there, grinning like a nervous schoolboy. His meeting with Hazel must have gone well.

Maeve was glad for him; she knew how much he enjoyed writing *Money Matters*. She would have to make an effort to get home earlier in the next few weeks so that he didn't end up doing all the work for it in the middle of the night. Not that that bothered him – he always said he worked best after dark. But if he was looking after the kids all day, he really deserved some time to himself as well. She forced herself to smile, and got out of the car.

She went around to the boot to take out the groceries she had picked up on the way home, and was surprised that Fintan didn't offer to help carry them. He was stuck to the spot, still wearing that idiotic grin. No matter, she only had two bags of shopping and her briefcase. She walked towards him and held out her cheek for a kiss, but he ducked inside to hold the door open for her. At last he took the two shopping bags and brought them into the kitchen. Maeve dumped her briefcase in the study and followed him. He had started unpacking the groceries.

"Well? How did it go?" she asked. And then, as Fintan seemed to be looking at her blankly, she added, "With Hazel?"

"Oh, that? Great." He gave her the details. He didn't seem as enthusiastic as she expected.

"That sounds better than you hoped. Are you having second thoughts? You only have to do one issue a month if two feels like too much."

"No, it's not that. I guess I'm just tired. It's been a long day, what with getting up early to come up to Dublin. And Darragh was sick last night – I was up a couple of times in the middle of the night to him."

"What's wrong with him? Why didn't you ring me?" Suddenly Maeve was alarmed, and felt guilty that she was only hearing about it now.

"It was in the middle of the night and he was a lot better this morning. I tried getting you today, but you were in meetings all morning. I didn't think it was important enough to disturb you."

"So tell me about it, Fintan." Maeve tried to remain calm; she felt that Fintan was deliberately excluding her in punishment for not being there at the time. "Was he throwing up, did he have a temperature? What?"

"No temperature. He just got sick a couple of times. I think he stole Fiona's beaker of orange juice before bedtime or else Fiona fed it to him. You know what effect that always has on him. Anyway, I told you, he's fine. I checked with Mum about an hour ago. I'd have let you know, but . . ."

"Yeah, I know, my phone was off."

Since he was a small baby, Darragh had been unable to tolerate undiluted juices, but he loved them. If he managed to get his hands on them, over the next few hours he inevitably threw up a glorious mess of juice, milk and whatever else was in his stomach. Maeve was so relieved she forgot to be annoyed with Fiona who loved to 'feed' her little brother with her cup.

Fintan occupied himself with unpacking the last of the groceries. He took some meat out to the freezer in the utility room and shouted back: "So how was your day? As hectic as Colm seemed to make it out to be?"

"Not too bad," she answered, "lots of meetings."

"I thought I might catch you in time to take you for lunch, but you were gone when I phoned. Colm said you'd be gone all afternoon, didn't seem to know where you were. He sounded a bit peeved about that."

Fintan was very busy in the utility room all of a sudden and Maeve suspected that he was annoyed that she hadn't been available to celebrate his good news with him. She really couldn't face this now.

"Oh, you know Colm," she answered casually, flicking through some bills she had picked up in the hall, "he seems to think he has a God-given right to know where I am every second of the day. It was no great mystery; I was meeting a new client. He'll get all the details on Monday. How are Fiona and Ciaran?" Just when Maeve didn't want to talk about work, it was all Fintan was interested in.

"They're fine." Fintan answered, still in the utility room. "Did you have any lunch?" "You left very early for an afternoon meeting. You shouldn't go skipping meals like that." He slammed the washing-machine shut and began to twist the dials as he spoke, but then waited as Maeve hesitated before she answered.

"I grabbed a sandwich on the way there and ate it in the car. Stop worrying – do I look as if I'm in danger of starving?"

Fintan came back into the kitchen and looked coldly at Maeve.

"Was the meeting productive?" he asked. "Did you land any new contracts?"

Why was Fintan suddenly so interested in new contracts, Maeve wondered. Less than a week ago he thought she was working too hard.

"No, it was a bit of a waste of time. Look, Fintan, I really don't feel like talking about work right now. I'm hot and tired, and I need a shower. We'll talk later."

She looked up to see Fintan staring at her with an expression she didn't recognise. Cold, almost hostile.

"I'm going to head back down to Courtown," he

said tonelessly. "With Darragh sick, I don't think it's fair to let Mum on her own with him."

He moved towards the door, hardly looking at Maeve.

"Hey wait!" she retorted. "You said he was better! Hang on a few minutes and I'll come down with you."

"I'm going now, and there's really no need for you to come too. Like I said, Darragh's fine. But as we're leaving the kids with Mum tomorrow night, for that charity dinner of yours, I wouldn't like her to get a sleepless night tonight. You stay here and enjoy your shower. And then I'm sure you have loads of work to do. Make the most of the quiet house."

Maeve could hear anger in Fintan's voice that she didn't recognise. She felt like screaming, or throwing something. Or just letting her legs give way under her, sliding to the floor and crying. She felt incapable of making a decision. Or of working out what she should do. She wanted to go down to Courtown and see the kids, but it was obvious Fintan didn't want her to come. Though if she didn't he would hold it against her. Neglecting her poor sick baby in favour of work. Suddenly Maeve had had enough, and took the easiest option. She had had a traumatic day and the last thing she needed was a petulant, sulking husband. If he wanted to play the martyr, let him. She kicked off her shoes, picked them up and walked upstairs. When she reached the top, she turned back to Fintan who was looking up at her, obviously trying to decide whether to say something or not. She waited to see if he was going to add anything to what he'd already said, then shrugged.

"Drive safely. I'll call and talk to you later and I'll see you tomorrow. We have to be at the Burlington for eight."

"Those kinds of things never start on time," Fintan snorted.

Maeve blew him a kiss as he put his hand to the front-door handle, turned towards the bathroom then stopped. "Fintan, I really am pleased about *Money Matters*. Congratulations, you deserve it."

He looked at her as if seeing her for the first time. "Yeah, whatever. Talk to you later."

Then he walked out the front door with his shoulders sagging and looking about six inches shorter than normal. He looked so miserable that Maeve was tempted to run out after him, give him a hug and ask him what was wrong. But what was the point? There was nothing she could do about work at the moment and to bring up the subject would only start another row. She undressed in the bathroom feeling utterly depressed.

Despite the heat of the day and her feeling of stickiness, Maeve needed a hot shower. She needed the comforting sting of scalding water on her shoulders. She scrubbed her hair until her fingers ached and she left her skin raw and tingling as a result of her efforts with the loofah. She got out of the shower and opened the window to let out the build-up of steam. She tried to wipe the mirror a few times to comb her hair properly, but it kept misting over, so she gave up and went into the bedroom. She looked at herself in the full-length mirror and let the towel fall to the floor. But it was as if she couldn't see anything in the mirror. Staring past her reflection, eyes fixed at some point in the distance, she began to remember her day.

The phone rang at around eleven and Maeve answered it herself. It was James. He was in Dublin to carry out some preliminary interviews on behalf of a Dutch electronics company and he wanted to meet her for lunch. She tried to put him off till the weekend. Wouldn't he rather come to the house for lunch on Saturday and meet Fintan? But he said he was only in Dublin till that evening and he really needed to talk to her about something. Reluctantly, Maeve cancelled an appointment and agreed to meet him at his hotel.

When she got there, James was waiting in the lobby. He kissed her on the cheek in greeting.

"The hotel staff are clearing the meeting-room – is it okay to have lunch in my suite?"

"You'd want to watch it, James. If I didn't know you better, I'd swear you were trying to proposition me."

Now that she was here, Maeve was glad to see James. After her hectic week, she could do with some of his easy good humour to help her get a sense of proportion again. He laughed, and steered her towards the bedrooms. They chatted about the weather on the way to his room and suddenly Maeve felt uncomfortable. There was an air of tension between them she had never before experienced with him. Even in the weeks and months after their break-up, they had quickly reverted to being good friends.

James led her into a large comfortably-furnished room with two floor-length windows but no sign of a bed, so Maeve assumed this must be the living-room side of his suite. There were two low, soft leather couches arranged at right angles to each other with a low table between them and three straight backed chairs scattered around the room. James stepped over to the table, lifted some paperwork and placed it on a desk near the window. There was a pile of what seemed to be prospectuses on the desk, and a closed laptop connected to a charger, so James was no doubt using this room as an office during his stay.

He waved to one of the couches, inviting Maeve to take a seat and then lifted two linen napkins off a tray of food.

"I just ordered sandwiches and salads for lunch, if that's okay? I didn't know whether you wanted to drink or not, so I have a bottle of wine and some mineral water." James was so busy acting the perfect host that Maeve felt like shaking him.

She accepted a glass of wine in the hope that he would have one too and loosen up a bit. Then she helped herself to a mineral water as well and gulped down half a bottle in one go. They were silent as they piled food onto their plates and then James asked her about the children.

His reserve vanished as he laughed about Ciaran's latest pearls of wisdom or Fiona's mad antics and suddenly, remembering what he had hinted at in Courtown, Maeve guessed why he had asked her here. He wanted her to hear it from him first! She began mentally choosing wedding outfits, wondering what time of the year James would get married. Maybe it was an English girl, and they'd all have to travel over there. Maeve hoped not – she hated to think that James would settle over there permanently.

"Well, James, what's this big news you have for me then?" Half a glass of wine on an empty stomach had unleashed her curiosity and her inhibitions.

James stopped talking, put down his drink, picked it up again, poured himself another glass, swallowed it back and replaced the empty glass on the table between them.

"I'm gay."

The flower-girl outfit Maeve had mentally chosen for Fiona, her own outfit, wide-brimmed hat and killer heels, all vanished in a confused mist in her brain.

"Are you sure?" Her mouth opened and closed a couple of times in a vain attempt to recapture the words that had escaped before she got her brain in gear. "I mean . . . how long . . . who?" She shook her head slowly. "But I don't understand . . . we . . ."

She waited for the explanation she hoped would untangle the emotional spaghetti in her mind. She flopped back into the comfortable armchair and cradled her wineglass in both hands. Then she looked at it with suspicion and put it down in a hurry before it laid her open to any other wild hallucinations.

"I know this must come as a bit of a shock," he said.

Maeve nodded helplessly. Not only did she not trust herself to speak, she seemed to have lost the ability.

"First question, yeah, I'm sure."

"I didn't mean . . . sorry if . . ."

"Only joking. Calm down. I know I've had longer to rehearse this. I'm not expecting any perfect reactions from you. Second question. How long? I guess I've known, deep down, all my adult life." He looked at Maeve's horrified face. "I don't mean, when we . . . I mean . . . we didn't actually ever . . . Oh God, in my worst nightmares I didn't imagine it would be this hard."

James stood up and began to pace the room. Irritated by Maeve's gaze following his progress like a ball in a tennis match, he stopped and stared out the window.

"Is that the bathroom?" Maeve pointed to the only other door in the room other than the one they had come in.

"Yes. Oh wait . . . hang on." James rushed into the small room, picked up a few dirty clothes and damp towels then opened a door on the opposite side of the bathroom and tossed the clothes into the bedroom.

"Sorry, I . . ." Maeve looked embarrassed.

"It's all right, just some clothes and towels. I don't have a man, or used condoms or anything hidden in there."

His attempt at humour failed miserably, leaving Maeve looking even more wretched. They just kept saying the wrong things to each other.

"Just go to the toilet and I promise I'll still be here when you get back." James must have thought she was hoping he'd have vanished, like a bad dream.

When she did come out, she sat back onto the couch, picked up her plate and tried to restore some sanity to the situation.

"Look, James, let's pretend I never said anything. Go back to your rehearsed version and we'll take it from there." She filled her mouth with smoked salmon sandwich, indicating her resolve not to interrupt again.

James told her that when he was younger he had often wondered if he was different. But at first he fought the idea that he might be gay, as much out of fear as out of a desire to please his parents. Since Maeve, no relationship had lasted more than a few weeks, and he admitted that most of the women he had told her about since his move to London were one-off dates or invented for her benefit. He had gay friends in England, and they all seemed to know he was gay long before he admitted it to himself. The turning point was when he met someone in the same position as himself. Together they started to go to gay clubs, and both had drifted in and out of short relationships. Gradually they realised that the reason they had been able to help each other was that they were in love, and they accepted that they wanted to spend the foreseeable future together.

"But that's wonderful, James," Maeve said, meaning it. She had always been a sucker for happy endings. "So when do we get to meet him? Tell me everything."

Suddenly James looked uncomfortable again.

"That was question three, wasn't it? 'Who?'" He couldn't meet her eyes. "It's Tony. And I've got to ask you not to say a word of this to Fintan – you know what Tony's parents are like."

"Tony! But . . ." All Maeve could think about was how Fintan used to tell her how he had envied Tony's easy way with girls, later women, and how he always had crowds of hopefuls hanging around. "He always . . ." That, on top of everything else was just too much to take in; Maeve couldn't put together the words.

"So I can't tell Fintan?" she asked at last, not sure why this made her so uncomfortable.

"I'd prefer you didn't," James answered. "You're the only person at home to know about this. And it's not really my decision. There's no way you could tell Fintan about my being gay without his guessing about Tony. I can't expect you to lie to Fintan, but if you can avoid the subject . . ."

"So why did you feel it so important to tell me?" Maeve wanted to know. She suddenly had a horrible thought: "You've told your parents, haven't you?"

She could see from his shamefaced expression that he hadn't. Suddenly the burden of being the only one to be told was too much for her and she repeated his question: "So why me?"

"Because we went out for so long. Because of what I felt for you, what I'll always feel for you. I needed to explain that what we had was in no way false or sham or anything. What we had was real, and right for who I was at the time. I suppose I just needed the reassurance that hearing this won't make you look back at those years and think I lied to you. Because I didn't, Maeve. Until the end, I really could see us together, ridiculous though that may seem now. Did I hurt you?"

Of course he had hurt her when they broke up, but Maeve wasn't sure if his revelations today changed that. She couldn't analyse her feelings about it now, with him here. She needed to get away, be on her own.

She stayed for a while longer to try and reassure James that she wasn't angry and then, unable to face the office or even home, she took refuge amongst the safe anonymity of Friday afternoon shoppers.

Then she came home and in the weird mood she was in, managed to upset Fintan by not being the perfect parent he was getting so much practice at being.

Maeve shook her head to clear it and looked again into the mirror. She examined her body, expecting it to look different from this morning. The only man she had ever loved apart from her husband, was gay. He loved men rather than women and yet they had sustained a relationship for five years.

She picked up the towel and wrapped it around herself again to protect her body from such disturbing scrutiny. She wished Fintan hadn't gone back down to Courtown. She needed to feel his arms around her. She wanted to fall into bed with him in this silent house and chase away the fear she couldn't name. She didn't want to be alone for the night.

When Fintan phoned later, Maeve could hear that he

was still annoyed with her, as he spoke in short clipped phrases. She was determined that the following evening at the dinner dance would be a success for them. She would be attentive to him rather than Danny's business guests, and she would promise to cut down on her hours. They would make the most of having the house to themselves that night and the next morning.

CHAPTER 32

Maeve stood in the lobby of the Burlington Hotel and looked around at the other guests as they wandered around greeting each other with exaggerated cries of delight, and embraces designed so that the recipient couldn't see you were looking over their shoulder for someone more interesting. So far Maeve hadn't seen anyone she knew and felt out of place amidst the cream of Dublin's Charity Committee Ladies. She was glad to see Fintan return, stuffing the cloakroom ticket into the inside pocket of his jacket.

"You see, I told you the black was the right choice."

She had been in agonies earlier and eventually agreed with Fintan that you could never go wrong in a black dress. Now she wasn't so sure. She seemed to be surrounded by LBD's, and most of them cost more than Maeve would spend on clothes in a year. And the women inside the dresses looked as if they had eaten nothing but rocket salad with balsamic vinaigrette since the early '90s.

Maeve forced herself to smile, not wanting Fintan to know how insecure she felt. He had arrived up late from Courtown, after getting stuck in a traffic jam, and was still in a foul mood.

"Let's go in and get some of that free champagne down our necks," he growled and dragged her into a huge ballroom, where they were greeted by waiters bearing trays of drinks. Fintan handed her a glass of bubbly and took one for himself. Then Maeve spotted Andrea and moved towards her in relief. As usual her friend was surrounded by a group of admiring bachelors, but for once she wasn't flirting with any of them. Danny was nowhere to be seen.

"Maeve, there you are at last!" Andrea broke free from the throng surrounding her, and met Maeve halfway across the room. "Why is it, that when you're actually with someone, suddenly there's a glut of available men. Where were all those gorgeous hunks six months ago?" She waved at the group of men she had just left.

"They're not that spectacular," Maeve argued, looking over her friend's shoulder. "Your standards must be dropping."

"Oh God no! You don't think it's because I'm nearly forty, do you?" Andrea asked in horror.

"Shut up! We haven't even hit thirty-five yet, so don't go starting rumours. It's probably because when you're looking at the menu without having to choose something to eat, all the dishes look . . . dishy!"

"If that's an extension of that witty saying about being on a diet but still being allowed to look at the menu, I'm afraid to say, I'm not on a diet. And not looking as if I'm going to be. Yet!" She looked peeved.

"Not progressing as fast as you'd hoped with Danny Boy?" Maeve asked sympathetically.

"Not progressing, period. I swear, things are almost exactly the same as they were ten years ago – best buddies, but nothing more. Do you think I'm wasting my time? No, don't bother answering that. Whatever you say, I'm not giving up yet."

"So where is our host?" Fintan asked, looking around just as he joined them. As he'd followed his wife over he'd noticed Andrea's empty glass and had gone looking for a waiter, so he now carried three glasses of champagne.

"Why can't I get a man like yours?" Andrea pouted, accepting the drink and kissing Fintan lightly on the cheek. "Oh, and in answer to your question, Ofiscom's sponsoring one of the raffle prizes, so Peter's dragged Danny off to get a photo taken."

The mention of Peter was enough to remind Maeve why tonight was going to be so much of an ordeal. A quick look at the seating plan showed her sandwiched between Peter and Jean-Paul, whose wife was with him on this trip. Mme Thiebaud was to be seated between Danny and Fintan. Maeve was glad she was not going to be sitting next to the Frenchwoman. She knew she was being a prude, but she found it hard to accept that Jean-Paul was only now introducing his wife to business associates who had met his mistress months ago. She wondered whether Mme Thiebaud was aware of the existence of the glamorous Sandrine, and if she knew her to be such formidable competition.

"Have you seen Cathy?" Andrea whispered to Maeve just as Danny approached them.

"No. Is she home for the weekend then? To support her mother's do?"

"Yes, and she's on the seating plan as being at her mother's table. Sitting with her brother, no less," Andrea added gleefully. "She obviously hasn't managed to replace Danny yet!" Then she added quickly as she saw Danny approaching, "Don't let him out of your sight for a moment. I don't want him running into her on his own."

"Come on over to the table," Danny suggested, leading the way. "The Thiebauds are already there."

Pascale Thiebaud was a striking-looking woman with strong French features, high, sharp cheekbones and an aristocratic nose. Maeve imagined she must have appeared somewhat ungainly when she was younger. She looked older than Jean-Paul, but then Maeve had never been able to figure out his age. All those bedroom aerobics helped him stay young, she thought wryly. She was determined to like Pascale, although it was hard to disapprove too fiercely of Jean-Paul. He had such a boyish charm.

Jean-Paul introduced his wife without blinking although he must have known that at least some of the company were thinking of his last trip to Dublin, and how he had abandoned most of his sightseeing plans in favour of exploring the delights of his room in the Shelbourne. He was even staying in the same hotel with Pascale and Maeve hoped the staff were discreet.

Pascale's English, better than her husband's, put the Irish to shame. She spoke with a perfect, almost BBC-quality accent and she was very much the society hostess. She remembered everyone's name so readily that Maeve was convinced she had learned them in advance, a belief reinforced when the Frenchwoman asked about her children by name. Maeve wondered if she had a little book in which she kept details of all Jean-Paul's business contacts. But she found she enjoyed talking to Pascale, and was surprised to learn that the Thiebauds' own two children, a girl and a boy, were only a few years older than Fiona and Ciaran.

As the guests in the ballroom began to take their seats, Peter rushed over with his escort in tow, a slim redhead who looked vaguely familiar to Maeve. Andrea seemed to recognise her as well, and tried to catch Maeve's eye with a look on her face that could only be described as sick. But they were unable to swap notes as Peter carried out loud introductions, presenting her as "my beautiful Irish colleen, Aoife".

The final couple at their table, swept along in Peter's wake, were John and Amy O'Callaghan, the husband and wife who had been part of Danny's legal team during the merger negotiations. As they took their seats, Maeve noticed Aoife waving discreetly at someone on the other side of the room and following

the direction of her glance, she saw Cathy Houlihan
making her way towards the ladies' room.

Suddenly Maeve could place Aoife. She was a friend
of Cathy's, the one who had accompanied her when she
was writing a series of articles on health and beauty
salons. The articles were cleverly written in the form of
a restaurant review – 'My companion chose to start with
a facial, followed by a full body massage, while I settled
for the mesh highlights topped off with aromatherapy'
– and the series might have been good except that
Cathy had seen them as her ticket to indefinite free
beauty treatments in Ireland's top salons and the
quality of her review depended on promises of future
preferential treatment. Andrea refused to give in to
blackmail, and threatened to sue if Cathy wrote
anything disparaging about Egans. She was only
bluffing, but being the daughter of one of Dublin's
prominent solicitors lent gravity to her threat.

So that was why Andrea had looked so sick when
she saw Aoife with Peter Fisch, Maeve realised.
Although to be fair, Aoife had turned up in person at
the salon later, to apologise for the misunderstanding,
and to assure Andrea that Cathy probably hadn't meant
to sound so aggressive. Andrea said later that Aoife
actually seemed quite nice and that she couldn't quite
understand what she and Cathy could possibly have in
common.

Meanwhile Cathy examined her reflection in the large
mirror in the ladies' room. She was wearing a sheath-

like glittering, multicoloured dress, which would have clung to her curves if she hadn't banished them by obsessive under-eating. These neon lights were so unflattering, she thought, they made her blonde highlights look almost brassy and they emphasised the dark circles under her eyes. Well, at least she was well on the way to doing something about those, she thought – revenge would soon have her sleeping like a baby again. She never had circles under her eyes until she discovered how she'd been cheated out of Danny's millions. And to add insult to injury, Danny had brought the Egan woman to the dinner tonight – no doubt that was also Maeve Larkin's doing.

Well, Maeve would pay. And whether they knew it or not, Peter and Aoife would help Cathy make sure she paid.

Cathy and Aoife had worked together on a small local paper before Cathy landed the job at 'WOW!' They had kept in touch since then, even though Aoife had neither moved on nor been as successful as Cathy. And Aoife, who was terribly shy, really appreciated Cathy's friendship, and was always ready to help her friend by doing some writing for her if she was running close to her deadline. Which was most of the time, it must be admitted. It had been her idea to do the pieces on the health and beauty salons, so Cathy had invited her along for the treatments. Aoife really appreciated that – and had done most of the work on the articles in gratitude.

So Aoife from Cathy's point of view was the perfect

girlfriend for Peter. And having given it a huge amount of thought, Cathy had decided that it was a girlfriend that Peter needed. Not only Danny would warm to him if he declared that he had fallen head over heels with a sweet little Irish girl (Danny was an incurable romantic; Cathy had nearly puked every time he had admired Maeve and Fintan's perfect marriage), but Cathy could keep an eye on Peter (whom she didn't entirely trust) and on what was going on at LBS. And now, through careful questioning of Aoife, Cathy knew more about the running of LBS than she ever had when she was going out with the owner. Aoife had a journalist's efficient memory and since she had fallen for Peter in a big way, she was providing him with an audience for all his stories about work.

And as Cathy got to know more about Peter, it hadn't taken her long to figure out how to poison his mind against Maeve. He was terrified that if he didn't do well in Dublin his future in Ofiscom was bleak, so Cathy hinted that Maeve might have complained about him to Texas. When he heard that, Cathy discovered to her delight, he didn't need much manipulation, but was more than Machiavellian enough for the two of them. And although it was strange that Peter never questioned her motives in helping him advance his career, Cathy simply figured that he was so busy trying to keep her happy while also dating Aoife, that his poor little male brain just didn't have any space left to consider more intrigue.

Cathy pulled in her stomach and examined her

reflection one last time in the full-length mirror. She admired the way the glimmering Lycra outlined her lower ribs. One advantage of all this worry, she thought, was that it had caused her to lose weight – soon she'd be able to rival any teenage catwalk model. As she walked into the ballroom and took her place at the top table beside her mother, she couldn't resist a glance in the direction of Danny's table and was pleased to see Aoife in place beside Peter. It amused her to think that Maeve had no idea what was going on.

After the meal, Maeve got up to go to the ladies' and Andrea followed. They returned via the bar so they could stop and talk.

"Is that Aoife really the same girl who was doing those beauty-salon articles with Cathy Houlihan?" Maeve asked.

"Yes, that's her alright. I wonder how she met Peter."

"You must have missed the story – everyone else at the table heard it about three times," Maeve groaned.

"I'm afraid I tend to tune out when Peter starts on one of his sagas. So, did Cathy introduce them?"

"Give me lessons in tuning out from Peter," Maeve laughed. "It could come in handy at work." Then she added somewhat sombrely: "Although, maybe I've been tuning out a bit too much. I should be listening in more to what he says."

"Listen?" Andrea sniffed. "And die of boredom? Whatever for?"

"I get the feeling he's up to something. But nothing to worry about." Maeve wasn't ready to answer Andrea's questions on office politics until she was sure of how things stood between her and Danny. "So, anyway, the tale of Peter meeting the beautiful Irish colleen: Cathy and Aoife were having lunch in Habitat, he happened to wander up to the café after ordering a new toilet seat and Cathy introduced them."

Andrea frowned.

"Maybe I'm being paranoid," she said, "but the fact that a friend of Cathy's is dating a colleague of Danny's just after Cathy and Danny's break-up . . . well, it gives me the heebie-jeebies. Especially when I'm after Danny myself, and everyone knows that I'm not that journalist's favourite beautician!"

"Yes, you are being paranoid!" Maeve replied. "Besides, I don't think Cathy and Aoife are really that friendly – I never met her any of the times we were dragged out to meet Cathy's crowd. It was probably a work thing – they may just have got together to do that series of articles you refused to co-operate with."

"I didn't refuse to co-operate. I refused to be blackmailed. I offered free treatments for the review, but that wasn't enough for Cathy. She claimed she couldn't endorse an establishment unless she could come back regularly to ensure standards were being maintained." Andrea was red with indignation as she remembered.

"But you did say that Aoife was really nice the time she came back and apologised," Maeve pointed out, "although she asked you not to tell Cathy, for some reason."

"I suppose so," Andrea agreed reluctantly. "Besides, the poor girl deserves our sympathy – look who she's going out with! Come on – we've hidden here for long enough, let's go back and join the party."

When they returned, Peter and Aoife were missing. The O'Callaghans were talking to some friends at the next table and Danny and Fintan were in deep conversation with Pascale. Maeve had no choice but to resume her seat next to Jean-Paul. The band was just starting up, and he took advantage of the background noise to lean across and talk to her.

"You are shocked, I think, that I bring my wife tonight?"

"Not at all, Jean-Paul, I'm here with my husband after all." She longed to make some sarcastic comment about his companion in April, but wasn't quick enough. Danny and Pascale turned to them, to share their conversation.

"I was just asking Pascale why she had never come to Ireland before," Danny said. "She's loved her stay so far – it's a shame she hadn't made it over before now."

Maeve hoped her embarrassment didn't show on her face. Suddenly she hated Jean-Paul for putting her in this position. She glanced at him, but he was quite oblivious to her distress.

"Pascale does not like to leave the children, and she finds my business travel so boring. Is that not true, cherie?" He smiled. "Of course, if she had met tonight's company before now, perhaps she would have a different opinion."

"How old are your children?" Andrea cut in. She could see that Maeve was almost having trouble breathing, so great was her effort to keep a neutral face.

The conversation returned to the safe topic of children until the group split up and went their own way around the room, mingling.

Before long Andrea caught up with Maeve again, and asked, "Is LBS doing any business with Brewer's auctioneers at the moment?"

"No, and we never have to my knowledge. Why?"

"It's just that Peter has been sitting at the bar with Malcolm Brewer for the last half hour."

"Well, maybe they're just chatting, discussing holiday plans or something," Maeve replied, irritated. She wanted a night off from worrying about what Peter might or might not be up to.

"Malcolm never wastes time on chat that won't earn him money or get him laid. Besides, he bought Peter a drink. I looked around for a journalist, but they're like buses, never around when you need them."

"Is it so unusual that this Malcolm guy would be sitting at the bar, buying someone a drink?"

"Very unusual," Andrea answered, "especially when they're foreign, and therefore unlikely to be entering the housing market."

Suddenly alarm bells began to sound in Maeve's head. "How well do you know this Brewer?"

"He went to school with my brothers. Not in the

same year as any of them, but he played rugby, so I saw a fair amount of him." Andrea had been a rugby groupie in her day. "I tended to steer clear of him though, he's a bit of a groper – 'The Octopus', we used to call him."

"Any chance you'd be able to find out, discreetly, what he and Peter were talking about? *Very* discreetly, in such a way that it doesn't sound like you're actually trying to find out?"

"Consider it done." Andrea's eyes brightened to the challenge. Information was her stock in trade. She looked into the bar and saw Peter stand up and shake hands with the other man. He left by the other door.

"That's my cue!" Andrea said, making towards Malcolm Brewer. Maeve followed her with her eyes. She was beginning to regret suggesting this course of action. She watched as Andrea touched Brewer on the shoulder and saw his face light up as he recognised her. His eyes roved up and down her body and Maeve could watch no more.

"Malcolm!" Andrea gushed. "Has that awful American left for good or do you need rescuing? When I came past half an hour ago, he'd just trapped you, and you're still here now. You poor darling, was it awful?"

"Oh he's not too bad really." Malcolm spoke with his 'reasonable man of the world' tone. "I was discussing some potential business with him actually."

"Business?" Andrea fluttered her eyelids – this was going to be too easy. "What could you possibly be trying to buy or sell from him? Of course you could sell sand to the Arabs, or in this case oil to the Texans!" She laughed musically at her own joke.

"He's thinking of settling in Ireland, and his girlfriend suggested he talk to me as I work mainly in the area he's interested in. He's not sure yet if he wants to buy or rent, but we handle both so we'd be ideal for him. But enough talk of Peter – how are you, Andrea? Can I buy you a drink?"

"Well, maybe a quick one, Malcolm, as long as Ciara doesn't mind." Ciara was Malcolm's long-suffering fiancée. They had been engaged for three years, with no sign of a date being set. By all accounts, Malcolm was reluctant to give up his outside interests.

"And what about you, Andrea, do you have to rush back to anyone?"

"I'm here with Danny Breslin tonight," Andrea said, trying to make it sound as if she was 'with' Danny, without actually saying it. Not that being attached would make her any less attractive to the lecherous auctioneer; in fact the reverse was probably true.

"And are all the rumours about Danny true?" Malcolm asked eagerly as he leaned closer. Andrea knew it wasn't her just cleavage he was interested in. "Is he really in for a huge windfall when he sells out to the Yanks? I tried to get something out of that Peter guy, but he plays his cards too close to his chest."

"Now you know me, Malcolm, I never had a head for business." Andrea laughed her girlie laugh and flicked the hair off her face. "It's hard enough for me to keep track of my own income and expenditure without worrying about the high finance of the city." She continued in this vein, parting with no information, but at the same time learning nothing new until she knocked back the last of her white wine.

As she walked back into the ballroom a hand gripped her arm and Danny pulled her towards him.

"Where have you been hiding?" he asked with a grin, leaning in towards her and putting an arm around her waist. "I've been looking for you for ages."

His face was lit by a warm smile and Andrea was annoyed to feel her knees weaken and her heart quicken as she felt the warmth of his body. Was this a new turn in their relationship? She was suddenly tongue-tied, terrified of saying anything to spoil the moment. How many times had she dreamed of this moment, and how many bright, witty answers had she rehearsed? All ten thousand of them failed her.

"I was just having a drink with a friend of my brother's," she said. "You seemed to be tied up networking, so I thought I'd better give you some space."

"I hope you don't think I've been neglecting you. Come on, let's dance."

Danny led her on to the dance-floor, where the band was halfway through a slow set. As they danced, he pulled her close, almost possessively, and whispered, "I could dance all night with you, do you know that?"

She felt as happy, with her stomach as fluttery, as a teenager just before her first kiss. This was ridiculous, Andrea told herself sternly, she was in her thirties and well used to men sweet-talking her, why should she be in such agony of excitement, just because it was Danny?

"It's nice to be dancing with someone tall for a change. I'm used to ending up with a crick in my neck after the first song," he explained, rather spoiling the romantic effect of his compliment by referring to his previous five years slow-dancing with Cathy. Not that Andrea cared. As long as he kept holding her, their two bodies swaying together in this so public of embraces, Danny could discuss the likely outcome of tomorrow's football and she would nod in agreement.

She lowered her head to his shoulder and was rewarded by one of his arms travelling down, to the small of her back, to pull her closer. The music stopped, the other dancers applauded gently and Andrea felt cheated as Danny moved away from her and began to clap. There was an announcement about the musicians taking a break, but she hardly heard it. She moved as if in a trance, back to the table, unsure she would have found the way if Danny were not propelling her gently along. She sat down with relief and beamed at him. He remained standing and leaned towards her to talk. Closer than he needed to now that the music had stopped.

"Don't go anywhere, I'm just going to get some drinks. You still on the white wine?"

Andrea nodded helplessly and Danny smiled.

"Back in a second."

He seemed to be gazing almost past her but, as he left, he squeezed her shoulder gently. The touch was casual, but so intimate that Andrea felt sure she had missed some vital step in their courtship, and that things had moved on without her noticing. For some reason, she felt drawn to look over her shoulder, in the direction Danny had been looking. She went cold. Cathy Houlihan looked away just too late to avoid meeting Andrea's gaze. Their eyes locked for a fraction of a second and Andrea could feel the hostility directed towards her as an almost physical force. She looked down at her hands, fiddling with the strap of her evening bag. She had to get out of this room, now! She saw Maeve and made her way across to her.

"Maeve, if you see Danny, would you tell him I had to leave in a hurry. I've got the most blinding migraine."

"Andrea, you don't suffer from migraine."

Maeve looked at her friend with concern. Andrea looked unhealthily pale, except for two bright red patches on her cheeks, and her eyes looked suspiciously bright.

"Just tell him, would you?" She pushed her way past Maeve, towards the hotel lobby.

"Andrea, wait!" Maeve called after her, and caught up. "If your migraine's that bad, you could get one of those dizzy spells before you get home. I'm going with you."

She said this for the benefit of Peter, who had somehow materialised at their side.

"I'll meet you at the cloakroom," Maeve continued. "I'm just going to tell Fintan what's happening. Now go!"

Maeve turned to Peter and smiled sweetly.

"Peter, I'm going to have to see Andrea home. Could you apologise to the Thiebauds and the O'Callaghans for me? I'll get Fintan to tell Danny what's happening."

She found Andrea sitting in the lobby near the cloakroom. Her coat was on her knees, and she was staring at some point in infinity. Maeve retrieved her own jacket and they set out on foot.

They walked in silence for the twenty minutes it took to reach Andrea's flat. Once inside, she collapsed into an armchair like a rag-doll.

"Thanks for seeing me home, Maeve, but I'm fine now, you don't need to stay."

"Well, I've nowhere else to go in a hurry and I told Fintan you might need me to stay the night."

"What on earth gave you that idea?" Andrea snapped irritably. "I can look after myself, thank you very much."

Smarting at Andrea's dismissive tone, Maeve was nonetheless relieved that she had at least roused her friend from a mood of seeming indifference to everything. She took off her jacket, and went into the galley kitchen to put on a kettle. "You said you were ill," she said calmly, "and I've never seen you in this state before. If you're not sick, then you've been really upset by something. You don't have to tell me what's wrong, but I'm not leaving until I'm sure you're alright." Maeve clattered mugs around the kitchen to stake a territorial claim. "Tea or coffee?"

"I'll have coffee," Andrea answered with a weak grin. "Although I shouldn't really, considering I've got migraine."

"How on earth did you decide on migraine anyway? What's wrong with a headache, a sick stomach, typhoid or bubonic plague as an excuse?"

"It was the first thing that came to my head," Andrea said sheepishly. "My mother's suffered from migraine all her life, and it's served her well . . . Oh God, Maeve, do you think people will fall for the migraine thing?" Suddenly she was worried that people might think she was running away. Which of course she was.

"Definitely," Maeve reassured her. "When I explained to Fintan what was happening, I told him to emphasise that this has happened before and that migraine can strike you like a bolt out of the blue."

"How good is he at lying?" Andrea asked warily.

"Lousy. But it's okay," Maeve added quickly, when she saw Andrea's expression of alarm. "Fintan doesn't know he's lying, not really. I told him it was years since you had one of these attacks, and although he suspects something, I know he'll cover just fine." Maeve didn't tell Andrea about Fintan's resigned 'I knew this kind of thing was bound to happen' expression as she told him she would be leaving with Andrea. Although she wished she were at home with him now, making up after yesterday's disagreement, a secret, ashamed part of her, was relieved to put it off till another time.

Maeve brought the coffee and a packet of Hobnobs into Andrea's living-room. "Start tucking into those while I get the milk."

They sat for a while, munching biscuits and slurping hot coffee to break the silence. Eventually Andrea spoke.

"I don't think I'll ever be able to face Danny Breslin again; I feel like such a fool." She stared at the brown liquid in her mug, searching for inspiration. "I should have known better than to believe in fairytale endings. I mean how could he suddenly have moved from indifferent friendship to romantic intention in the space of half an hour? I should have known there was a more realistic explanation." She told Maeve all about the dance, and the way Danny suddenly seemed all possessive of her.

"And this is bad. Why?" Maeve was confused. "I've listened to you moan for the last few months about how you never seem to be getting through to Danny, that you don't seem to be able to get beyond the level of friendship you've had for the past ten years. And when he acts more than a little interested, you flee across the city under cover of darkness, pleading migraine. Have I missed something obvious here?"

"It was all an act. He was only acting."

"How can you be so sure?"

"When we left the dance floor," Andrea explained, "and got back to the table, and Danny was standing so close to me, touching me . . . I thought I imagined him looking over my shoulder." She stopped, unable to continue.

"Maybe something, or someone, caught his eye. You can hardly write him off for one little glance at the wrong moment," Maeve offered.

"It was Cathy. He was looking at Cathy. I saw her looking at us."

"Well, if Cathy came into his line of sight," Maeve argued, "it would be hard not to look at her. She was lit up like a Christmas tree in that dress."

"Don't you see?" Andrea said in exasperation. "She was watching us the whole time. And Danny must have known it. The whispers, the touches, the dance – it was all for her benefit; he couldn't resist looking at her to see how she took it. And I went along with it like a fool." Andrea stood and kicked off her shoes, then she turned to Maeve, hands on her hips. "The most annoying thing is – if Danny had only told me he wanted to rub Cathy's nose in it, I'd have given an Oscar-winning performance. I'd have been all over him like a rash. But he didn't, he used me, and I thought he was serious." She was pacing around the room now. "And do you know what the worst thing was?"

Maeve shook her head, stunned into silence.

"He must have been sure enough of me to know he could pull it off. He must have realised how I feel about him, and he chose to wait until now to do something about it. When he knew Cathy was watching."

Maeve went quiet, choosing her words carefully. When she spoke at last, it was cautiously.

"You've known Danny forever. You've been close friends for the past ten years. Do you honestly think he's capable of doing something like that to you?"

"If you'd asked me that two hours ago," Andrea answered wearily, "I'd have said no, not in a million years. But I know what I saw. And you have to admit he's taken this whole split from Cathy very calmly –

and that's not like him. Maybe he was just waiting for his chance to get back at her."

"If that was his plan," Maeve insisted, "do you not think there were plenty of other people he could have asked to the dance tonight, rather than a friend he risked hurting?"

"I don't know. Maybe he didn't set out with a plan in mind, but when he saw Cathy watching him, he couldn't resist it. What do you think, Maeve? You know him as well as I do, if not better."

Maeve wasn't sure what to say. She was sure that Danny hadn't set out this evening to use or hurt Andrea. But could she honestly say he couldn't have done it out of stupidity and total insensitivity? With all the banter about Cathy over the past few months, he might have assumed Andrea would know what he was at. Or it could have been a spur of the moment thing. Then there was the possibility that Andrea had read the situation all wrong, and Danny was genuine in his display of attraction. This was the scenario Maeve decided to put to her friend.

"You know, we could be over-analysing this. Danny is a man after all – a simple creature by nature. Maybe the only reason he was acting as if he fancied you was . . . because he does! And it took a few drinks and a romantic slow set for him to pluck up the courage to show it."

For a moment Andrea clung to this hope, then the spark disappeared from her eye and she seemed to sink into even deeper despondency.

"I wish I could fool myself into believing that. Oh, God how embarrassing! While I was on the dance-floor with him, and afterwards, for those few moments before I saw him looking at Cathy, I did believe it. And I'm sure he knew it too."

"Oh come on, how would he have known?"

Andrea looked at Maeve as if she was an idiot. She had the grace to blush. "Well, maybe he'll think you saw Cathy too, and were playing along."

"So at least now you admit that's the most likely explanation for his behaviour tonight." Andrea found no joy in her victory.

"I didn't say that. To be honest I don't know what to believe. I may as well let you know, Danny's been behaving really strangely lately, so I suppose anything's possible. But to treat you like that . . . well, I really don't know . . ."

"What do you mean he's been behaving really strangely?"

Maeve had no choice but to tell her friend the whole story of what had been going on at LBS. Andrea looked horrified.

"Danny's been keeping you in the dark at work? Wow, he really has lost his marbles, hasn't he? You'd have thought his sense of enlightened self-interest would have kicked in long before now – he knows he can't run the place without you. Now I understand why you were so interested in Peter's movements."

Maeve was glad she had told Andrea. Apart from being able to share her fears, her friend was so indignant that she seemed to have forgotten her own woes.

"Incidentally, I didn't get much of interest out of Malcolm. He seemed to think that Peter was planning on staying in Ireland, and interested in property in the Dundrum area." Andrea saw Maeve's look of shock. "Or maybe that is relevant? But why on earth, even if Peter were planning on staying in this backward, godforsaken country, where you can't even get CNN, would he be interested in Dundrum? I'd have thought he was much more your trendy-apartment-in-town type.'

"Dundrum would be the perfect place to commute to Sandyford from." Maeve had already explained to Andrea about the new office and the possibility that operations would be split between the two sites. "I had kind of hoped that I could arrange to spend most of my working week based in Sandyford. It would be much closer home and would cut my commuting time right down. I might even get home for lunch the odd day to see the kids."

"Did you tell Danny what you wanted?"

"No, as I said, when the suggestion came from Ofiscom that we might need more office space, I suggested Sandyford, but I've heard nothing since. I didn't even know if we were going to split the operation, or move lock stock and barrel to a new location."

The two women talked on until Fintan phoned, and arranged to pick up Maeve. They exhausted all possible conspiracy theories and finally settled on the only plausible explanation: Peter Fisch was an alien who'd come to steal Maeve's job, and then move on to destroy the world computer industry in order to facilitate an alien invasion. And Danny was having a mid-life crisis, exacerbated by radiation from Peter's Mother Ship.

Their humour was a poor attempt at covering over Andrea's sense of despair and the panic that had overtaken Maeve.

CHAPTER 33

The date of the merger passed although the official launch of the new company wasn't due until the big party at the end of August. Maeve was getting more and more worried about what was going on between Peter and Danny. They were still spending a lot of time locked up in Danny's office.

Andrea had decided that now would be a good time to take the holiday she'd been promising herself. So, before Danny could come calling at her door to check on her migraine, she disappeared off to visit her brother in the Cayman Islands, leaving Maeve with no one to confide in. Fintan was still communicating with Maeve in monosyllables and she couldn't figure out why. She knew they ought to sit down and sort it out, but she hardly ever saw him any more. He spent half his time in Courtown and, even when he was home, if Maeve finished work early Fintan would make the most of her being home to research and write his *Money Matters* review. As soon as Maeve walked in the door, Fintan disappeared into the study. He had also taken to eating with the children. Because he couldn't be sure what time Maeve was going to get in, he claimed it made more sense to eat early than have his stomach grumbling till all hours. And although she had to admit it made sense, Maeve missed their late-night dinners with a glass of wine.

They were living parallel lives. At night Maeve missed his long, comforting body in the bed beside her as he had taken to working until late on *Money Matters* and she was usually asleep by the time he came up. But, during the day, she appreciated the new smooth pattern to their lives, which allowed her to concentrate on her job and spend whatever time she could with the kids.

And Fintan expected nothing of Maeve at the moment. He must have realised what stress she was under and was doing his best to alleviate it wherever he could, but she worried that it was driving a wedge between them. She was glad that, now the merger was through, everything would soon settle back to normal, and Fintan would return to work. She couldn't help feeling that part of their problem was down to his missing his job. Despite everything, Maeve couldn't imagine ever stopping work, and she guessed Fintan was feeling the strain.

The week before the launch party Maeve asked Fintan if there was any possibility that his parents could keep the kids in Courtown for the Saturday night. They had spent so much of the summer there that it made more sense than trying to organise a baby-sitter.

"Why do we need a baby-sitter?" he asked.

"For Saturday night. The launch party?" Maeve wondered had Fintan forgotten about it or was he being deliberately obtuse.

"But surely you don't need me at the party," Fintan answered. "This is your night of glory. Enjoy it – I'd just get in your way." He turned away from her and began to busy himself with folding towels.

She stared at him in disbelief. Had Fintan come to resent the company she worked for so much that he wouldn't even attend one of its functions with her?

Ciaran appeared at the kitchen door in his pyjamas, holding a dog-eared book of favourite fairytales under his arm.

"Mummy, you said you'd read me a story!"

"I'm talking to Daddy, Ciaran," Maeve said gently. "Go back upstairs and I'll be up with you in a moment."

"You did promise him a story, Maeve," Fintan said in an expressionless voice, "but if you're too busy I can do it."

"Of course I'll read his story," Maeve sighed, "but I need to talk to you first."

"I'll still be here when you get down," Fintan pointed out reasonably. "Ciaran might have fallen asleep by the time you get to him. Although the thrill of having Mummy at home during the week to read his story should be enough to keep him awake."

Fintan folded the last towel, picked up the pile and moved past Maeve toward the stairs. She stood motionless in the kitchen, shivering despite the warmth of the evening.

"Mummy, Mummy, *Mummy!*" Ciaran yelled from upstairs.

"Coming, honey!" She finally roused herself.

While she was reading a tale about dragons and witches, Fintan poked his head around the door of the boy's room.

"I'm just going to pop over to Hazel's. I said I would let her see the next issue of *Money Matters* before I send it off to print and this evening's the most practical time."

"But you said . . ." Maeve gasped at his retreating back.

"Won't be long. Bye!" Fintan called from the bottom of the stairs. Then he was out the door before Maeve could catch her breath.

"Will you finish my story now?" Ciaran asked with huge worried eyes.

"What? Oh yes, of course, where was I?" Maeve hugged him and tried to chase away the fear at the back of her mind. She knew the kids could pick up on things like that.

Somehow she finished the story, and got back downstairs before bursting into tears. What did he mean he wasn't coming to the launch party? She'd been talking about this for months and at the beginning Fintan had even been quite encouraging about it.

Then she dried her eyes quickly and decided it was a just silly disagreement that she'd sort out as soon as he got home.

Maeve tried to call Andrea who, although she had extended her stay in the Cayman Islands and had experienced some difficulty getting a flight home, was due home this week. There was no answer. Then she nearly dialled her mother, but what could she say?

I'm having a row with Fintan, I don't know what it's about, but it's probably to do with the amount of time I'm spending at work. She could hear Anna's silent 'I told you so' without even talking to her. She stared at the phone for a few moments longer, then jumped when it rang.

"Hello? Oh hi, Hazel. No, Fintan's not here. He's on his way over to your house."

"With *Money Matters*?" Hazel asked. "Thank God for that. I was afraid we wouldn't have this issue out on time and I'd have to face a whole load of smug faces at the next management meeting. I should have known Fintan wouldn't let me down."

"Always punctual. You know Fintan," Maeve agreed, feeling uncomfortably as though she were evaluating a junior member of staff for promotion.

"I'd say you'll be glad to see the back of that merger," Hazel said next. "Fintan tells me you've been working all sorts of hours, you must be exhausted. And what with him doing this work for me, you must hardly ever get any time to yourselves anymore."

Maeve was about to make reassuring noises and say

that everything was fine, when she realised that not only were things not fine, but that she had no idea how much this woman, a woman she hardly knew, had been told about her marriage. She was trying to think of something to say when Hazel continued.

"Although of course, I have to say, I was really surprised at the change in Fintan. He loves this whole stay-at-home Dad business, doesn't he? To hear him talking about sleep routines, walks in the park and family mealtimes, would almost make me broody again." Hazel laughed out loud. "Would you listen to me? And me with my childbearing years so far behind me . . . Oh there's Fintan now, I can just see him pulling up. Bye Maeve. Talk to you again sometime. And do try to make things a bit more difficult for Fintan at home. I'm not sure I like the way he changes the subject every time I mention him coming back to work for me full-time."

Maeve stared at the silent phone in her hand until an interrupted dialling tone made her drop it back on its cradle as though it was hot.

Something didn't make sense to her, but she was too tired to try to figure out what. She shook her head and walked resolutely into the study. She wasn't going to sit around worrying until Fintan returned. The house was quiet – she would work on proposals for new clients.

Several proposals later she stood up to switch on a light and rubbed her eyes with the strain of staring at the computer screen. She was surprised at how dark it was outside and glanced with annoyance at her watch.

Fintan had said he wouldn't be long. She went into the kitchen to make a cup of tea, then heard his key in the lock.

"I'm just putting the kettle on. Can I make you something?" she called out when he pushed open the door.

"No thanks, I'm fine," he said automatically. Then changed his mind. "Maybe if you're making a pot of tea, I'll have a cup, please."

"What did Hazel think of the review? I bet she liked it."

They were being very polite to each other.

"Fine, just a few changes."

Fintan leaned up against the work surface and watched Maeve move around the kitchen.

"Did Hazel have any news?" Maeve asked. "You were gone a long time. Catching up on office gossip?"

"Not really. We talked about the review for a while then Gerry insisted I try one of those gourmet beers he's started drinking. They're quite good, we'll have to get some."

The silence crackled between them for a moment, then the kettle began to hum.

"I'll get the mugs," Fintan offered in a hurry.

"I'll have my big yellow one; I could do with a long drink."

Fintan reached into the cupboard and got out the huge mug decorated with chickens and daffodils. It had been a Mother's Day present from Ciaran, which Fintan had insisted he chose himself.

"Maeve . . ." Fintan said carefully, "if you really want me to, I'll come to the launch party with you." He was obviously making a huge effort.

"No, you're probably right, you'd be bored out of your skull," Maeve admitted and instantly wished she hadn't. She really wanted him there.

"Okay, so." He half-smiled with relief. "The weather forecast's good for the weekend, so I think I'll take the kids down to Courtown anyway. It'll probably be the last chance before Ciaran starts school. Do you think you can make it down on Sunday?"

"I doubt it. The crowd over from Texas will be in town for the whole week. I can't really go vanishing, just in case."

"In case of what?"

"I don't know, but these guys don't exactly work nine to five, Monday to Friday."

"I'd noticed," Fintan snapped.

"And while they're here," Maeve continued as if there had been no interruption, "they might not take too kindly to my not being available. Besides, Peter will make himself all too available and I don't want to take my eye off him. Especially with Joe MacPherson around."

MacPherson was Ofiscom's business-development manager and therefore the person from the Texan parent company that LBS would have to work closest with once they began to implement their expansion plans. He was due to arrive in Dublin the day before the launch party and had a series of meetings scheduled with LBS staff the following week.

"Now you're sounding paranoid again. What exactly do you think Peter's up to?" Fintan asked.

"I wish I knew. He and Danny are preparing a presentation for Joe next Tuesday, and if I offer to help, Danny just tells me he's got everything under control."

"So he probably has. Don't forget, Danny might be feeling a bit vulnerable at the moment. It's not his company any more. He may feel he has to justify his salary, and he can't do that with you looking over his shoulder all the time." Fintan picked up his mug of tea. "I'd really better get down to work on these revisions. Have you finished with the computer?"

"Just let me update my laptop, and it's all yours."

Maeve knew the conversation was closed.

Ten minutes later, she sat on the bed and wondered why Fintan kept closing down on her like that. Anytime they talked it was the same. Was she really so obsessed with work that she was driving him away? But she couldn't even get him to talk about non-work-related things. On Sunday, she had tried to raise the subject of how he was finding his role as house-husband. She had been feeling guilty that in the six weeks since he had given up work they hadn't really discussed it at length. Fintan gave her a few non-committal comments and changed the subject. At the time Maeve took it as meaning that he didn't really enjoy it but wasn't going to say anything, but tonight Hazel had told her how much Fintan loved being at home.

She took her mug downstairs to put it in the dishwasher and put her head through the door of the study where Fintan was working. She admired the speed at which he filled the screen with words. Although Maeve could type much faster than his two-finger technique she could never form sentences, paragraphs or documents with Fintan's fluency. He didn't even work from notes or rough drafts. Once he had a concept clear in his mind, he had no trouble translating it into easy-to-read text. She envied him that.

"Fintan . . ." she said softly.

"Hmm . . ." came the reply.

"We are okay, aren't we?"

"Yeah, sure." He didn't look up.

"I mean we're not having problems or anything, are we?"

For a moment he didn't move. Then he twisted round the swivel-chair to face her.

"I don't know. What do you think?" All trace of emotion was missing from his voice. His face was tense, expectant.

"It's just work, isn't it? I mean we'll have more time to ourselves soon. Everything will get back to normal soon, won't it?" she pleaded.

For a moment Fintan's face crumpled with what looked like disappointment, but he recovered quickly and turned back to his work.

"Of course. I'm sure you're right. We're under a lot of pressure at the moment."

He hammered at the keyboard and didn't seem to notice that Maeve stood for an age at the door, staring at his back, before trudging back upstairs.

As she undressed for bed, Maeve found herself once again in front of the full-length mirror. She seemed to be consulting it more often than usual lately. She tried to find some fault with herself – had she put on a few pounds lately? But Fintan had never worried about her weight. In fact she was pretty sure he was genuine when he said he preferred her not to diet. So why had they not slept together in so long? Anytime she asked that question she found it impossible to ignore James' revelation. Of course Fintan didn't know about it, but maybe she was so confused by it that she was giving off insecure vibes? Or maybe Fintan had somehow guessed that James was gay, and this had somehow coloured his view of Maeve. No matter how often she told herself she was being ridiculous, the fear returned. It was as if her whole self-image was in doubt.

Her mind returned to a weekend over ten years ago, before she and James broke up. They were going away for what Maeve had decided was to be their first 'dirty weekend'. After more than four years she reckoned it was about time and booked them into in a small anonymous tourist hotel in West Cork. It was a disaster. James told her she wasn't ready to sleep with him and that he wasn't going to push her into something she might regret later. She seethed with frustration, but felt strangely relieved. It had been the beginning of the end for them and, when they finally split up, Maeve had wondered if she would always repel men. Was there something wrong with her?

It was the one thing she couldn't forgive James for.

He had let her believe, in the months of heartbreak after they broke up, that she was at fault.

Now, as she looked back, Maeve wondered if it was this uncertainty that had pushed her so enthusiastically into Fintan's arms a few short months later. She hated herself for even thinking like that, but wondered was she unconsciously pushing him away now. As she stared into the mirror she knew that no matter what they had said earlier, their marriage was in trouble. And much as Maeve would have liked to blame work, she knew she was missing something.

CHAPTER 34

On Saturday night, Maeve stood in the middle of a crowded room, utterly alone. Although she had organised the whole event, Danny and Joe MacPherson were understandably hogging the limelight. She was glad she had opted for a restaurant for the cocktail party rather than a large hotel. It restricted the guest list, and reduced the number of people she had to be polite to. All she wanted to do was get through the night.

"Why are you so serious, Maeve?"

Jean-Paul Thiebaud's rolling French rrr's grated on Maeve's nerves. How did he manage to be in Dublin every time there was free drink on offer? He was such a big client now that it was impossible not to invite him.

"And where is your husband tonight?" Jean-Paul asked, making the question sound like an accusation.

"With the children, on a seaside holiday," Maeve answered. "Ciaran will be starting school in a couple of weeks, so this is their last chance. I haven't seen Pascale, is she here?"

"*Non.* She decided not to make the journey this time. Like your husband, she must get the children ready for school."

Again Maeve felt she was being measured up and found wanting.

"So, we will have to amuse ourselves tonight," he continued. "Your glass is empty; permit me to get you another drink."

Before she could object, Jean-Paul stopped a waiter and, draining his own glass in a way she felt showed a lack of respect for good champagne uncharacteristic of a Frenchman, he produced two new drinks with a flourish.

"I see Danny is enjoying his new-found wealth." Jean-Paul pointed to the label on the champagne bottle, a good vintage.

"I think he is making the most of the fact that Ofiscom's picking up the bill for this one," Maeve laughed.

She was aware that her mood was improving rapidly with the amount of alcohol she consumed and that she would have to be careful. She moved on to circulate with other guests.

Maeve wished Andrea were here. But although Andrea was back in Dublin since yesterday, her flight had been via several other European cities and she was exhausted.

"Maeve, finally I've caught up with you. You're very popular," a familiar voice drawled. "You've done us proud here. I gather most of this is your doing."

She turned to face the tall, smiling man in a pale suit. He was slim, and his clothes hung loosely on him, but it had the effect of making him look as if he had dressed deliberately casually. The pale suit would have looked wrong on any other man as fair as he was, but he had such an air of confidence that he could carry it off.

"We had a very good PR firm, thanks, Joe," Maeve replied.

Joe MacPherson looked around the room in admiration. He approved of the number of journalists present. He had spoken to most of them and was pleased to note that there was a good mix of business and society columnists present. He was a great believer in making a brand familiar in whatever way you could.

"I'm looking forward to Danny's presentation on Tuesday. Peter Fisch tells me they've come up with some interesting proposals for restructuring."

Maeve looked around nervously. Fortunately none of the other staff were within earshot.

"Whatever you do, don't mention restructuring. It's a dirty word at the moment," she explained in a low voice. "I assume you're talking about the new office space we're taking up in Sandyford? It should be ready by Christmas, but we haven't really come up with any formal plans yet on how to reorganise."

"Oh?" Joe looked surprised. "I'm sure Peter said that they had come up with a division which would suit everybody."

"Well, of course we have to consider his proposal, but like I said, nothing's been decided yet." Maeve tried to sound like she knew what Joe was talking about. Whatever her differences with Peter, she didn't want Texas to know that she didn't trust him. "So, Joe, will you see anything of Dublin while you're here?"

Maeve safely steered the subject away from sensitive topics, and chatted to her new boss for the next fifteen minutes. She liked Joe. He was easy to talk to and seemed genuinely interested in whatever she had to say. Before long he returned the conversation to LBS and was asking her opinion on a number of fairly safe topics. She enjoyed the conversation. She described how they had built up the company, especially in the last ten years since Danny had taken over. It was a subject she was passionate about. As Fintan was fond of saying, the company was her hobby as well as her work. And although Joe was familiar with most of the details from company documents, he liked to hear about the more human side of the story. When he was dragged away for a photo call, she was sorry to see him go.

"A penny for your thoughts, Maeve?" Peter appeared beside her. How long had he been standing listening, Maeve wondered, glad she had steered clear of any controversial topics.

"A penny, Peter? Talk may be cheap, but my thoughts are worth more." She cringed at how stupid that sounded and only hoped Peter had had as much to drink as she had.

"So, how do you find the new boss?" he asked.

"Danny's still officially our boss, Peter; at least he's

yours as long as you stay over here with LBS. But Joe's a lovely man. I had a long chat with him about the company. He was telling me all about your presentation on Tuesday."

Oh God, Maeve thought, why had she said that? She was too drunk to be playing games with The Fish right now. However, she had the satisfaction of seeing Peter pale slightly before dashing off in search of Danny to whisper urgently in his ear, only to be brushed off with irritation. Shortly afterwards, Danny came over to find her.

"Maeve, congratulations on a wonderful evening. The months of work you've put into this have really paid off."

"Don't thank me, you'll be picking up the bill from the PR company."

"Not me, the Great Bill-Payer in Texas. You have no idea what a relief it is not to be responsible for the finance of the company any longer. It's bad enough going to bed worrying about one mortgage – thirty-three is really pushing it."

Suddenly he sounded like the old Danny again.

"Well, I'd say there's a fair few substantially smaller mortgages since the share pay-out." Maeve smiled. "You must feel like Santa Claus!"

"Oh, come on now, Maeve. Credit where credit is due. You did most of the negotiation. You helped make me a very rich man. Cheers!" Danny clinked his glass unsteadily against hers. "You were talking to Joe for a long time. Anything interesting?"

"No, we were mainly talking about old company history. I was telling him about some of the colourful characters who helped make us great!"

"I just hope you didn't tell too many anecdotes about Dad!" Danny laughed. "The Americans believe eccentricity is hereditary! They'll have me down as a nutter!"

"Your dad was no nutter. Ahead of his time maybe, mildly eccentric in that he treated his staff like human beings, but no nutter. Besides, I never really worked with him. He'd virtually retired when I joined you."

"I keep forgetting that. It feels like you've been with us for years."

"Less of the *years* please, Breslin! You hired me, remember? And this was my first real job – you'd been around for centuries before then. Old man!"

"You're right. I am feeling old," Danny admitted. "Maybe it's time I took a step back and enjoyed some of the money I've just made."

"Very funny, Danny. You retire? You'd be bored stupid." Maeve didn't take him seriously.

"I know, but the past year has left me feeling exhausted. I haven't enjoyed the wheeling and dealing. I used to love coming into work each day. Now, well . . ."

"Give it six months, boss. Before you know it you'll be enjoying it again. We've all been under a lot of strain lately. Now that the merger's through, with more money behind us, and the opportunity to expand, we'll get a chance to concentrate on what really makes you tick, business development. Just promise me you won't rush into anything without talking to me first," she added, just in case he might be thinking about it.

"Since when have I ever made any decision which would affect this company without consulting you first?" he asked.

"I don't know, Danny. I get the feeling there's a lot going on that I don't know about. Take this presentation on Tuesday. What's that all about?" She hadn't intended bringing this up tonight, but as he'd raised the subject . . .

"Oh, don't worry about that. Peter's just trying to justify his existence over here, so he's come up with some proposals for reorganising the company once we're working from two sites. That's all they are though, proposals. He seems really to have fallen for Aoife in a big way, and wants to spend at least another year in Ireland. I'm just humouring him really. Don't worry about it. He said he'd give you a summary before the meeting so you can get a chance to go over it. So, if you want to make any points, you can be prepared."

Maeve had a feeling she would want to go over Peter's proposals with a fine-tooth comb. She was also fairly certain that she wouldn't get to see them until minutes before Tuesday's meeting.

"Maeve, you don't have to answer this if you don't have to . . ." Danny looked nervous, "but have I done something to offend Andrea? I've been trying to get in touch with her since that night in the Burlington. I know she went on holidays, but I can't believe she hasn't checked her messages. Not when she's away from the salon for that long."

"Maybe she's ringing the salon directly," Maeve suggested. She hadn't been expecting this. Danny had seen her dozens of times since that night and hadn't said anything. Did he know Andrea was home?

"I've left messages there too. I wish I could get in touch with her. I need to talk to her and I'm terrified I'll leave it too late."

"Too late for what, Danny?" Maeve was intrigued. Although her instincts told her not to get involved, Veuve Clicquot 1990 was telling her this was too good an opportunity to miss.

"You're a good friend of hers, aren't you?" Danny asked. "I mean you'd have a good enough idea of what's going on inside her head, wouldn't you?"

I'm also a good enough friend to know when to keep my mouth shut, Maeve didn't say. She merely nodded sympathetically at Danny to go on.

"Well, I thought I was really getting somewhere that night in the Burlington, but I think I may have scared her off. If she doesn't want to get involved, fair enough, but I don't want to lose her as a friend."

"I'm not sure what you're talking about, Danny," said Maeve cautiously, hoping he would elaborate.

"Promise me you won't repeat this, but my feelings for Andrea have moved beyond the mere platonic."

Only Danny could sound so Victorian in the middle of a room full of drunken businessmen, Maeve thought.

"I only really realised it for certain the night of the charity dinner," he continued. "I suppose seeing Cathy there, and discovering that I was well and truly over her. In fact I'd probably been over her long before we split up," he sighed. "Then I saw Andrea in the bar talking to a really good-looking guy, younger than me . . . I couldn't believe what I felt, Maeve . . ." He looked into the depths of his glass, leaving her wondering how many of them he'd consumed. "I totally panicked. I was afraid that I'd been neglecting her all evening, and I deserved it if she was picked up by someone else. I asked her to dance, and on the dance-floor I could have sworn . . . well . . . what do you think, Maeve? Do I stand a chance? You must know, you're her best friend." Danny was almost pleading.

"I haven't spoken to Andrea since the night in the Burlington either, Danny." Maeve crossed her fingers behind her back. "So I don't know what to say to you. Andrea isn't one for wearing her heart on her sleeve; she never tells me about things like that." He was a man, he'd fall for that. "All I can suggest is that you tell her how you feel, and see what happens."

"I couldn't, Maeve," Danny protested. "She left so fast that night that I even wondered if she suspected what I was thinking, and got out before I made a fool of myself. I don't want to lose her friendship."

"You've been friends for years, Danny. Besides, the reason she left so fast was that she was worried she was going to throw up." Maeve hoped Andrea would forgive her the exaggeration. "She gets terrible migraines."

"But why haven't I been able to contact her since?"

"I haven't been able to talk to her either." The fingers behind Maeve's back were now twisted into a tortured knot.

"Have you any idea when she might get back?"

Maeve hesitated. In the mood he was in now, if she sent Danny over to Andrea's he would fall at her feet, and hopefully they would live happily ever after. If he left it until he sobered up, he might chicken out. She took a decision.

"I'll try to ring her mother for you."

"I've tried that." He looked utterly dejected. "She says that Andrea's having trouble getting a flight so she's no idea when she'll get home."

"When did you last ring her?"

"A couple of days ago."

"Well, I'll ring her now," Maeve said. "I'll just go somewhere quiet." Danny seemed to be about to follow her, so Maeve added: "The ladies' room might be a good idea. I'll tell you how it goes when I get back."

"Andrea, Andrea, pick up, I know you're there!" Maeve hissed into her mobile phone in the sanctuary of the ladies' toilets. "Andrea, stop pissing about and pick up. Life or death!" The answering machine droned on about leaving a message after the beep. "Andrea!"

"Yes, Maeve, and this better be good! I've just drenched an expensive carpet to get to the phone."

"You always take the phone into the bathroom with you."

"Not when I'm screening. Now what do you want? If I stand here much longer I'll flood the flat downstairs."

"How do you feel about being at home? If someone like Danny were to drop by?"

There was silence at the other end of the phone. Then, "What have you told him, Maeve? You promised . . ."

"Relax, I haven't said anything. I'm phoning from the ladies' toilets. I said I was calling your mother to find out when you'd be home."

"Well, I'm not, not to Danny. I told you earlier how I felt about the prospect of seeing him again, and I haven't changed my mind. It'll be bad enough running into him socially without having to face him on his own."

"Give him a chance. I think you may have misread him that night. He's just spent the last twenty minutes trying to find out when you'd be getting home – he said he needed to talk to you."

"What else did he say?"

Maeve hesitated. She was tempted to tell Andrea exactly what Danny had said, but reckoned that if they both knew they were on similar wavelengths, it would take a lot of the tension out of their meeting. And all of the romance.

"Nothing." She said at last. "He just said it was important."

"It took him twenty minutes to ask when I was getting home?"

Andrea clearly suspected her friend was being less than one hundred percent forthcoming.

"You know Danny – he'd never come straight out and ask anything – it takes him ages to get round to it."

"So do you think I should admit to being home? Meet him tonight?" Andrea asked after a long pause.

The longing in her voice was audible and Maeve knew she had won.

"Definitely. Strike while the iron's hot and all that."

Maeve returned to Danny.

"Her mother says Andrea's at home!" she announced proudly. "That she got back yesterday and that she was completely exhausted and isn't answering the phone. So, it's up to you now."

"What do you think I should do?"

"I can't tell you what to do Danny, you know that. You and Andrea are two of my best friends and I can't get caught in the middle. However . . ." she added as he frowned with exasperation, "if it was me, I'd go for it!"

Danny looked around the crowded restaurant where his clients and colleagues were falling about in various stages of inebriation.

"How much longer do you think I need to stay here?"

"The photographers are gone, the journalists who are still here are probably too drunk to return any decent copy by now and the clients are pleasantly sozzled. This evening has served its function. You could always get a headache." Maeve nearly said a migraine. "I'll make sure everyone here is kept happy."

"Thanks Maeve, I owe you one."

"So, Maeve. Alone again?"

She jumped. She was standing near the window and hadn't heard Jean-Paul come up behind her.

"If I didn't know better, I'd say you were scaring all the men away."

"Maybe I am Jean-Paul. Maybe I am."

Now why had she said that? Watching Danny leave for his encounter with Andrea had left her all gooey inside. She wished Fintan were here to share the feeling with her. She wished she could leave this gathering and drive straight to Courtown.

"Your glass is empty again, Maeve." Jean-Paul tutted. "Irishmen have no idea how to treat their women. What can I get you?"

Maeve longed to say that she was nobody's woman or something cutting along those lines, but she was gasping and too lazy to go looking for a waiter.

"A mineral water would be lovely, thank you, Jean-Paul."

That would take him some time to find. The waiters' trays seemed to be loaded down with alcoholic beverages only. Was no one driving tonight?

Jean-Paul was back at her side rather too soon, touching her elbow possessively as he handed her the glass. Maeve made an effort to talk to him by asking about his children. They talked for a while about schools and holidays and the differences between France and Ireland, when suddenly Maeve became aware that he didn't seem to be listening to her at all, but staring at her in a daze.

"Is something the matter, Jean-Paul?"

"I can't help wondering how any man could let a woman as beautiful as you come alone to a gathering such as this." He smiled charmingly. "Your Fintan must be a very trusting man. I would be insane with jealousy to think of you in a room with all these men."

For the first time all evening, Maeve realised that most of the guests were indeed male.

"I don't think he has too much to worry about, Jean-Paul. I don't see queues of men lining up to steal me away. Now perhaps if I had the looks of your friend Sandrine, maybe then he would be here tonight."

What was she saying? If she was fishing for compliments, she was sure Jean-Paul would be happy to supply them. But the price tag might be a bit exorbitant. He surprised her by not rising to the bait.

"So why is Fintan not here? Truthfully?" he asked, his eyes appearing to look right into her mind. "I see I have shocked you. Apologies."

He drew back a little and Maeve realised how close to her he had been standing. She could feel the cool space he left behind.

"Pretend I said nothing," he continued. "Fintan is at the seaside with the children. *N'est ce pas*?"

"He didn't really want to come tonight," Maeve admitted at last. "A bit like Pascale, I suppose."

"She would have had to travel much further, and I am to be here for two weeks on this trip. If I remember correctly you live no more than two or three kilometres from here. Not quite a valid comparison. But it is none of my business, *non*?"

He was right; it was none of his business. But Maeve found herself confiding in him nonetheless. If only because his attention was focused entirely on her and it felt like a long time since she had felt so much the centre of someone's attention. Anyone's attention.

"I've been spending too much time at work lately and Fintan resents it. He offered to come tonight, but with such bad grace that I thought I would be more comfortable without him."

"And it is so unfair, is it not?"

"What?"

"That just because you are a woman, and he a man, he has the right to resent the time you spend at work."

"It's not like that at all." Maeve felt her anger rising. "He's right, I have been spending too much time working. All the changes the company's going through, having to keep old clients on board, keep growing . . . he's right, it has been a strain. But it'll get better soon. He'll be going back to work soon too. Everything will get back to normal." Who was she trying to convince?

"I just think he should be careful that he doesn't drive you away with all his resentment. A woman can not be expected to wait forever . . ." Jean-Paul left the sentence hanging and moved closer to Maeve again.

A flush rose through her. She looked around in panic and noticed that the room was emptying. Surely it was alright for her to leave too?

"It's getting late. I had better be going. I have a lot of work to do in the morning. Yes, even on a Sunday!" she added in response to his raised eyebrow. "Goodnight, Jean-Paul!"

She turned abruptly and hurried towards reception to ask them to book a taxi.

To her dismay, only a short while later, she saw Jean-Paul also approach reception and collect his coat.

"Still here, Maeve?" he asked when he noticed her. "I thought you had left."

"I'm still waiting for my taxi. It's a bad time of night. You're not hoping to get one at short notice, are you?"

"*Non,* I have a car and a driver on his way. One of the advantages of being here on business."

A large black car pulled into the car park as he spoke and a uniformed driver stepped out and made his way towards the door.

"Ah, here we are! But I insist on driving you home – you could be waiting all night for a taxi. I remember my last trip to Dublin."

He took Maeve's coat from her and almost forced her arm into the sleeve. She was too tired to resist. All she wanted to do was get home.

If the driver was surprised to be picking up an extra passenger, he didn't show it. After all, he was probably used to Jean-Paul by now. Maeve gave him her address and sank back into the comfortable seat. The car was enormous, so by sticking close to her door she was able to leave a safe distance between her and the too-charming Frenchman. She wondered why she had never noticed before tonight how good-looking he was. He had a face best described like the hero in some cheap romantic novel: sculpted features, strong jaw and dark hair. His eyes were a haunting dark almost navy blue, which seemed to draw you in if you looked at him for long enough. He had an athletic build, and obviously kept fit.

"Where on this road is the house, madam?" the driver asked.

"Next turning to the right, and to the end of the cul-de-sac." Maeve leaned forward to point out the house. It was the only one in total darkness. When she left it had still been bright and she hadn't thought of leaving a light on. If the rest of the family were home, the toilet and landing lights would at least throw some kind of welcoming glow into the night.

"Let me see you in safely, Maeve."

Before she could object, Jean-Paul was out of his door and around the car to open hers. The driver switched off the idling engine and leaned his head back on the headrest. Maeve stayed in the light of the car to search through her bag for her key, then led the way to the front door. Jean-Paul leaned into the car before closing the door. If he spoke to the driver, she didn't hear him.

She opened the door, then rushed in under the stairs to switch off the alarm within the fifteen seconds she was allowed. She took off her coat and was surprised to see that Jean-Paul had stepped into the hall. She flicked on the light and he blinked, dazzled. "Thank you for seeing me in. I think I'm safe now. No doubt I'll be seeing you in the course of the next two weeks. Those computers we ordered for you should get here on Monday, and I have a team of technicians lined up to get your systems up and running."

He didn't move, although Maeve imagined that the expression on his face changed from one of almost tenderness to careful neutrality. He studied her for a moment.

"You must always try to drive away those who would be your friends, Maeve," he said at last. "If you do this all your life, you will be very lonely." Jean-Paul spoke sadly, as though from personal experience.

"What kind of friendship were you looking for, Jean-Paul? The kind you have with Sandrine, your glamorous air-hostess? Your standards must be dropping, I'd hardly measure up." Maeve was surprised at her own bitterness. She sounded jealous of the other woman.

"Maeve, I do not see you like that. Although you are much more beautiful and sexy. No, wait, do not interrupt. You do not realise your own attractiveness – you drive a man crazy. No, I admire you, and I would like you as a friend. But I suspect my pride would take a battering if I were to proposition you. You are too in love with your husband. I am right?"

Maeve realised that she had been hoping he would 'proposition' her. She had wanted to turn him down, but at least feel wanted. And she would have turned him down, wouldn't she? At least she would have had the option.

Her eyes filled with tears.

"Maeve, Maeve, do not cry. I did not mean to upset you." He rushed over to comfort her. "What did I say? Can I help?"

Maeve wished he would go – she was on the verge

of a dangerous flood of emotion. Instead he touched her chin and lifted her face towards his own. She flinched away from the contact, but his eyes kept hers locked into his. Then he stood back, keeping eye contact.

"If you want to talk, I am here. No strings, as you say in English."

"I think it would be better if you left, Jean-Paul. I'm not sure I can cope with too much talking right now." To Maeve's horror, her eyes filled again. "You're right when you say I love my husband. I love him more than you can imagine."

"But . . .?"

"But nothing, I love him. Things are just difficult at the moment."

Was it the champagne, the lateness, the lonely empty house, or the fact that Jean-Paul genuinely seemed to care? Maeve heard herself tell him the whole story of the past six months. From losing her childminder, to Fintan giving up work, to discovering James was gay, and to the horrible, terrible cooling there had been between herself and Fintan.

"Maeve, listen to me." Jean-Paul lifted one of her hands and held it between his. "This is important. Whatever has happened has nothing to do with this old boyfriend of yours discovering he is gay. That is him, not you. You did not believe me when I said earlier that I thought you were beautiful, sexy? Well, it is true. You are so full of life, so enthusiastic, so . . . physical. You need not even try – you mesmerise any man who looks at you." Suddenly he looked embarrassed.

"Go on, this is doing me the world of good," Maeve joked weakly.

"I have made you smile again. Maybe I can claim some small measure of friendship?" He let go of her hand. "I can't begin to guess what has gone wrong between you and your husband. You may be right when you say it is work. If it is, do something before it is too late. But forget this James, the only way he could be affecting your marriage would be if Fintan were jealous of him. But as he is gay – no worries for him there." He buttoned up his coat. "I had better leave now, before my poor driver falls asleep. I will be needing him early in the morning again. Like you, I work tomorrow."

"Goodnight, Jean-Paul, and . . . thank you," Maeve said as she let him out the front door.

"There is nothing to thank me for, my friend." He lifted her hand and kissed it lightly.

"Thank you anyway, *mon ami*."

CHAPTER 35

Given the champagne of the previous night, Maeve felt a lot better than she should have on Sunday morning, or rather Sunday afternoon by the time she managed to drag herself from bed. She tried to phone Fintan and the children as soon as got up, but his phone was 'switched off, or out of range'. Finally, to drive away the depression that engulfed her each time the computerised voice denied her the comfort of their voices, she decided to phone Andrea.

As she began to dial the doorbell rang. Maeve cursed, crept into Ciaran's room to peep out the window, then let out a sigh of relief when she saw Andrea's red BMW in front of the house.

"Well? How did it go?" Maeve asked, "Last night, with Danny?"

Andrea stood on the doorstep looking tanned, healthy and relaxed. She was holding a flat parcel and a bottle in a bag.

"Are you going to let me in, or leave me standing on the doorstep?" Andrea pushed past Maeve, put down her bundle, gave her friend a huge hug, then stood back and examined her critically. "He's right; you *have* been working too hard. No tan, circles under your eyes and you haven't been eating properly – you could do with putting on some weight. Come on. Let's do something about the eating anyway. I assume you still shop at least? Is there anything in the house that would go down well with Pimms?" She waved in the direction of the kitchen.

"Is there any kind of food that *wouldn't* go down well with Pimms?" Maeve asked "But it's much too early to start drinking, even on a sunny day like this."

"Nonsense," Andrea replied. "I'm still working off Cayman Islands time. And if you drank even half the amount of champagne Danny did, your hangover won't even have started to kick in yet, so start drinking before it does."

By now Andrea was rooting through the cupboards looking for lemonade and food. "Pringles, three packets! How have you lost all that weight while I've been away?"

"They were on special offer, buy two get one free," Maeve said sheepishly. "Who could resist an offer like that? I thought I'd stock up for Christmas."

"Christmas!" Andrea harrumphed. "Even I couldn't come up with as deluded an excuse as that for binge-shopping. Okay, I'm all stocked up: lemonade, Pimms, jug. Which flavour Pringles do you want to bring out, or will we take all three?"

"How about the low-fat ones?"

"Yeah right! The low-fat ones," Andrea snorted with derision. "Come on! You grab a bowl of ice and I'll meet you in the garden."

She led the way out. Maeve was more than willing to relinquish control of her life for the next few hours. She switched on the oven and took a quiche out of the freezer. She emptied a bag of prepared salad into a large blue bowl, and shook croutons on top. They might as well make at least a token attempt to soak up the alcohol. With two large frosted glasses, and the bowl of ice her friend had ordered, Maeve followed her into the garden, dying to hear her news.

But first Andrea rushed back inside to bring out the flat parcel she had been carrying when she arrived. Inside it was a beautiful oil painting. It was about twelve inches by eight and showed a dark-skinned woman hanging washing along a fence, against a backdrop of a sapphire ocean. The white sheets she was struggling with seemed to jump off the canvas in the wind, and Maeve longed to reach out and hold them steady so the woman could finish pegging them in place.

"It's beautiful, Andrea. Really, it's too much. This must have cost a fortune! I love it." She continued to stare at the painting, gasping with delight as she spotted new details that caught her eye. A child playing on the sand, a brilliantly coloured bird taking flight, disturbed by the woman's activity.

"I thought you'd like it. It's by a local artist out there.

A very good-looking local artist, I might add." Andrea grinned wickedly. "I spent rather a lot of time in his studio. The artist was as soothing and exciting as his paintings. Very good therapy for a confused mind!"

"Come on, tell all! And me feeling so sorry for your broken heart that I had to go and send Danny over to you the moment you got back." Andrea was incorrigible!

"What happened on the Caymans will stay on the Caymans. Let me just say that I didn't get up to anything I'd be ashamed to tell my mother!" she said with a suspect giggle.

"Oh, alright. But at least tell me all about what happened when Danny called over last night."

"I can't, I'm sorry, but I just can't say another word."

"Why not? Did it not go well?" Maeve was alarmed.

"It went very well, but if I'm going to tell you the whole story, I don't want to be interrupted, and suddenly the smell of that quiche is making me hungry!"

"Quiche, Madame? Certainly Madame." Maeve stood up to go inside. "But may one ask first what did Madame's last slave die of?"

"Alcohol poisoning," Andrea replied, frowning at Maeve's untouched glass, "but there's no danger of you going the same way. You wimp!"

Maeve returned a few minutes later carrying a tray laden with the quiche, salad and plates. There were also two fresh glasses and a bottle of mineral water, which Andrea pointedly ignored as she helped herself to food.

"You could have warned me how absolutely

gorgeous Danny would be looking when he finally arrived at my door last night," she giggled between mouthfuls. "You didn't tell me that launch party was a formal affair. You know what men in tuxedos do to me, especially gorgeous hunks like him." She was almost salivating with the memory.

"I'm sure you didn't let it show."

"Are you joking? I had just spent the previous half-hour in front of the mirror perfecting my cute, tossed, just-out-of-bed look. And while I was at it I practised my 'Who the hell is calling at this time of night?' scowl. I had it so well rehearsed, I nearly scared him off completely. He was so apologetic standing there behind his petrol-station bunch of flowers and a box of chocolates. He looked like he was waiting to take me to the debs."

Andrea smiled at the memory.

"So you let him in, I presume?" Maeve finally prompted, to get the story going again.

"Hmm? What? Oh yes. Eventually. I let him stew on the doorstep for a minute or two, asked what on earth he thought he was doing calling on people at that time of night. He said he'd only just heard I was back, and that he needed to talk to me. Then he said if it was a really bad time, he could come back tomorrow. By then I reckoned I'd done enough to convince him I wasn't really expecting him, so I let him in."

"You're very cruel, do you know that? You deserve to spend your life alone and unloved." Maeve was laughing in spite of herself.

"Shut up, you, or I won't tell you the rest of the story. You've been so long married, and happily settled that you just don't remember the rules. Anyway, I showed Danny in to the living-room, sat him down and went to put on something less revealing than the loose T-shirt and knickers I had been wearing."

"You didn't answer the door like that?" Maeve gasped.

"Don't forget," Andrea reminded her, "Danny didn't know I knew he was coming. I had to look as if I was just out of bed and not expecting anyone. Besides, it had the desired effect. He couldn't take his eyes off me. Then I came back after changing, sat on the other side of the room from him, and let him begin talking."

As she told the story Andrea made it sound like she had been totally in control of the situation. But in reality her heart had been pounding and she'd felt sick.

The butterflies which had been fluttering playfully in her stomach before the doorbell rang transformed into large South American fruit-bats who threatened to tear out her insides with their vicious swooping. She hadn't actually intended answering the door in T-shirt and knickers, but the shrill bell froze her to the spot and when she finally regained control of her limbs, there was no time to change into the black leggings and rugby shirt she had picked out.

When she returned after changing into these Danny looked up in appreciation, seeming only slightly less enthusiastic then he had been about the first outfit. The shiny black material of her leggings owed a lot to the miracle of Lycra in the way they clung to her long, slim legs. The rugby shirt, old and frayed, was obviously a man's one. The open neck gave the odd tantalising glimpse of a white lace bra and there was a tear along the side seam allowing him a peep at her tanned waist. The shirt looked like an old and well-loved garment and Danny tried to remember which teams her brothers had played for after leaving school. He wasn't sure if she was trying to say something by appearing before him wearing another man's clothes.

"I'm really sorry to wake you, Andrea. I was at the launch party for the new LBS, and Maeve let it slip that she thought you were home, and I rushed over without really thinking what time it was."

The small clock on Andrea's bookshelf pinged, making them both jump.

"I don't know if you've been checking your messages, but I was trying to reach you while you were away. . ." Danny got stuck.

Andrea just shrugged, not trusting herself to talk.

Danny tried to remember whether he had rehearsed this moment during the past month, but he had never felt so unprepared in his life. If this was a business meeting, he would have covered the subject from every angle, and then gone in without any prepared speech, just given a quick presentation and then let the client take over. His preparation and enjoyment of his work gave him an air of confidence which won him contracts against formidable competition. Now his confidence failed him. He sobered up rapidly and wished he were a million miles away. What on earth was he going to say to this beautiful, bewitching woman who had so occupied his mind for the past weeks? He couldn't remember ever being in this position before. His good looks and affable personality had meant he was usually the one pursued by the opposite sex.

"I was worried when you dashed off that night in the Burlington." He tried to get Andrea at least marginally involved in the conversation.

"I'm fine now; it was just an attack of migraine."

"I know," he said, "but I was worried that I might have done or said something to upset you."

He paused, indicating that she could jump right in there and say something useful. She didn't.

"The thing is, Andrea, we've been friends for so long now. I'd hate to do anything to upset that friendship . . ."

Andrea's face remained calm, not betraying the presence of the cold hand which gripped her heart.

"But that night in the Burlington, Andrea, I could have sworn that I wasn't the only one who felt that maybe we could take this beyond friendship."

There, he'd said it! And to his relief the woman on the couch opposite him didn't look as if she was about to take flight again. Her face relaxed and the small smile which crept along her lips was reflected in her eyes. Some of the caution he had read in her tense body melted away.

"What about Cathy?" she asked before she could let caution go completely.

"Cathy? What about Cathy?" he repeated. His look of genuine confusion told her what she needed to know before he said it. "Cathy's history, Andrea. I know it sounds awful, only a few months after the break-up of a five-year relationship, that I can say I'm totally over her, but I am. And I didn't realise it until that night."

He leaned towards her, trying to narrow the gap between them.

"You know, when I decided to go ahead and take up the table I'd booked from her mother before Cathy and I broke up, I think somewhere in the back of my mind I thought 'That'll show her!'. I wanted her to see that life went on without her. I could still enjoy myself with my friends. I could even use her mother's charity bash as an opportunity to get a bit of publicity for my own company. And all the time I was there, I was half-aware of where she was. Was she watching me? Could she see how carefree and happy I looked? Could she see that I was there with one of the most beautiful women in the room?"

Aware that the guarded look had clouded Andrea's face again, Danny rushed on. He got to his feet and paced up and down Andrea's small living-room. Four strides took him to the end of the room where he had to turn around and head in the opposite direction like a demented Duracell bunny.

"But then I saw you talking to that good-looking man in the bar, and I forgot all that."

For a moment Andrea was confused, then remembered her brother's estate-agent friend, and smiled. Malcolm Brewer had his uses.

"You were so comfortable with him," Danny continued, "and he seemed to know you so well. I thought I'd blown it. I'd been rushing about like a blue-arsed fly all night, and now some other man was going to steal you from me." He stopped and looked at her. "Then we danced and . . . when we finished dancing, I saw Cathy staring at us, and that's when I realised I was really over her. I didn't care what she thought. I even felt a bit sorry for her, because I couldn't remember a single occasion during our five years that I'd felt as happy as I did right then. Does that sound big-headed of me? If it does, I'm sorry."

Andrea shook her head, but he wasn't looking at her – he had to keep his eyes on the carpet so as not to collide with the walls as his pacing resumed.

"Tell me I was imagining it, that I was wrong to think that maybe you shared a tiny bit of what I felt, and I'll walk out of here. We'll try to pretend this conversation never took place. We can put it down to the champagne, or the full moon, and just go back to being friends –"

"You don't need to go, Danny," Andrea interrupted.

At last he stopped and looked at her properly. The small smile on her face erupted into a grin when she saw the effect her words had on him. His mouth was opening and shutting in an attempt to capture words to form an appropriate reply. She laughed. A happy, bubbly, musical laugh. And a contagious laugh. Danny had to sit down as they both laughed, the tears rolling down their cheeks. When they stopped, neither of them asked what had been so funny. Andrea got up to make a pot of coffee, and it seemed the most natural thing in the world for them to be sitting together on the small couch, drinking coffee, eating stale biscuits, talking.

"So, what did you talk about?" Maeve asked, pushing aside her plate with the quiche, which had seemed so appetising when she started on it, only half eaten.

"What? Oh, everything." Andrea replied, tucking into her own meal with energy. "We talked about everything. About how we used to caddy for our dads when we were younger and about the terrible crush I had on Danny even then. About our jobs, about friends, holidays. About kids . . ."

"Kids? Aren't you jumping the gun a bit there?" Maeve laughed.

"Oh, we just talked about kids in general. I can't remember how the subject came up. Oh yes, he was telling me a story about one of the best holidays he'd ever had. A week with his brother in the States. They took his kids to Disneyland."

"So have you decided how many children you're going to have? Aim high – I can guarantee that after the first two you'll lower your estimate."

"Very funny! But seriously, we talked for hours and it felt so right. At about three, he left. He could see I was falling asleep in front of him and he apologised for keeping me up so late. We arranged to meet for lunch tomorrow and take it from there."

Maeve looked at her friend in disbelief.

"You're telling me that you spent three hours curled up on the couch with him, after you both agreeing to take your relationship 'beyond friendship'. Then he goes home, and nothing happened?"

"Well, he kissed me on the way out."

"He kissed you?"

"Yes, and a very nice kiss it was too. Stop looking at me like that, Maeve." Andrea threw a handful of Pringle crumbs across the table at her. It was about all she had left uneaten. "I don't ravish every man who makes the mistake of crossing my threshold. Besides, I think this is it. The big one. I didn't want to rush things. I want to make a whole lot of memories about the start of our relationship to bore our grandchildren with." She ignored Maeve's gagging noises.

Maeve tidied the table, and brought the plates inside. She looked out at Andrea who was sitting with her eyes closed, her face turned to the sun and her legs stretched out to catch as many of the tanning rays as possible. She looked as happy as Maeve had ever seen her. She thought back to her own early days with Fintan and remembered exactly when she had decided he was the man she wanted to spend the rest of her life with. They had been walking down Dun Laoghaire pier, the wind almost blowing them into the sea. Maeve couldn't even remember what they had been talking about. As they reached the end of the pier and stood on the sea-wall looking out at the waves battering the rocks, Fintan held onto her protectively, as if afraid the wind would steal her away from him. She had felt so safe, so loved. When they kissed, it was the first time they had kissed properly. Their kiss was long and soft; they were barely breathing. They came down off the sea-wall and sheltered on the lower part of the pier to continue their kiss. Maeve couldn't believe they couldn't recapture whatever they seemed to have lost since then.

Andrea was trying not to drift off to sleep. Instead she replayed the night before in her head. She had been honest with Maeve about the time Danny left at the night before, but she didn't add that when he left, it wasn't for good. After closing the door behind him she had leaned against it, sighing like a lovesick teenager. She couldn't remember ever feeling happier. She wasn't sure how long she had been standing there when she heard a gentle scratching on the door. She looked through the peephole; it was obscured by the back of someone's head, someone leaning with their back to the door.

"Danny?" she said gently through the door.

"Yes, it's me, sorry, I'll be gone in a minute."

Andrea opened the door and Danny stood there, looking sheepish.

"Sorry, I didn't trust my legs to take me where I wanted to go. Or rather, I'm sure they'd take me where I want to go," he peered over her shoulder into the flat, "but they wouldn't take me home yet."

She stood back to let him in. Before the door was closed behind them, he had taken her into his arms and was kissing her hungrily. His jacket fell to the floor, followed by her rugby shirt. He gasped when his hands could feel nothing but skin, and they explored her lower back moving upwards until they were stopped by her bra-strap. The lacy garment detached itself from its owner as if by magic and Andrea began to unfasten the buttons of Danny's shirt with clumsy fingers.

"Bedroom?" he asked, his voice husky, almost inaudible.

"Down the hall, the door at the end."

But they didn't make it that far. They had to pass the living-room door and it was so much nearer.

"This may sound terribly corny, Andrea, but I really do feel like I've been waiting for this moment all my life," Danny said as he held her as close as physically possible. The two of them were wrapped around each other on the deep pile rug on the floor.

"Really?" she asked, as she began to untangle her body so that she could switch on the gas fire to keep them warm. "You were very good for a first-timer."

"I didn't mean . . . I mean . . ." He was flustered.

Andrea was amused to note his blush spread to parts she had never seen blushing before.

"It's okay. I know what you meant." She snuggled down beside him again. She enjoyed the closeness as he began to run his hand absentmindedly up and down along her thigh. "I think I feel the same."

They didn't speak for a while.

"I didn't plan on this, you know," Andrea said finally.

"On what?"

"You know, this, tonight."

"How could you have? You didn't even know I'd be here tonight until I showed up at the door."

She looked at him quickly. Had he guessed that Maeve had phoned her? But his face was guileless and she decided it was an innocent comment.

"No, I mean, I was glad after you left, that nothing had happened. I liked the idea of taking things slowly. Going out for lunch, maybe dinner, going for walks whatever, seeing how things developed." She couldn't explain it properly.

He pulled away from her, and sat up.

"I've rushed you. I'm sorry. When you let me back in that time . . . I thought . . . I swear, I wasn't standing outside plotting this . . ."

"Hey, stop that, come here!" The look of anguish on his face was too much for her. She sat up too, and leaned back against his chest. She picked up his arms and wrapped them around her. "I wouldn't change a thing about tonight. I suppose what I was trying to say is that even though nothing had happened, I knew it was only the start of something. I wasn't afraid to let you go away. I knew you'd be back. Does that sound big-headed?"

"Not at all. You couldn't have kept me away." He sounded joyful, and pulled her closer. "I know what you mean about it being special though. From the moment I walked in the door, and saw you for the first time in nearly a month, I wanted you so badly it hurt. But when I left, it didn't matter, because I knew I could wait any amount of time for you." He began to kiss her

411

neck, and nuzzled up to her ear. "But I'm very, very glad I didn't have to wait too long," he whispered. "I'm going to remember this night for the rest of my life. When we're too old for all this, we'll keep each other warm with the memory of tonight."

"Mmm," Andrea agreed, "but we'll never be too old for this."

CHAPTER 36

Maeve looked out at Andrea who seemed to have fallen asleep in the sun. She decided not to wake her. Even asleep, she looked deliriously happy. Maeve wondered if she was dreaming about Danny.

The phone rang.

"Mummy, hello. This is Ciaran."

"Hello, sweetheart! Are you having fun with granny in Courtown?"

"We went swimming today," he answered, "and Daddy said we can go again later, if we're really good, and after the *babies* have had their nap."

"Do you miss me? I miss you." The moment she said it, Maeve regretted it. She didn't want to put thoughts in his head, but she needn't have worried.

"Yes, I miss you. I miss telly too."

"Which do you miss more?"

There was a pause.

"You, I miss you more."

Maeve wasn't sure whether to be worried that Ciaran had to think about it or relieved he had given it proper consideration rather than parrot off the expected response.

"Granny says that when she was small, there was no such thing as telly," her son continued.

"That's right."

"That was a long time ago, wasn't it?" Ciaran thought about it for a moment. "Were there still dinosaurs when Granny was small?"

"No, there were no dinosaurs."

"So it was after the dinosaurs were extincted," he said sagely. "Was I born?"

"No, you weren't born."

"Okay."

Now that he had accurately dated his grandmother's televisionless childhood as falling between dinosaur extinction and his own creation, Ciaran moved on to weightier matters.

"Will the telly ever go extinct?"

"I don't think so. No, I'm sure. The telly won't go extinct." Maeve was emphatic; it was the kind of thing that Ciaran could get nightmares about.

"Granny wants to talk to you. Bye, Mummy." Before she could blow her son a kiss down the phone, Maeve's mother-in-law was talking to her.

"Maeve, how are you? How did your big launch go?"

They chatted about her news and the kids, before Maeve asked to talk to Fintan.

"I'll just bring the phone out to him in the garden. He doesn't know you're on the phone or I'm sure he'd be in by now. Ciaran's been nagging us all day to phone you and eventually I couldn't handle his whining anymore. I reckoned you'd be well up by now, no matter what Fintan said about letting you sleep. After all, the reason you didn't come down today was that you wanted to do some work."

Was that what she had said to Fintan? Maeve couldn't remember. She felt guilty that she wasn't going down to see the kids, but he hadn't seemed keen to have her come down either. There was some mumbling in the background before she heard Fintan's voice.

"Hi, how did the party go?"

"Oh, you know these things," she answered. "As they go, it was okay. I got away before midnight, which was a relief."

"Are you getting much work done? It seems a shame to waste such good weather."

"Well, I got a bit done this morning," she lied, "but Andrea's here now. And I have less to do than I thought I would. Peter's virtually hi-jacked the whole agenda for Tuesday's meeting, so I intend to keep my presentation fairly short. Hopefully it'll be appreciated after they're all bored to death by Peter."

Maeve could hear a hissing sigh as soon as she mentioned Peter, indicating Fintan's irritation. She changed the subject.

"Are you coming back up tomorrow?"

"No, I thought there wouldn't be much point," he

answered, "if you're going to be tied up with getting Tuesday's presentation ready. We'll drive up that afternoon."

"I don't really need to do too much, so if you want to come up on Monday . . ."

"No, the kids would be disappointed." He was firm. "I promised them a trip to the funfair tomorrow so we'll stick to the original plan. Tuesday. What time do you think you'll get home?"

"You could always go to the funfair this afternoon, after the naps," Maeve said in a small voice. She felt on the verge of tears.

"It would be mad on a Sunday, with all the day-trippers," Fintan answered. So quickly that it almost sounded rehearsed.

"Alright, stick to the original plan," Maeve agreed. "I just thought that maybe the kids might be missing me."

"They haven't time to, they're being run off their feet," Fintan said. "Look, this is Mum's mobile phone, and you know how worried she gets about bills, so I'll say good-bye. See you Tuesday."

"Bye, Fintan." Her voice got very small. "I miss you."

Had Maeve said it too quietly, or had he already hung up before she said it? The phone was silent.

She was still sitting on the couch, phone in hand when Andrea came in to use the bathroom.

"There you are – I'm just going to the . . . Maeve, what's wrong? You look miserable."

"Nothing, I'm fine." She tried to force a smile.

"Bullshit! Look, I really have to pee, but I'll be down in a minute, and don't think you're getting out of telling me the whole story." Andrea took the stairs two at a time. When she got back downstairs, Maeve hadn't moved.

"Alright, let me do a bit of detective work. You were just on the phone?" She pointed to the handpiece. "You had a row with someone?" Maeve shook her head. "You got some bad news? Come on, Maeve, help me out here."

"I don't know if there's anything wrong at all, not really. I may be just imagining it."

"You're not imagining being that miserable. Come on outside and let's get to the bottom of it. And you'd better tell me everything," she warned, "otherwise – I'll have to administer the truth serum!" She pointed to the bottle of Pimms.

In her usual, easy way, Andrea extracted Maeve's story of the past weeks, how Fintan hadn't wanted to come to the launch and how things seemed awkward between them.

"Danny did say last night that Fintan hadn't come to the party and that he felt guilty at the number of hours you'd put in lately, but I didn't think things could have got this bad."

Andrea was worried. Fintan and Maeve were her idea of the ideal couple. She couldn't conceive of anything going wrong between them and hearing that they could hardly even talk to each other on the phone was terrifying.

"You were talking about me to Danny?" Maeve was horrified. "What were you saying?"

"Hang on, let's not get things out of proportion here. He wouldn't have been in my flat at all last night if you hadn't been talking to him about me. Glasshouse-owners, please take note."

"It's not the same. He's my boss; you're my best friend. You shouldn't be talking about me." Oh God, Maeve thought. Is this going to be a problem?

"I don't think Danny considers himself to be only your boss – he's also a friend," Andrea pointed out. "One of your best friends. Don't forget he's godfather to one of your children. And he was talking last night as your friend. He's worried about you and it sounds like he might be right. He says that no matter what he does to try to cut down on your workload, you find something else to do."

"Trying to cut down on my workload?" Maeve protested. "But he hardly seems to do a thing anymore!"

"I don't know. He said something about delegating the boring stuff to Peter. He even has meetings with the creep to keep him out of your hair. Now if that's not the act of a true friend, I don't know what is."

"Oh that? Is that what he said they've been up to?"

"What had you been imagining?"

Maeve told Andrea about her uneasy feeling about Peter, and how he always seemed to be trying to undermine her.

"That's why I've been working so hard. Apart from the merger, I've been gathering in new clients, so that if there is a shake-up once we open this new office, I'll be in a stronger position."

"What kind of a shake-up?"

"That's just it. I have no idea. We agreed not to discuss it until everything had settled down. It was making the staff paranoid, and we didn't want everyone jumping ship as soon as they had cashed in their first shares. But now I hear that on Tuesday Peter and Danny are presenting proposals about the division between the two sites, and I haven't a clue what to expect."

"How can it affect you so badly?"

"Well, for one thing, you know I had hoped I would be able to work part of my week from Sandyford. But it's more serious than that. Peter is planning to stay over here, working with LBS for longer than planned."

"What's the problem with that? Surely there's enough work to go round?"

"What kind of work? Peter's not a computer guy, he's not in marketing. He's management. Pure and simple."

"So?"

"I manage LBS. It's *my* job to run the place."

"But you do a hell of a lot more than just manage the place. You joined as a marketing graduate."

"I enjoy what I do. I don't want to get tied back into just one area. And if Peter is given management responsibility here, that's just what he'll try to do. We're going to have big money in the company for the first time. We'll have a really exciting time developing new products, taking the company in different directions. I want to be a part of that . . . Hell, I want to be in charge if it."

The two women were quiet for a while. Then Andrea spoke.

"I don't know how real your fears about Peter are, or whether you need to worry at all. I know Danny would never knowingly shaft you and –"

"But that's just it. Is Peter using him?"

"Let me finish. And the one thing that jumps out at me is the fact that we started this conversation trying to figure out what was happening to your relationship with Fintan, and we end up talking about your job."

Andrea didn't need to say any more.

"I guess you've hit the problem on the nose. I just can't focus on anything but work. As soon as all this settles down, I'm sure everything will return to normal. I'll be able to spend more time with Fintan and the kids."

"Maeve Larkin. Wake up and smell the coffee. You're being so dense I could shake you."

"What . . .?"

"If I told you to wait until Christmas to see what was going to happen with LBS, you'd give me a hundred reasons why you had to do something before then. Do you not think you marriage deserves the same effort?"

Maeve looked at her, stunned. Andrea was red with anger.

"But don't you see . . . work is the cause of the problem . . ."

"I see nothing of the kind. And nor do you. You haven't really tried to work it out, have you? You just keep going back to the simplest solution. Even if you're right, and it is all about work, what have you done about it?"

"What can I do?"

"You found plenty to do when you thought you had a problem at work. Now apply that brilliant mind to more important things."

Maeve looked so upset that Andrea took pity on her.

"Look, I don't want to preach, but you have to admit things have got a bit twisted. Let's sit down and work out what's really gone wrong. You say things are awkward between you and Fintan. Describe exactly what you mean."

"Well, he seems to resent everything to do with work –"

"No, don't go giving him motives. Let's assume for a moment we don't know why he's behaving the way he is, or why you're behaving the way you are. Just stick to facts. How are things between you? What do you talk about when you're together? When did you last do something romantic together? Do you still leave each other those lovely soppy notes around the place? Do you kiss each other properly, or is it just the duty-pecks on the cheek when you come in and out? When you make love, is it real or just mechanical?"

Andrea was so intent on what she was saying that she didn't notice the tears rolling down Maeve's face. She was shaken from her monologue by the sound of a sob as her friend put her head in her hands and began to shake.

Andrea rushed over to comfort her and when Maeve's sobbing finally subsided she tried again.

"Come on, tell me everything."

She listened without interrupting as Maeve told her all about how she hardly ever saw Fintan any more. Any time she was home, he seemed to go out of his way to avoid her. She described the meals she ate on her own, because he insisted on eating earlier in the evening with the kids. She shared with her friend the discomfort she had felt when she heard that Fintan had discussed with Hazel how he loved being at home although he hadn't said anything to her, leaving her to blame his new life at home for their problems. With a flush of embarrassment, because she never discussed her sex life with anyone, she explained that there was nothing to discuss. With a stab of pain she admitted, to herself as much as Andrea, how he almost seemed to flinch away from her, if she tried to hug him, or even stand too close to him. The only thing she failed to tell her friend was about James's revelations, and how she wondered if they somehow affected her, that maybe she was subconsciously pushing Fintan away.

Andrea was horrified.

"How long has all this been going on?" she whispered. "Why didn't you tell me any of this before I went to the Caymans? I'd never have stayed away so long if I knew you needed someone to talk to."

"I thought it had crept up slowly, but now that you ask me, it's only really got bad in the last few weeks. In fact, I don't think there'd have been much to tell you before you went away." She stopped to think for a minute. "That's right, if I had to put a date on it, I'd say the weekend of the dinner in the Burlington." And that's when I learnt about James, she thought miserably.

Neither of them spoke for a while. To break the silence Maeve suggested coffee, although she didn't feel like drinking any, and Andrea nodded absentmindedly. As Maeve stood to go into the kitchen, Andrea caught her arm. She grinned to take the sting out of what she was going to say.

"You know, if I didn't know better, I'd swear Fintan suspected you of having an affair."

Maeve collapsed back down into her seat.

"You don't think *he* is, do you?" she asked. The fear she had only allowed voice itself in the small hours of the morning, in the dark, took all the heat out of the August afternoon for her.

"No way. That is not the behaviour of a man having an affair." Andrea spoke with the authority of experience and a thousand magazine articles. She went on to reassure her friend that the cheat lavishes more attention, not less, on his unsuspecting wife. As Fintan was neither showering her with flowers to assuage his guilt, nor making mad passionate love to her to allay her suspicions, they could safely assume that he was not straying.

"But even assuming you were right, and he suspects me, who on earth could he think I'd have an affair with? Where would I find the time?"

"What about someone at work. Danny, Colm?

Maybe he thinks all the protests about Peter are to hide something else?"

Maeve didn't even take that possibility seriously.

"What about a client? I wouldn't kick that dishy Frenchman out of bed for eating biscuits." Andrea was surprised to see Maeve blush scarlet. "Maeve? You're not . . ."

"Don't be ridiculous, but . . ." She told Andrea about the previous night, how Jean-Paul dropped her home and how she thought he was going to make a pass at her. She admitted that she had wanted him to.

"I would have turned him down, Andrea," she continued, "you've got to believe me. But he made me feel good, the centre of attention, admired. I haven't felt that for a long time. You think I'm awful and I deserve to lose Fintan."

The tears began to trickle down her face again.

"Stop it!" Andrea commanded. "Feeling sorry for yourself is going to get you nowhere. Let's get back to the question at hand. I have to admit, when I said Fintan sounded like he suspected you of having an affair, it sounded ridiculous as soon as I said it. But think hard, can you think of anything which might have made him jump to the wrong conclusion?"

Maeve couldn't.

"Besides, if he suspected me of having an affair, would he not be trying to catch me out rather than leaving me on my own for days on end while he goes down to his parents? No, I can't believe that's the answer." She refused to believe that the trust between them had broken down that far. "It has to be something to do with work," she repeated mantra-like. If she noticed the look of annoyance that flitted across Andrea's face, she ignored it.

"Right. So what are you going to do about it?"

"What can I do? I can't exactly give up my job – we're living off one income here."

"Listen, Larkin. If you want me to bash your head against that wall over there, you're going the right way about it. Stop being such a wet dishrag. This is so unlike you. Maybe you should just toss in the job, if this is what it's doing to you. Start making some decisions; pretend this is a problem in the office. When does Fintan get home?"

"Tuesday evening. What do you think I should do?"

Andrea hid her exasperation. "I don't think anything. What are you going to do?"

"Ask him what's wrong; force it all out in the open."

"That's a start. How are you going to do that?"

"Make him sit down, and tell him that he's not getting up until we talk everything through."

"Great. When?"

"As soon as he gets in. I'll be sure to get home before him."

Maeve was amazed how much better she felt, now that she was making some plans.

"Right, so he walks through the door, three tired and cranky kids in tow, after a drive in the afternoon sun, and you sit him down to sort out your marriage." Andrea looked at her with raised eyebrows.

"Sorry, you're right. I've got to plan this properly," Maeve agreed. "I'll make sure I have a meal ready for the kids, feed them, get them off to bed, tell Fintan to relax while I get our dinner ready, and then sit down over a nice meal and a bottle of wine." She looked to her friend for approval. "What do you think I should say to him?"

"You don't need me to tell you what to do. You're on your own." Andrea stood up. "And if you keep thinking about this for the next two days, you're going to drive yourself insane. Come on. Let's go for a long walk, then a meal in that brilliant Chinese restaurant you took me to before. Your treat: consider it payment for the therapy session."

"You don't have to stay," Maeve said. "I'm sure you'd much rather be going to meet Danny. I'm fine now, honestly." She didn't sound convincing.

"I told you, I'm going to meet Danny for lunch tomorrow. He's not around today. He and Peter are taking that group from Ofiscom up to see Newgrange." She saw Maeve trying to wipe a worried look from her face. "Stop being paranoid! I think I can offer you a fairly cast-iron guarantee that they're *not* about to set up a rival office in a stone-age settlement in County Meath."

They both grinned, even if Maeve's smile was a little watery. Then they began to pick their meal from their memory of the menu, and by the time they left the house, their mouths were watering and they agreed on a short walk and a long meal.

CHAPTER 37

On Tuesday morning, Peter Fisch paced up and down the office assigned to him. He was nervous about the presentation he was about to make – it was make or break time for his career. He felt a bit guilty that he had to shaft Maeve Larkin to get what he wanted and he didn't entirely believe all the things Cathy Houlihan had told him about her, but Peter was pragmatic. There was only room for one top manager in this company and he was determined it should be him.

He had given a lot of thought to creating an alternative job for Maeve and he was sure she'd like what he'd come up with. And she would thank him when she got used to the idea. Much less responsibility, less pressure and less commitment. She'd be able to concentrate more on her family. Maeve gave him the creeps the way she was so devoted to her job. His mom had been a real apple-pie and Little League mom – it was unnatural for a woman to focus so strongly on a career. Peter quite liked the husband too – he must be sure to invite him for a round of golf sometime, so that Fintan could thank Peter properly for freeing up Maeve.

Peter's office was a small room with its window partly obscured by a metal bookcase. He had a feeling it had been a storeroom before his arrival, but no one would admit that to him because Ofiscom had insisted that he have his own private office and access to a direct phone line. He had been horrified when he saw the space he had been allocated and only slightly mollified when he realised that everyone in the company worked in the same cramped conditions. Only Danny had an office of any decent size. The only other person to have her own office was Maeve Larkin, and that wasn't much bigger than this, even if it had a bigger window, and wasn't hidden down the end of a corridor, past the coffee room.

Of course at first he had consoled himself that he would only need to make use of this cramped cupboard for a few months. Then he would return to headquarters in a blaze of glory and certain promotion. That was the only reason he had gone after the posting. When rumours spread that Ofiscom's latest planned acquisition was in Dublin, Ireland, Peter had checked its location in the atlas to put himself a few steps ahead of the others when it came to looking knowledgeable on the subject.

Not that there had been huge competition – not everyone had Peter's inside knowledge. His uncle, who sat on the board, had warned that there were soon to be drastic reductions at middle-management level, and Peter would do well to be out of the way when the axe swung. Either that or make his mark in the company so that he would be considered worth keeping. Peter had decided on the easier option of being out of the way. It was only when he came to Ireland and realised that LBS could well become the jewel in Ofiscom's crown, that he realised he could achieve both objectives.

It hadn't taken him long to decide that he was going to extend his stay. His problem was to find a niche for himself. The company was already extremely well run by Maeve. Any time he tried to get more involved, or asked Danny if he could help out with something, Danny blustered and said he was sure Maeve had it under control. And he would hear no criticism of her either; Peter had learned that to his cost early on. He had voiced his concern over this cosy working relationship to his boss in Texas in one of his earlier memos, but had basically been told - if it ain't broke don't fix it. In fact, the powers in Texas were so impressed at how efficiently the place was run they asked him to do an analysis of LBS's management structures. This was a problem because there were none. And Peter could hardly admit that, because the only thing he was qualified to do was manage. If he wanted to stay here, he'd have to find something or someone to manage.

For the first few months he was in Dublin Peter had looked in vain for a job he could do within the company, which would justify his staying over for a year or more after the merger. He reckoned that was the minimum of time he would have to stay if he was going to claim the credit for what he saw as the inevitable success of LBS. He didn't know a huge amount about computers or software, but he knew enough to realise that there were some wonderfully innovative programmes in development and, with Ofiscom's cash, they were going to be huge.

His problem however, was as much Danny as Maeve. Well, more Danny really. He couldn't connect with the guy. Danny knew nothing about baseball, he thought football was soccer and his real passion was rugby, which Peter thought a wimp's version of real American football. But then Peter had a stroke of luck. A stroke of luck called Cathy. As narcissistic and self-serving a person as Peter had ever had the (mis)fortune to come across. The wonderful thing about Cathy (apart from her bedroom gymnastics) was that Peter realised very soon that she was so self-centred, that she made an instant assessment of anyone she met and didn't bother to take the trouble to re-form her judgement because that would mean showing an interest in people far beneath her. Which suited Peter. He could see that like most Europeans, Cathy had decided that Peter was just another thick Yank. And the heavier he laid on the Texan drawl, the more outrageously stupid she seemed to believe he was and the more he could get away with. Peter couldn't believe his luck. Cathy pointed him in a direction so obvious that he couldn't believe he had missed it himself: golf. She moaned about how Danny used to abandon her for hours on end to belt a little white ball around a few acres of grassland. Peter had never played golf before, but on hearing that Danny was a fanatic he took some coaching, persuaded Danny to take him out and . . . bingo! Within two rounds he had the other man's trust. He couldn't believe it had been so easy.

Cathy knew disappointingly little about the company, but she was a mine of information on Maeve Larkin. Peter realised she had a grudge against the woman, but although he couldn't figure out why, he realised it coloured everything Cathy said about her. When she suggested that Maeve had tried to get him recalled to the parent company, saying she couldn't work with him, he wasn't sure if he completely believed her – but there was no smoke without fire, so he reckoned it justified any steps he wanted to take to make his position in Dublin secure.

And dating Aoife, at Cathy's insistence, hadn't been such a drag after all. She was sweet and relatively pretty. And if she was a bit unadventurous in bed, well, that was due to lack of experience – nothing the right training couldn't fix. She was also so in awe of Cathy that it never occurred to her to suspect that Peter's meetings in London all took place in Cathy's flat. Peter stopped his pacing for a moment, as he remembered his last 'meeting' with Cathy. He had to sit down behind his desk in case anyone came into his room and wondered why rehearsing his presentation should cause such a tightening of his trousers.

He looked at his watch. One hour to the meeting. He

wondered if he dared delay any longer in giving Maeve a summary of his main points. So far his excuse was that his laptop was jammed shut, that he'd sent it to maintenance and couldn't get into the file. She looked vaguely annoyed, but not as worried as he'd expected. He wasn't sure if that was a good or a bad sign. He took a floppy disk out of his drawer and buzzed on the intercom. He asked one of the girls outside to send Colm into him. He had been assigned a share in a secretary when he had arrived in LBS, but he knew it annoyed Colm when he ordered him around, and Peter couldn't stand him. He couldn't understand how any guy could tolerate taking orders from a woman all day.

"Colm, could you print off this file for me," he ordered, holding out the disk from behind his desk. When he saw the other man about to object he added, "Maeve's been waiting for this for hours. The tech guy just dropped back my laptop, so I was able to run her off a copy. I don't think she'd appreciate being made to wait any longer."

He left the disk on the edge of the desk and looked down at the notes in front of him, aware that Colm was debating whether to storm out or pick up the disk. Eventually his loyalty to Maeve triumphed – as Peter had known it would. He picked up the disk and dashed off to the nearest printer. He would have slammed the door on the way out except that whoever had laid the carpet in Peter's cupboard hadn't bothered shaving anything off the door to make it move smoothly.

Peter walked into the meeting-room and felt his

stomach lurch with apprehension. Apart from Joe MacPherson, his boss, he had never met any of Ofiscom's board members before Saturday at the launch party. In Texas these guys were gods. It was a testament to how important they believed LBS to be, that so many of them had made the trip. This meeting would be the making of him. He glanced quickly at Maeve. She looked less worried than he had hoped.

Peter could see that everyone was waiting for him to begin.

He stood at the top of the small group and made his presentation. It had come about after one of his sessions interrogating Cathy. Although she knew very little about the business of LBS, mind-blowingly little considering she'd dated the owner for five years, she did remember that there was one thing on which Danny and Maeve disagreed on. Danny wanted staff to specialise; he wanted to subdivide the company into sections. Over the course of several rounds of golf, Peter flattered Danny into believing that he had been right all along, so Danny had given his blessing and his help in preparing his proposals for today. So Peter proposed locating all the programming and design staff in Sandyford, leaving the technical and training staff in town. Then he magnanimously praised Maeve, complimenting her on her management skills.

Big deal, she thought, but he looked too smug for her liking. Her copy of his presentation, which she had scanned through before coming in to the meeting, gave her no cause for worry – it was too vague and woolly.

"But, my proposal goes beyond that."

Maeve looked up, mildly alarmed now. She had reached the last page in her handout, but Peter began to read from notes that everyone in the room seemed to have apart from her.

"I think we should add a computer-training centre to the Donnybrook office."

He went on to outline how their own and client's staff could make the trip here to be trained in a dedicated environment. The central location would be ideal for all their clients. Maeve managed to conceal her horror when she realised he was offering her a future as supervisor to the technicians and course co-ordinator for their training centre. He wanted her to ensure that the clients' tea and coffee got to them on time when they were ready for their break.

And Peter intended to run the Sandyford office, managing the programmers, to be in control of future development. For some reason Peter made no mention at all of Danny. He obviously wasn't quite cheeky enough to go proposing what the boss should be doing to justify his salary.

There was silence when he finished. Peter looked around the room, avoiding Danny because he knew that he had taken his idea one step further than the man was expecting. There was no way he would tolerate Maeve being sidelined like that, but it might not be up to him. Power was now held by the men in this room.

To Peter's relief, some of the board members seemed to be nodding their approval. Danny looked furious and was avoiding looking at Maeve. She was busy scribbling on a sheet of paper in front of her.

Joe MacPherson took over as chair of the meeting; Danny seemed to have forgotten that he had agreed to do it.

"Any questions anyone?"

Silence.

Suddenly Maeve realised what he had said.

"Yes, Joe, if you don't mind, I have a few questions for Peter."

Joe MacPherson looked at her, waiting for her to speak, but she didn't see him; she was busy scribbling on the pad in front of her.

This is brilliant, thought Peter. She looks like the worst sort of incompetent idiot.

Maeve looked up, realised all eyes were on her and blushed with embarrassment. Peter grinned.

Joe stood up.

"Peter's presentation went on longer than expected," he said in a slow and measured tone. "If we're going to give it the consideration it deserves, I think we ought to break for lunch and come back and discuss it afterwards. Maeve, let's go and see if your assistant can persuade that restaurant to take us early."

He went to the door and held it open for her while she gathered her notes. They didn't speak on the way to her office where she called Colm and asked him to phone the restaurant. Then Joe closed her office door.

"Was that an ambush?"

"Sorry?" Maeve played for time. Although her first

impressions of Joe had been good, she wasn't sure how far she trusted him. Nor did she want to be the girl who ran for Mummy when the big boys pulled her hair.

"Was that an ambush?" he repeated. "Had you seen those plans before Peter presented them to the rest of the group?"

"I saw some of them."

"When?"

She hesitated.

"Come on, Maeve," MacPherson said. "I've been in business long enough to know what happened in there and I want the truth. When did Peter give you a summary of his proposal, and which bits did he leave out?"

She told him.

He stared out the window for a few seconds. When he turned around again his face was angry.

"I don't want you to think that this is the way we do business in Ofiscom. Especially in my section. If it was up to me, Peter would be packing his bags for pulling a stunt like that. Unfortunately, he has a little more job security than I'd like to mess with." He explained that Peter's uncle had managed to get himself into a very powerful position on the board, and although he hadn't made the trip to Ireland, he was known to be supportive of his nephew. "It's well known that Bart Fisch and I don't see eye to eye, so if I give you any support this afternoon, they'll all assume I'm trying to score points over him when he's not here. I'm afraid you're on your own."

Colm came back in to say the restaurant booking had been changed.

"All I can do," Joe continued when Colm had gone back out again, "is to keep them at lunch as long as possible, and make sure they don't drink too much. If you're going to turn this around, both for your own sake, and so that I can get the prick back to Texas where I can keep an eye on him, you need to work your butt off for the next two hours. The rest of the board want us to come back to Texas with firm proposals for the future of LBS, so although no decisions are going to be taken this afternoon . . ." He didn't need to say that her future with the company depended on the next few days.

Maeve didn't even wait for MacPherson to leave before she began to pull out files. She called Colm into her office and the two men nearly collided in the door.

"Cancel any lunch plans," she ordered when Colm came in, closing the door behind him.

When he opened his mouth to object, she gave him a brief outline of what had just happened. His face lit into a grin at the thought of finally taking Peter on.

"And don't worry, Maeve. Before you say it, I know – this is strictly between us."

She gave him a list of jobs and, as he scurried off to his own desk, she called after him:

"Get hold of Paul Hyland and tell him I want a one hundred-word summary of his progress to date on the research I asked him to do." Paul was one of the brightest stars in the company. "And tell him I want it by half one. If he protests tell him his whole project is in danger of going down the toilet if he doesn't manage it. I want you to print off ten copies of it as soon as you have it."

"Do you not want to check it first?"

"I won't have time. If it's not what I want I won't use it, but print it anyway."

Colm scuttled off and Maeve got down to work. There was a tap at her door. Danny stuck his head through and she looked at him in annoyance. She really hadn't time for this, but she thought she ought to listen to what he had to say.

"Maeve, honestly, I had no idea that he was going to propose that training-centre thing. And leaving you to run things here. Although I agree with him on some points . . ." He held up his hand as she began to object. "You'll get a chance to have your say this afternoon."

"Yes, but Peter's presentation has the advantage of carrying the weight of your endorsement. Everyone knows he's been consulting with you on this for months."

"Yes, but he didn't tell me everything he was going to say. I can say I don't agree with all his points."

"No, you can't. It would make you look incompetent – not checking in full what he was going to say on your behalf. When you were offered the opportunity of making a presentation, you declined. No, the only way out of this is if I can come up with an alternative."

"You have one?" Danny sounded hopeful.

"I wasn't planning to have to fight for my life in there, but yes, I have some outlines of where I would like to see us go. And I'm going to have to add some things in response to Peter's masterpiece without it looking like I'm opposing it directly. But yes, I think I can handle it. *If* I get some peace and quiet to work on it."

Danny began to back towards the door.

"Maeve . . ." he said as he was leaving.

Her head was down and she was concentrating.

"Yes?" she answered, without looking up.

"Nothing, I'll tell you later."

"Danny, if you want to say something, say it now."

"No, honestly," he said. "It can wait until after you've finished this afternoon. Can you spare me a few minutes this evening?"

"Yes, whatever," she promised, without her own words registering in her brain.

At half two the meeting reconvened and Maeve was in the room before the rest of the group arrived back. Colm had just finished putting together the last of the folders and was distributing them around the table. Most of the material she had already assembled, but two pages were new. Maeve hooked up her laptop to the projector and uttered a small prayer before she flashed up the first slide. It looked perfect on screen. She switched it off again and sat back, looking more confident than she felt.

When the room was full, and everyone seated, Joe MacPherson got up to speak.

"As you are aware, the only other person to be making a presentation today is Maeve Larkin. I suggest we let her speak first and then open the floor to discussion of both presentations."

Maeve stood up and launched into a fluent delivery of her ideas. Within thirty seconds of starting, she had forgotten Peter and began to draw the listeners into her vision of the future. It was clear that she had a grasp of the market they worked in far superior to his, and she didn't once refer to his plan. She listed opportunities she felt LBS would be in a perfect position to grasp and she included developments up to five years down the line. She was able to give an analysis of the major European markets and she listed possible new openings in cities like Paris, Brussels and Frankfurt. She gave a comprehensive overview of their current staffing levels and where they needed to recruit and retrain. Without referring to Peter's specialisation plan, she concentrated on flexibility within their workforce. Where he had prefaced every sentence with 'I suggest . . . I believe . . . I think . . .' her presentation used phrases like 'Our future', 'We should be prepared' and 'The market dictates that we'. She continued for twenty minutes, but a few minutes into her talk she was aware that she had the attention of everyone in the room, awakened from their post-lunch stupor. Before resuming her seat, she referred to the last two pages in her handout.

"I received this report in at lunch-time; I hadn't expected this much progress so fast."

Paul Hyland had done her proud on the pet project they shared. Instead of the one hundred words she had asked for, he already had a two-page report which he had intended to give her at their next meeting.

"Online training is an area which we cannot afford

to get left out of." She referred to Paul's report, which outlined a feasibility study and a pilot programme with two clients already signed up to take part. Only now did she allow herself to glance briefly in Peter's direction. He sat crumpled in his chair, his body language conceding defeat. In allowing himself to be swayed by Cathy's vindictive rhetoric, he had seriously underestimated Maeve.

The discussion that followed was lively. Maeve did not get an easy ride; the four men and two women representing the board of Ofiscom knew their business well. Their questions were probing and relevant. Most of them Maeve could field, some she had to promise answers for at a later date, but the meeting revolved around her. There seemed to be a consensus that the least said about Peter's presentation the better. When Maeve finally left the small boardroom of LBS at five o'clock she was exhausted but exhilarated. She flew through the office, stopping only to give Colm a quick hug, thank him and tell him everything was going to be fine.

Then she ran to her car, determined to get home before Fintan and the children. She was dying to see them, and in the mood she was in she knew that everything was going to be fine.

CHAPTER 38

Maeve had already shopped for her planned dinner with Fintan, so didn't need to stop on the way home. But because of a bus breaking down on the dual carriageway, it was after six before she got home. Fintan had arrived before her, but not long before because he was still unloading the car. She cursed that part one of her plan, to get home first and have everything ready for him, had already gone awry.

She helped him unpack the last few bags after a brief greeting muttered in short explosive sentences.

"Hi, Maeve. I'll get all your news later. I have to get this stuff unpacked. The kids are on their own in the garden. They're in a foul mood. The drive took us two hours. Remind me never again to buy a car without air-conditioning."

He didn't need to add that he shared the children's mood.

"You go and have a shower, then take a drink into

the garden," she said. "I'll get the kids to bed and make dinner. I've a small rack of lamb and I'm going to make your favourite rosemary sauce to go with it."

Fintan looked as if he was about to make a cutting comment, but at the last moment noticed the tension in Maeve's face.

"That'll be nice. Are you sure you don't need any help?" A trace of a smile crossed his face.

"No, I'm fine. You relax. If you really feel you have to do something, open a bottle of wine. Something decent."

"Okay, I'll open some of that Spanish stuff Andrea got us for Christmas."

Now he really was smiling. One of his old smiles, not the kind she had nearly got used to lately, the kind that stopped well short of his eyes. It was going to be alright. They were going to get everything sorted out this evening, Maeve was sure of it.

She sang to herself as she prepared the dinner, then she pulled Ciaran from in front of the television, and put him to bed. When he was settled, Maeve put the lamb with the potatoes and vegetables scattered round it in the oven to roast, and checked the cookbook one last time. She decided she would have time for a quick shower while it cooked. She was glad to note that Fintan was still smiling when they met on the landing.

She ran a comb through her wet hair and went downstairs just as the oven timer began to beep. Fintan was coming out of the study, frowning. He jumped when he saw Maeve looking at him.

"Anything wrong?" she asked.

"It's nothing." He looked as if he was going to say no more, but thought better of it at the last minute. "I was just checking the messages on the machine. There's one from Hazel – some problem with *Money Matters*."

"If you want to ring her now, you'd better make it quick. The lamb's ready." The timer was still beeping.

"It can wait until tomorrow. It's only work after all."

Maeve's felt this was intended as a reproach. She rushed into the kitchen to serve the dinner.

They chatted while they ate. Politely. Fintan described the few days by the sea, Maeve told him about her meeting. Neither of them had drunk a full glass of wine by the time she cleared the plates.

Fintan was about to get up.

"Sit down and top up the glasses – I think I have some cheese here." Maeve's stomach felt as if it would throw the cheese straight back at her it was churning so hard, but she had to do something to keep him at the table.

"I think we need to talk," she said into the fridge.

Then she turned to look at Fintan and put a plate with a piece of Brie and two old heels of unidentifiable cheese in front of him.

"Yes?" he answered.

Maeve rummaged in the cupboard for some crackers. She sat down without having found any.

"We're out of crackers. Would you like some bread?"

"No, thanks." Fintan made no move to help himself to the cheese, but reached for his glass. He cradled it in his hands, waiting for Maeve to speak.

"I don't know about you," she said, "but I've been pretty miserable these past few weeks. Something's gone very wrong between us and I can't figure out what. I want to get everything out in the open so we can try to work things out."

She looked at him for some acknowledgement of what she'd said. He just nodded, his face almost blank.

"Have you anything at all to say?" Maeve said in frustration.

"You go first."

"Alright." She wasn't sure where to start. "I know things have been hectic at work lately, and I promise, I never intended for you to get landed with so much at home, but there was nothing I could do about it. It turns out my instinct about Peter was right, and if I hadn't put in those extra hours, my future at LBS might have consisted of running a training centre. But that's all out of the way now, and hopefully things will return to normal. I promise I will cut back next month. Just let me get the board members safely back to Texas and I'll be more in control of my own fate."

Maeve stopped and waited to see if Fintan had anything to add. He was silent so she continued.

"I thought part of the problem was that you hated being at home, and that you were being noble by not telling me. So I thought that once you went back to work everything would begin to fall back into place. But it seems I was wrong." She told him about her conversation with Hazel. "Why did you not feel you could talk to me about anything? Why did I have to hear how much you loved your new role from your boss – someone I barely know? That really hurt, Fintan."

"You never asked."

"There was a time we didn't need to interrogate each other to get at our feelings," she retorted.

"There was a time we shared everything – we didn't keep anything from each other." His first full sentence was filled with bitterness.

"Keeping things from each other? What's all this I hear from Hazel that you'd love to stay off longer? When were you thinking of discussing that with me?"

"Anytime I tried to bring up the subject we seemed to end up talking about Peter or Danny or LBS or Ofiscom."

"So it is a possibility," Maeve said. "Not just some vague impression Hazel formed during some long cosy chat. Why didn't you say something?"

He was mute.

"Okay, tell me now." Maeve was trying hard to stay calm.

"That contract for the two issues a month of *Money Matters* would take me beyond November. Hazel claimed it was standard stuff, but she suspected I might want to stay off longer."

"And do you?"

"Yes, I've been thinking about it seriously."

"Great! So you, and Hazel have been planning the future of this family and no one thought of consulting me."

Maeve was suddenly aware that the conversation

was getting confrontational. This was not what she had intended. According to her master plan, they should be kissing and making up about now. She tried another tack.

"Look, if you're sure that's what you want, I'll support you, you know that. We can more than afford it. With what you're being paid to write the reviews, and what we'd be saving on childcare –"

"I wasn't aware I needed your permission."

The coldness in Fintan's voice took Maeve completely by surprise.

"I'm not talking about permission, but I thought we could have discussed this; I thought that was what we were doing." She was fighting off tears now. "You said we should be able to talk about anything, keep nothing back from each other."

"James rang while you were in the shower."

Fintan was dismayed to see a quick look of caution cross his wife's face.

"Why didn't you call me?"

"He said there was no need. He just left a message. Asked if we'd both be in tomorrow evening. He and Tony are in Ireland at the moment. He said they have some stuff to sort out, and that he'd like to call to see us on their way back to the airport tomorrow. He gave me the impression it was important that we both be in."

"What did you tell him?"

"I said I assumed we'd both be in. Will we be?"

"Yes, that's no problem, but let's forget James for the moment. We were talking about us."

"We were talking about not having any secrets."

"And what has that got to do with James?"

"Why don't you tell me?"

"What do you mean?" Now her face was guarded.

"I know about it, Maeve. About James."

Fintan looked more miserable than Maeve had ever remembered seeing him. He looked like a little boy who was about to burst into tears. Maeve was torn between a longing to rush over and comfort him and a feeling of intense irritation at what she felt was sulky childishness.

"Oh for God's sake, Fintan, are you trying to tell me that this whole silent treatment for the past month was because I didn't tell you about James and Tony being gay? I'm sorry if it upset you, but James asked me not to say anything. It wasn't just for him, but for Tony. You know what your aunt and uncle are like. If it's any consolation, I'm the only person in Ireland to know. In fact, I think I'm supposed to act surprised when they tell us, because James never let on to Tony that he was telling me . . ."

Her voice faded off as she realised that her husband was grinning like an idiot opposite her.

"What?" she asked.

"James and Tony," Fintan laughed. "*Of course!* I've known for years without really knowing. James, gay. . . Tony. . ."

His laughter was getting hysterical, tears of giddy mirth filled his eyes. Maeve looked at him, baffled. Suddenly she remembered Andrea's words and she felt sick.

"You thought . . ." She could hardly put the words

together. "You thought that . . . James and me . . ." She shook her head. She was having difficulty breathing.

"But I was wrong. Oh God, I was wrong! Oh Maeve, you don't know how happy that makes me!" Fintan stood up and came around the table towards her. She jumped up, backing towards the door.

"Stay away from me!" There was a feral savagery to her voice.

Now it was his turn to look puzzled. "But it's alright now . . ."

"Stay back!"

"Okay, okay." Fintan held up his hands in surrender. "What's wrong?"

"What's wrong? You sit there and tell me you thought I was having an affair, and then you ask me what's wrong?" Maeve's eyes glistened, tears of anger replacing the feeling of hopelessness she had felt earlier. "How could you, Fintan?"

He slumped back down onto his chair. His shoulders drooped, he opened his mouth once or twice to say something, but words failed him. They stared at each other in silence.

"You know, Maeve, it wasn't an unreasonable conclusion to jump to," he muttered at last.

He hadn't known her face could grow even more hostile. "I mean add up the facts . . ." His voice got belligerent.

"The facts?" Maeve's voice caught as she spoke.

"Well, you and James go up to his hotel room – the receptionist says he asked not to be disturbed . . ."

"So you're following me around now?"

"You knew I'd be in town that day. I wanted to take you to lunch to celebrate my success with Hazel. I missed you at the office, and saw you pull into the hotel."

Maeve's expression remained unchanged, so he continued.

"By the time I found parking, I was just in time to see you vanish through the resident's door . . ." The pain of remembering shocked him, adding to his aggression. "I asked you about the afternoon, Maeve, when you came home that evening. You lied. You said you were in meetings all day. What was I supposed to think?"

"I'd have thought that eight years of marriage would have given me the right of reply at least. Or did those vows mean as little to you, as you clearly think they meant to me?"

"I don't think anything, Maeve. I was wrong. I've said I was wrong. What more do you want me to say?"

"I wish I knew. If I had the words which would make this all go away, believe me, I'd tell you."

Maeve sat on another chair, as far from Fintan as possible. She didn't trust her legs to hold her up much longer.

"It wasn't just that, Maeve. If you think about it, you've spent hardly any time at home since then. You hardly speak to me any more." Although Fintan knew he was probably making things worse, he couldn't stop. "And I couldn't help wondering if that meeting in Courtown was completely coincidental. You know, when you and James spent the afternoon together and you came back convinced that my taking time off was the right solution after all. I couldn't help thinking that it freed you up to do whatever you wanted. I wondered was that his idea."

"It's ironic really." Maeve looked up at last. Her eyes were icy. "You believed I was having an affair, you pushed me away, you left me so miserable that you nearly drove me into the arms of another man." She exaggerated out of a need to hurt him, to help her resist the urge to pick up something and throw it at him. To inflict real pain.

"Who was it?" he asked

"It doesn't matter who. Nothing happened. Nothing would ever have happened."

She was glad to see that her barb had hit home. Fintan's jealous expression was replaced by one of remorse. Maeve stood up and Fintan made as if to follow her, but she shook her head violently.

"No, I'm going to bed. Goodnight."

"It's early," Fintan said. "I'll just tidy up here, set up for breakfast and follow you up. We can talk some more."

"No, I'd rather you slept in the spare room."

The words hung between them like a threat. In all their years of marriage, even when one of them was coughing or sick, when Maeve was at her most pregnant with Darragh, and tossing and turning all night keeping her husband awake, they had always shared a bed. They stared at each other, each willing the other to break the silence.

"What will I tell Ciaran in the morning?" Fintan asked finally.

"Whatever you like." She turned to go out the door, but added: "Tell him you've got a cough, and you didn't want to keep me awake all night."

"How long do you think my cough's going to last?" Fintan asked her. He didn't get an answer.

CHAPTER 39

Maeve felt like she hadn't slept all night. She knew she had, because she had taken two antihistamines and drunk the better part of the bottle of wine left over from dinner. She could remember no dreams, but knew she must have dreamt because she woke terrified and sweating and it took her a few minutes to remember why Fintan's side of the bed was empty. It was half six. She decided to get up and attempt to get out of the house without seeing anyone because she couldn't face trying to keep up a front in front of the children.

At seven, she slipped out the front door, feeling guilty. She had heard Fiona beginning to stir and knew there would be tears later, when the toddler realised Mummy was already gone. Let Fintan deal with it, she thought savagely. When she hit the main road, she realised she had no idea where she was going. It was too early to go in to the office and there was nowhere open yet for breakfast. She decided to go for a walk along Dun Laoghaire pier.

The sunny spell of the past week had broken and there was a brisk breeze chasing white stormy clouds across a leaden sky. The threat of rain added urgency to Maeve's pace as she walked. She was surprised how many other early morning walkers there were, and how they all seemed to know one another. They nodded and smiled in greeting, or fell into step for a few yards to exchange pleasantries before resuming their own pace. Their easy camaraderie rubbed off on Maeve and she felt much more optimistic after her mile in the fresh air. She reached the end of the pier and saw the bit of the sea wall where she and Fintan had sheltered, that first time they had kissed. She was relieved that she didn't feel like crying.

When she sat down at last for coffee and a croissant in a local café, she allowed her mind to replay the scenes of the night before. Her head told her that she was overreacting, that Fintan had jumped to the conclusion any husband would have. But her heart argued back that she didn't want a marriage like any other, she wanted her own marriage back. The kind of marriage where the word affair could be joked about because it didn't have any currency.

She knew she would go home this evening, and that she and Fintan would patch things up as best they could. He still loved her, his jealousy and misery had shown her that. And if she thought about it hard enough, she was sure she still loved him. Besides, they had three children to think of. But the words 'as best they could' terrified her.

She delayed as long as possible over a breakfast she couldn't taste because she didn't feel like facing work. She had a sense of anti-climax after yesterday; since last night, her job was suddenly less important. To her surprise she found herself entertaining the fantasy of someone offering her a choice: her job or her marriage back. She would have no trouble choosing, but she knew that there was no fairy godmother waiting in the wings to solve all her problems. She was tempted not to go to work, to call in sick, but the alternative, staying at home all day, was even less attractive. Maeve wanted to let Fintan stew in his own juices for the day before letting him off the hook. And let him off the hook she knew she would, because she could see no alternative. She couldn't live without him, and she couldn't live with this resentment forever. She wished he would make some grand gesture to make it all up to her, make her feel like before, but she had no idea what such a gesture should consist of.

When Maeve arrived at LBS, Colm was jumping up and down with excitement. He ushered her into her office and made a great show of closing the door behind him.

"Everyone's gone home to Texas except Joe MacPherson. The Word Is that the meeting yesterday told them all they need to know about the company, and he's just staying on to tie up lose ends. He's in Peter's office now." When Colm saw that Maeve wasn't about to share his jubilation at the thought of The Fish getting a severe dressing-down, he continued, "Joe asked me to cancel all your appointments for this morning and he wants to see you as soon as he's finished with Peter." He noticed Maeve's thunderous look. "Well, actually he asked me to check with you if he could tie you up for the morning. And I did try, but your mobile was switched off. And your only appointments were with our own staff, so I didn't think you'd mind me cancelling them."

"Alright, Colm. But I want to talk to Paul Hyland. Can you get him on the phone for me?"

"He's in the office. I think he was hoping to see you, but I told him you'd be busy all morning –"

"Now, Colm. And bring us two cups of coffee, please."

She brought Paul up to speed with what had happened in yesterday's meeting. She reckoned he deserved to hear it before the rest of the staff, because his work had done so much to promote her vision of the future of the company.

"No promises, Paul, but I don't think it'll be long before I can give you the green light on that pilot programme. If you want to start lining up people to help with it . . ."

Colm stuck his head through the door, and said that Joe MacPherson was finished with Peter, and was looking for her. He said the word 'finished' with particular relish.

"Tell Joe I'll be with him as soon as I'm done here." Maeve waved at Paul to get him to sit down again. They talked for another ten minutes. The twenty-four-year-old programmer was brimming with enthusiasm. He quickly drew up a list of staff he wanted on his team, and Maeve negotiated downwards so that they'd have a few people left to see to their current business.

"And Paul," she added with a smile, as he finally got up to leave, "you don't have to start dressing all formally just because you're going to be heading up a project." He had discarded his usual jeans and designer T-shirt in favour of a shirt and tie, worn over trousers that looked suspiciously like the lower half of a suit.

"I wasn't . . . oh, alright, I suppose I was trying to impress the top brass." He tore at the knot in his tie. "I borrowed the suit from my brother. He's an accountant," he added as if apologising for having a relative who owned a suit.

The door didn't close when Paul left and Joe MacPherson tapped lightly on it, then came in. He had obviously been waiting nearby for Maeve to finish.

"Sorry to keep you waiting Joe, but . . ."

He put up his hand.

"Don't apologise. I appreciate your rearranging things to see me. That's your on-line training guy?" He nodded his head towards the door. Maeve didn't ask him how he knew. Joe had been in Dublin for a week, and she'd bet there was very little about LBS she would need to tell him. He was chatty, and the staff all liked him. He spent a lot of time in the coffee room, and had time to talk to everyone. She knew she would have no trouble working with him and she hoped he had enough influence on the board of Ofiscom.

"What can I do for you, Joe?" She was surprised that he wanted to see her, and that he had put aside so much time for it. They had spent much of the previous week going over how LBS and Ofiscom would interface, and she assumed he wouldn't be able to tell her much about the future direction of the company until the board met.

"I gather Danny didn't get to talk to you last night," Joe said.

"No, I had to rush home after the meeting." Maeve remembered Danny saying something about wanting to talk to her when she finished up yesterday evening, but he hadn't made it sound important so she'd put it to the back of her mind. And then forgotten it.

"He wanted to tell you this himself, but there'll be a formal announcement at lunch-time on Friday."

"What? Where's Danny now?" Maeve suddenly realised she hadn't seen him. She would have expected him to be in her office first thing, to debrief after a meeting like the one they had yesterday.

"He's at the Airport Hotel in a meeting with Marian." She was the personnel manager who had travelled over with the Ofiscom contingency.

"Why couldn't they meet here?"

"Marian's catching a plane out at midday so it suited better. Besides, they needed a bit of privacy."

Maeve grinned, acknowledging that privacy was a hard commodity to come by in the cramped LBS offices.

"Danny's retiring out of LBS, Maeve," Joe said. "Effective next week." He let it sink in for a few moments. "I'm sorry he couldn't tell you before now, but we asked him to keep it quiet until the merger went through. We know the loyalty of the staff is to you and Danny and we didn't want to lose anyone before we've a chance to convince them to stay."

The news was so unexpected that Maeve couldn't take it in fully. She knew she should be feeling something other than confusion, but she couldn't. So she settled for gathering facts.

"When was all this decided? I mean when did he –"

"From the very beginning, as soon as he entered into negotiations to sell to us."

"Peter knew, didn't he?" Maeve began to feel anger.

"He'll swear he didn't, but I'm pretty sure his uncle must have told him. No one was supposed to know."

"So Peter's presentation was a pitch for Danny's job." And he needed me out of the way, Maeve thought.

Joe shrugged.

"Peter's coming back to head office with us. I'm going to set him a project on rationalising the use of printer paper in our branch offices. He'll be able to put his imagination to good use there. From talking to Danny last night, I gather Peter has rather a good line in bullshit."

"Well, I suppose it beats sorting paper-clips." Maeve was aware that her laugh sounded more like a nervous giggle. Her heart beat fast as the implication of Danny's retirement sank in, but she was unwilling to let herself get excited.

"Who's going to . . . ?" She didn't know how to phrase the question.

"We were kind of hoping you would, Maeve," Joe grinned, "if you're asking me who's going to run this place? That is unless you have any better suggestions?"

Suddenly Maeve remembered the promise she had made last night. How would this affect the number of hours she needed to work?

"I wasn't expecting you to jump up and do a dance, but I was expecting some kind of positive reaction from you." Joe watched as a series of emotions battled in Maeve's face. "Do you need time to think about this? Do you have any questions? Although, if you're about to tell me that you've been planning your retirement too, I think I'll just go out and shoot myself." He looked across the desk at her.

"Sorry, Joe, but this is just a bit unexpected. You guys have all had a lot longer to get used to the idea. When did you decide I was the right person to take over?"

"Danny was rooting for you from the start. Needless to say we had some reluctance from the older, more conservative . . ." He hesitated.

"Male?" suggested Maeve.

"Yes, alright, male members of the board. But yesterday you won over any doubters in that room."

"So now if I turn around and ask a question like what does this new position mean to the number of hours I have to put in, and how is it likely to affect family life, I'll be back to square one when it comes to reinforcing their prejudices."

"Whatever you say to me remains confidential. But

I can assure you that we don't encourage overwork in our top executives. It's too expensive to replace you when you burn out. The job will entail a certain amount of travel though. A few trips a year to the States, and once you get things moving in Europe . . . well, whatever you find necessary yourself."

"How much control will I have over what I do? How tight a control does Ofiscom intend to maintain?"

"I'm sure Danny will have told you that we intended everything to go on being run much the way you've been doing up to now. Of all our subsidiary companies, you're the most efficient, so everyone's terrified of meddling and screwing that up! If you accept this post, it's hands off from Texas, I promise. And if you don't . . . well, we'll cross that bridge when we get to it. If we get to it, which I hope we won't." He became business-like, and withdrew a manila folder from his briefcase. "This is a copy of your proposed contract, as chief executive of LBS. I'd advise you to get legal advice on it." Joe pushed the folder across the desk. "I don't like to put pressure on you, but we'd kind of like an answer by Friday, if we're going to announce Danny's retirement."

"And if I say no?"

"We'll cross that bridge when we come to it," he repeated giving Maeve the feeling he was fairly sure she'd accept. As he didn't know her well enough to know that the company was her life, she guessed the terms in the manila folder were too good to refuse.

"I'll have to talk to my husband."

"Of course. I'd be worried about your long-term

commitment if you rushed in without giving the whole thing proper consideration."

"I'll get this checked out, and give you a definite answer tomorrow afternoon at the latest."

"I'd appreciate that." He handed her a card. "This has my private mobile number on it. As soon as you decide, one way or the other, let me know. Day or night." Joe got up and shook hands with her, and left the office without looking back.

Maeve took a deep breath as she turned the key in her front door two hours later. Fintan was in the hall when she walked in.

"You were gone early this morning." He tried a smile.

"I needed some fresh air before I faced work so I went for a walk along the pier."

"We haven't been along there for ages. We should take the kids down at the weekend."

"That's a good idea," Maeve agreed. "Although this rain looks set to last."

"Ciaran heard you going out this morning," Fintan told her. "He was in a bit of a huff that you'd gone without saying goodbye."

"Sorry. I just needed –"

"I wasn't trying to –"

"I know."

Unsteadily they laid the groundwork for a truce.

"Where is everyone?" Maeve asked.

"Darragh and Fiona are taking a nap and –"

At that moment Ciaran came hurtling along the hall and threw himself at Maeve's legs.

"Mummy, Mummy, Mummy! Auntie Orla's having a wedding so that I can be a pageboy and I'll wear a suit and a big hat. And I'll mind Fiona, 'cos she's a flower-girl and she'll be too small to know what to do." His face beamed with excitement and pleasure as he looked up. Maeve picked him up to give him a cuddle.

"Come into the kitchen and tell me all about it."

"Orla got home from London this morning. She wanted to surprise everyone," Fintan explained. "She and Matt have driven down to Courtown to tell Mum and Dad."

"Have they any definite plans?" Maeve asked, glad of the distraction; engagements and weddings were an easy topic to discuss.

"They're hoping to get married next spring or early summer. They'll wait and see what suits best from the point of view of Orla's college term. Have you had lunch?"

"No, I was drinking coffee all morning and I couldn't face anything to eat."

"I made a pasta bake, and some salad. I'll just reheat the pasta. Sit down." Fintan began to lay the table, setting two places.

"Have you not eaten yet either?" It was nearly three.

"When you rang to say you'd be taking a half day I thought I'd wait so we could eat together." It was a small thing, but Maeve felt absurdly grateful to him.

"Danny's retiring," she said when they sat down to eat.

"Retiring? He's a bit young for that, isn't he?"

"Well, he's retiring from LBS. I don't know what his plans are for the future."

"Did he say why?" Fintan asked.

"I haven't spoken to him. Joe told me."

"Oh." Fintan could sense that there was more to come.

"I've been offered the job of chief executive of LBS."

"That's brilliant." Fintan's face lit up with pride. "Not that you haven't been running the place for years, but at least now you'll get the credit for what you achieve. Congratulations!"

He felt he should be getting up to give her a hug. He longed to, but was afraid she would push him away. Instead, he reached across the table, took her hand and held it between the two of his.

"I take it you've accepted?"

"I said I'd talk to you first. And I've sent the contract to be checked out by the O'Callaghans."

"What's there to talk about? You're perfect for this job. You're already doing it, for God's sake. You do want it, don't you?"

"I don't know what I want any more."

The silence between them was broken only by the sound of Ciaran laughing at the television.

"We've got ourselves into a bit of a mess, haven't we?" Fintan said finally.

Maeve nodded, not trusting herself to speak.

"We're going to get through this, Maeve, I promise you. I know I've hurt you, and I know you're angry with me."

"I'm not angry, not any more," she shrugged.

"Okay, you're not angry."

Fintan stopped, unsure of how to go on. He stood up and moved his chair closer to hers.

"I think you should accept this job," he said carefully. "In fact, I know you should. This is what you want. What you've always wanted, even before you knew there was any chance of getting the job. Am I right?"

Maeve nodded.

"Well, then, you've got to take it. We're grown-ups and we have got to solve our problems in the real world. We can't afford for you to give up work. And even if we could, you don't want to. You don't honestly think that the only way of sorting out our marriage somehow involves you giving up a job you love?"

"I guess you're right." But Maeve couldn't help remembering her fantasy of that morning, about choosing between job and marriage. Superstitiously she wondered if by accepting Fintan's logic was she dooming her marriage. "And it's not as simple as that. I'll be more in control of my job, and the hours shouldn't be anything like what I've put in the past few months . . . but you know there'll be times when things will get mad in there, and it'll be my responsibility to sort it out."

"And who's always done it up to now?"

"I'll need to be very flexible about my working hours. I may be able to do some from home, but I may also have to rush into work at a moment's notice . . ."

"We'll manage. You still haven't given me any good reasons why you shouldn't take it."

"There aren't any. I suppose I just want some kind of guarantee that I'm making the right decision."

Fintan leaned forward and brushed a strand of hair from Maeve's face. He tucked it behind her ear, but didn't follow the gesture, as he always did, by stroking her jaw with his finger. The omission made Maeve look up in surprise.

"There are no guarantees, Maeve," he said. "You know that. But it's as right as it possibly could be, so you'll have to settle for that."

"And what about you? What do you want to do now?" Maeve left the question deliberately open.

"About work? I'm not sure. I suppose I'd like to try taking a year off. If you don't mind."

"Mind?" Maeve smiled for the first time since sitting down. "I'll be the envy of every working woman in Ireland."

The doorbell rang and they both jumped. Maeve wasn't sure if she was relieved to be interrupted. They were on the verge of getting into a deeper discussion and she wasn't sure if that was a good or a bad thing.

"Wow, that smells good!" Danny burst into the kitchen. "All I had for lunch was a lousy sandwich. I'm not disturbing you, am I?" he asked as he noticed the plates of food on the table.

"There's loads more if you'd like some," Fintan offered.

"No, thanks – it may have been a lousy sandwich, but it was a big one, and I'd better save my appetite for tonight, Mum's cooking a big dinner. I take it Joe gave you the news?" Danny turned to Maeve. "I wanted to tell you last night, but you shot out of the place so fast that I reckoned you had something important planned."

"Congratulations on your retirement," Fintan said at last, realising that Maeve seemed stuck for words. "No doubt you'll have your golf handicap down to single figures by Christmas."

"You *are* going to accept the job?" Danny had suddenly realised how quiet Maeve was.

Maeve looked at Fintan. "Yes, I'll be taking it."

"Thank God for that! You know if you hadn't accepted it, I'd have had to stay on for one more year until a replacement was found."

The doorbell had woken Fiona or Darragh and Fintan went to check on them.

"It came as a bit of a shock, Danny," Maeve said quietly after Fintan had left the room.

"I'm sorry, Maeve," Danny was contrite. "I had no choice. It was the only way I could get them to agree to my stepping down as soon as the deal was finalised. If it became known that I was leaving they were afraid that we'd lose staff, clients . . ."

"Why do you want to get out?" she asked. "What are you going to do?"

"Nothing for about six months. After that I have a few ideas. I'd like to get back into the programming side of the business. You know I never intended to take over from Dad so young, but when he got sick I had no choice. I'm not complaining; it's all worked out for the best, and I definitely enjoyed the past ten years, but now I'll have the money and time to do so some of the things I want to do for a change."

They could hear Fintan laughing with Fiona.

"Did you get things worked out?" Danny jerked his head upwards.

"Get what worked out?"

"Whatever you needed to." His face was troubled. "We're friends, Maeve, and now that I'm not your boss anymore, you can moan all you like about me and the job. Is that what's made things difficult between you?"

"I think we're going to be fine, Danny. Thanks. And no, it wasn't all down to work."

"I'm here if you need to talk."

"Thanks." They both knew she wouldn't take him up on it. Their relationship was going to enter a whole new phase. Danny was no longer her boss, but it looked like he was going to be the partner of her best friend while she would be the custodian of the company he and his father had built. New rules, new ways of relating to each other would all have to be hammered out in the months ahead and Maeve felt that the past was best left out of it. Suddenly she was nostalgic for their old, easy friendship. But that had died a few months ago when she stopped trusting him entirely as her boss.

Danny stayed for another hour or so, and the house was filled with the sound of the children laughing as they tortured 'Uncle Danny'.

"I'd better be off," he said finally. "I've got to pick up Andrea at six. She's coming to dinner tonight. I don't know how Mum worked out that things had got more serious between us, but she insisted on inviting her out. She's thrilled of course, and she's started talking about getting the house decorated and moving out to give me space."

Danny laughed, not the slightest bit worried that his mother seemed to be marrying him off.

"I was supposed to be meeting Andrea earlier, but she had to meet James. Is that the same James you used to go out with, Maeve? Before you started with LBS?" Danny asked as he pulled on his coat at the door. "Andrea said it was a childhood friend, but I didn't make the connection until just now."

"Yes, it must be. James is coming out to visit us later tonight," Fintan replied and put his arm across Maeve's shoulders. It looked like a natural gesture of affection between any couple, but his arm was laid so lightly that she could hardly feel it. His muscles were tense, as if he were expecting to have to pull his arm back suddenly, but he relaxed slightly when she neither stiffened nor pulled away from him. When the door closed behind Danny, she put her own arm around his waist and squeezed gently before letting go and walking to the kitchen.

Chapter 40

Cathy Houlihan sat looking at the answering machine in her flat. She was sitting on the floor because her legs seemed to give way when she played her messages. She was home early from work, having pleaded a migraine, and had planned an evening of relaxation before ringing in sick tomorrow and flying to Dublin for a long weekend of sex and celebration with Peter. She wasn't too worried about upsetting her bosses with her frequent sick leave because she reckoned she wouldn't be staying much longer in London. Her father had sold the ad agency, so the flat in London would soon be on the market and Cathy's mother had made it more than clear to her that there would be less financial support now that her father was retiring. Living in London on a budget was unthinkable.

It was a good thing that she had lined up an avenue of retreat in the form of Peter Fisch, Cathy thought. His meeting was yesterday, so by now he was probably running the company with that bitch Maeve Larkin back in her place. So Cathy would sail back to Dublin, saying that she couldn't possibly live in a different city to Peter, that no man would ever compare to him. He was narcissistic enough to believe that, and it wouldn't be too much hardship living in his designer flat until something better came along. Or at least that had been her plan. When she got in, there were two messages on her machine.

The first was from her father. The company had found a private buyer for the London flat, and they hoped to complete soon. As she had never paid rent, they did not feel they needed to give her notice.

The second message was from Peter. "Your plan was a complete disaster; it's landed me neck-deep in shit. I'm going back to Texas, so this is goodbye. By the way, I lied: those extra two pounds don't make you look feminine – they make look you fat."

Andrea was absurdly nervous. She knew Mrs Breslin, Danny's mother, very well. The two families had been friends for as long as she remembered. But tonight's invitation to dinner was not as the daughter of old friends. Danny had been so frustratingly slow to make a move that his mother seemed to be making up for lost time. When she rang Andrea she had used some phrase along the lines of 'Now that the two of you have finally got it together'. Andrea couldn't remember her exact words, but Mrs Breslin seemed to know a lot more about the future of the relationship than she knew herself.

Andrea was flustered. Danny was late, and she had dashed around like crazy to be ready on time; she had got back later than intended after her drink with James.

When James had rung out of the blue to say that he would love to meet her for a drink, she assumed he was just killing time before a flight. But the serious, hunted look on his face when she arrived in the pub made her realise that she was in for more than a quick drink.

When he finally came out and told her why he had wanted to see her, Andrea laughed out loud and hugged him. "At long bloody last!"

He looked at her in amazement. "You knew already. Who told you – Maeve?"

"I didn't know she knew."

"I told her last month. No one else knew until . . ." James looked at her. "How long?"

"Since we were teenagers, I guess," Andrea answered. "I didn't know exactly, but I sure as hell knew that you shouldn't have been going out with Maeve."

"So she didn't say anything to you about it since I told her?"

"You know Maeve. If you asked her not to say anything – loyal to the death. I doubt she even told Fintan."

Andrea shivered now as she remembered why James would have asked Maeve not to say anything to Fintan. She had only met Fintan's aunt once, but knew that the chance of Tony's new lifestyle being accepted by his mother was slim. This meant that he would be cut off from his father too; Brian Larkin would never go against his wife.

As she finally answered the door to Danny, Andrea was glad that James had saved the visit to Maeve and Fintan for last; she knew that they would give the couple the reception they needed to go back to London in a slightly more upbeat mood.

James pulled away slowly from the kerb. He waved at Maeve and Fintan who were braving the torrential rain to see them off. Tony began to visibly deflate again in the seat beside him. Although he had cheered up in the time they had spent with Maeve and Fintan, the rest of the day was catching up with him and he looked miserable. Between gear-changes, James laid a hand briefly on his knee. He longed to say something like 'Give them time, they'll come round', but he knew it wasn't true. Tony's parents had reacted to the news of his sexuality with a concerned offer to get him a referral to a psychiatrist. His mother's brother, Father Anthony, whom he had been named for, worked with the mentally ill and they were sure he could recommend someone good. When his parents saw that he was not only not ashamed about this shocking discovery about himself, but celebrating it, they promised to include him in their prayers, but thought it might be a good idea if he didn't visit Dublin too often until he was over this phase.

The Kirbys' reaction to their only child's news was the complete opposite. James was surprised how matter-of-fact his mother had been.

"I never really expected you to make me a grandmother," she said. "It's a pity; you would have made a good father." And that was the closest she came to expressing regret in the two hours they spent talking.

"So when do we get to meet this Tony?" his father had asked when he was leaving. His parents would have liked him to stay longer, but they understood his need to make this a flying visit.

"Whenever you're ready, Dad." James didn't want to rush his parents into anything so he and Tony had told their parents separately.

"Well, our fortieth wedding anniversary party is at the beginning of October, so if I'm going to introduce your young man to all our friends, I'd like to look like I hadn't just met him."

James had felt a lump in his throat the size of a large plum, and he hugged his father for the first time in over twenty years.

And now as he handed back the keys of his rental car at the desk in the airport, James decided he would invite his parents to London, and put them up in the small hotel down the road. That way they could get to know Tony in the anonymous bustle of the city, and Tony wouldn't have to endure being welcomed into James's parents' house, knowing that his own home, less than ten miles away, was closed to him.

Their flight was delayed by an hour, so James linked his arm through his partner's and dragged him off for a drink. He was glad to see a trace of a smile on Tony's face, which strengthened into a resolute grin, as they strode together through Dublin airport as a couple.

Fintan retreated behind Maeve into the house, struggling against the wind to shut the front door. He followed her into the living-room, where she flopped onto the couch, her legs stretched along the length of it. He didn't pick up her feet, put them on his lap and rub them, as he would usually have done, but chose the armchair by the window instead.

"Tony was pretty gutted by your aunt and uncle's reaction," Maeve said when the silence between them had stretched to thirty seconds, and she could bear it no longer.

When he had opened the door earlier, Fintan was so upset at the sight of his cousin's red-rimmed eyes that he had abandoned all pretence of not having been told, and threw his arms around him. It was the right thing to do. Within minutes they were all relaxing in the kitchen and giggling under the effect of the champagne Maeve had chilled in the fridge. Tony made a huge effort not to put a damper on the evening, and James, who was the only one not drinking, kept filling up his glass and steering the subject away from parents. They nibbled on some reheated Indian snacks, and Maeve and Fintan accepted several invitations to come and visit the couple in London. The alcohol flowed so freely during their brief visit that Maeve confessed to her fleeting fantasy about James getting married, to the dress she had chosen for Fiona and her own matching hat. She asked Tony would he mind ever so much choosing her daughter as flower-girl if he ever decided to do the decent thing and make an honest man out of her ex-boyfriend?

But now Maeve and Fintan were alone again and emotionally drained. They had fed off the emotions of others all day. Danny had talked about how happy he was to have finally realised that he and Andrea were perfect for each other. Orla and Matt had phoned to allow Maeve and Fintan to share the sound of the champagne being uncorked to celebrate their engagement. James and Tony were so obviously in love that the Larkins felt foolish not to have noticed it in Courtown.

Maeve wished she had never come in to the living-room and sat down, but to get up again now . . . with Fintan in the other chair . . . So she did the only reasonable thing in the circumstances and reached for the television remote control. After the news she stood up, stretched and said she felt like an early night. She handed Fintan the remote before going into the kitchen to put the glasses in the dishwasher. She did her usual pottering then went upstairs. On the landing she stopped and went into the spare room. The clothes Fintan had been wearing yesterday were thrown over a chair. She gathered them up automatically to put in the laundry basket. Then she stopped, pulled back the quilt and dumped his jeans and T-shirt on the middle of the bed. She stripped off the duvet cover and pillowcase and put them with Fintan's clothes. As she was pulling off the bottom sheet and wrapping it around the bundle of laundry, Fintan stopped in the doorway.

"I heard you overhead," he said and saw what she was doing. "Are you sure?"

She nodded and moved towards the door with the armful of bed-linen.

"I'd hate Ciaran to worry about your cough," she said without looking at him.

He stepped aside to let her past and Maeve drew in her stomach, making herself as small as she could so as not to brush against him. Fintan followed her into their own bedroom. He took the sheets from her, dumped them on the ground and pushed her gently so she sat on the edge of the bed. Then he knelt down in front of her, took her hands in his, and tried to get her to meet his eyes.

"What can I do, Maeve? You know I'd do anything to make this right," he asked finally when it was obvious that she was not going to give up her examination of her knees. "We have to make this work again, don't we? Not just for the kids – I couldn't imagine a life without you."

He waited for some sign she had even heard him until last she looked up at him.

"I'm trying, Fintan, but I can't help remembering that every time you looked at me for the last month you must have been imagining me with James . . ."

"I wasn't. I can't really explain it. I didn't really believe that there could be anything between you, not like that . . . maybe deep down I realised he was gay."

Fintan stopped. Now he was the one who couldn't meet her eyes. He got involved in a detailed examination of her hands, which he was still holding. He began to rub them absent-mindedly between his own.

"I don't really know what I thought, Maeve. It all kept coming back to the fact that whatever had happened that afternoon, you couldn't tell me about it."

"Could you not have asked me straight out?"

"I was afraid to."

"Afraid of what?"

"I just kept hanging on to the belief," he said, "that what we had together, was bigger than anything else. By forcing whatever it was out in the open, it might make it real."

"What did you think it was?" Maeve insisted. She had to hear him say it.

"Unfinished business. Between you and James." Fintan looked distraught. "Do you remember, when we were going out together first, you asked me was I ever jealous that James was still so much a part of your life? I said I wasn't and it was true – for some reason I knew it was over between you. But it wasn't until years later that you told me that you and he had never actually slept together, and when you told me I felt special."

He got to his feet and stared out the window so Maeve wouldn't see his tears.

"I knew I was the luckiest man in the world to have you and I was afraid that James had only just realised what he'd let go." He turned to face her now. "I couldn't believe I'd ever lose you, so I thought that if I just waited, it would all blow over, and you'd come back."

"I never left. You pushed me away."

"I know that now." He turned away again, and tried to build up the courage for his next question. "You know you said last night that I'd nearly pushed you into the arms of someone else?"

"Nothing happened, I told you."

"But what could have happened?"

"I thought someone was about to make a pass at me."

"Who?"

"It doesn't matter."

Fintan seemed about to object then realised that she was right.

"So what did happen?"

"I thought he was going to make a pass at me and, when I realised I was wrong, I was disappointed." Maeve paused to let that sink in, then took pity when she saw the pain in his face. "I would have turned him down and I'm glad it didn't come to that, but that night, I needed to feel wanted."

"I never meant to make you feel unwanted."

"But you did. And don't forget that I had just found out that the only other man to have loved me had now decided he preferred men." She tried a grin. "Not the kind of revelation designed to give a girl confidence in her desirability."

"You . . ." Fintan came over and knelt at her feet again. "You know, no matter what, I'd have waited for you. No matter what."

"What did you say?" Maeve asked. Suddenly her whole chest ached.

"I said I'd have waited for you," he answered. "If

you'd been with James, if you'd succumbed to whoever it was who didn't make that pass at you, I'd have waited till it all blew over."

Maeve looked at him and wondered how he could say something like that. She tried to imagine Fintan sleeping with another woman and she was fairly sure she wouldn't be that forgiving. Maybe he was just saying it to win her over, she thought. But then she remembered: when Fintan believed she was having an affair with James, he hadn't confronted her – he had stood back. He'd even spent time away from home as if to give her space. He'd waited!

Never in Maeve's life had she felt as loved as she did that moment. Suddenly she knew she'd been given what she was looking for. The grand gesture she had hoped would restore her faith in her marriage had turned out to be something Fintan had been doing all along – just waiting for her.

At last the tears began to flow. Not the angry, acid tears she had cried last night, but a torrent of salt, forced out by sobs which exhausted her and broke down the last of her resistance. Fintan came to sit beside her on the bed and pulled her against his chest. He stroked her hair over and over and kissed the top of her head, waiting for her shaking to subside.

"I love you so much," she gasped, "and I was so afraid I was losing you."

"I love you, too Maeve," he whispered into her ear, "and I'm going nowhere. In fact I'm afraid you're stuck with me for the rest of our lives."

"I'll hold you to that," Maeve sniffed. And with a watery smile, she detached herself from Fintan's embrace for just long enough to pull back the covers on the bed. "But in the meantime, come here and I'll show you just how much I've missed you."

THE END